Praise for #1 *New ~~York Times~~* bestselling author
L~~isa Jackson~~

"Lisa Jackson takes my breath away."
— #1 *New York Times* bestselling author
Linda Lael Miller

"When it comes to providing gritty and sexy stories, Ms. Jackson certainly knows how to deliver."
—*RT Book Reviews* on *Unspoken*

"Bestselling Jackson cranks up the suspense to almost unbearable heights in her latest tautly written thriller."
—*Booklist* on *Malice*

Praise for *New York Times* **bestselling author**
B.J. Daniels

"B.J. Daniels is a sharpshooter; her books hit the target every time."
—#1 *New York Times* bestselling author
Linda Lael Miller

"Daniels is a perennial favorite on the romantic suspense front, and I might go as far as to label her the cowboy whisperer."
—*BookPage* on *Luck of the Draw*

Lisa Jackson is a #1 *New York Times* bestselling author of more than eighty-five books, including romantic suspense, thrillers and contemporary and historical romances. She is a recipient of the *RT Book Reviews* Reviewers' Choice Award and has also been honored with their Career Achievement Award for Romantic Suspense. Born in Oregon, she continues to make her home among family, friends and dogs in the Pacific Northwest. Visit her at lisajackson.com.

New York Times and *USA TODAY* bestselling author **B.J. Daniels** lives in Montana with her husband, Parker, and three springer spaniels. When not writing, she quilts, boats and plays tennis. Contact her at www.bjdaniels.com, on Facebook at www.Facebook.com/pages/ BJ-Daniels/127936587217837 or on Twitter, @bjdanielsauthor.

#1 *New York Times* Bestselling Author

LISA JACKSON

LONE STALLION'S LADY

⟨H⟩HARLEQUIN® BESTSELLING AUTHOR COLLECTION

ISBN-13: 978-1-335-01511-2

Lone Stallion's Lady

First published in 2000. This edition published in 2019.

Copyright © 2000 by Harlequin Books S.A.

Intimate Secrets
First published in 2000. This edition published in 2019.
Copyright © 2000 by Barbara Heinlein

Recycling programs for this product may not exist in your area.

Printed in U.S.A.

CONTENTS

Also by Lisa Jackson

Visit the Author Profile page
at Harlequin.com for more titles.

LONE STALLION'S LADY

Lisa Jackson

Prologue

Kincaid Ranch Whitehorn, Montana

"Well, Laura, I've got some bad news," Garrett Kincaid said as he poured himself a cup of coffee from the enamel pot resting on the remains of the campfire. Dark embers glowed red and the wide night sky twinkled with thousands of stars above this ridge of the Crazy Mountains. Somewhere, not too far away, a coyote howled.

Of course Laura didn't answer. She'd passed away years ago, but after nearly half a century of living with and loving her, he sometimes had to talk to his wife. He believed that a part of her still lingered nearby, if only in his heart.

Squatting near the fire, sipping the hot, bitter brew, he tamped down the loneliness that never quite left him and glanced at his painted stallion, Ricco, who was grazing just beyond the glow of the campfire.

"Now, Laura, even though Larry was our firstborn, you and I both know that he had more than his share of faults." Garrett squeezed his eyes shut. "Larry never thought the rules applied to him. He drank, gambled, smoked and womanized his way into an early grave." A lump filled Garrett's throat and he wondered, not for the first time, if somehow he'd failed his only boy, if he'd been too arrow-straight and unbending for his wayward son. But it was too late for regrets. "Darlin', now that he's gone, too, I hate to bad-mouth him. Hell, I loved him almost as much as you did. I just hope he knew it."

Frowning, Garrett stretched out one leg on the long grass and heard the rush of water from the creek, swollen with the spring runoff that cut through these hills. "Anyway, I've been goin' through his things. I found a strongbox where he kept a lot of personal papers and such. It seems our son didn't quit sowing his wild oats when he was a teenager. Not only that, but he fathered himself a passel of boys. Six. Well, maybe even seven, but I'm not sure about that. I've got a private investigator looking into it."

He paused and watched the moon begin to rise in the broad expanse of sky. Yes, this sure was God's country.

"The investigator's name is Gina Henderson. She's a cute thing, and smart as a whip. Right off the bat she found six of our illegitimate grandsons, Laura. Helluva nice girl, she is. You'd like her." Garrett's lips curved into a smile at the thought of the feisty redhead. "She's gonna come here next week and try to locate Larry's youngest, if the boy really does exist. Anyway, in the meantime I've got to call all our grandsons and tell them about their father, even though they don't have a clue they have Kincaid blood running through their veins." He sighed as a night breeze crept through the hills, rustling the branches of the lodgepole pines at the edge of the meadow.

"Yes, Laura, it's a mess. I sure wish you were here to help me out. I just want you to know that I'm going to make it right, straighten things out with Larry's sons. It darn near breaks my heart to think that our boy was so…well, damned irresponsible—but then, we always knew it, didn't we? Right from the get-go, Larry was a wild one."

Garrett envisioned his wife's pretty face and thought maybe it was better that she hadn't known about all of Larry's indiscretions, hadn't experienced the heartache of realizing there were so many children abandoned by their father. Garrett rubbed his neck and suddenly felt all of his seventy-two years. He drained his cup and tossed the dregs into the fire, causing the coals to sizzle and smoke.

"I'm going to start by calling Trent Remmington. He's not the firstborn by a long shot, but he seems to be the one who most needed a decent father figure in his life. I'm afraid he might be a lot like Larry. Trent's a rebel, struck it big in the oil business and doing okay now, but as a kid, he barely finished high school and gave his mother fits. He and his twin brother, Blake, were passed off as another man's kids and raised by governesses and the like." Garrett snorted at the thought and emptied the coffeepot onto the grass. "Blake, he towed the line. Trent was hell on wheels. A real maverick. Still is, I think." Straightening, Garrett's knees popped and he felt the flare of arthritis in his hip. He kicked dust into the campfire and packed the remains of a sandwich and his coffeepot into his saddlebag. How did you go about telling a man that everything he'd held true in his life had been a lie?

Well, you just did it. Garrett packed up his few belongings and stuffed them into the saddlebag, too. The fire died and he glanced down the hill to the heart of the ranch where a half dozen lights glowed in bright warm patches from the bunkhouse and stables. The silvery illumination of three security lamps reflected onto the roofs of the sheds and the front of the main house. It was empty now. Had been for years.

Well, that was going to change.

God, he missed Laura. She'd been rock-steady throughout all the good and bad times in their marriage. He'd never wanted to outlive her, but a man didn't choose his way into the world, or out of it, either.

Deciding to call Trent in Houston this very night, he ignored the ache in his hip, walked over to Ricco and patted the white splash on the stallion's neck. "Let's go," he said, slinging the saddlebag over the saddle horn, grabbing the reins and swinging himself up.

He heard the coyote's lonesome cry one more time and looked to the sky. A shooting star sizzled across the heavens. Garrett smiled, imagining it a sign from his wife.

"Thanks for listening, darlin'," he whispered into the wind. Pulling on the reins, he and the big stallion headed downhill.

Chapter 1

"Just slow down a minute, would you?" Trent Remmington half yelled into the crackling cell phone at his ear. Rain pounded the windshield and the crack of thunder was louder than the roar of traffic in this part of Houston. "Who are you? What do you want?" He thought the old man had said something about being his grandfather, but that was impossible.

He maneuvered his BMW through the streets, which were beginning to flood with the sudden torrent. Water sprayed from beneath his tires, the windshield wipers slapped, and some old Garth Brooks's tune pulsed through the speakers. Headlights flashed in his eyes as he turned quickly onto the street where he lived in a high-rise apartment building that he owned outright.

"—Kincaid...my son...your father...dead now and I just found his papers...."

Hell, he couldn't hear a word. "Hang on," he growled, snapping off the radio as the apartment building came into sight. He pressed the automatic parking gate opener, drove into the underground lot and pulled into his private space. The phone went dead.

"Great. Just great." He snapped the phone shut, stuffed it into the pocket of his suede jacket and got out of the car. The shoulders and collar of his jacket were wet, the result of his mad dash from an attorney's office to the car, and the underground garage with its hissing pipes and cement floor was hot and muggy.

Listening for the damned phone to ring, he walked to the elevator, used his key and took a quick ride to the top floor where his suite of rooms—the place he called home in the city—opened up to him. The blinds were up and beyond his leather couches, tables of rosewood, glass and brass was a panoramic view of the city. The windows were steamed, the air-conditioning running full-blast, and through the partially clear glass he could see lightning fork down from the heavens and flash in a brilliance that vied with the glow of Houston's city lights.

He shucked his wet jacket and poured himself a quick drink, wondering if he should sign on the dotted line to sell off half the wells he owned in Wyoming and net more than ten million before taxes. At one time he would have felt a deep satisfaction with the deal, that he'd proved wrong all the nay-sayers who'd thought him a complete failure. Now he didn't really give a damn.

As the Scotch—which cost more per bottle than he'd made in a day's wages when he'd first started out—slid down his throat, he leaned a shoulder against the window-pane and wondered who had called him. Probably some prank or wrong number. The connection had been lousy.

He felt unsettled. Or maybe it was his bad mood. Lately his entire life had turned a corner and he wasn't certain he liked the new direction it was taking. At thirty-two he was restless and edgy, just as he had always been, but he no longer felt the rush from meeting the challenges in his life.

Turning from the window, he tossed back his drink. This change of attitude had all started a few weeks back in Dallas, at an oilmen's convention. It had been boring as hell, until he'd met the redhead. Celia O'Hara. He'd spied her in the patio bar of the DeMarco Hotel and he'd been fascinated. She was sexy, a bit shy, with legs that wouldn't quit and wide green eyes that shifted from sly to naive in a heartbeat. From the minute she'd entered the bar, he'd been hooked. Arrogantly he'd assumed she, like so many other women, would fall for his charms.

But the whole night had blown up in his face.

He wondered what had happened to her—she'd disappeared from his bed in the morning—had even gone so far as to make inquiries.

He should have forgotten her, but he hadn't. He'd even contacted a private investigator. He wasn't used to taking no for an answer, especially when she'd said yes the night before.

The cell phone rang, shattering his thoughts. He pulled it out of his jacket pocket and flipped it open. "Remmington."

"Trent?"

"Yep."

"I called a few minutes ago." Trent recognized the deep voice with the slight Western drawl. He sat on the edge of the sofa. "Don't know how much you heard earlier, so I'll start over."

"That would be a good idea."

"My name's Garrett Kincaid and I'm your grandfather."

Trent sat stock-still, holding the phone to his ear with one hand, the ice in his glass melting in the other.

"I know you think Harold Remmington is your dad and, hell, he should get all the credit, raising you and your brother as he did, but the truth of the matter is that your mother was involved with my son Larry. You two boys were the result."

The man went on and on, and though Trent wanted to call him a raving lunatic and slam the phone shut, there was enough truth peppered into the guy's story that he didn't. Maybe Kincaid was a nutcase, but if so, he was a thoughtful, slow-speaking one, and Trent could detect a note of regret in his voice; honest, down-to-earth remorse.

"…there are others, as well. I want all of you to meet."

"'Others'? I don't get it." The guy was talking about Blake, his twin, of course. Or were there more?

"You will."

"Maybe I don't want to. You know, this is way beyond bizarre, Kincaid."

"You're not telling me anything I don't know. Look, I'm hoping you can arrange your schedule so that you could fly up here to Montana in a week and we can sit down and talk. All of us."

Trent's head was pounding, his ears ringing, and flashes of his childhood whipped across his mind's eye. He and Blake learning to ride bikes, being taught by a baby-sitter. Their mother, Barbara, hadn't been around much. A state commissioner when they'd lived in Montana, she'd been a real go-getter who'd had little if any time for rambunctious twin boys. Boarding schools and

governesses had been Barbara's means of parenting.
Trent had spent most of his time getting into trouble,
calling attention to himself. His twin, however, had tried
like hell to be perfect, hoping his mother and father
would notice. They hadn't. Barbara had been wrapped
up in her career; Harold Remmington had never really
given a damn.

"...so much we need to talk about," the caller went
on. "I've got plans for you boys—"

"I'm used to making my own plans."

"I know. That's not what I meant." The geezer continued, "But since we're a family now, I'd like to meet
all of you."

"'Family'?" Trent sneered. "You think you're part
of my family?"

"Yes, son, I do."

"Give up the Aw-shucks-cowboy routine, would you?
I mean, this is one helluva lot to digest, and I don't even
know if you're legit or a first-class nutcase or someone
intent on shaking me down. An hour ago my life was
just the way it's been for thirty-two years, and now you
expect me to buy that everything I believed in is wrong."

"That's about the size of it."

"Damn."

"Come on up to Whitehorn. Meet the rest of the family out at the ranch. It's the only way you'll know for
sure if I'm the real deal or—what did you call me?—'a
first-class nutcase.'" The old man's voice sounded a bit
crafty for the first time. His gravelled chuckle seemed
like pebbles rattling inside a wooden box. "Well, maybe
I am. Anyway, you may as well come to the ranch. What
have you got to lose?"

"Well, that's a good question, isn't it?"

Kincaid ignored the sarcasm, gave him directions to the ranch and hung up.

Trent swallowed the remains of his watery drink and walked directly to the bedroom closet. No way would he wait a week. He pulled out a battered leather bag and flung it onto the bed. Ignoring the suits and sports jackets hanging near the power ties in his closet, he went to the bureau, found a couple pairs of scruffy jeans and some shirts that did the jeans justice and tossed them onto the bed. He only paused long enough to leave a few long-winded voice mails for his secretary and his foremen, giving last-minute instructions and telling them to reach him via his cell phone or e-mail. Then into his bag he threw one pair of slacks and a decent shirt, his travel shaving kit and a bottle of Excedrin.

He called the airport. The first flight anywhere close to Helena wasn't until morning.

Fine.

Tomorrow he'd be off to Whitehorn, Montana, wherever the hell that was. He wouldn't warn the old man that he was coming ahead of time. Nope, he wanted to catch Garrett "Grandpappy" Kincaid off guard.

Trent believed in striking first, blindsiding his opponent. Unfortunately Kincaid had done just that to him. It was now time to turn the tables. From memory, he dialed the number of a private investigator he'd used in the past.

"It's me," the recorder stated. "You know the drill. Leave a message after the tone."

Trent waited, then said, "It's Remmington, again. I still want you to find out whatever you can about Celia O'Hara, the paralegal from L.A., but now I want you to check out a couple of guys from Montana. Garrett Kincaid and his son Larry. They hail from a small town called Whitehorn, somewhere east of Helena, located off Highway 191 near the Laughing Horse Reservation. Find out anything and everything you can about these guys and e-mail me or call me on the cell. Thanks." He hung up, discarded the idea of a second drink, stared at the lightning through the window and waited for dawn.

As she drove her rented Ford Explorer across the ranch land of western Montana, Gina glanced at her watch and smiled to herself. She was making good time from the airport, and her job was just about finished. She'd helped Garrett Kincaid locate six of his son's illegitimate children. The only question that remained was whether Larry had sired a seventh.

She was willing to bet her life on it. There was that notation in the date book/journal Larry had kept. It read simply, "Found out former flame had baby boy. Check into this. Could be mine. Timing seems perfect." It could have been idle scribbling, but Gina didn't think so; it wasn't Larry's style. No, there was a baby, all right, and she imagined, given Larry's track record for fathering illegitimate sons, the boy was a Kincaid. The date book had been stuffed into the box of Larry's personal effects, the one relating to all of his bastard sons. Gina had a feeling that another child had indeed been born, just in the past year or so, a seventh illegitimate son. Because of Larry's whereabouts in his last year, Gina would bet dollars to donuts that baby was somewhere in the state, probably not too far from the town of Whitehorn. Well, she thought with the determination she was known for, she'd leave no stone unturned to find the kid.

Though she'd never met the man, Gina held a particular dislike for Larry; he'd been the antithesis of his father, Garrett. A hard-drinking, womanizing, gambling man, Larry Kincaid had swaggered through life without a bit of empathy, understanding, or interest in anyone else. He'd fathered illegitimate children as if he were in some kind of contest, then pretty much ignored the offspring as well as the women who had borne them. Garrett, on the other hand, was decent and straitlaced, a man of strict morals, a man as steady and true as Montana, the vast land that had spawned him.

All in all, she'd enjoyed locating Garrett's lost grandsons...well, except for one. The hellion. But she wouldn't think of Trent Remmington now. She'd compromised her own rules when she'd met up with him last month—lying about who she was—and that thought still stuck in her craw.

She'd made a mistake of biblical proportions on that one and nearly lost her heart in the process.

"Fool," she muttered, kicking off her sandals to drive barefoot. She reached into her open handbag sitting on the passenger seat. Squinting, and avoiding a truck speeding in the opposite direction of this long stretch of highway, she dug into her purse, found her sunglasses and managed to slip them out of their case and onto her nose.

A few years ago, just out of college, she'd begged her brother Jack to let her work with him as a private investigator. He'd balked at first, but finally agreed, and she'd sworn then that she would never get involved with any of her clients.

It hadn't been a problem. Until she'd met Trent Remmington.

"Stupid, stupid woman," she berated herself under her breath as she flipped on the radio. Listening to what little news there was, she leaned an arm out the window and felt the hot May wind pull at the strands of her hair. Acres and acres of rolling ranch land stretched as far as the eye could see under the deep blue Montana sky.

Fences sliced fields spotted with all shapes and colors of cattle and horses. She smiled at the sight of a Brahman calf with its tiny hump mounted over its shoulders and wide, curious eyes watching as she passed. Spotted longhorns ambled along a creek bank and a frisky colt in another field lifted his tail like a banner and ran, kicking its black legs and shaking its head as he joined a small herd of Appaloosas.

The wide expanse was a far cry from the crowded confines of L.A. It was quiet here, maybe too quiet for her, but a nice change of pace. She would only be here awhile. Garrett had invited her to stay at the ranch as she peeked under every as-yet-unturned stone in her search for Larry's baby. She'd decided to take Garrett up on his offer. She'd always wanted to spend a week on a real working ranch, and now it seemed she was going to get her fantasy chance. She wouldn't stay longer than a week; not when she knew that the rest of Larry's brood would show up soon and she'd come face-to-face with Trent Remmington again.

Somehow she was going to avoid that. Though Garrett had been making noises about her sticking around, meeting the sons and explaining her part in finding them all, she was going to politely turn him down.

There was just no reason to stay.

She spied the turnoff to the Kincaid ranch, just as Faith Hill's voice wafted from the speakers. Cranking hard on the wheel, she headed down a long lane of twin ruts. Tall dry grass grew between the parallel trails of sparse gravel, brushing the undercarriage of the car. Potholes and rocks dotted the dusty laneway and Gina smiled at the pure, raw grit of this part of the country. She spied a tractor chugging in one field, and farther ahead, climbing to the sky, craggy mountains spired over rolling, pine-covered foothills.

Gina slowed as the lane curved toward what appeared to be the heart of the spread. Clustered around the perimeter of a hard-packed parking area were the stables, undergoing some kind of renovation, a bunkhouse, and a variety of buildings including a weathered pump house and a variety of machine sheds and the like. The most commanding building of all—despite its disrepair—was a once-stately two-storied ranch house that dominated the parking area. Once beautiful, it was slowly going to seed. Shutters missing slats sagged near the windows, the once-white paint was beginning to peel, and more than one windowpane had been boarded over. A broad porch skirted the first floor and a man was standing on the steps. A tall man with broad shoulders, dark hair and…and—

"Oh, God."

Gina slammed on the brakes and the Explorer shuddered to a stop.

There, big as life—no, make that bigger than life—was Gina's own personal nightmare.

Trent Remmington was waiting for her.

And, from the looks of him, he was mad as hell.

Chapter 2

Gina slowly eased her foot from the brake and shut off the engine. How could this have happened? Trent wasn't supposed to be here until next week.

"Give me strength," she whispered, her palms suddenly damp as they clenched the steering wheel. Through the open sunroof the Montana sun streamed down in what felt like harsh, merciless waves. Heat crawled up the back of her neck and images—a kaleidoscope of dark, seductive pictures—played through her brain. In her mind's eye she saw all too vividly his tanned skin, rippling muscles, bare, broad shoulders and oh, so much more as he lay next to her on the bed in Dallas, kissing her, touching her, making her tingle inside....

Stop it!

Though it was only the middle of May, she was suddenly as hot as if it were late August. She couldn't think of their night together in Dallas. Wouldn't. Gritting her teeth, she reminded herself that she was a grown woman, a private investigator, for crying out loud. She didn't have to feel an ounce of shame or obligation or…or even kid herself that she'd been in love with him. No way. No how.

So why was her stomach doing a slow roll of anticipation at the mere sight of him?

Crossing her fingers, Gina blinked and silently prayed that she was seeing things.

She wasn't.

Trent Remmington was here at the ranch. All six feet, two inches of him. He stood on the front porch of the rambling, two-storied ranch house, his arms folded across his chest, his lips drawn into a thin line of disapproval. His eyes squinted against the bright spring sun, his jaw was set, and the hank of dark hair she'd found so fetching fell across his forehead as he glared at her.

Well, like it or not, she had to deal with him. Now. He would certainly demand answers she wasn't prepared to give. Her feet scrambled into the sandals and for a fleeting second she thought she might have gotten lucky. Maybe the man on the porch wasn't Trent, but his identical twin Blake. That would explain the uncharacteristic jeans and faded denim shirt.

No, she was only kidding herself. She'd researched both brothers. Blake and Trent, though they looked alike, were as different in personality as night and day.

Blake, a pediatrician now living in Southern California, was kindhearted, well-meaning, without the hard edge of his irreverent renegade of a twin. This tough-as-leather man glaring through the dusty, bug-spattered windshield at her was Trent Remmington. No two ways about it. He might have discarded his two-thousand-dollar suit and designer tie, but he still wore the same arrogant attitude of the maverick oilman he was.

To make matters worse, he obviously recognized her. If looks could kill, Gina Henderson, a.k.a. Celia O'Hara, would right now be six feet under and pushing up daisies.

She shoved open the door to the Explorer and stepped out onto sparse gravel. "Give me strength," she whispered to any guardian angel who happened to be passing by. Leaving her briefcase, laptop computer and overnight bags in the car, she forced some starch into her spine as she marched across the lot. She was suddenly aware of her rumpled khaki skirt and sleeveless blouse that she'd thrown on hours ago in L.A. Her lipstick had probably faded and her hair was a tangled mess from the wind that had caught hold of it through the open windows and sunroof of the Explorer, but there wasn't time to repair any of her feminine armor. Not that it mattered, anyway.

An old shaggy dog, with more shepherd than Lab in his gene pool, was lying on a patch of bare ground near the porch. In the shade of a shrub, he gave off a soft "Woof" as she approached.

"It's all right," she told the mutt, though she didn't believe it for a minute herself. He thumped the ground with his tail and didn't bother climbing to his feet.

She stood in front of the stairs and looked up. "We've got to quit meeting like this," she said to break the ice.

He didn't so much as crack a smile.

She didn't blame him.

"What the hell are you doing here?"

So much for pleasantries.

"Looking for me?" he continued.

"What?" She nearly laughed. If he only knew that

she would have run in the other direction if she'd but guessed he was here.

"I don't believe in coincidence." Blue eyes drilled into her.

"Neither do I." His voice brought back memories of laughter and seduction, memories she quickly cast aside. Her smile faded and she cleared her throat as she stared into a square-jawed face branded forever in her brain. "I'm actually here to see Garrett Kincaid."

"You know him?" His eyes narrowed as she reached the bottom stair. Yet he didn't make a step toward her, didn't move, didn't offer the hint of a smile, just stood, jeans-clad legs apart, denim shirttails flapping in the honeysuckle-laced breeze, arms folded across that broad expanse of chest she'd known so intimately.

This wasn't the time for lies. "I work for Garrett," she admitted, and could almost see the gears whirring in his mind with this new information.

"You work for him?" he repeated, assessing her all over again.

She mounted the steps and stood close enough to touch him for the first time since ducking out of the De-Marco Hotel five or six weeks ago as the first light of dawn had crept over Dallas. She blushed at the thought of their last meeting, but managed to keep her eyes trained on his.

"He hired me."

"Then I take it you're not a paralegal."

"No," she admitted, wishing she could drop through the battered floorboards. "I'm a private investigator, hired to locate all of Garrett's grandsons."

Deep grooves bracketed his mouth. "Anything else you lied about?"

"Oh, yeah," she admitted, blushing as she nodded and cranked her chin up a couple of notches. "Quite a few things, unfortunately. It, um…" She met his gaze, then looked away in embarrassment. "It seemed appropriate at the time, but… Well, I don't see any reason to beat around the bush now, but I think maybe Garrett should be involved in this conversation."

"Why?"

"This is his gig. He hired me and I don't know what he's already said to you, if anything. There are things he might want to tell you himself."

"I'll bet."

She glanced at the house. "I take it he's not here?"

Trent shook his head and the afternoon sunlight touched the thick mahogany-dark strands that brushed his collar and tops of his ears. "The foreman said he's gone into town for some supplies."

Wonderful, she thought sarcastically. Now she was stuck here. With Trent and her lies. "But you have met him."

"Not yet." Uncompromising blue eyes appraised her. "He called, invited me to come here next week, and I decided to jump the gun a bit."

No wonder Garrett hadn't warned her that Trent would be here. He hadn't known himself.

"So, you live here in Whitehorn?" Obviously the inquisition wasn't over.

"No," she said quickly. "The L.A. part was the truth."

"What wasn't, Celia?"

She cringed inwardly at the name she'd come up with on the spur of the moment. "For starters, my name is Gina Henderson."

One dark eyebrow cocked, encouraging her to go on.

She glanced at the barn where a tractor pulling a trailer piled high with bales of hay had rumbled to a stop. Two ranch hands seated high on the mountain of hay jumped off and began unloading the bales, tossing them onto a conveyer that was positioned to move the bales upward and dump them into an open doorway on the second story of the barn. She could see other workers standing at the ready to stack them in the hay loft.

"Anything else I should know, *Gina?*"

"Oh, yeah, probably a lot, but let's just wait and Garrett can explain all the sordid, gory details," she suggested, wiping away a drip of sweat that had slid down the side of her face.

"All right. We'll play it your way. But when he gets here, I expect to hear the truth."

"You probably won't like it."

His smile was as cold as a November rain. "I'm sure I won't," he agreed. "I'm damn sure I won't."

"Wait a minute," Jordan Baxter insisted, leaning back in his desk chair and studying his daughter, Hope, with a jaundiced eye. Propping the heel of one polished boot on top of a neat stack of deeds, he narrowed his eyes on the one good thing he'd accomplished in his life. "You're telling me that Garrett Kincaid is gathering all of Larry's bastard children, here in Whitehorn?" His stomach turned at the thought. From the first time Dugin, one of those uppity Kincaid brothers had called him "white trash" back in grade school, Jordan Baxter had hated the whole family.

Hope slapped a file onto the edge of her father's desk and leaned a hip against the corner. "I'm only telling you what I heard down at the Hip Hop Café at lunch today. It's probably not true, anyway."

Jordan hoped she was right. Hip Hop was gossip central in Whitehorn. Some of the information bandied about over elk hash, blueberry pie and hot coffee was right on; the rest was just the talk of bored, small-town minds ready to make a little excitement for themselves.

Hope lifted a slim shoulder as if she didn't care what her father thought. Wearing black slacks and a T-shirt, her wheat-colored hair pulled back in a ponytail, she looked even younger than her twenty-five years. She was on the naive side, but, given the way her father had protected her over the years, that was to be expected. She was smart as the proverbial whip.

"Six bastards?" he repeated with a long, low whistle. "And all boys?"

Hope offered an indulgent smile. "I'm not sure, Dad. It's just what I heard, and now you're getting all worked up again." She sighed and moved from his desk to lean against the door frame to the outer office. "I shouldn't have said anything." She actually looked as though she regretted confiding in him.

"Listen, honey, this is the kind of thing I need to know. In a small town, fortunes can be made or destroyed by one little bit of information. If it's true. So, who was talking about it—and don't tell me Lily Mae Wheeler. That old battle-ax lives and breathes gossip and none of it's reliable."

"I overheard Janie talking with Winona Cobbs."

"Winona? Well, that explains it." Jordan let out a puff of disgusted air. "With all her psychic mumbo-jumbo, that woman should be locked away instead of being allowed to sell junk on the interstate." He glanced up and saw Hope trying to swallow a smile. "What? You know as well as I do that she acts as if she's been smokin' peyote."

"Janie was the one who had the information. And you'd better be careful, Dad," Hope said. "Talk like that about Winona could get you into trouble. It's called slander, I think."

Jordan let his feet fall to the floor. "I just call 'em as I see 'em." But if Janie Austin was passing along the information on the Kincaids, then there might just be some truth woven into the local gossip. Janie usually knew her stuff. Bright and pretty, she had access not only to all the information that was passed from table to table at the Hip Hop Café, but she was married to Reed Austin, the deputy sheriff, who knew just about everything going on in the county. Nope, Janie wasn't someone to create grist for the ever-turning gossip mill of Whitehorn.

So it could be true.

Whitehorn might be about to have a huge influx of Kincaids.

Stomach acid burned in Jordan's esophagus and he reached into his desk drawer for a package of Rolaids tablets to help with the heartburn. He shoved back his chair. "I guess I'll just have to check this out myself."

"You do that," Hope advised as she returned to her desk in the reception area.

Jordan grabbed his hat and caught his reflection in the mirror mounted near the door. At forty-six he was a long way from over the hill, but the silver in his dark hair and the lines around his eyes and mouth reminded him that he wasn't getting any younger. He exercised regularly, was fit, didn't even have the hint of a gut, but the years were beginning to show. He'd hate to think how many of those gray hairs and wrinkles were the direct result of dealing with those damned Kincaids. That family had been the bane of his existence all his life and the thought that there were six more heretofore-unknown brothers about to appear in Whitehorn did nothing to improve his mood.

"Don't forget that Jeremiah Kincaid killed your grandmother," he said, passing his daughter's desk.

Hope rolled her eyes. "C'mon, Dad, that isn't fair. The coroner said she drank too much and was smoking in bed. That's what caused the fire, not some devious plot by the Kincaid family. You're the only person in the entire State of Montana who thinks Jeremiah was behind it."

"He was." The bastard. Rich, powerful, and deadly, he'd taken Vera Baxter to his bed, then cut her free. When she wouldn't accept his rejection, she'd ended up dead in a conflagration that Jordan didn't believe she caused for a minute.

"Does it matter? They're both dead now. Let it go."

"I'll think about it," he lied, as his fists clenched in frustration. Slowly he straightened his fingers. He wanted to argue, to bring up every incident where a Kincaid had screwed over a Baxter, so that his daughter would understand the legacy of pain every Baxter had borne, but he didn't. Hope wouldn't believe him, anyway. She was just too damned naive for her own good.

"I hope you're wrong about this," he said, straightening his tie.

"Me, too." She held his gaze for a second. "I don't want to see you get all crazy about it."

"I won't." Well, not crazy, but his blood did curdle at the thought of even one more Kincaid in the area. Jeremiah had been a half cousin to Garrett, or something like that. The way those Kincaids screwed around it was hard keeping 'em all straight. Not that he really wanted to.

"So, Larry fathered six kids out of wedlock. It figures." He chuckled without a hint of mirth as he squared his hat on his head and reached for the doorknob. "I bet that just about killed Garrett when he found out."

"The way Lily Mae tells it, Garrett's planning to divide up the Whitehorn ranch among the heirs. To make amends or something."

That stopped him short. He let the doorknob go, and faced his daughter. "I thought you said Janie Austin had the information."

"She did, but Lily Mae put her two cents in."

Jordan's back teeth ground together as he thought of the Kincaid ranch—the place where he'd worked his tail off as a kid, the ranch that had been promised to him. "You know that spread is supposed to be mine. Ours. It used to be called the Baxter place before the Kincaids swindled it from us."

Hope sighed and a sadness settled in her eyes. Once again he felt an incredible urge to protect her, for she was the light of his life.

"Why don't you give it up, Dad?" she asked. "What's your fascination with the Kincaid place, anyway? I know when Uncle Cameron owned the ranch he promised it to you, but that was years ago. And you've got so much already."

That much was true. Jordan had made his own fortune years ago working for an investment firm in New York. Young, fresh out of college, and determined to put his poor roots behind him, he'd taken to investment banking like a fish to water. But his roots were here. In

Whitehorn. Though he now owned thousands of acres in the county, none meant anything to him. The old Baxter place did. When times had been tough, it had been his home. He felt a lump rise in his throat and steadfastly swallowed it back.

"You know, Dad, you could buy and sell a dozen places around here. All of them would put the Kincaid ranch to shame."

"It's not about money, darlin'," he said, wishing his only child understood, but then, she hadn't experienced the grinding poverty he had, nor endured the taunts from some of the wealthier kids in Whitehorn that he'd heard while growing up. The worst had been the disparaging remarks and mean-spirited gibes that had been cast his way by the Kincaid boys. "Nope, it's not about money at all, Hope," he repeated, his voice a little rough. "It's about pride. Family pride. That's all that matters in this world and it's time you knew it."

"When did you say Garrett was due back?" Gina asked, wondering how she could possibly make small talk with this man.

"I didn't. The foreman—"

"Rand Harding," she said automatically.

Trent nodded. "He wasn't sure, but didn't think it would be long."

Gina mentally crossed her fingers. The less time alone she had with Trent, the better.

"So, I guess this would be a good time for you and I to get to know each other," he suggested, resting a hip against the railing. "If I recall correctly, we have some unfinished business between us."

More than you know, she thought, her mouth suddenly desert dry. She decided it would be best to keep her secret to herself. Until she was certain.

"You're talking about Dallas." Her heart kicked into overdrive as she thought about that night. He stared at her so hard she found it difficult to take a breath. Oh, Lord, why wasn't she immune to him? Why hadn't she forgotten him after that one star-spangled night they'd shared? Why was she such an idiot where he was concerned? "I don't think we should go into that."

"Why not?"

Unspoken accusations fairly crackled in the warm spring air. "Because there's no point to it. We had a night together, it was a mistake, and that's the end of it."

He grabbed her arm as if he expected her to flee. "Not exactly the end. We're both here now."

"So we are," she said, wishing she was anyplace else on earth other than standing toe-to-toe with him, sandal to scruffy boot, feeling his work-roughened fingertips on her skin and smelling the faint seductive scent of the aftershave he'd been wearing when she'd first met him. For a second she thought he might kiss her the way he had in Dallas. Her throat caught and it took all her strength to yank her arm free of him. "But I don't think we need to go into all that."

Thankfully, the old dog ambled up the steps to lay at her feet. "Some watchdog you are," she said, grateful for an excuse to not stare into Trent's silently accusing eyes. She reached down and scratched the mutt behind his ears. His dark eyes regarded her warmly, a wet, pink tongue slid out of the side of his mouth and he rolled over, offering her his belly to be rubbed.

"Seems like you've made a friend for life," Trent observed.

And right now I need each and every one, she thought.

The sound of a truck engine reached Gina's ears and she turned to see a big pickup lumbering down the lane. Piled high with sacks of grain, the bed sat low over the tires. Behind the wheel, aviator sunglasses in place, was Garrett Kincaid, the patriarch of a brood of six, maybe even seven, illegitimate grandchildren. Gina had never actually met any of the grown men and women who had Kincaid blood running through their veins.

Except for Trent.

And that meeting had proved a disaster of monumental proportions. In his case—and in his case only—she had let her personal curiosity overcome her self-imposed rule to distance herself from her clients.

"See, now, you didn't have to wait so long, after all," Trent said sarcastically. "Let's go have a chat with Gramps, shall we?"

He grabbed her wrist, making her pulse jump. With long, ground-eating strides he half dragged her as he made his way toward the stables where Garrett had parked beneath a solitary pine tree.

"Just wait a minute," she said as she jogged to keep up with him. She jerked her arm free. "I, um, I think it would be best if Garrett didn't know anything about what happened between you and me in Dallas," she admitted, feeling her cheeks stain with color that had nothing to do with the intensity of the sun. He didn't say a word, just waited, eyes narrowed, cords at the back of his neck standing out above the sun-bleached collar of his shirt.

"He wouldn't approve?"

"It's not that, but—"

"Don't worry about me, darlin'. I'm not the kind to kiss and tell." Trent's smile was pure saccharine.

She felt like a damned fool. "Good, because what happened between us had nothing to do with you being Garrett's grandson. You're the only one I ever met and... well..." She let her voice trail off; there was just no reason to go into it any further.

"Only one. You mean, you didn't meet Blake?"

She nodded. "Nor any of the other brothers."

He froze. "'Other brothers'?"

She hesitated. "Garrett didn't tell you?"

His jaw slid to one side. "Why don't you?"

In for a penny, in for a pound, she supposed. He'd learn soon enough. "Larry Kincaid fathered six sons out of wedlock, quite possibly seven."

Trent's eyes narrowed suspiciously. "Are you trying to tell me that, besides me and my twin, there are five others? That I've got five half brothers?"

"Well, actually, you have six half brothers, excluding your twin, and a half sister. Larry had a son, Collin, and daughter, Melanie, with his wife Sue Ellen. The rest were the result of his affairs with several different women."

Trent stared at her as if she'd gone mad. "That's impossible," he said as the conveyer loading the hay bales rumbled and a calf in a nearby field bawled plaintively. "No one's that stupid. Not in this day and age."

"It would be better for Garrett to explain this," she said, realizing she'd said too much. "He can tell you about your father."

"Let's get one thing straight," he said slowly, his nostrils flaring just a bit as he leaned down to drill her with those incredible blue eyes. "Larry Kincaid is *not* my father. It takes a helluva lot more than a one-night stand for a man to earn that title."

"I suppose." She swallowed hard at the irony in his words.

He glanced to the parking area near the stables where Garrett was climbing out of his truck. "And as for what happened in Dallas, I'll keep it to myself. For now."

"Good."

"Now I think it's time to get a few things straight with the old man." With that he strode toward the truck and left Gina behind, feeling like an utter fool.

Trent zeroed in on the man who claimed to be his grandfather as the older man walked around a dented fender of the truck.

"You must be Trent." Garrett removed his sunglasses, stuffed them into a pocket of his faded plaid shirt and extended his hand. "Here a bit early, aren't you?"

"I guess I just couldn't wait."

"Fair enough." Garrett's smile was rock-steady "Glad to finally meet you. Sorry it took so long."

Trent took the older man's hand. Garrett's clasp was strong and sure, his face weathered, his straight hair nearly silver. There was a trace of Native American in him, the coppery skin and high cheekbones giving testament to it, but his eyes were a startling blue. Intense enough that, Trent guessed, they could cut through any amount of bull slung in the old man's direction. "So, what do I call you? Gramps?" He couldn't hide the sarcasm in his tone. Trent had learned long ago not to rely on family. A man made his own way in the world. Period. He relied on no one.

"Garrett will do."

"Good."

"I guess I should start out by apologizing for my son." Pain stole through the old man's eyes. "I had no idea that you or any of the others existed." He lifted his hands and from the corner of his eye, Trent noticed that Gina had joined them in the shade of the tree and the old dog had followed suit, ambling across the sun-dappled gravel to sit at Garrett's feet.

"It's not your fault."

Garrett rubbed his chin. "No, but it doesn't mean I don't feel bad or obligated to make it up to you and the others."

"Maybe no one wants anything."

"Maybe." Garrett didn't seem convinced, and Trent realized this was a sincere man, one who was embarrassed by his son. Trent's biological father.

It seemed that Larry Kincaid was a far worse choice for being a father or role model than Harold Remmington, the man Trent's mother had passed off as his and his twin's father. Harold had been a decent enough guy, Trent supposed, if you liked wimps. Trent didn't.

But, hell, Larry Kincaid?

"You've met Gina, I see," Garrett said, hitching his chin in the woman's direction.

"Just."

Gina—if that was her real name—managed a smile that seemed well-practiced at best. Oh, she was a looker, he'd grant her that. He'd noticed her right off in the De-Marco Hotel's patio bar. She'd walked into the bar, alone, and he'd felt something like the soft touch of a finger at his nape. He'd looked up and found himself staring at the most beautiful woman he'd seen in a long, long while. Her red hair, cut in soft layers, had framed a perfectly oval face of white skin dusted with a few freckles. Her eyes, a deep green fringed with gold-tipped lashes, had seemed to sparkle in the moon glow. A pouty little smile that he'd found absolutely fascinating had been his undoing. From the first second he'd laid eyes on her, he'd determined that he would seduce her.

Right now, he noticed the rosy glow that had come to her cheeks. So she was embarrassed. She should be. She'd lied to him. And gotten caught. Trent had no use for liars. They were worse than wimps.

"We've actually met once before," she admitted, shaking Garrett's hand with a familiarity that bothered Trent. It was as if they were in on a very private secret—one that involved him. "Briefly. In Dallas."

Garrett raised a silver eyebrow, but didn't comment.

"Maybe we should go somewhere and sort this all out," Trent suggested, suddenly uncomfortable. He looked to the sky and saw a hawk circling and high above that, the fading wake of a jet slicing across the wide Montana sky.

"Good idea. We'll meet up at the house," Garrett suggested. "I suppose you both brought your things."

"Mine are in the car, but I'll take a room in town," Gina said quickly.

Garrett scowled. "Nonsense. We've got plenty of room and I'd like you close at hand."

She was moving in? Here?

"Let's get your bags inside."

"What about you?" He slid a glance at his grandson.

"I already talked to Rand. He showed me up to a room at the main house. He seemed to think it would be okay with you." Trent glanced at the two-storied home sitting upon a slight rise.

"More than okay. Just as long as you're all settled in."

"For a while," Trent said. He scratched his forearm and asked a question that had been bothering him. "I suppose you contacted Blake?"

"Yes. Talked to him this morning. Said he'd give you a call."

"I guess he missed me."

"And you didn't call him?"

"No."

Trent shook his head and didn't elaborate as he, along with Garrett, walked Gina to her Explorer. No reason to get into his problems with his twin right now. He had a feeling it would all come out soon enough.

"Blake will be here next week," Garrett said as Gina opened the back of her car. "So will the others."

Trent was faced with half a dozen bags. This lady didn't know the meaning of traveling light. "A regular family reunion." Trent pulled out a medium-size bag.

"Or irregular," Garrett corrected.

Trent's eyes narrowed as he considered the man who had sired him. "Eight kids by six different women. Didn't Larry know anything about birth control?"

"I guess not." Garrett scowled as he grabbed a bag. "And I'd say it's damned lucky for you that he didn't."

Chapter 3

Gina dropped her suitcase onto the bed and mentally kicked herself from one side of the sparse room to the other. Trent Remmington—why was he the one who'd shown up unannounced? What kind of cruel irony was that? Any of the other heirs she could have dealt with, but not Trent. Not until she was ready to face him again... and then again, maybe not ever. But all that had changed.

She hung up her few dresses in a closet about the size of a coffin, then refolded several pairs of jeans and T-shirts and placed them in a tall oak bureau. Glancing at her reflection in the cracked oval mirror attached to the bureau, she saw the wild state of her hair and the remainder of what had once been her makeup.

"Great," she groaned. She was cranky and out of sorts—probably just because she'd had to face Trent again. Certainly there was no other reason, right?

Biting her lower lip, she touched her tight, flat abdomen.

Was it possible? Could she be pregnant? Seeing Trent again only reinforced her worries. She'd never been one of those women whose menstrual cycle was like clockwork, but even she was overdue for her period.

"It's just your nerves," she said, picking up her brush and working it through the tangles in her hair. "This case has got you in knots."

But she wasn't convinced as she twisted her hair and pinned it with a clip, then applied a fresh sheen of lipstick and called it good. Sighing, she sat on the edge of the narrow bed and wondered how long she could stand to call this room her home. A sun-faded rug covered the wood floor and a small desk, shoved into a corner, doubled as a nightstand. The room smelled faintly musty, so she threw open a window, letting in a breeze that billowed ancient lace curtains.

From her vantage point on the second story, she watched the old dog sniff his way to an oak tree where he stopped to eye a squirrel scrambling in the overhead branches. On the other side of the fence, sedate mares grazed in one pasture, their coats shining in the sun while spindly legged foals frolicked and scampered, sending up puffs of dust. Not far off, in a field so large she couldn't see the fence line, a herd of cattle lumbered along the banks of a creek that sliced through the lush grassland.

Gina wondered about the men and women who lived here, so far from a large city. She watched as Garrett and a strapping man in a cowboy hat and dusty jeans unloaded the sacks of feed from the back of the pickup. The conveyer had stopped moving and one of the hands had hopped back onto the tractor. With a growl and plume of black smoke, the old John Deere headed through an open gate.

Horses nickered, cattle lowed, and a wasp buzzed as it worked hard on a muddy nest hanging just under the eaves. Gina inhaled the fresh air laced with the scents of spring flowers and new-mown hay, then sighed.

"Heaven on earth," she heard, and whipped around to find Trent standing in the doorway, one shoulder propped insolently against the jamb, his arms folded across his chest.

"Looks like it."

"Even to a city girl?"

"Especially to a city girl."

To her surprise, he strode into the room and swung the door shut behind him. "I think we'd better talk," he said, grabbing the desk chair. He swung it around backward, straddled the seat and leaned his arms across the back. "You start."

"By?"

"By telling me what's going on. With the old man, with you—whoever you are. Let's start with Dallas."

"That was a mistake," she said, meeting his gaze evenly. "I think we both know it."

"It wasn't a setup?"

"Excuse me? A setup? What…?" She stared into his angry blue eyes and suddenly understood. "You think I planned meeting you and…and what?"

"Seducing me."

She nearly laughed. The man was out of his ever-lovin' mind. "Don't flatter yourself, Remmington. I'd had too much to drink, so had you. I had no idea you'd be in that hotel bar that night and—"

"And you knew who I was. An advantage, I'd say."

"It wasn't a game."

"No?" He scowled and rubbed his chin. "Sure feels like one now. One that I somehow lost." His gaze drilled deep into hers. "Believe it or not, I'm not used to losing."

The man was damned irritating, but someone she had to deal with, like it or not. "I understand."

"That's right. You know all about me." He stood and crossed the few feet separating them, looming over her to the point that she nearly backed into the open window, but somehow stood her ground. "And I know nothing about you, do I?"

"Except what I've told you."

"Exactly. So let's get one very important thing straight, shall we? I don't like anyone snooping into my life. Period. And I don't trust people who lie to me. So you already have two strikes against you in this little 'non-game.' The way I see it, three strikes and you're out."

She told herself not to lose it. To grab on to the rags of her temper and hold tight. But she couldn't. It wasn't her nature. "Look, Trent—I can call you that, right, considering the circumstances. 'Mr. Remmington' seems a little formal. Yes, I was hired by Garrett to find you, not to pry into your personal life, but to locate you and determine that you were one of Larry Kincaid's sons. That's all. I lied to you that night in Dallas because I—I—"

"Didn't want to blow your cover?"

"Well, yeah, that's kind of a TV-cop way of describing it, but I'd told myself I wasn't going to meet any of the Kincaid heirs, that I would keep this as professional as possible and then…okay, I blew it. I have to confess, when I stumbled into you that night and you started flirting with me, I couldn't resist. I guess you're just too damned irresistible. Is that what you wanted to hear?"

He stared at her as if he couldn't believe a word. Neither could she, but she couldn't stop herself and she was far from finished.

"So, in answer to your question—" she closed the gap between them to mere inches and glared up at him as if she wasn't shaking inside "—meeting you wasn't part of some nefarious scheme or shakedown or whatever you want to call it. It was, as I said before, a mistake. Maybe it's one that we should just get over, okay?"

A huge hand snaked forward to clamp possessively over her forearm. "Get over? I don't know about you, lady, but that kind of thing doesn't happen to me every day of the week."

"Oh, save me." She glanced down at the hand encircling her arm. "And remove that now. I'm not going for any of your Neanderthal tactics."

His fingers released and she walked around him, picked up her laptop computer case and unzipped it. "Was there anything else you wanted to grill me about?" she asked, glancing over her shoulder as she placed the sleek little computer on the desk near her bed.

"I just wanted to clear the air."

"Consider it cleared." She found the outlet and plugged in her machine, then, ignoring the drumming of her heart, looked around for a phone jack.

As if he understood her dilemma, he said, "There aren't any connections in the rooms. I already checked." With a thumb hooked toward the wall, he added, "I'm in the next room."

Her stomach tightened. He was close, too damned

close. Just one door down the hall? In a house that had seven bedrooms. Just…great.

"I've already talked to Garrett and placed a call to the local phone company to have a few more lines installed, but it'll take a while." He walked to the door and swung it wide, then strode through and said over his shoulder, "As I said earlier, 'This ain't exactly L.A.'"

So it was true, Jordan thought as he shoved his plate to one side of the table. He'd eaten a long, late lunch, listening to the gossip buzzing around him like a swarm of mosquitoes on a stagnant swamp. Garrett Kincaid had, with the help of a private investigative firm from somewhere in California, located Larry's illegitimate brood. He'd also managed to get control of the ranch that Jordan considered his own private legacy. Of course, he'd been screwed out of it. All those promises his uncle Cameron had made weren't diddly squat. Once again, the Kincaids had kicked the Baxters.

Hell.

Frowning darkly, Jordan stirred his coffee and his blood boiled, but he somehow managed to hold his tongue. He'd learned a long time ago it was better to get even than to get mad, but that took considerable self-control.

Jordan took a long sip from his cup, eyed the desserts that were slowly cooling in a rotating display case, and eased back in his booth. He was alone, which was fitting, he supposed. Since returning to Whitehorn a millionaire several times over, he'd collected a lot of "friends," but he didn't trust any of them. He knew they only liked him for his money and what he could do for them. Yep, he was becoming a powerful man here in Whitehorn and he'd been feeling pretty good about himself until Wayne Kincaid hadn't accepted his offer to buy back the ranch he should have inherited.

"How about a piece of pie?" Janie asked, dragging him out of his vengeful thoughts. She was a cute thing and efficient as all get-out. Her blond hair was pulled back into a ponytail and her perennial smile was tacked neatly in place. Head waitress and would-be manager, she ran the Hip Hop Café these days. "We've got fresh strawberry-rhubarb, and isn't that your favorite?"

"Yep, but I think I'll pass."

"Your loss," she teased, and refilled his cup.

"Hey, what's this I hear about Garrett Kincaid buying the ranch from Wayne and fillin' it up with the grand-kids that Larry left all over the country?"

Little lines formed between Janie's eyebrows and she hesitated. She wasn't one prone to gossip, unlike most of her clientele. "That's the word. I haven't talked to Garrett myself about it, though, so, I guess it's still just hearsay." She slapped Jordan's check onto the table as the front door opened and a group of teenagers walked in. "If you reconsider about the pie, flag me down."

"Will do." He reached for his wallet and eyed the crowd. There was Lily Mae, the town's premier gossip, dressed to kill, as usual, in a tight lavender sweater and matching slacks. At another table Winona Cobbs's graying head was ducked low as she engaged Christina Montgomery, the mayor's younger daughter, in a quiet conversation.

From different tables of the packed café he heard the name Kincaid mentioned several times.

"Six of 'em, can you believe it?" Lily Mae was saying. "All with different mothers, aside from the twins, that is." She was spouting off to a woman Jordan didn't recognize. "And there's talk of another one. I tell you, say what you will about Larry Kincaid, he was certainly a charmer."

Jordan snorted and finished his coffee.

He'd heard enough. Larry Kincaid's bastard sons were about to descend upon the town. He left several bills, including a healthy tip, and tossed his napkin onto the table. That's just what the town needed. More Kincaids, and bastards at that.

Well, really, he thought bitterly as he jaywalked, dodging a sports car that was speeding down Center Avenue, weren't they all?

Why did he let the woman get to him? Trent wondered as he helped unload a sack of feed and stacked it in the stables. So she'd sneaked around, so she'd lied to him, so he hadn't been able to resist her that one hot night in Dallas. So what? Forget her. He just had to put up with her for a few days here in Whitehorn and then he'd fly out and leave her forever.

Right?

He gritted his teeth and using his body, slammed the sacks of feed nearer the wall, straightening each stack. He tried to ignore the feeling that Gina was different, that she wasn't just the love-'em-and-leave-'em kind of woman he associated with one-night stands. His jaw clamped tight. Years ago he hadn't thought one way or the other about meeting a woman and bedding her. But as he'd aged, he'd become more selective, more careful, restraining himself. He'd learned that people, women included, always wanted something from him, something more than he was willing to give.

So he'd been cautious. Until that damned night in Dallas.

"Something wrong?" Garrett asked as he dragged the last sack from the truck and flung it on top of the pile. For an old man he was strong, a hard worker, though Trent did detect a hint of a limp and glimpsed the sweat that ran down the back of his neck. Garrett yanked off his battered leather gloves and set them on top of a barrel of oats. "You look like something's eating at you."

"Got a lot to think about."

"Don't we all?" Together they strode through the fading sunlight to the main house. They kicked off their boots on the back porch and walked into the kitchen where a pretty woman with dark upswept hair was overseeing boiling pots on the stove and peering into the oven. "The chicken's about done," she said, looking up at Garrett with dark, shining eyes. "I'll just whip these potatoes and you can gather in the dining room. Oh, hi." She spied Trent, wiped a hand on her apron and extended it. "I'm Suzanne."

"Rand's wife," Garrett said quickly. "My grandson, Trent Remmington. I called Suzanne in to pinch-hit with the cooking until I can find someone to take over. Suzanne, here, is an accountant in town."

"That is when I'm not playing Julia Child," she teased, then laughed at the pseudo-consternation twisting Garrett's features.

"Actually, I don't mind," she said as she found a couple of pot holders and carried a kettle of boiled potatoes to the sink. She poured most of the water down the drain, saving a little in a smaller bowl. "Since my baby, Joe, was born, my career's slowed down. I just do the books for a few people now. There." She set the pot of

potatoes on the counter and, opening the oven door, re-
trieved a couple of golden-brown chickens. "I'll make
the gravy, then serve up in about fifteen minutes. After
that I'd better hurry home. I left Joe with my brother."
She rolled her eyes and grinned.

"Mack's a good kid, but there's only so much 'quality time' he can stand with his nephew." She laughed
brightly at the thought. "He's seventeen and all thumbs
around the baby, but I figure it's time he learned about
kids before he gets wrapped up in some girl and has
one of his own."

"Best form of birth control there is," Trent observed.

Suzanne's smile slid away and Garrett's expression
turned sober. "We'd better wash up."

Realizing the old man was apparently having trouble
with his son's indiscretions, Trent didn't say anything
else. He walked through a long hallway to the main stairs
but at the archway leading to the living room, his footsteps slowed. He heard Gina's muffled voice.

"I said I'd be back as soon as this was finished, Jack,"
she said hotly, then paused for a few seconds while the
guy on the other end of the line had his say. "Yeah, I
know, I know. I'll wrap this up as soon as I can."

Another pause.

Trent told himself to move on, that she deserved some
privacy, but then he reminded himself that she hadn't
been all that interested in preserving his. For all he knew,
she'd dug into the most intimate details of his life.

*And didn't you try to do the same to her? Didn't you
hire a private investigator to find Celia O'Hara and
when that didn't pan out, have him look into Garrett
Kincaid's life?*

He ignored the attack of sudden conscience.

"I'm not sure, Jack," Gina said with a long-suffering sigh. "I'm still looking into it. But I'll be back soon, I promise." She laughed then, that deep, throaty laugh that had caught his attention in Dallas, and he felt a moment of jealousy. "Yeah, I miss you, too... Oh, come on, you know I do. What? ... Now, listen, quit worrying! I can take care of myself." He must've said something incredibly amusing again because this time she chuckled. "Fine, I'll remember. If I'm not gonna be back in a couple of days, then you'll just have to carry on without me, and yes, I'm sure it'll break your heart, but believe me, Jack, you can handle it." She listened again, then sighed theatrically. "Me, too. Okay, I've gotta run. I'll call again." Another minute's hesitation while the guy on the other end of the telephone line said his goodbyes. "Love you, too," she said as she hung up.

Trent, feeling like the eavesdropper he was, considered climbing the stairs and high-tailing it to his room. But that seemed a little sneaky and he'd always prided himself on being a straight shooter.

Jamming his fists into his pockets, he sauntered into the living room and found her nestled in the corner of a floral couch that had seen better days, staring at the cold grate of the fireplace. "Boyfriend?" he asked, startling her.

"What?"

He pointed at the phone. "I overheard the tail end of your conversation with your boyfriend. Sounds like he's missing you."

A smile tugged at the corner of those full lips. "Oh, he is." She nodded, her green eyes flashing with amusement, as if she'd just pulled a fast one on him.

"Special guy?" He couldn't help but ask and tried to ignore another jab of unlikely jealousy.

"Very." He could see the pride in the way she held her head. She cared about the man very much. Sunlight pierced the windows and caught in the fiery strands of her hair.

"Known him long?"

"All my life."

That bothered Trent. This guy Jack had watched her grow up while he'd only met her a few weeks earlier. "So, he's kind of a boy next door?"

"You could say that." She was more than amused now, he thought. Curled up on the faded sofa, her bare feet tucked beneath her, a notepad on her lap, she looked cozy and warm, as if she belonged in this rambling old house with its out-of-date, yellowed wallpaper and odd collection of memorabilia. There were all manner of guns mounted on the walls, antlers and animal heads, trophies from long-ago kills now collecting dust in the den and even, down one hallway, a showcase of old Western costumes and Native American paraphernalia.

Trent walked to the fireplace. "This guy—Jack," he said, nodding toward the phone. "Does he know about me?"

"He's heard of you, yes."

"About Dallas?"

She blushed and shook her head. "Nope. And I hope he never finds out." She set her notebook aside, hesitated, and finally said, "I thought we were going to let what happened go."

"Can you?"

She bit her lip. All hint of amusement left her face. "I don't know," she said, and it was the first statement she'd made that he believed. "But I'm going to try. Hard. It might be difficult the next couple of days since we'll both be here, but I'm going to see if I can rise above it." Her eyes narrowed a bit. "That is, if you would quit throwing it up in my face. You know, it wasn't as if what happened was all my fault. As the old saying goes, 'it takes two to tango.'"

"But one of us didn't lie about it."

"So flog me with a dozen cat-o'-nine-tails, or toss me in the pillory, or blaze my shirt with a scarlet A... or, oh—" She snapped her fingers and shot to her feet. "I know something even better! Why don't you keep bringing it up and trying to throw some guilt on me, huh? How about that?" With that she turned on a bare heel and stormed out.

He started after her and she sent him a look over one stiff shoulder that was guaranteed to freeze mercury. "Don't, okay? Don't run after me, don't say anything more, and next time I'm on the phone, don't put a glass to the window or listen at the keyhole. It's really none of your business."

"That's where you're wrong, darlin'," he drawled. "You were the one who started poking into my life. Remember? Not the other way around. So I think whatever you do here just might be my business."

"Just stay out of my way."

"That might be impossible."

"Give it a try, okay?" She was out of the room and up the stairs like a shot.

Trent wondered where a man kept his whiskey around this house, and cringed when he heard Suzanne Harding call, "Okay, dinner's on. Come and get it."

Garrett had no idea what had gotten into Trent and Gina, but he didn't like it. No, he didn't like it one bit.

All through Suzanne's tasty meal of chicken, mashed potatoes and gravy, applesauce and green beans, they'd both picked at their food, tried their damnedest to ignore one another, and forced smiles onto faces that were both strained and drawn.

Something was up.

If he didn't know better, he'd think they were having themselves some kind of lover's spat. For that's sure what it looked like. But that was impossible. They hardly knew each other.

Trent, shoving his plate aside, finally said, "Okay, so tell me about these other 'brothers' that I've got. How'd you find out about me and them?"

Garrett pushed his chair back from the long table and walked the few steps to the sideboard where Suzanne had left a pot of coffee. Filling three cups, he set them on the table and said, "I was going to explain all this to everyone at the same time, but being as you're here now, I guess I may as well get down to it." He settled into his chair again, felt a pinch of arthritis in his hip and ignored it. This was the tough part, trying to explain his only son's irresponsible actions. "Let's go outside, and sit on the back porch."

Though the two hadn't said a civil word to each other all night, they followed Garrett through French doors to a picnic table and benches. Gina took a seat at the table with Garrett. Trent stood on the porch, bracing his back against a pillar that supported the roof.

"Okay, so shoot," Trent suggested.

Garrett cradled his cup in his hands. This was the hard part. Trying to explain about his son. It pained him. When Larry had been born more than fifty years ago, Garrett had been proud enough to pop. A son. A healthy, good-looking, robust boy. But as the years had passed, Larry had proven to be wayward and ornery, selfish and lazy. Even worse, he'd never been able to keep his hands off women, even as a teenager. But that had been a long time ago.

"This isn't easy, you see. Burying a child, no matter how difficult he was, is painful." Garrett frowned and stared into the dark depths of his coffee. "When Larry died, it about killed me," he admitted, acknowledging that black hole in his heart. "It hadn't been long after Laura had passed away and I was just thankful that she wasn't alive." His lips folded over his teeth and he tamped down the pain that was always with him when he thought of his wife and firstborn. "Anyway, I went through all of Larry's things after he died and I found a safe-deposit box key for a local bank. Larry had asked me to sign on the box years ago and I'd forgotten about it. When I opened it, I discovered a letter from Larry to me or Collin—"

"Who is his legitimate son?" Trent guessed.

"Right. Anyway, there was a smaller box inside the one in the bank and the most important document in that was a letter that explained about the other kids Larry had fathered." He lifted one hand. "There were names, dates, and some addresses, pictures and canceled checks, notes, baby photos, birth certificates…even copies of old report cards. He must've kept everything he ever laid his hands on, and I guess he kept it in the safe-deposit box so when he died someone in the family would know about you and your brothers."

"Thoughtful of him," Trent said sarcastically.

"It was something. Not much, I'll grant you that,"

Garrett admitted, wishing there was some way he could defend his son. "But at least I found out about you."

"No one else knew about us?"

"Just the mothers, near as I can figure, and they all kept their mouths shut."

"Why?"

"I don't know."

"Some of them were paid," Gina said.

"You're trying to tell me they bribed him or they were given hush money? Is that it?"

Gina lifted a shoulder.

"Who knows," Garrett said. "I didn't figure I should bother them. It's between them and their boys."

Trent let out a snort of disdain. "This family exceeds the limits of dysfunctional." He tossed the rest of his coffee onto the parched grass.

"Then I guess it's time we fixed that."

"Or maybe it's too late."

"Well, I guess we won't know until we try, now, will we?" Garrett asked as Trent cast Gina one last look and strode inside.

Gina attempted to act disinterested but Garrett had been around enough men and women in his life to recognize when two people were interested in each other. In Trent and Gina's case, they were way beyond interested.

Gina had admitted to meeting Trent in Dallas.

Garrett wondered what had happened. But he didn't ask. He figured he might just be better off not knowing.

Chapter 4

So much for the quiet of the country lulling her to sleep. Gina tossed off the covers in her tiny bed and padded barefoot across the room to grab her robe—a short cotton thing that worked better as a beach cover-up but was lightweight and easy to pack. Without making a sound, she walked downstairs and out the back door. The moon rode high in an inky sky littered with millions of stars— more stars than she'd ever seen.

Wrapping her arms around her, she hurried along a well-worn path to the stables and there, leaning over the fence railing, she watched the dark shapes of the horses shifting in the night. The air was warm, a light breeze dancing across the fresh-mown hay and playing in the overhead branches of a pine tree.

Peaceful. Serene. Panoramic. So different from the bustle of L.A., a city that was filled with the hum of traffic, beep of keyless locks and scream of sirens at all hours of the night. Here, the chirp of crickets, croak of frogs and occasional nicker from the horses were the only obstructions to a pure, almost ethereal silence.

And Trent Remmington was sleeping in the room next to hers at the main house. Unbelievable! Her fingers tightened over the top rail. So much for tranquility or peace of mind. How had she been so stupid as to get involved with him—if that's what you'd call it. Crueler tongues might dub what had happened between them as a one-night stand or a bar pickup.

She flinched inwardly at the terms. She'd never been one to get involved easily, and, if any name had been fitting for her, it had been Ice Princess as she'd always had a hands-off attitude toward men. At least during the first few dates. She'd grown up watching her divorced mother struggle to make ends meet and eventually marry a man for financial security. Gina had decided then and there that it wasn't a path she'd ever take. No way. No how. Not for her. She would never sacrifice her happiness nor her self esteem for a man—any man—and so, she'd never found one that had really interested her.

Until Trent. Blast the man. She'd been intrigued with Trent Remmington from the first time she'd opened Larry Kincaid's box of memorabilia. The "bad twin," Trent had been as rebellious and wild as his brother Blake had been good and conscientious. Trent drank, smoked, rode motorcycles, boats and horses at breakneck speeds and had the citations, bruises, and scars to prove it.

He'd gone through baby-sitters and governesses like water, even managed to get kicked out of more than one boarding school. When Gina had read his profile, she'd been instantly attracted to the sexy, irreverent rebel. At fifteen he'd "borrowed" an idling bus and tried to drive it through the drive-in window of a local burger hut. At sixteen he'd jumped on a boxcar and rode across the country. At seventeen he'd climbed the ivy-enshrouded halls of his exclusive boarding school to steal a test and been expelled. A few years later, after dropping out of college, he'd bluffed his way through a high-stakes poker game to win. He'd put up the title of his sports car and had come out not only still owning the car—he had still owed Blake the five thousand dollars he'd borrowed for it but also with the deed to a scrap of property on which he'd eventually discovered oil.

So the hellion who had come within a hair's breadth of landing in jail had ended up a wildcat oilman who had struck it rich without benefit of a higher education or a grandfather or a father to grease the way for him. He'd made his millions by luck, grit and brains.

Trent had not only been strapping, good-looking and blessed with a killer smile, he had also been a child lost, a hellion of a teenager, and a man who, against all odds, had made good.

In retrospect, Gina decided on this starry night, she'd been well-primed, ready to fall victim to his very serious set of charms.

It had been a night not much different from this one when she'd chanced to run into him. She'd had one last night in Dallas where she'd located Trent Remmington at a convention. Having already checked out his Houston-based corporation, Black Gold International, she'd come to Dallas and got a glimpse of the man himself. Gina had been ready to return to L.A., where Jack was waiting for her to wrap up this case, but, suddenly feeling in the mood for celebration, she'd gone downstairs to the patio bar for a glass of wine.

She'd drunk two glasses of wine in less than an hour. Which wasn't so bad, except for the fact that having not eaten since breakfast, the Cabernet had immediately gone to her head. Seated at a table near a planter, she looked across the dance floor toward the bar and spied none other than the object of her most recent hunt: Trent Remmington.

To him, she was a stranger, but from months of researching his life, she felt as if she already knew him. She'd spent weeks tracking him down and piecing together his life as the fifth illegitimate son of Larry Kincaid. She'd seen pictures of him, read every article ever written about him, been fascinated by him.

On this spring night she couldn't help but stare as he sipped what looked like a Scotch and water. When he'd glanced her way, she'd dropped her eyes and decided to leave before she did something stupid like introduce herself to him.

She started to leave, but before she could sign off on her tab, the waiter appeared with another glass of wine. "Compliments of the gentleman at the bar."

Her stomach dropped to the floor. She didn't have to look to know that he meant Trent, who, though not staring at her directly, was viewing her in a beveled mirror suspended above the bar.

This is a mistake, she told herself, but managed to smile at the waiter and accept the drink. She glanced at Trent again and, heart knocking ridiculously, held the glass aloft and mouthed, "Thanks."

He nodded, but remained on his bar stool, nursing

his drink. A live band tuned up in the corner and a few brave couples, some with incredible dance skills, took over the floor. Gina finished her wine, felt a little light-headed and was about to leave when another glass of Cabernet appeared.

"Oh, no, I couldn't," she said, shaking her head.

"The gentleman insists."

"But—" She started to argue, but the waiter breezed away, taking an order at a nearby table, and Gina was left with the drink. She didn't have to drive, only had to make it up to her room where she'd already asked for a wake-up call, but she didn't need another glass of wine. Didn't want one.

She looked over to the bar and Trent was assessing her, his blue eyes bright in the reflection of the mirror. There was amusement in his gaze, the hint of a smile toying with his lips, and she felt an instant surge of anger.

He was getting off watching her try to decline the stupid glass of wine. And what would happen if she downed it? Would he send over another? Spying the challenge in his silent gaze, she sat, drank the wine and rose again.

Another appeared, just as she'd expected.

"I really couldn't," she insisted, but the waiter wouldn't take no for an answer and she was left with a glass of expensive wine on the table in front of her.

Again the look in the mirror.

Great.

Though a part of her brain nagged at her that she was making an incredible, irreversible mistake, she felt bolder than she should have. Picking up the stemmed glass and carrying it carefully, she wove between the dancing couples and made her way to the bar.

"I suppose I should thank you for the drink—no, drinks," she said, unable to hide a trace of sarcasm in her voice.

"My pleasure." A crooked grin slashed across his jaw.

Damn the man but he was enjoying this. The twinkle in those blue eyes gave him away.

"Have a seat." He patted the vacant stool next to his.

She knew she shouldn't, but found it impossible to resist. "Trent Remmington," he said. To her horror she found his boyish grin incredibly endearing.

"Uh, Celia..." she said. Though tipsy, she realized she couldn't admit her real name or true calling. Besides, she was just thanking the man for buying her a glass of wine. "Celia O'Hara."

"In town for the weekend?"

"Yes."

"Business or pleasure?"

"Just visiting my sister," she lied, telling herself she was getting into this way too deep. "You?"

"Convention here in town."

"Business, then?"

"For the most part."

"You live around here?"

"Houston, actually. As I said, just here for a convention." He finished his drink. "Want to dance?"

She hadn't danced in ages. "Dance?" She was certain she shouldn't. It wasn't a good idea to be this close to Trent Remmington when she was sober, let alone when she was feeling a little giddy. However the wine seemed to control her tongue and actions and she angled her head up and flirted outrageously.

"Why not?"

A million reasons raced through her head. This is

dangerous. He's your client, for God's sake, whether he knows it or not. He's got a reputation for living on the edge. If he finds out you lied to him, it will be a disaster. A calamity! But she didn't stop herself.

The song was a slow country tune that she should have recognized but didn't. Trent's fingers touched her elbow, guiding her to the floor, and she felt her pulse leap. Oh, God, this was worse than she thought. He folded her into his arms and she realized she was in trouble. Big trouble. Kincaid-handsome, he was strong, smelled faintly of musk and he felt warm and, oh, so right. Her stupid heart began to race, and as his breath brushed her hair, she imagined kissing those blade-thin lips that she'd seen in so many of the photographs Larry had hidden away.

Of all the Kincaid heirs, Trent was the one who had touched her, who had reached through the reams of paper to find her heart. She felt as if she already knew him intimately, had shared his most private secrets, his quiet pain.

But that was crazy.

Or was it?

As the band's lead singer crooned an old love song, it seemed so natural to be held close to him and imagine she could hear the beat of his heart over the music, the buzz of conversation and the clink of flatware. Hundreds of tiny white lights winked through the boughs of the potted trees placed strategically around the patio and a soft, warm breeze caressed her face.

Though she wasn't the greatest dancer around, Trent made the steps seem easy. He held her close without crushing her, twirled her through the other couples without any effort, and never once did she even step on his toes. All in all, it was a miracle. A blessing. A...catastrophe! She couldn't be dancing with one of her clients, one who didn't even know he was the object of her search, one to whom she'd already lied.

When the song stopped, he held her a little too long and she could barely breathe. Her skin tingled and her heart was drumming in her ears. She wanted to sag against him, but fortunately he released her. She took one deep breath, then he took her hand and, after snagging their drinks from the bar, led her to a booth in a darkened corner where he settled onto a bench beside her. She tried to convince herself that she had to leave, that she couldn't trust herself this close to him.

"So tell me about yourself," he suggested, his thigh pressing against hers. Deep inside she started to melt. Swallowing hard, she picked up her glass and took a sip of wine that she suddenly wanted to gulp. "Are you married?"

"No." She held up the bare fingers of her left hand as proof and told herself that she was getting into hot water.

"Ever been?"

She shook her head.

"Why not? And don't give me some line about not meeting the right guy."

"Okay, I won't. I'm just a wallflower by nature."

His eyes narrowed on her and she had to swallow a smile. She'd worn a tight black minidress, strappy high heels, and added gold earrings and a necklace. She'd even gone so far as to twist her hair onto her head, letting only a few soft wisps fall around her nape and face.

"Wallflower," he repeated, then shook his head. "Nice try, Celia. But I'm not buying."

She lifted a shoulder. "You asked. How about you?"

"Been lucky so far. Never even gotten close."

She knew this, of course. He had a reputation of short-term relationships that never developed into anything serious.

"So are there any exes lurking in your past?"

"Not much of a past to lurk in, I'm afraid," she admitted, and he seemed skeptical.

"Got a job?"

"Paralegal. Thinking about becoming a lawyer." Jeez, how did these lies fly out of her mouth so quickly?

He cocked a dark eyebrow and took a sip from his drink.

She pretended she didn't know a thing about him. "So you're trying to convince me that you don't have an ex-wife and a dozen kids stashed away somewhere." Candlelight cast gold shadows across his bold features.

"No, I was lying earlier. I've really got four ex-wives and, get it right, fifteen children. Not just a dozen." He chuckled and his smile seemed more sincere, his interest obviously piqued.

Careful, Gina, you're treading in dangerous waters here, the sober, nose-to-the-grindstone private investigator part of her mind screamed. But the other part, the feminine, ludicrously romantic side, wanted to wade ever deeper and couldn't resist stepping closer to the whirlpool that she sensed was so near.

"So what do you do for a living that allows you to support all those kids and still leaves enough change left over to buy strange women glasses of expensive wine?" she asked innocently, wondering if he would tell the truth.

"Well, I'm a millionaire several times over, have oil wells and real-estate ventures all over the state, and saw you sitting all by yourself and thought you looked interesting."

She smiled and sipped her wine. "Does this line of yours usually work?"

"Usually." He said it without a trace of arrogance.

She wanted desperately to keep this game going, but she knew instinctively that she would only cause herself the kind of problems she didn't want or need in her life. She leaned over as if to kiss him, but said instead, "Well, it's not working with me. Not tonight."

"And you're a lousy liar."

"No, I—" With one hand he reached up and cupped the back of her head, and held her face firmly close to his. His eyes were suddenly so close she noticed the different shades of blue fusing together. His lips were near enough that when he spoke they brushed against hers.

"As I said, a lousy liar."

She gulped as she stared into those laser-bright orbs and tried to come up with some quick comeback. Was he going to kiss her? Oh, God, right here in the bar? With the dancers and the band and the other patrons? Pulse racing, she was suddenly and desperately out of breath. She licked her lips.

"Thought so," he said arrogantly. His hand dropped.

So he'd been toying with her!

Like a frightened colt, she bolted. As she stood suddenly, her elbow hit her glass, splashing wine on Trent's shirt and suit, on his face, on the table.

"Oh, I'm—I'm sorry," she said, trying to swab up the spills and feeling her face turn as red as the wine. "Your suit…"

"It's all right."

She was mopping furiously with a napkin. "You've

got to clean that before the stain sets. I'll pay the dry-cleaning bill."

"It's all right."

"No." She was insistent. "I mean, please, I feel like an idiot. The least I can do is pay for this." She motioned feebly to the red stain on his shirt and the drips still clinging to his jacket. "If you take it to the cleaner's you can send me the bill—" No, that wouldn't work. Even though she was a little tipsy, she knew she couldn't give out her real name or address; he'd catch her in her lie. "Or better yet, why don't you just give me the suit and I'll have it cleaned here at the hotel and get it to you tomorrow."

"Great idea. Let's go." He was on his feet in an instant. His fingers circled Gina's wrist as he dragged her with him. She wanted to argue, but when she started to protest, she saw the light of challenge in his eyes, the lift of one of his cocky eyebrows, the absolute belief that she wouldn't take him up on the offer.

"Lead the way," she said, fighting back all her rational instincts that told her she was not only flirting with the man but danger, as well. "If that's what you think we should do."

He sent her a glance that was pure sexual energy. "Oh, yeah. I do think." He said to the barkeep, "Put it on my tab." Then with Gina in tow, her head spinning from too much wine, he made his way to the elevator. Once in the car, he punched a button for the penthouse floor.

Her stomach knotted. What was she doing? Alone with him as the elevator sped to the top floor, she felt her feet beginning to chill. By the time the elevator car landed on the uppermost floor and the doors opened,

Gina had a severe case of cold feet. "I'm not sure this is a good idea."

"I know it isn't." Still pulling her, he led her into a suite with a panoramic view of the city. The lights of Dallas blazed. Stars twinkled. Her head spun.

What am I doing here? she wondered, and nearly fell into one of two small leather couches angled around a glass-topped table that held a basket of fruit and an ice bucket with a bottle of chilling champagne. A gas fire hissed from a marble-faced fireplace and through double-glass doors she caught a glimpse of a king-size bed. Soft music played through hidden speakers.

Get out of here, Gina. Get out of here before you do something stupid!

"Pour yourself a drink. Anything you want." He motioned to a minibar tucked inside the wall unit as he walked into the bedroom.

"I think I've had enough. Done enough damage to your clothes."

"Suit yourself." He was already unbuttoning his shirt and rather lone even be tempted to look at him, she walked to the windows and stared out at the city, where the traffic hummed and a few clouds dared venture across the moonlit night.

Just get out, Gina. As fast as you can! Take his clothes, send them down to the cleaner's and then go back to your room and forget him. He's a client, or more precisely, the object of a client's quest. Don't forget it. It was crazy that she was anywhere near his hotel room, especially considering how she felt about him, the mental picture she'd drawn of him, the way she empathized with his rebellion and felt pride at what he'd accomplished on his own terms.

She had to leave and fast.

She heard him emerge from the bedroom and turned to find him in a clean pair of slacks and polo shirt. Barefoot. He strode to the table and without saying a word, opened the bottle of champagne and as it popped and foamed, poured two glasses. Carrying one in each hand, he walked to the bank of windows where she stood. She hoped she didn't look like a frightened doe caught in headlights.

Her pulse quickened with each of his steps and she forced her eyes away from the neckline of his shirt and the dark chest hairs springing from the open collar.

"Another bad idea," she said when he held out a long-stemmed glass.

"I guess I'm just chock-full of 'em."

"Appears so."

Reluctantly she accepted the glass. "How about a toast?" she suggested, intending to take one sip and bolt.

"You go first."

"Okay. How about, 'Here's mud in your eye'?"

A smile touched the edges of his mouth. "I expected something a little more original."

"Such as…?"

"To chance meetings." He touched the rim of his glass to hers and her heart did a silly little flip.

They both sipped and she managed to stare into his erotic blue eyes. "Or how about, 'To the art of dry cleaning'?"

"Why not?" Again he tapped his glass to hers. Again they sipped.

He didn't stop there. "Or to—let's see—how about 'To women who aren't always what they seem'?"

"Are you talking about me?" she asked, ignoring the increased tempo of her heartbeat.

"If the shoe fits…"

"Easy for a barefoot man to say," she teased, and he chuckled deep in his throat. "You don't know anything about me."

"Whose fault is that?"

"You wouldn't want to know."

One eyebrow elevated and the hint of a dimple creased his cheek. "Try me."

"I don't think so. Just trust me on this one." She was warm inside from the wine but feeling guilty for the lies she'd so glibly told him. But there was no way out of them now. That was the trouble with lies; one bred another and another and so on. She set her half-drunk glass on a side table where a vase of irises, birds of paradise and lilies overflowed. "I think I'd better leave. Where's the suit?"

"In the bedroom."

"Maybe you'd better bring it out."

She half expected him to invite her to go get it herself, but he nodded curtly and, leaving his glass beside hers, walked through the open doors again and returned with the black suit and shirt. "You don't have to do this," he admitted.

"Of course I do."

"It was an accident."

"I know, but I'd really feel better if you'd let me take care of it." She didn't want to argue, just make tracks.

"Why?" he asked. "Why would it make you feel better, since we both know you didn't mean anything by it."

"Accident or not, it was my fault." Oh, this argument was stupid.

He shook his head, tossed the suit onto a couch, cast a guilty glance at Gina and then out the window. "Maybe I should be honest with you."

Gina cringed inwardly at the words. "You haven't been?"

"Nope."

"You're not really a millionaire, is that it?" she said, though the joke fell flat and she already knew it was the truth.

"Nah, that's not what I was talking about." His blue eyes met hers with such an urgent honesty she nearly gasped. "I wanted an excuse to get you up here."

"Oh?" She swallowed hard.

"The dry cleaning was just a ploy. I don't give a damn about it."

"And once you got me up here?" she asked, sweating a bit, her heart knocking. Was it her imagination or had the temperature in the suite just gone up about fifteen degrees?

"I just wanted to get you alone."

Her heart began to jump now. "Why's that?" she asked, but she saw the passion in his gaze.

"Because, darlin', I think you're the most interesting woman I've seen in a long, long time."

"You…you don't even know me."

"But I'd like to." His expression was sincere, but she warned herself not to believe him.

"I bet you say that to all the girls who pour wine on your clothes."

His lips twitched. "You're right. All of them."

She felt an unlikely stab of disappointment.

"And all of them are right here."

"Imagine that. All the klutzes in one suite. Gee, Mr. Remmington, how did you manage that?"

"I'd like to say it was skill, but it was probably just dumb luck."

She giggled despite all her reservations. What was there about him she found so damned alluring? So sensual? Intriguing enough that she would cast down her natural defenses and throw all caution to the wind? She could rationalize from now until eternity, tell herself that it was because she "knew" him from everything she'd read and researched about the enigmatic bastard son of Larry Kincaid, but there was more to it than that. She was smitten with this stranger. Felt a bond with him he didn't even know existed. She was a fool, that was it. And she had to leave now.

As if he'd read her mind, he said, "You could stay."

Her heart nearly stopped. She was tempted, but no, she couldn't.

"I don't spend the night with strangers."

"You could get to know me first."

"I think, Mr. Remmington—"

"Trent."

"Okay. I think, Trent, it would take more than a couple of hours to get to know you."

"I can be very charming."

"Oh, please. Good night."

To her surprise and chagrin he didn't try to stop her.

He lifted a shoulder. "Whatever you think's best, Celia."

That name again. Reminding her of her duplicity. "Just don't tell me I'm missing out on the opportunity of a lifetime," she said, scooping up the soiled suit, shirt and tie.

"Wouldn't dream of it."

He didn't so much as take a step closer to her. Again that ridiculous stab of disappointment. "Well, thanks for the drink, the conversation, and the champagne. I'll see that these are delivered before you check out."

"Thanks."

Feeling suddenly silly, she started for the door, then crossed the room and stood in front of him. Still holding the bundle of clothes, she said, "It's been interesting."

"Amen."

Impulsively she kissed his cheek. "Good night." That was the mistake.

He grabbed her then. He wrapped his strong arms around her, dragged her close, slanted warm, possessive lips over hers and kissed her so hard she couldn't breathe, couldn't think, could only hear her own heartbeat thudding in her ears.

Gina felt dizzy. She dropped the suit on the floor. His hands splayed across her back as if he owned her. Her mouth opened and he groaned as the kiss deepened. Somewhere music was playing and the room seemed to shrink. He tasted of Scotch and champagne. Her knees went weak, her resistance fled, and before she knew what she was doing she was kissing him back, molding her body into the tight fit of his, her knees turning to jelly.

Don't do this, Gina. This is pure madness. Get out. Get out now. While you still can!

But the alarms in her head went unheeded. She wrapped her arms around his neck and heard him groan as he lifted her off her feet and carried her through the French doors to the bedroom.

He didn't ask.

She didn't protest.

They kissed and touched and she remembered hearing the hiss of her zipper as it slid down her back, feeling a cool breath of air against her bare skin, discovering the wonder and strength of his body as her fingers explored the ridges and planes of hard, sinewy muscles.

She knew she was making an irreversible error, but she didn't care. She'd always been so cautious when it came to men, but this time, for this one night, she flung her reserve and distrust aside. She knew him, she rationalized as he kissed the crook of her neck and she began to ache inside. Strong, calloused fingers slipped her dress down her body and his mouth and tongue followed, his hot lips brushing her breasts, his warm breath blowing against her abdomen as he slid the silky fabric quickly off her body.

She sighed as every nerve in her body tingled expectantly.

She felt the corded strength of hard muscles pressing against her; reveled in the feel of her fingers playing in the soft matt of hair on his chest; kissed anxious lips that couldn't seem to get enough of her. Through the panes of the French doors, firelight sparkled.

She heard him kick off his pants, felt the strong muscles of his legs against her own, and experienced a wanting heretofore unknown to her. He breathed against her ear, the soft whisper of air tingling her ear, and as his fingers dipped past the lace of her bra, she wanted more. Everything. To discover what it was to be a woman— fully loved, if only for one night.

Closing her eyes, she moaned softly as his tongue and lips caressed her, seeking out each dimple in her skin. His hand parted her legs. She ached inside. Her back arched and she clung to him, her fingers digging into his shoulders. He touched her intimately, expertly, finding a place that stopped her breath.

Heat sang through her bloodstream and she'd never in her life felt such fever. She'd never known such want, such hunger.

By instinct she moved beneath him, swallowing against desire, needing the feel of him within her.

Hot. She was hot. Dots of perspiration broke out on her skin as he stoked heat in the most intimate part of her. She was clinging to him, gasping, opening. Desire thundered through her veins, throbbed in her brain. The room seemed to spin, or was it her soul? "Trent," she whispered, her voice hoarse, unrecognizable.

"Right here, darlin'."

"I—I want…"

"I know."

Desire pounded through her brain. She moaned—or was it his low, raspy voice she heard? He shifted, slid upon her and, kissing her hard, thrust deep inside her.

She gasped as she felt a jab of hot pain. But as he began to move, pain quickly became pleasure. He was everywhere at once, moving within her, kissing her neck, her eyelids, her lips, his hands caressing her as her mind spun out of control and the center of the universe existed in the spot that fused them together.

Faster. Harder. Hotter. She couldn't breathe, couldn't swallow, caught his rhythm, moving furiously with him. A billion stars flashed behind her eyes. Her mind spun with wild, erotic images and she cried out as the world seemed to shatter into brilliant shards of light. Body and mind convulsed.

He threw back his head and with a primal cry spilled

into her, releasing himself. Letting go. He fell against her and sighed, his fingers twining in her hair as he kissed her cheek. "Celia."

The alias hung in the air.

Her lie.

Her deception.

She opened her mouth, determined to set the record straight. He kissed her again and all her good intentions fled. For this night, she would give in to the desperate urges of her body and when it was over, she'd leave. He'd never know the truth....

Until now, she thought as she stared at the broad expanse of Montana sky. High above, the moon gilded the Kincaid ranch with its pearlescent light. Somewhere far off a coyote cried and Gina rubbed her arms. How could she ever explain what happened? To Trent? To herself?

Was it possible?

"What's going on?" a deep male voice asked, and she visibly jumped.

Whirling around, she found herself face-to-face with Trent Remmington. Moon glow cast his face in silvery shadows and yet she was able to read his harsh expression and knew that whatever he had to say, it wasn't going to be pleasant.

"Nothing. I—I just couldn't sleep. Thought maybe some fresh air would help."

"Did it?"

"Not so far."

"I couldn't get any shut-eye, either," he admitted as he walked to the fence and leaned against it. "I kept thinking about the night we met in Dallas and how you lied to me."

Here it comes, she thought, expecting him to lambaste her for keeping her identity a secret. Instead, he blindsided her.

"I didn't realize it until the next morning," he admitted, obviously irritated with himself. "But that night we were together, it was your first time, wasn't it?" He sounded disgusted. With himself? Or her?

"I don't understand…" She let the sentence drift into the shadows.

"Sure you do. You'd never been with a man before, had you?" His lips compressed. "You—Celia, or Gina, or whoever-the-hell you are—were a virgin."

Chapter 5

"Excuse me," she said, and even in the moonlight he saw the blush staining her cheeks.

"You neglected to tell me you were a virgin."

"You didn't bother asking."

She met his gaze boldly, almost daring him to make some inane comment about being over twenty-five and saving herself. For what? Him? He doubted it and felt like a heel.

"Did it matter?"

"To me?" He shook his head. "But I thought it might to you." She lifted a shoulder beneath the white terry-cloth of that short little robe thing in what he considered measured nonchalance. Any woman who'd held off that long didn't take going to bed with a man lightly. And yet she was the one who had disappeared before dawn.

"It's not that big of a deal."

"What about Jack?"

"What?"

"The guy you were talking to on the phone. What about him?"

She snorted. "My sex life isn't any of his business."

He digested this, listened to the sounds of the night—a horse snorting in a nearby field, frogs and crickets competing for air space while a bat swooped from a hidden roost. "So what's your relationship with him?"

"If you want to know the truth…"

"Well, that would be a nice change of pace."

Her lips flattened together for a heartbeat, then she added, "Jack and I are very close. Extremely. He would understand. Now, if you'll excuse me, I think I'd better try and get some sleep." She started to march away, but he was tired of her flouncing exits.

"No way, lady," he said, grabbing hold of her wrist, spinning her back to face him and feeling how small the bones were beneath his fingers. "I think I deserve some answers."

"Why?"

"Because the ones I got in Dallas weren't exactly on the up-and-up."

"Maybe you just asked all the wrong questions," she fired back and jerked her arm away from him. He watched as she huffed off toward the house in a blaze of self-righteous and, as far as he was concerned, undeserved indignation.

"Women." He wanted to dismiss her, but somehow she'd gotten under his skin. She had from the instant he'd seen her sitting across the dance floor, alone, at a table, sipping wine and dressed to kill. At first he'd assumed she was waiting for someone. A knockout redhead like

Gina wasn't likely unattached, but when the date he'd thought she was waiting for didn't show up, he'd taken a chance and sent over a drink.

The rest, as they say, was history. He'd helped her "spill" her drink, had plotted to get her up to his room, but sensed that she wasn't comfortable, wasn't used to one-night stands. Hell, neither was he. Not any longer. But from his initial glimpse of her he'd known she would be different. Interesting. Intriguing. And she hadn't disappointed. Just thinking of their night together made him hard. He'd woken up and found her gone, which was unusual. No note, no trace of her. He'd called the front desk and gotten no information on Celia O'Hara.

She'd just disappeared.

He'd decided to track her down, and felt like a fool. Never in his life had a woman walked out on him. Never. And he hadn't liked the feeling. So he'd gone so far as to call a private investigator who'd done identity checks on people he was considering hiring for Black Gold. The man had come up empty. Celia O'Hara, the paralegal from Southern California, had disappeared.

Or, as he learned later, had never existed. Then out of the blue he'd gotten that life-altering call from Garrett Kincaid telling him he wasn't Harold Remmington's son, after all. Hell, no, he was Larry Kincaid's bastard.

He'd been about to shelve looking for the woman, had even called his own private investigator and told him to quit searching—and now she'd fallen into his lap. Not as Celia O'Hara, the paralegal intent on becoming a lawyer, but Gina Henderson, a P.I. who had pulled the wool over his eyes and been investigating him, for crying out loud!

He kicked at a rock and sent it careening into a fence post. From the porch the old pooch gave up a soft woof.

The worst part of it was, he was still attracted to her. She'd lied to him, deceived him, played him for one helluva fool, yet Trent could hardly be around her without getting an erection that just wouldn't quit. It was ridiculous. Foolish. His reaction to her was way out of line, as if he were a horny nineteen-year-old kid instead of thirty-two and supposedly an adult.

But then everything about his life was a little out of whack right now. He'd considered phoning Blake and talking over the entire situation with him, but had decided against it. He and his twin, though identical in looks, were worlds apart in their thinking. Trent had always wondered about those twins who grew up wearing the same clothes, being each other's best friend, riding matching bikes. He couldn't imagine it. He'd been into leather jackets, jeans and T-shirts in high school. Blake had gone for a preppier look. Trent had ridden a motorcycle hell-bent-for-leather whenever he could, picked up more than his share of speeding tickets and was lucky he'd never spent a night in jail. Blake had driven their mother's car when they lived at home, a dependable sedan when they were away at boarding school, put his nose firmly to the grindstone and with the idea of becoming a doctor chiseled into his brain from a young age, had put his goal in front of everything else. He'd even married well, a girl from a socially acceptable family, then moved to California where he'd set up practice as a pediatrician.

Trent had almost envied his brother's vision for his life, but that vision seemed to be blurring as Blake had divorced and, if Trent had read the last telephone conversation correctly, Blake was looking for more in his life.

Whatever the hell that meant.

With a final glance at the stars, Trent slapped the top rail of the fence and walked toward the house. The smell of fresh-mown hay lingered in the air but was laced with the trace of Celia—damn, he had to get it right—Gina's perfume. If he listened real hard, he was certain he heard the rush of water through the creek that cut through some of the pastures. Horses nickered softly, grass rustled and the wind sighed through the few sparse trees. The old Kincaid house rose out of the land and sprawled wide.

Home?

Trent snorted and examined the mansion with a jaundiced eye.

He didn't think so.

"Okay, so where are we?" Jack asked from their office in L.A. as Gina, sipping coffee and fighting a headache from too little sleep, wedged the phone between her shoulder and ear. She was sitting in a worn leather desk chair in the den and was looking through the open window to a view of the stables and several interlocking paddocks.

"Garrett's talked all of the brothers into coming here. They start arriving early next week. Well, except for Trent Remmington. He kind of jumped the gun and showed up before I got here." Leaning back in the chair, she watched Trent and Garrett talking to Rand Harding, the ranch foreman. They were seemingly discussing the small herd of cattle that had just been driven into one of the pens, dusty coats catching rays of early morning light. Disgruntled, they bawled as the men who, deep in conversation, pointed from one steer to another.

"Gina?" Jack's voice brought her back to the present. "So, all of Larry's sons will be there?"

"Just the illegitimate ones, I think. Garrett didn't say a word about Collin or Melanie, the kids Larry had with his wife. So we're expecting six, five more. I still haven't located the baby or his mother." She frowned as this little mystery was the only part she hadn't been able to figure out. Who was the last woman Larry had been involved with and where was she? Gina had always relied on gut instinct and feminine intuition. Right now she had a feeling that Larry's youngest child, who was little more than a baby, was nearby.

"If the baby exists." Jack was skeptical. One note in a personal journal didn't mean that there was a seventh illegitimate son, or so he'd said time and time again. "Six is enough, don't you think?"

"I know, but searching through Larry's things, it just seems that there might be a much younger sibling." She took another swig from her now-cold coffee and frowned. "One who was born in the last couple of years."

"You're sure about this?" her brother asked, and her nerves were instantly strung tight. Jack was well-meaning but overprotective. He was often second-guessing her and always cautious, to the point that she wanted to scream. Eight years her senior and having spent time working for the Los Angeles Police Department, he was forever afraid she might get hurt.

"I'm not sure about anything," she admitted, blowing her bangs out of her eyes. "But I have this gut feeling that there's another son."

"Here we go again. Instinct over facts." He laughed and she imagined his hazel eyes crinkling in amusement.

"It's worked before."

"Can't argue with that."

"But you'd like to."

"Ah, baby sister, you know me well," he teased.

"Unfortunately," she cracked.

"So, how're you going to go about locating the kid?"

Gina's eyes narrowed as she thought. "I've gone through the regular channels, checked hospital records, birth announcements in the paper, adoption agencies and lawyers, so now I'm going to listen to some good old-fashioned gossip. There's a place where everyone in Whitehorn seems to gather—a diner called the Hip Hop Café."

"So what if that tack doesn't work?"

"Well, I don't know. Back to square one. I guess I'll just have to talk to Winona Cobbs, she's something of a psychic around these parts, I hear. Maybe she can just read some tea leaves or gaze into a crystal ball or read a few palms or something."

"Oh, brother."

"No, in this case, it's 'Oh, half brothers.'"

"Very funny," he drawled, then chuckled. "Listen, take care of yourself and—"

"Don't do anything dangerous. Watch your back and call you if there's a hint of trouble. Have I got it down, Jack?" She couldn't help needling him.

"I guess. Hey, one more question. How're you getting along with Remmington?"

She glanced back to the window and discovered Trent was no longer with Garrett and Rand. "That's a tough one," she admitted, "considering the circumstances."

"Well, keep me posted."

"Will do."

"Love ya, kiddo."

"Love ya, too, old man," she teased and, as she hung up, glanced at the date on the display of her laptop computer. It had been more than a month since the night she'd spent in Dallas with Trent and… Oh, Lord. A familiar worry wormed through her brain again. Her throat tightened as she stared at the date, then brought up the screen for April. There it was, big as life—the little mark she always made that reminded her of her last period.

More than six weeks ago.

Her heart sank.

She'd never been this late. Never.

Nor have you ever slept with anyone before…and unprotected sex at that. Oh, Gina, what were you thinking? You're smarter than this.

There had to be some mistake. Had to.

So she either was sick or she was pregnant.

It was time to find out which.

Winona prided herself on her ability to read people. It wasn't just their expression or their body language that gave away their inner thoughts. Oh, no. It was much more. She was certain each person's aura manifested itself, and if most people took the time, they, too, might view what she found so obvious.

As she walked down the dusty street, she noticed more than most people. Jordan Baxter had paused in the awning of the bank building, checked the lazy flow of traffic, then jaywalked across the street. He was concentrating so hard, his eyebrows cinched together under the brim of his hat, his lips all drawn up as if he'd been sucking on lemons. Anyone who glanced in his direction could tell that he was as mad as a nest of hornets just shot with a hose. But Winona knew there was more to it than simple ire. The look on Jordan's face was reserved for those times when he had to deal with the Kincaids. He'd never gotten over the fact that his mother had been just another notch on Jeremiah Kincaid's belt. Poor Jordan, he was forever trying to prove himself as good as the Kincaids. No doubt he'd heard a whole passel of them were due to arrive.

Jordan blew past and didn't even shoot his disdainful once-over her way. But then, he was a little intimidated these days. He'd tried to buy her land on the highway, attempted to force her out of the Stop-n-Swap, but she'd told him to leave her alone, that she'd ricochet all his bad energy back in his direction if he tried it. He'd laughed at her until a few little "accidents" had occurred all around him. Unnerved, he'd taken her advice to heart, backed off, and seemed to now save his frustrations for the Kincaids.

Well, good luck. In Winona's opinion, bad karma begat only bad karma. As long as Jordan dwelled on the negative, he'd never prosper. All his money and possessions would give him little joy.

She wiped at her head with a handkerchief and paused on her way to the bank when she noticed a rig pull into a parking spot in front of the Hip Hop Café. A tall redhead practically flew out of the shiny Ford. She was a pretty girl with a strong stride, determined set to her chin, and a no-nonsense attitude that caught Winona's eye. But there was more to her than that, Winona thought. This gal looked like a woman on a mission.

That was the trouble with the young people today; they were all moving way too fast. The young woman, whoever she was, had better slow down because if she didn't she was headed for a fall. Winona had a sixth sense about these things.

* * *

"Oh, that Larry Kincaid, he loved women. Didn't matter if they were married or not. He charmed the socks off 'em. Well, the socks and a whole lot more." Seated at the first booth of the Hip Hop Café, Lily Mae gave an exaggerated wink, showing off an eyelid covered in bright blue eyeshadow.

"I'm tellin' ya, Gina, if there was a female within fifty miles of him, she was fair game as far as he was concerned," the little old lady said with a smug I've-seen-it-all smile. A friendly thing, Lily Mae was anxious to give out as much information as she could, but even she couldn't keep up with Larry Kincaid's exploits.

From her side of the both, Gina nodded and noticed that she was the object of more than one curious glance. "I'm talking about a woman he might have been seeing a couple of years ago, or a year ago, not long before he died."

"I'm thinkin', I'm thinkin'." Lily Mae swirled her iced tea and a slice of lemon pirouetted through the cubes.

"There were so many, it's pretty hard to keep them straight." Lily Mae glanced around the crowded café, always on the alert for the makings of more gossip. "Haven't you found a passel of his sons, already? All of 'em have different mothers, don't they?"

"Just about." Aside from Trent and his twin brother Blake, the other four men had been brought into the world by different women. Gina tapped her fingers anxiously on the edge of the table until she realized Lily Mae was taking note of her case of nerves.

"Somethin' botherin' you?"

Only that I slept with the grandson of my client. That I lied to him and now have to face him every day, and that I might just be pregnant with his child. Other than that, things are just peachy. "I'm just trying to wrap this up," Gina said. That much was true.

As the waitress passed by, Lily Mae held up her half-full glass. "How 'bout a refill, Janie?"

Janie managed a patient smile as she quickly jotted an order from a nearby table onto her pad. "Coming right up," she said to either the two men from the sheriff's department who were seated at the next booth—or to Lily Mae, Gina couldn't tell which. The café was crowded, Janie nearly running herself ragged as she breezed from one table to another.

"They need another waitress here," Lily Mae mumbled. "Janie can't do it all herself."

"I think they're looking for one." Gina nodded to the Help Wanted placard taped to the inside of a window.

"Well, it better be soon."

"So, tell me about the women in Larry Kincaid's life."

"That would take forever. Oh, thank you dear." Lily Mae smiled brightly as Janie came by with a pitcher of iced tea. "Can I get you anything else?" she asked. "We've got fresh strawberry-rhubarb pie today."

"Oh, I shouldn't…" Lily Mae said, then lifted a shoulder, "but I can't resist. Bring me a piece with some ice cream. Vanilla."

"Anything for you?" Janie asked Gina as the ceiling fans slowly turned overhead.

"No, thanks."

"Oh, come on," Lily Mae insisted. "People come from miles around for the pies and donuts here."

"Fine," Gina agreed, more to be amiable than from hunger. "The same."

"You won't regret it." Lily Mae winked again as

Janie refilled her glass then hurried off. "Now, as for the women in Larry Kincaid's life, let's see…" Lily Mae wriggled her fingers and started rambling on, her version of Larry's colorful life a mixture of fact and fiction. She paused only when the two slices of pie were delivered.

Gina was amazed and took mental notes of anything that seemed the least bit true.

"You know a lot about Larry Kincaid," she said.

"Well, that's true. I make it my business to know." Guileless, the older woman waved her fork at Gina. "Whitehorn's a small town. I just keep my eyes and ears open."

"So, who was the last woman Larry was involved with?"

Lily Mae was cutting off another bite from her wedge of pie. She stopped and thought for a second, little lines furrowing between her eyebrows. "You know, I don't really recall." Then, as if she'd let herself down, she shook her head. "I'll have to do some checking around."

So will I, Gina thought. *And I'm going to do it quickly.* The sooner she could get out of Dodge—er, Whitehorn, and away from Trent Remmington, the better!

"So, tell me about Gina," Trent suggested as Garrett surveyed the progress on the indoor arena that he'd ordered built as he hoped to train horses during the harsh winter months ahead. The framework was finished, the roof in place and the siding started. Frowning, pulling on a two-by-four to test its strength, he seemed satisfied that he was getting his money's worth from the construction crew he'd hired to update the paddock and repair the ranch house.

"What is it you want to know?" From beneath the brim of his hat, he slid his grandson a glance.

"You hired her to find Larry's sons." He just couldn't make himself call the son of a bitch who'd sired him "father." No way.

"Yes."

"And she did."

Garrett straightened, swatted at a horsefly, then rubbed his thumb over the head of a nail that had been driven into one of the two-by-fours. "That's about the size of it. Actually, I hired her brother."

"Brother?"

"Jack. He's really the owner of the private investigation firm. Gina works for him."

Trent's jaw slid to one side. So much for her mysterious relationship with Jack. He should have figured she'd lie to him again. "Does she?" he asked, and didn't bother hiding the sarcasm in his voice. He couldn't wait to confront her with this little bit of knowledge. He'd heard her talking to Jack on the phone yesterday morning and jealousy, ridiculous as it was, had burned in Trent's gut. He couldn't help himself. Where she was concerned, he was fast becoming a fool.

Garrett's gaze narrowed on his grandson. The grooves around the corners of his eyes deepened. "Well, there's more to it than that, I'd say. They're almost partners. Jack worked for the L.A.P.D. for years and he takes the more dangerous cases, mainly because he's protective of his little sis. But she's no slacker. I have the feeling she'd like more dangerous assignments, but she's gifted at what she does. She's developed quite a reputation for finding lost family members." He shoved the brim of his hat up with a thumb. "Found you pretty quick, now, didn't she?"

"I suppose."

"And that bothers you."

"Nope."

"Then maybe it's the woman herself that bothers you." It wasn't a question. The old man was pretty intuitive, Trent would give him that. "And I don't blame you. She's one good-looking, smart lady."

And a liar, Trent silently added. He wondered if he could believe anything that passed between those perfect white teeth. "I'm not in the market."

"How do you know?"

"I know."

Garrett didn't respond, just patted one of the posts and turned toward the house.

"Tell me about Larry. What's up with all these illegitimate sons?"

All amusement died in the older man's eyes and Trent, though he'd been loath to bring up a sore subject, felt he deserved the truth.

"I wish I knew." The old man sighed as they passed a corral where horses grazed in the late afternoon sun. "I sometimes think it might have been my fault, you know."

"How?"

"Oh, well…" Garrett's mouth twisted into an ironic smile. "Larry's mom was pregnant with him when we got married. I wonder if Larry thought, once he was old enough to do the math, that it was his license to promiscuity."

Trent snorted. The more he learned of the man who had sired him, the less he liked him. Whereas Garrett seemed to stand for truth, justice, the American way and everything good in this part of Montana, Larry had been just the opposite. "Probably he was just a bad apple."

"We've had more than our share," Garrett admitted, then stopped short and watched the lowering sun for a few minutes. "You may as well know, there's a lot of good blood in the Kincaid family, and a fair amount of bad."

"The way it is in all families," Trent observed.

Garrett raised a skeptical graying eyebrow. "We'll see. When the rest get here."

Great, Trent thought with more than a trace of sarcasm as he reached into his pocket and withdrew his keys. Just damned great.

Chapter 6

So what had she learned? Gina asked herself as she urged the palomino mare up a dusty trail in the foothills.

Only that you can't get Trent Remmington out of your head.

"Fool," she muttered under her breath. She clucked to the horse, encouraging the little mare into a gentle lope as they crested one of the hills on the western portion of the Kincaid spread. She'd been at the ranch for three days and hadn't gotten any closer to finding Larry Kincaid's seventh child than she'd been when she'd left L.A.

But she had a feeling that she was getting closer. Just being near Whitehorn spurred her female intuition into overdrive. Her fingers gripped the reins a little harder. She'd already scoped out the town, met some of the locals, delved into local history. She began to understand, for the first time in her life, why people chose to settle down in a small community over the fast pace and excitement of the city.

Or was it because of Trent? She could hardly turn around without running into him. He was either at the desk in the den of the house, running his business via fax, modem and telephone or helping Garrett and the work crew with the chores. She'd heard him argue with an investor one minute, then watched as he'd tugged on work gloves to help repair a barbed-wire fence the next. He'd gotten his hands greasy helping Garrett fix an oil leak in the old tractor, helped Rand cull calves that needed to be immunized another day, and offered Suzanne a cup of coffee, insisting that she "take a load off" and sit with Gina and Garrett at breakfast just this morning.

The playboy millionaire was far more than met the eye, a man who wasn't afraid of work, women or much else.

And she was falling for him.

"You're a case," she derided herself. She was here to do a job. Period.

And what if you're pregnant?

She closed her eyes for a second. Yes, what? Her mind spun at the thought. Breathing deeply of the pine-scented air, she felt the mare tense. Gina's eyes flew open as a startled bird flew across the path in a whir of feathers. She watched as the pheasant took cover in a copse of long-needled branches. Rays of sunlight piercing the overhead canopy spackled the trail with splotches of sunlight and shifting shadows.

Gina clucked to her horse. She'd decided to take this ride to get some exercise, explore the ranch a little and work the knots out of her mind. But she was failing. And the tangles she'd been trying to loosen only seemed to become more stubborn and tight.

Ears pricked, the mare accelerated into a bone-jarring trot and Gina tried to put order to the facts on the case. She'd found six of Larry Kincaid's sons, true, and there was evidence that he'd had another. There were unsubstantiated rumors that Larry had had a fling with a woman who lived near Whitehorn, but no one seemed to know with whom or if the rumors were true. Who was the woman he'd been involved with? Where was the baby? Gina had checked the birth records at the closest hospitals, read birth notices in papers of small towns surrounding Whitehorn, surfed the Internet and had come up dry.

And you're supposed to be a specialist when it comes to finding people, her P.I.'s mind nagged at her.

She had hoped to wrap up this case and move on. And get away from Trent Remmington. "Yeah, yeah, I know," she admitted to herself. But she'd failed. Her back teeth gritted at the thought. Failing was a word she didn't want in her vocabulary.

The path veered sharply to the right. Spindly trees gave way to a grassy meadow where wildflowers bloomed in profusion, speckling the sea of tall grass with small purple and white blossoms. A late afternoon breeze caressed her face and caught in Gina's hair. Now *this* was the Montana she'd read about, the place of romantic fantasies and cowboy tales.

And of maverick oilmen? She frowned at the thought and quickly banished it.

Soon she'd be faced not only with Trent but the other five sons Larry Kincaid had hidden from the world—grown men she'd found. She wasn't looking forward to meeting them. She still thought it best to keep a professional distance from the objects of her search.

How would the half brothers react? Until just a few weeks ago none of them had realized they'd been sired by a ornery cuss of a man who hadn't bothered to be a part of their lives. Yep, Larry Kincaid had been a piece of work.

She doubted any of the men would be thrilled to meet her. She pulled hard on the reins near a creek that tumbled and splashed its way downhill. Hopping off the mare's back, she let the horse graze and took a seat on a large flat rock at a bend in the creek. From atop the sun-baked stone she gazed downward to the heart of the Kincaid ranch. The indoor arena, nearly complete, was by far the largest building, and in the distance, she made out the foreman's house. Cattle and horses grazing on the surrounding acres were small dots in the rolling fields.

Gina kicked off her boots, rolled up her jeans and let her feet dangle in the icy water. She sucked in her breath. "God, that's cold." It all seemed so peaceful. Serene. Uncomplicated. She watched a butterfly flutter amid the blooms of wildflowers along the creek bank. It was a lie. Serenity was only an illusion. She had only to think of Larry Kincaid and the mess he'd made of his life and all the lives around him. Seven illegitimate sons. And never a thought to them.

Again she considered Trent. What would she tell him if she was pregnant? "Don't even think like that," she warned herself. So she was late in her cycle. So what? She was stressed-out. Majorly so. That was it. As soon as she could she would buy a home pregnancy test and that would be the end of that.

Unless she was going to become a mother.

Oh, Lord. She felt a moment's elation before she re-minded herself that a baby wasn't exactly the kind of blessing she was expecting right now. Babies came well after a person was married and secure in a relationship. Right? Pregnancies were planned, unless you were a person like Larry Kincaid. Frowning at the thought, she absently rubbed her abdomen, then caught the gesture and stopped. There was just no reason to borrow trouble.

She had a job to do here in Whitehorn and she planned to finish it as quickly as possible, then return to L.A., her apartment near the University of Southern Califor-nia, where she still took an occasional night class, and the private investigation firm where she worked with her brother. Inwardly she cringed when she thought about Jack. He would be devastated if he had any inkling she thought she was pregnant.

"Stop it," she growled just as she heard the sound of hoof beats. The mare's golden head lifted and she nick-ered. Gina glanced over her shoulder. Astride a roan gelding, Trent appeared.

Gina's throat caught at the sight of him, back-dropped by the blaze of a setting sun. Scrambling to her feet, she used her hand as a visor and squinted up at him. "You know, Remmington, we've got to quit meeting like this," she said as much to break the ice as anything.

The hint of a smile twisted his lips. "My thoughts exactly." He slid from the saddle and advanced upon Gina. Her heart knocked wildly and she thought he was as purely male and sexual as men came. His hair was windblown, his jaw darkened by a day's growth of beard. In faded jeans, boots and a shirt that had seen better days, he seemed a part of this raw, rugged land, at odds with the smooth-talking, slick businessman she'd met in Dallas.

"How'd you find me?" she asked, ignoring the heat she saw in his blue eyes.

"Just my infinite tracking skills."

"Oh, right."

"I think…no, I'm sure I have some Native American blood running through my veins. Isn't that right? Or maybe in a past life I was a tracker."

"Give me a break."

He laughed and the sound was deep and true, rising above the babble of the creek. "Okay, so maybe Rand saw you riding this afternoon and pointed me in the right direction."

"That sounds more like it," she admitted, and found his slash of a smile as infectious as ever. Why was it she couldn't resist him?

"It didn't hurt that you took a main trail."

"So how do you know about it, and don't give me any of that B.S. about being a native guide, okay? I'm not buying it."

His grin slid from one side of his jaw to the other. "Well, now, you know, I'd like to take all the credit, but I think my old pal Chester —" he patted the stallion's neck "—wouldn't much approve."

"And the reason you followed me is?" she asked.

"I thought we needed to talk."

"Uh-oh. Look, if it's about me lying to you about who I was, I think I already apologized. I made a mistake."

"*We* made a mistake," he said.

She inwardly winced. He was right, of course. Falling into bed together was wrong. Too much wine, too little experience, and a curiosity about the sexiest man she'd ever met had been a lethal combination.

"There's no reason to rehash it to death." She felt her palms begin to sweat a little and she was rambling. "I don't know what to say. I'm sorry I lied, it won't happen again. We had some fun and— Oh!"

His arm snaked out, he grabbed her wrist and yanked her hard against him. "Don't."

"Don't what?" she asked, breathless with surprise.

"Don't fake all this nonchalance, okay? Don't act like it was just fun and games or a quick roll in the hay."

"But it was," she countered, refusing to be seduced by words she wanted to hear. She ignored the denial drumming in her head. "What it was, Trent, was a one-night stand."

"That was your choice."

She felt as if he'd slapped her. "Wait a minute, are you trying to say that you and I would have…what? Dated? Gotten involved? What?"

"You didn't stick around long enough to find out, did you?"

"I thought it was time to leave."

"Maybe I should have been consulted." His gaze bored down at her with such intensity she wanted to squirm away. But she held her ground and swallowed hard when she noticed how dangerously close his lips were to hers.

Don't think that way, Gina. That's what got you into trouble in the first place.

"I, uh, I thought it was best to leave things as they were."

"Because you lied about who you were."

"That was part of it, yes."

"But someone who waits until they're twenty-seven years old…" He paused and must have witnessed the flash of surprise in her eyes, because he nodded. "Oh, yeah, I know how old you are. I've done my own little investigation since Dallas. How does it feel to be the one under the microscope?"

She jerked back on her arm, but he wouldn't let go. He just kept driving his point home.

"Anyone who's a twenty-seven-year-old virgin doesn't fall into bed lightly."

Angling up her chin, she said, "So you're telling me that because I happened to end up in bed with you, it had to be because you were someone special, someone I'd saved myself for, someone—"

"Oh, hell!" He kissed her then. His arms surrounded her and dragged her tight against him. Before she could protest or start to struggle, his lips pressed urgently against hers. Anger fired through her bloodstream, outrage sang through her mind, but her wanton body wouldn't fight back, *wanted* to melt against him.

Desire, friend or foe, caused her to ache inside, brought an intense sexual awareness that caused a weakness in her knees and a hunger in the most primal depths of her.

Oh, but she wanted to make love to him, yearned to have his hard body driving deep into hers. White-hot images of making love to him flashed behind her eyes, branding her brain. She saw taut, bronzed skin, a washboard of abdominal muscles and a thick mat of chest hair stretched across raw bone and sinew. Her breathing was suddenly shallow, her heart jackhammering.

Don't do this, her mind warned. *Gina, for heaven's sake, think! You lost yourself to him once before, don't let it happen again.* And yet her free arm wrapped around his neck. Her fingers brushed the hair at his nape as his tongue pressed urgently against her teeth and she opened to him. Kissing him felt so right, and yet was oh, so wrong.

She closed her mind to that hideous voice in her head that was screaming she was about to make yet another, life-altering mistake.

He sighed into her mouth and she felt one of his hands splay against the curve of her spine, the tips of his fingers tantalizingly close to her buttocks. *Oh, Trent, let me love you,* she thought wildly, though she hardly knew the man.

He lifted his head, twined strong fingers in her hair and forced her to look into his hot blue eyes. "You make me crazy."

She smiled despite herself. "And here I thought insanity was just one of your natural charms, that maybe it ran in the family. Now *I'm* the cause?"

"Yep." His lips twitched.

"I'm not buying it."

One of his dark eyebrows cocked. "Maybe I should convince you."

"Oh, and how do you propose to do that?" she asked, flirting outrageously, daring him.

"Want me to show you?"

No!

"Absolutely."

"You're asking for it, lady."

"Am I?"

"Oh, yeah." Again he kissed her. Again her blood heated fast. Again her heart raced. His lips were hot, hard, demanding. What was wrong with her? He devoured her mouth and she did the same, kissing, nipping, biting until she felt his weight drag them onto the carpet of new grass.

"You know, Remmington, this is a good way to get grass stains," she managed to say.

"Is it? Hmm. I can't think of a better one." His hands rubbed her shoulders as he kissed her neck and cheeks. She trembled inside. His breath was hot against her skin. In between presses of his warm lips against her flesh, he said, "But if you're really worried about it, maybe we should take this off." He was already bunching the hem of her T-shirt in his hands, yanking the fabric over her head, baring her skin to the cool kiss of spring air.

Stop this. Stop it now, her mind screamed, but the warnings were lost to her.

"Then it might be wise for you to do the same. I already wrecked one set of your clothes."

"The suit and shirt are fine."

"And the tie?"

One side of his mouth lifted as she started unfastening the buttons of his shirt. "It's history."

"I was afraid of that," she said, her fingers fumbling as she tried not to stare at his hard-muscled chest or the alluring thatch of dark hair that nearly covered it. Flat nipples peeked out of springy nearly black curls and it was all she could do not to kiss each one.

"As I said, this is insane," she whispered as he settled next to her and traced the lacy outline of her bra with one lazy finger. Her stomach did a slow, sensuous roll. He leaned over and kissed the top of one breast and she watched the sunlight catch a few strands of red in his thick brown hair.

"Can't argue." His breath caused goose bumps to rise

on her skin and the feeling was divine yet wantonly unholy. Her head was spinning, her body craved more.

"I mean… We should maybe go back to… Oh—" She half-closed her eyes as his tongue followed the path his finger had taken. Within the soft cup of her bra, her nipple hardened and ached.

He looked up, noticed the want in her eyes and kissed her again. With a deftness that only comes with practice, he unhooked the back strap and the lacy scrap of unwanted fabric was tossed aside.

He touched the tip of one nipple and watched in fascination as it puckered. "You are beautiful."

Blushing, she attempted to roll over to hide her nakedness, but as she turned, he pushed her back onto the grass and stared directly into her eyes. With a calloused thumb, he circled her nipple and she moaned with a desire she'd never known existed.

How she wanted to feel his naked body on hers. She imagined the length of him stretched out upon her, touching her, kissing her, his erection pressing hard as he made love to her as he had before. Deep inside she melted, and as he kissed her breast, his tongue caressing and tugging at her nipple, she moaned, her eager fingers digging into the muscles of his shoulders, her body arching in an insistent demand for more.

His lips found hers and her mind began to spin. As if from a distance she heard the stream gurgling and a woodpecker drilling into the bark of a tree.

He lay upon her, the fly of his jeans hard against hers. Heat roared through her. She held him fast. He began to move and rub against her, denim against denim, friction mounting.

Somewhere not too far off, over the drum of the

woodpecker she heard hoof beats. The mare snorted. Trent stiffened and lifted his head. "I think we've got company."

She froze. "No."

"Yes."

"Terrific," she muttered, scrambling for her clothes and feeling every inch of her skin turn red.

Trent rolled to his feet and tossed her clothes to her. She stuffed her bra into the back pocket of her jeans and pulled on her T-shirt. She didn't have time to tuck in the hem. In an instant Garrett Kincaid, astride a painted stallion, rode out of the woods.

Gina was certain her face was the exact hue of her hair. The man wasn't an idiot. It wouldn't take him too long to figure out what had been going on as she stood barefoot, her hair mussed, her clothes wrinkled. Trent's shirt was on, but not buttoned, its shirttails flapping in the breeze.

The expression on Garrett's face said it all. He wasn't pleased. Hard lines surrounded his mouth as his eyes narrowed on his newfound grandson. "Thought I might find you up here," he said as he swung to the ground as easily as if he'd been forty years younger.

"You were looking for me?" Trent asked.

"Yeah. Rand said the two of you had headed up this way. You got a call from your secretary. Said it was real important. Talk of a strike."

"Hell."

"Thought you'd want to know."

"I do."

Garrett's harsh, uncompromising gaze swung in Gina's direction. "And Jack's been calling for you." If he noticed her disheveled state, which, unless he was blind he couldn't have missed, Garrett had the good manners not to mention it.

"Guess we'd better get back." Trent tucked the tails of his shirt into his waistband.

Garrett's jaw slid to one side. With a curt nod, he walked back to the paint and pulled himself up into the saddle. "Might not be a bad idea, all things considered." He kneed his horse and the rangy stallion took off.

Gina wanted to die. The last thing she needed was for Garrett to think she'd compromised her professionalism. "Well, that was certainly embarrassing," she said, dusting off the seat of her jeans and walking to her mare.

"Nah. He didn't think a thing of it."

"What makes you so sure?"

Trent snorted. "He's Larry's father, right? Garrett Kincaid's already seen it all."

But Gina wasn't convinced as she felt her breasts swing free beneath her T-shirt. It wasn't that she was a prude, not by any means, but she was bending her own rules of professional conduct a little too far for comfort.

The trouble was, she decided fatalistically as she mounted the mare, when it came to Trent Remmington, she didn't seem to have a brain in her fool head.

Chapter 7

"So what's goin' on with you and Gina?" Garrett asked as Trent, seated at a battle-scarred desk in the den, finally hung up from a long conversation with his secretary. Garrett had walked in, taken a seat in a folding chair wedged into the corner and waited for Trent to finish his phone call. Renovations were going on in the main house and the sound of saws, hammers and men talking between themselves could be heard as they worked to update the old Kincaid homestead.

"Between me and Gina? Not a whole helluva lot," Trent hedged, not wanting to admit that from the moment he'd first seen her in the bar that night in Dallas, he'd wanted to go to bed with her.

"Don't kid a kidder." Garrett leaned forward, clasped his hands together between his knees and favored Trent with an eagle-eyed stare that was becoming all too familiar. "I've got eyes, you know, and though you might find this hard to believe, I wasn't born yesterday."

"And you might find this hard to believe, but I'm a grown man, can make my own decisions and don't need anyone to tell me how to run my life."

"That's just exactly what Larry told me years ago," Garrett countered. He rubbed his hands together, pursed his lips and looked as if he had something more to say.

"What is it?" Trent asked, certain that he wouldn't like the answer.

"I just hope you don't turn out like him."

"Ha!" Trent barked out a laugh. "Like Larry? No way."

"You didn't know him."

"Sounds like that might have been a blessing."

Guilt shadowed Garrett's eyes and he stood, his knees popping as he walked to the window and gazed past the bunkhouse, stable, machine sheds and paddocks. But Trent guessed Garrett's eyesight wasn't focused on the vast acres of ranch land that swept up to the forested foothills. Nope. His grandfather—hell, that was still hard to swallow—was looking inward, to a time and space only he could see.

"Larry had more than his share of faults, I can't deny it," Garrett said as a skill saw screamed from another wing of the house, "but I loved him nonetheless. Yeah, he was a womanizer, a hard drinker and a gambler. He gave me more white hairs than any son should, but he wasn't all bad. At least, I can't believe he was."

"Or you won't."

Garrett lifted a shoulder and rubbed the back of his neck. "That's probably more like it. Anyway, just be careful. Gina's a nice girl."

"No, Garrett, she's a grown woman."

The older man turned on the well-worn heel of his boot and leveled a blistering blue glare at his grandson. "A *nice* grown woman. Now, listen, I'm offering you some sound advice here—"

"I don't remember asking for any," Trent interjected.

Garrett ignored him and barreled on. "Don't do anything stupid. That's all I have to say. Use your fool head and keep your pants zipped." With that, he left.

Trent, still seated at the desk and holding a pen, clicked it several times in frustration. His jaw was clenched so tight it ached, and for the first time in years he felt like a schoolboy who'd just been chastised by the principal. He hadn't liked it then, he didn't like it now. Probably because his own thoughts had taken the very same path.

He swivelled in the creaky chair and stared through the watery panes of glass. Outside, about to climb into his truck, Rand Harding had paused at Suzanne's appearance from the back of the house. One booted foot propped on the running board of his pickup, he leaned against the open door, as if he was about to climb behind the wheel. Suzanne stood in the shade of a live oak, holding their baby on one out-thrust hip. Smiling and laughing, she winked at her husband as he moved toward her. Trent couldn't hear their conversation but witnessed their expressions—amusement and deep-seated affection—so evident in the curves of their lips and sparkles in their eyes. The discussion was short and when it was finished, she leaned forward and he kissed her, hard. As if he meant it. Even though they were married. She blushed like a schoolgirl, the baby put up a wail, and Rand, his cowboy hat pushed back on his head, grinned widely, as if he was the bad boy in high school who'd just stolen a kiss from the prom queen.

Trent dragged his eyes away. He'd never been a romantic, never seriously considered settling down. Well, maybe once, when he'd thought a girlfriend had been pregnant. Beverly, a willowy blonde, had told him about the baby, then suddenly, the next week, informed him that it had all been a mistake.

He'd had conflicting emotions at the time. Beverly had been a stockbroker and was used to making her own decisions. Sophisticated and hardheaded, she'd been exciting and clever, but he'd never been in love with her. When she'd said she was carrying his child, Trent had felt an odd mixture of emotions: an elation he hadn't expected, a surprising sense of propriety and protection. He'd decided to be a part of the baby's life, either by marrying Beverly or by demanding joint custody, but he hadn't had the chance. Though she denied it vehemently, even laughing at his discomfiture, he suspected Beverly had either lied about being pregnant in the first place, to manipulate him, or had decided on her own to have an abortion. Either way, he'd ended the short-lived affair because he'd been certain she'd put her career above her child. In his scope of the world, that just didn't pan out.

Oh, sure, he'd heard a lot about quality time, about how a woman these days could have it all, but he didn't think there was enough of one person to go around when the demands of husband, kids, job and house were thrust upon her. He'd seen enough of that firsthand. His own mother, a career woman who hadn't had time for her twin sons, had convinced him that he never wanted to tie the knot—especially not with some woman already bound to her job.

So he'd had his share of flings and one-night stands. No strings attached. He'd been careful—except for the night with Gina. That night had been different on so many levels. Truth to tell, he was more than irritated that Gina—well, Celia at the time—had summoned the gall to slip away from him while he was sleeping in that hotel room in Dallas. Loving and leaving had usually been his M.O.

But then, she'd been different from the get-go. He'd seen her, wanted to seduce her, and managed to pull it off. That accomplished, he hadn't been satisfied. He wanted more. Now, it seemed, he couldn't get enough of her.

Frowning, he dropped the pen into a cup on the desk and slid one more glance at Rand and his wife. The foreman had taken his place behind the steering wheel, started the engine and had turned around, looking over his shoulder as he backed out. Suzanne, a wide smile across her face, waved and urged the baby to hold up his tiny fist and open and close his chubby fingers in a mimic of his mother's goodbye.

Trent felt a heretofore unknown clench around his heart, as if he were actually envious. God, he was a fool, and yet he continued to stare voyeuristically at the tight-knit little family.

Rand's truck disappeared in a cloud of dust, and Suzanne, usually serious from what Trent could discern, held little Joe up high in the air and twirled around, spinning them both. The baby threw back his head and mother and child laughed merrily, as if they hadn't a care in the world.

For the first time in his life, Trent wondered if any part of that homey little scenario would someday be his.

Jaw clamped tight in disgust at the turn of his ludicrously maudlin thoughts, he snapped the blinds shut. He wasn't a Peeping Tom, for crying out loud, and he had no interest in the seductive illusion of the Norman Rockwellian picture of family life. He had no time for envy, not in this lifetime.

Marriage and kids and the whole ball of family wax was fine for Rand and Suzanne. Hell, it was fine for most people.

Just not him.

Ever.

Running down blind alleys. Barking up the wrong trees. Winding up at dead ends. Every one of those clichés proved true as Gina shut down her laptop and winced against a headache that was building behind her eyes. Positioned on her bed with a long phone cord connected to one of the three lines running into the house, she rotated her neck and hated the thought that she'd been defeated.

That baby was out there. Somewhere. She just had to find him. Ever since she'd ridden back to the heart of the ranch yesterday, she'd avoided Garrett and spent hours at the keyboard, searching the Internet, using every available source, hoping for some clue as to Larry's seventh illegitimate son.

There was another reason she'd holed up in her room, she admitted reluctantly. She'd needed time to pull herself together. How had she let herself fall victim to Trent's charms all over again? Hadn't she learned anything?

She turned her attention back to the problem at hand—that of finding the elusive Kincaid. So far she'd come up dry. Rubbing her temples, she turned to the small metal box lying open beside her on the bed. All she had was a notation in Larry's handwriting indicating there was a possibility of another baby—a boy, but nothing else. Just a supposition because the timing was right. Nowhere did he indicate the name of child or mother, not even the date of birth. Gina had looked through all of Larry's belongings, hoping for a letter, a birth announcement, a copy of the birth certificate…and she'd ended up empty-handed.

"It's impossible," she muttered under her breath, then caught herself. She had to find the baby.

So much for being an ace detective, she chided herself. Think, Gina, think! She flopped back onto the bed and closed her eyes, but instead of clearing her thoughts as she'd hoped, resting only muddled her head with images of Trent dressed in a killer suit in the Dallas hotel, in jeans and a T-shirt on the ranch, with nothing but a sheet draped over his naked body. "Oh, you're hopeless," she said out loud, and decided it was time to face Garrett again. She couldn't very well hide in her room forever.

Besides, she had some other business to attend to—a little matter of purchasing a pregnancy test. She was about to grab her purse and keys when she heard the sound of footsteps on the stairs. Within seconds Trent was standing in the door frame and her stupid heart jolted at the sight of him. Handsome, rugged, and sexy as all get-out.

"Something I can do for you?" she asked as he stepped into the room, which seemed to shrink.

"I just wondered how long you were planning to stay here at the ranch." His eyes were dark. Unreadable.

"I—I don't know. Does it matter?"

"Probably not."

"I hadn't planned to stick around, but I've got this problem," she admitted, climbing to her feet. "I don't like leaving a job undone. Until I can figure out if Larry had another child, I'll probably hang out here. Is that a problem?"

"Could be," he admitted, folding his arms across his chest and frowning. "You and I…we got off on the wrong foot in Dallas."

Oh, Lord, where was this going? Her pulse began to pound. "Yes, I know, that was my fault—"

"Both our faults." His tone was sharp.

"I shouldn't have lied."

"No, but neither should I have," he admitted, and she noticed a tic throbbing near one eyebrow. "You weren't the only one who stretched the truth."

"No?"

His jaw slid to one side. "Nope. The fact is that from the moment you walked into the bar, I noticed you. Thought I'd like to meet you and…" He sighed through his nose. "Oh, hell, Gina," he said, his eyes drilling into hers. "From the second I laid eyes on you I had one thing on my mind."

"Which…was?" she asked, standing only a few feet from him and staring into the most erotic blue eyes she'd ever seen.

"That I wanted to go to bed with you."

She swallowed hard. "Well…"

"I don't think that's a surprise."

"Just that you're being so…forthright… I mean, usually people don't discuss this kind of thing."

"It doesn't usually happen." He took a step closer. "At least not to me."

His lips were thinned. Pursed. As if he were disgusted with himself. For a second she thought he would kiss her. For a second it was all she could think of, all she wanted.

"But you changed that, lady."

Part of her was flattered, the other scared to death.

"I would have done anything," he said, reaching forward, touching her arm with those warm strong fingers, "anything to get you up to my hotel room."

Heat crawled up her neck. Invaded her cheeks.

She started to say something, but he placed a finger to her lips. "And so we both deceived each other. I'm coming clean because I think we should start over. With a clean slate. No lies."

Oh, God, she wanted to fall through the floor.

Tell him, her mind nagged, *tell him you suspect you're pregnant! Now!* But the words wouldn't come to her lips. What if her worries were all just a false alarm, that her cycle was just messed up, that there was no baby?

"Deal?" he asked, so close his breath fanned her face. He dragged his finger down her lips and lower, over her chin and throat.

She could barely breathe. "D-deal," she repeated, and a hint of a smile touched his eyes.

"Fair enough." He hesitated a second, as if he was thinking about kissing her or pulling her close or tossing her onto the bed and making love to her, but he didn't. Instead he walked out the door and Gina was left with the fragments of another lie still hanging in the air. A much bigger lie.

There was a possibility that Trent Remmington was going to be a father. She leaned against the wall and bit her lip. If she chased after him now and breathlessly told him her fears, she'd look like a foolish, desperate woman. No, she had to wait.

Until she was certain herself.

Janie stared at the girl at table six. Seated all alone, reading a paperback while she waited for her food, she seemed out of place in the bustle of the dinner crowd. Nearly every table was full and there was so much conversation that the music from the jukebox, some old Patsy Cline song about heartbreak, was barely audible. Cutlery and glassware clinked, conversation buzzed and laughter rippled as the ceiling fans whirred overhead and the deep-fat fryer sizzled in the kitchen.

The girl, all of twenty-two or twenty-three, Janie guessed, was dressed in black slacks and a white blouse with the sleeves rolled up. Thick glasses were propped on the end of her nose, wavy red-brown hair was clipped to the back of her head, and she wore little makeup. Every few minutes she glanced up from the novel that didn't seem to be holding her attention, then took a quick look around the diner, as if she were sizing up the crowd.

Some of the Hip Hop regulars had shown up. Lily Mae Wheeler, Winona Cobbs and Homer Gilmore, the old guy with long gray hair and equally long beard who spent as much time in the hills spotting aliens as he did in town, had claimed their usual spots. Most of the patrons Janie recognized and called by name, but a few strangers were sprinkled about and more streamed in, filling up the booths and tables faster than the busboy could clear them.

Janie breezed between the tables, took orders, brought drinks and food and tried to ignore the fact that her feet were beginning to ache from the long hours she'd put in this week.

The girl with the paperback absently chewed on the edge of her lip and every once in a while eyed the Help Wanted sign taped to the front window. "Order up," the cook yelled, and Janie scooped up four platters of steaming food. Balancing the plates carefully she wended her way through the tables to a booth in the corner. "Chicken-fried steak?"

"Right here," a cowboy with red hair, freckles and Western-cut shirt said. He was a regular who hired out as a ranch hand on several of the nearby spreads. As she set a couple of Reuben sandwiches and a Cobb salad in front of each of his friends, the cowboy used two fingers to motion Janie closer. His gaze was fastened on the girl at table six. "Don't suppose you know the gal over there with her nose stuffed into a book, do you?" he asked.

"No." Janie shook her head. "This is the first time she's been in."

His brow creased. "Think she's just visitin'?"

"I wouldn't know. Is there anything else I can get you?"

His friends shook their heads and dug into their food, but the cowboy was distracted.

"Order up!" A bell rang as the cook yelled just as the Patsy Cline tune ended.

"I guess I'll just have to find out," the cowboy said as Janie hurried back to the counter to pick up an order of burgers and fries.

From the corner of her eye she noticed the cowboy saunter over to the bookworm's table. Grabbing the coffeepot, Janie headed to Winona Cobbs's table.

Winona was eyeing the girl with the paperback when

Janie came to refill her coffee cup. "Who's that one?" Winona asked as she tore open a small package of cream. White clouds appeared in her cup as she drizzled in half the packet. She hitched her chin in the direction of the girl.

"You're the psychic," Janie teased. "You tell me."

"All right." Small lines appeared between Winona's graying eyebrows. "To tell you the truth, I think she looks like Lexine Baxter."

Janie nearly dropped the carafe of coffee. "Lexine? No way!" Lexine was pure evil and now in prison for crimes ranging from prostitution to murder. It was Lexine who had killed several of the Kincaid clan, including her husband Dugin and father-in-law Jeremiah. Janie shivered at the thought of the beautiful, seductive, and depraved woman. Thank God, she was locked away forever with no chance of parole.

"Yep." Fiddling with a crystal pendant that swung from a chain around her neck, Winona cast another look at the girl at table six.

Obviously embarrassed by the cowboy's attention, the newcomer blushed and swallowed, forced a smile she obviously didn't feel, and looked as if she wanted to drop right through the floor.

"Well, I'm talkin' about when Lexine was younger, before she had all that plastic surgery and she discovered that blondes really do have more fun." Winona narrowed her eyes. "Take off that one's glasses, dye her hair, and I'm tellin' ya, she's a dead ringer for Lexine."

Janie wouldn't believe it. She shuddered inwardly.

"You're way off on this one."

The door opened and more customers streamed in.

"Don't think so. There's Baxter blood in that one, unless I miss my guess, and there's something more. Look at the way she's trying to ignore the boy who wants to flirt with her. It's not natural."

The cowboy had placed a hand on the table and was leaning close, obviously interested, but he wasn't getting any kind of positive response. Finally giving up, he returned to his seat, grabbed his knife and fork and tore into his steak.

The poor girl stared at her book, but Janie noticed she didn't bother to turn a single page. Something was troubling her, and Janie knew the signs all too well. Worried glances, pursed lips, shadows darting through her eyes—all accompanied by heavy sighs. "You know, I'd bet that she's here in town to mend a broken heart. She could have just broken up with someone." Then, hearing herself, Janie shook her head as Elvis began to croon through the speakers. "Not that it's any of my business."

"I'm still saying she looks like Lexine in her younger days," Winona insisted, sipping from her cup. "I mean, without all that bad energy she conjured up later."

With a wave of her hand, Janie dismissed Winona's comments. Besides, she wasn't about to lump all the Baxters into one immoral pot. While Jordan had started out poor and made the best of a bad situation, returning to Whitehorn a prosperous, if not a kind man, his cousin Lexine had taken to a life of heinous crime. Though there was no doubt that both Lexine and Jordan hated the Kincaids, their need for revenge and the same grandparents were about all Jordan and Lexine had in common.

To think that the girl in the big glasses looked anything like the murderess was more than Janie could imagine.

"Take care of table eight," she told the busboy just as

the bell over the door rang again and a group of teenagers swaggered in, laughing and joking, before sliding into a corner booth.

Sweat prickling her brow, Janie started for the table, but the girl who had been reading caught her attention as she was about to hurry past. "Excuse me." She looked up at Janie. "I don't mean to bother you, but I couldn't help but notice the sign in your window and I thought... I mean—"

"You want the job?"

"Yes. I'd like to fill out an application." Large hazel eyes gleamed behind pop-bottle-thick lenses.

"Do you have any experience?" Janie asked the younger woman.

"A little."

"Tell you what," Janie said. "Go grab an apron from a cupboard by the back door. The cook will point you in the right direction. There's a pen and receipt book in the pocket. Then come back and start working." She gave the newcomer quick, basic instructions.

"I—I'm hired?" the girl asked incredulously

"For tonight. Think of it as a trial run."

"Wow." She brightened, and Janie motioned to the busboy to clear her table.

"Just one more thing," Janie said as the girl started for the kitchen.

"What's that?"

"I'm Janie Austin. I'm the manager here. What's your name?"

"Emma. Emma Stover."

"Nice to meet you, Emma," Janie said with a smile as she wiped a droplet of sweat from her forehead with the back of her hand. "Welcome aboard."

* * *

"What do you mean, 'real friendly'?" Jack Henderson asked as he held the telephone receiver to his ear and paced in front of his desk. Glancing out the window, he spied cars whipping up and down the palm-lined street just a couple blocks off Sunset Boulevard. A thin layer of smog had Los Angeles in a choke hold, but that didn't stop roller-bladers and pedestrians from walking on the bright sidewalks.

"I mean, I saw Gina and Remmington dancing there in the hotel bar, oh, about five, maybe six weeks ago." Herb Atherton laughed, and the sound was nearly dirty. Jack had never much liked Herb, whose credentials included a law degree but who did little in Jack's opinion to improve the legal system. Herb was and always would be a taker, a man who had the morals of an alley cat and yet had cultivated the ability to look down on others as if he were related to God. Herb didn't know the meaning of the word loyalty, but, if the price were high enough, he was willing to do whatever it took to win a case—right or wrong.

"Is that right?" Jack felt the vein above his eye begin to throb. Gina hadn't mentioned meeting Remmington. In fact, he'd thought she had planned to go to Montana, locate that last heir, if he really existed, then get out. She hadn't been interested in meeting Larry Kincaid's brood of illegitimate children, had even balked when Garrett had asked that she be present when they all arrived in Whitehorn.

"Yep, *real* friendly, if ya know what I mean."

Jack wanted to reach through the phone and strangle the smug attorney, but he somehow managed to hang on to his patience. "Gina didn't mention it."

"I'll bet she didn't. She spilled wine all over the guy, then gushed and apologized and ended up going up to his room—you know, to get the stains out or something." Another nasty laugh that ended in a coughing fit.

"Was there something you wanted?" Jack asked, trying to hide his irritation.

"Yeah, I need a little help trackin' down a dead-beat father," Herb said, suddenly very serious. "The jerk up and left the ex wife and five kids high and dry about six months ago. I thought maybe you'd want to team up and help me out."

"That's really Gina's department," Jack said, the muscles tightening at the base of his skull whenever he heard about a man walking out on his family. Losers, every one of them—his own father included. "I'll have her give you a call when she gets into town."

"Do that." Herb hung up and Jack was left with a bad taste in his mouth. He didn't like Herb Atherton's insinuations about his kid sister, but then, Herb wasn't one to spout off without at least a seed of truth to back him up.

"Damn it all," Jack growled, wishing Gina would wind up the Kincaid case and hightail it back here. He was always a little restless when she was gone, though he knew he was being overprotective, just as he'd always been. Yet he couldn't help but feel responsible for her. He was the one who'd started the agency when he'd had it up to his eyeballs with the red tape of working for the L.A.P.D. Domestic violence, drugs and gangs had jaded him and at the first opportunity he'd quit the force and gone into business for himself.

Gina, after graduating from college, had begged to join him, and he'd reluctantly agreed to let her be a part of the team. He figured that at least he would be able to keep an eye on her. The kicker was that she'd proved herself to be one helluva investigator, especially when it came to tracking people down, and eventually Jack had made her his partner.

Until now she'd proved herself to be levelheaded, smart, efficient and professional.

So what was she doing with Trent Remmington?

He picked up his cup of now-cold coffee, walked over to a potted avocado plant and tossed the dregs into the soil.

When their old man had left, Gina had only been four years old. Jack, all of twelve at the time, had decided then and there that he'd take care of her. And he had.

Until now. Or so it seemed.

Swearing under his breath, he reached for his Lakers' cap and strode out the door. It slammed with a bang behind him and the heat of the city hit him full-force. Not that he cared. He'd go for a run along the beach at Santa Monica, think long and hard, then call his sister in Montana and ask her what in the hell was going on.

Chapter 8

"Just tell me this, Gina, and give it to me straight. Are you involved with Trent Remmington?" Jack demanded from the other end of the line.

Gina's back muscles tightened as they always did when her brother pushed his way into her personal life. But, standing in the middle of the kitchen, she couldn't get into it with him now. She twisted the cord around her as she turned her back to the table where Garrett and Trent nursed cups of hot coffee and mopped thin pancakes through rivers of maple syrup. Suzanne, humming softly, was already stripping off her apron as the scents of bacon grease and java were blown around by a breeze rolling through the open windows.

"I don't see that it's any of your business," she said, keeping her voice low.

"Hold it. Stop it right there, Gina. We had a deal, you

and me. We *don't* get involved with clients, or subjects of our searches or—"

"Murder victims?" she teased, trying to lighten the mood while silently praying that Trent wasn't listening. He and Garrett had been talking about Blake before the phone had jangled.

"Don't try to be cute, okay? I'm not in the mood," Jack growled.

She could envision the lines of disapproval bracketing his mouth. "And don't you blow a gasket. I know what I'm doing."

Her brother snorted and she wished she could reach through the phone lines and shake some sense into him. "I am twenty-seven, you know."

"Old enough to avoid a mistake like this."

"Just trust me," she whispered. With any luck, her words were drowned out by the shouts of workers who had already arrived, intent on getting on with the job of renovating the place. Hammers pounded and a tractor started up outside, the rumble of its engine adding to the curtain of noise. "This is my life," she reminded her brother.

"Damn it all, Gina, you *are* involved!" He swore a blue streak before somehow managing to retrieve a bit of his composure. "You should know better."

"And you should butt out."

"Didn't you say that Trent Remmington is a rich playboy? A maverick oilman? A gambler?"

With each charge she cringed. If her brother only knew that she worried she might be pregnant. What would he say then? Well, he couldn't find out. He'd have a stroke, Garrett would go through the roof, and Trent would probably think she was using the baby to blackmail him into a relationship. Oh, Lord, what a mess. The hammering stopped and the tractor drove off, the sound of its engine fading. Again she lowered her voice. "I know what I'm doing, Jack," Gina lied, unconsciously crossing her fingers. "I would appreciate you having some faith in me."

"Holy Toledo." There was a moment's pause in the conversation, then he sighed loudly and she pictured him running stiff, frustrated fingers through his brown hair while his hazel eyes darkened with concern. The little scar on his chin, a result of a tango with a knife-wielding crack addict, was probably more pronounced as his anger rose.

"And, by the way, since when did you start listening to gossip?"

"Oh, give me a break, Gina."

"You give me one. Herb Atherton? Please!"

"Okay, so Atherton is slimy, I'll grant you that, and he'd sell his grandmother if he thought it would guarantee him a judgeship, but he usually gets his facts straight."

"The jerk should mind his own business. And so, brother, dear, should you."

"I am, Gina," Jack said, his voice tightening into the big-brother timbre she recognized and resented. "This is my agency and—"

"And I thought we were partners."

"We are but—"

"Then for God's sake, trust me, and don't come unglued. I'm handling everything, okay?"

She hesitated. Was it her imagination or had the kitchen become suddenly so still you could hear the proverbial pin drop?

She cleared her throat. "The rest of the half brothers are arriving in a few days, so if you're done, I think I've had my fill of browbeating for the rest of the day. But call back next week. I'll probably be under quota by then." She slammed the receiver back into its cradle. Turning, she found Garrett and Trent pretending to show interest in their clean plates while Suzanne, hanging her apron on a hook near the back door, lifted a curious eyebrow before saying, "I'll be back in a few hours." The screen door slapped shut behind her.

"Trouble?" Garrett asked as Gina settled into her chair where her breakfast of fried eggs, bacon and pancakes had congealed into a swamp of melted butter and syrup.

"Nah." She shook her head.

"I heard the browbeating comment," Trent remarked, and there was a tension near the corners of his mouth she'd never noticed before.

"Oh, it was just my brother. He can be a real pain sometimes."

Trent nodded but didn't seem convinced. He took a long swig from his cup. "I know about brothers."

"And you'll get to know more, real soon, unless I miss my guess," Garrett observed, rising to glance out the window as a sleek black Acura purred into the yard. "Looks like the first one's just rolling up now."

"Already?" Gina asked.

"Yep." Garrett's eyes narrowed as the man behind the steering wheel stepped out into the bright Montana sunlight. "Appears that twins are more alike than they might want to admit."

Gina moved to stand beside Garrett and braced herself. Trent scraped back his chair without so much as cracked smile.

The new arrival pulled a smooth leather suitcase from the back seat, and when he straightened, Gina caught sight of his features for the first time. Straight brown hair, high cheekbones, thin lips—identical to those of the man striding to the back door to greet him.

Blake Remmington had arrived in Whitehorn.

"So I'm not the first," Blake said as Garrett and Trent strode across the parking lot.

Trent forced a smile he didn't really feel. He and Blake had never gotten along. He didn't expect their relationship to change just because they now knew that their mother had lied to them and that they were, in fact, Larry Kincaid's sons. True to form, Blake was dressed in tan slacks, an open-necked polo shirt, and polished loafers. No jeans and boots for this guy, Trent thought, not even in Montana.

Garrett stretched out his hand. "Garrett Kincaid. Your grandfather. It's probably easier if you just call me by my first name."

Trent noticed an entire gamut of emotions run across Blake's strong features as he took the old man's outstretched hand. "Glad to meet you."

"Same here."

Blake's gaze moved past Garrett to land full-force on his brother. "Trent. You're here early, aren't you?"

"Just couldn't stay away," Trent drawled, knowing he shouldn't bait his twin, but unable to stop himself. "What about you?"

"Once I got the phone call, I took care of business, threw some things in a bag and started driving."

"Pretty spontaneous for you," Trent observed.

"Yeah, well, maybe I've changed."

"Is that just after hell froze over?"

"Right before." Blake gave his brother an exaggerated wink. "Give it a rest, okay?"

"I'll try. No promises."

"Fair enough." Blake nodded curtly but not one of his perfectly combed strands of hair had dared fall out of place. Though more people than Trent wanted to admit had insisted that he and his brother were dead ringers, they didn't have a whole lot in common.

Unless, of course, you excepted that their mother had been a lying, social-climbing witch whose only concern was the advancement of her career and their father had been a womanizing cheat. They did have those terrific traits to share.

Trent winced inwardly at the thought of how much his night with Gina had mirrored his biological parents' meeting. Their mother had been a Montana state commissioner when she'd had the bad luck to run into Larry Kincaid at a Ranchers Association convention. After too many drinks and a roll in the hay, she'd found herself pregnant. Somehow, Barbara managed to convince Harold Remmington the boys were his and they'd married.

"Trent arrived a few days ago," Garrett explained casually.

Blake's blue eyes, so much like his own, found Trent's and, though the slight tensing of his brother's shoulders or the touch of disapproval in the curve of his lips was hardly noticeable, Trent saw it. He'd also bet that the old man hadn't missed a single strained nuance between the brothers.

"Trent was never known for his patience." Blake

forced a handshake. It was strong, firm, and brief. "How've you been?"

"'Bout the same," Trent drawled. He'd never been one to confide in Blake. Oh, sure, whenever he'd gotten himself into a mess now and again, he'd had to turn to Blake, but that had been years ago.

"Still wildcatting?"

"Yep. What about you?"

"Well, things have changed a bit since Garrett called."

Trent heard footsteps behind him and Gina appeared. "Excuse me," she said, and stuck out her hand. "You must be Blake."

To Trent's irritation Blake's blue eyes sparked and his smile widened. "And you're…?"

"Gina Henderson," Trent said quickly before Garrett could make introductions. "Seems Gina was hired to track us down."

"Congratulations," Blake said so warmly and smoothly that Trent thought he might be sick. The guy was like warm pudding. Trent had forgotten how women had fallen at his brother's feet. Even now. Gina wasn't immune.

"Let me help you get your things," Garrett offered. "You can either stay up here in the main house or in the bunkhouse. Plenty of room in either."

"Doesn't matter where." Blake took a sweeping view of the place and as his gaze moved from the two-storied house to the stable, bunkhouse and outbuildings, he actually smiled, as if he liked the raw, rugged acres that unfolded in a patchwork of fields. "It's pretty up here."

Garrett practically beamed. "I think so."

"Bet you're not the only one," Blake said.

Garrett, rather than nod proudly, sobered. "No," he said, but didn't elaborate. "Let me help you with these."

Along with his suitcase, Blake had brought a briefcase, laptop computer and another smaller bag, all of the same matching leather, every piece engraved with his initials. Probably Blake's ex-wife Elaine's doing.

"Stayin' awhile?" Trent asked.

"I think so, yeah." Blake squinted against the morning sun as a warbler sang from a nearby tree and carpenters banged their hammers at the site of the new arena. "If that's all right with you," he said to the weathered man who claimed to be their grandfather.

"The longer, the better," Garrett said, grabbing Blake's laptop. "I think we all need to get to know each other."

"What about your job?" Trent asked. He'd never seen his brother so laid-back before. For as long as Trent could remember, Blake was always on a schedule, or a regimen. The son with a plan. As far as Trent knew, his twin had never faltered in his path.

"I'm taking a month off. At least. Maybe longer." They started toward the main house and Blake eyed the horizon. To the northwest the jagged snowcapped peaks of the Crazy Mountains loomed upward to a few hazy clouds. "Even doctors need some time off." He glanced at his brother. Deep lines creased his forehead. "Thing's haven't been great."

"I heard about the divorce."

Sadness touched his brother's eyes. "It wasn't meant to be, I guess. Elaine and I..." He shook his head and frowned. "Well, it's all water under the bridge now."

For the first time in a long while, Trent felt a pang of sorrow for his brother. Even though Trent could have told Blake way back when that social-climbing Elaine Sinclair wasn't the kind of woman who would want to stay home and raise the couple of kids his pediatrician brother longed for. Elaine had liked money, social events, and knowing who was doing what. She'd had visions for her doctor-husband and herself that didn't include her getting pregnant and fat or baking cookies or coaching soccer or attending dance recitals for a "snot-nosed brat." Why Blake hadn't seen it, Trent had never understood.

Blake had married Elaine and, upon her urging, taken a job in Southern California. Life in the fast lane of Los Angeles hadn't been Blake's cup of tea. Trent had known it from the get-go, but Blake hadn't asked his opinion at the time and Trent probably wouldn't have given it if he had. He figured each man made his own mistakes and paid for them.

At that thought, he glanced at Gina. God, she got to him. Even now, dressed in a pair of dark shorts and a pale yellow sleeveless blouse, she was sexier than any woman he'd met in a long time. Her hair turned to flame in the morning light and her little nose, spattered with those nearly invisible freckles, wrinkled when she laughed. Her smile was infectious and her legs, slim and tanned, seemed to go on forever.

Yep, he was hooked, he thought as he climbed the steps and held open the door.

And it ticked him off. Just as the spurt of jealousy he'd felt when she smiled at Blake bothered him. He'd never been the jealous type. If anything, he'd been the one who inspired jealousy and now that the tables were turned, he didn't much like the new feeling.

Once inside, Garrett led Blake up the stairs and offered him a room next to Gina's. Not that it mattered,

Trent told himself as he set the bags he was carrying on the rag rug near a small bureau. Yet Trent's damned jaw hardened to the point it ached.

"Fixin' the place up?" Blake observed as two workmen carrying buckets of paint walked toward the back of the house.

"A bit. It was pretty rundown." Garrett placed Blake's laptop on his bed and glanced out the window. "Looks like Rand might need me," he said, spying the foreman striding toward the house. "Why don't you have Trent and Gina show you around? They've been here a few days." Garrett started to turn toward the door, but Blake grabbed him by the shoulder.

"Thanks, Garrett," he said, as if he were genuinely glad to meet the older man and embrace this chaos of a family. He threw out his hand again and clasped Garrett's palm hard. "I'm really glad to be here."

"That's good to know, son." Garrett's smile touched his eyes. He clapped Blake on the shoulder. "Good to have you."

Trent strode out of the room. He couldn't stand another second of all this fake family togetherness over Larry Kincaid's bastard sons.

He'd never really gotten along with Blake and didn't think he'd fare any better with the rest of his half brothers. But then, he'd always been a loner. Finding out that Larry Kincaid had been his father hadn't changed things.

He left the room and hurried down the stairs to the den where he could bury himself in the faxes and e-mail that were streaming in. He heard Gina's laugh follow after him and he scowled to himself at the thought of her being amused by his brother.

Man, you've got it bad, he thought, jealousy sneaking through his veins again. And for a woman who lied to you, hopped into bed with you and then snuck away in the middle of the night. She played you for a fool.

Inside the den, he kicked the door shut and snagged up the receiver, intent on calling his secretary, lawyer, accountant, and an outside investor, but his fingers hesitated over the buttons and he listened for the sound of Gina's voice, only to get angry all over again.

What the hell was happening to him?

When it came to that damned woman, he seemed to be cursed.

Chapter 9

Garrett mopped the sweat from his brow and swatted at a bothersome mosquito that wouldn't leave him alone. Walking through the orchard, he paused and looked back at the main house where patches of light glowed from the windows as dusk settled over these vast acres he'd worked so hard to keep in the family name. "I think I might have made a mistake," he admitted to no one in particular, though he realized he was thinking of Laura again. God, he missed her and at times like this, when he needed help wrestling with a decision, the ache within him was raw; as if she'd left this earth just yesterday rather than years earlier.

The old dog that was padding after him whined and Garrett reached down to scratch the shepherd's ears.

"Yes," he said, imagining his wife's encouraging smile. "Don't get me wrong, I think it was a good idea to find all our grandsons, but I didn't expect some of the complications. Jordan Baxter's making noise that he was cheated out of this place and I have a feeling he's not going to rest easy about it. There'll be trouble, sure as shootin'." Garrett snorted and the muscles in the back of his neck tightened. "I don't really know why he's so angry, but it seems as if Jordan thinks he was owed the place, that his uncle promised it to him on his sixteenth birthday."

Garrett straightened and looked at the first stars beginning to wink overhead. "If that's true—which I doubt—it was a long time ago and Cameron Baxter must've changed his mind or he wouldn't have sold it to our family. Hell, it's a mess..." He reached into his shirt pocket for a nonexistent pack of cigarettes, an old habit as he'd quit smoking years before.

"That's not the worst of it," he admitted as he started along a trail leading back to the house. "It's Trent. He's got something going with Gina. I see the way they look at each other, even caught them getting cozy up on the ridge the other day and then just yesterday I surprised them. They were alone in the barn and well, you know..." A wistful smile tugged at the corners of his mouth. "They remind me of us, Laura. The way I couldn't keep my hands off you." He sighed, remembering how hot and randy he'd been at Trent's age.

He passed by an open window of the ranch house and country music, punctuated by static, reached his ears. "Trouble is," he went on, "Trent's never been one to settle down. Too much of his daddy's blood in his veins, I reckon, so I'm afraid someone's going to get hurt...and it won't be our grandson."

His eyebrows slammed together at the thought. As

he was nearly at the house, he quit speaking out loud. He'd have trouble explaining that he was talking to his dead wife, so he clamped his mouth shut, but he was still concerned. Trent and Gina were involved—no question about it—and though the relationship in and of itself wasn't a problem, Garrett was just sick at the thought that Trent might break Gina's heart. That spunky red-head deserved a whole lot better.

On top of all that, Trent and his brother Blake didn't seem to get along. They looked identical, but were, in fact, as different as night to day.

Yes, he thought as he walked up the steps to the back porch and the scent of early blooming roses from the overgrown garden reached his nostrils, things were only going to get worse. At the back door he inched off one boot with the toe of another.

In the next few days the rest of Larry's boys would arrive.

Contrary to what he'd hoped, the homecoming might not be filled with brotherly love. In fact, considering the escalating tension in the house between Trent, Gina and Blake, and the gossip in town running rampant about Larry's illegitimate offspring, to say nothing of Jordan Baxter's determination to make trouble, it was probably a damned good bet that all hell was about to break loose.

The door to her room was ajar and the sounds at night were becoming familiar. The old clock in the foyer ticked off the seconds, a television, the sound low, rumbled down the hallway, and Trent's voice, muted as he was on the phone in the den, was barely audible. He'd insisted on installation of extra telephone lines. Between the running of the ranch, Trent's business and hers, a single line hadn't cut it. Now, because Garrett had agreed and three extra lines had been installed just this past week, faxes could get through while he was on-line and talking on the telephone all at the same time. Garrett hadn't objected as he hoped several of his newfound grandsons would stay on at the ranch for the summer. Most of them would have to conduct their business from the ranch.

All in all, it was a nightmare, Gina thought as she sat on her bed and rubbed the kinks from her neck. She'd spent the past several days trying—and failing—to avoid Trent. They'd shared meals together, bumped into each other in the house, and while she'd helped Suzanne in the kitchen, he and Blake had pitched in whenever Rand had needed an extra hand or two. He'd spent a lot of time in the den and so she'd taken to working from her room.

She'd passed him in the hallways, tried to smile and act nonchalant, but there was always more between them than a cursory nod or "Hello," "How's it goin'?" or even "Did you sleep okay?"

Just yesterday she'd found him alone in the barn when she'd been searching for Garrett.

"Garrett?" she'd called, stepping into the darkened interior that smelled of dry hay and cattle.

"Don't think he's here." Trent's voice had startled her and he'd stepped out of the shadows. His boot heels, ringing on hundred-year-old floorboards as he approached, echoed through the chambers of Gina's fluttering heart. "I'm looking for him myself."

"Oh." She hadn't been able to conjure up a ghost of a smile as a barn owl, disturbed, had hooted from the rafters and dust motes had swirled and danced, appearing golden in the shaft of daylight piercing a solitary round window. She'd looked into his face and her breath had suddenly lost itself between her lungs and her throat. Bladed cheekbones, square jaw, and thick eyebrows guarding eyes so blue that even in the half light she swallowed hard.

"Not in the stables, either. I checked."

"Then…then maybe he went into town."

"His truck's here." He'd been so close she could smell the hint of his aftershave, all male and musk as it mingled with the other odors of the barn.

"Then I'll check the bunkhouse."

"Wait." He'd reached for her hand and as his fingers had caught her wrist a shock had run up her nerves. Sweat had beaded between her shoulder blades. "I think I've been a little rough on you."

"Rough?"

He'd frowned and she'd wanted to kiss those blade-thin lips. Frustration and bewilderment, emotions she didn't normally attribute to him, had been drawn into the lines of his face. "I don't think so."

"The truth is, you bother me, Gina. I don't know what to do with you."

She'd laughed nervously. "Nothing. There's nothing to do."

"No?" He hadn't been convinced, his thick eyebrows cinching together as the owl hooted again, flapped its wings and hid deeper in the rafters.

Oh, if he would just quit touching her. But his fingers had been warm on the inside of her wrist and the air between them had seemed to grow thicker still, heavy with unspoken emotions. She'd immediately thought of their lovemaking, of the fact that she might be pregnant and wanted to confide in him. But she hadn't—she couldn't. Not until she was certain. Maybe not even then. As if he'd read the doubts in her mind, he'd tugged gently on her arm, pulled her closer. His head bent and his lips had hovered over hers in delicious enticement. "I—"

With a creak of hinges the sliding door was suddenly rolled back. As sunlight streamed through the opening, Gina had pulled her hand away from Trent's. She'd turned quickly to find Garrett, Blake and Rand just outside. "That's right, I think we should check with the vet, make sure we have all the serums for inoculations," Garrett had been saying as the bright light flooded the barn's interior. Gina had tried to appear calm and Trent had actually stepped forward.

"Gina and I have been lookin' for you," he'd said without preamble, as if he wasn't the least bit disconcerted that once again they'd been discovered in a nearly compromising position. "I took a call from Wayne, he wants you to get in touch with him, and Gina—" He'd turned to her and with a cocky half smile, said, "She needed something, as well." Raising a dark eyebrow, encouraging her to take over, he'd cocked his head toward the three men as they'd walked inside.

Her mind had gone blank. For the life of her she hadn't been able to remember why she'd been searching for the elder Kincaid.

"Somethin' up?" Garrett had asked. Rand had walked past them and into the barn, Blake had smothered a knowing smile, and Gina, fighting the urge to slap Trent for tossing the ball in her direction, had forced her head to nod and hoped to high heaven that her face was still in the shadows, that her blush was hidden.

"It's not that important if you're busy. I just wanted to ask you some questions about Larry—where he was about a year and a half ago. I mean, I know he spent some time with you and Wayne going over this place, so he was here in Whitehorn, but I wondered about side trips he might have taken." They'd been over this territory before, but she'd wanted to double-check her notes, and Garrett was the best source of information she had.

"Just give me a minute and I'll meet you up at the house," he'd said. The owl had flapped his wings, shedding feathers that had drifted to the floor as Gina, embarrassed all over again, though she'd told herself she was being overly sensitive, had walked stiffly back to the house.

Garrett hadn't been able to shed any more light on Larry's whereabouts during the time when the seventh son had been conceived, nor had he brought up either time he'd caught Gina and Trent embracing. But he wasn't happy about the situation; Gina's feminine intuition was working overtime these days and she sensed Garrett's disapproval.

"Great," she muttered as she pulled one leg under her and leaned against the wall. Well, she didn't have much more time here. The other sons were due to start rolling into the ranch in the morning and if she could just locate that last one, or prove that he didn't exist, she could hightail it. Garrett wanted her to meet all of the men she'd located; she wasn't sure that was such a fabulous idea. Look what had happened when she'd made the mistake of accepting a drink from Trent. One thing had led to another and now…

Oh, she couldn't, wouldn't, dwell on the consequences of that first fateful meeting. Not while she had so much to do. Using her pencil, she scratched her head where the rubber band of her ponytail pulled tight. She spread the files she'd made of each of Larry's offspring beside her on the wrinkled covers. On the desk, her laptop glowed ghostly blue.

Where was that baby?

She'd spent days trying to track him down, to no avail. She had, again, come up dry.

"So much for your sharp investigative mind," she muttered to herself, wondering if there really was a seventh illegitimate son. She flipped open the journal. Could it be a hoax? Did some woman try to pawn off her baby as Larry's to scare him, or to shake him down? Was it all a twisted, cruel joke? Larry Kincaid had certainly used and cheated on any woman he'd contacted, maybe someone had just turned the tables on him.

She tapped her eraser against her teeth and ignored the sound of Trent's laughter rolling up the stairs. She wondered who he was talking to, then reminded herself she didn't care.

"Think," she admonished, and flipped through her notes about the other brothers, scanning the files, searching desperately for some thread that might tie them together, some reason Larry chose the women he did, a commonality aside from the fact that they were all Larry Kincaid's sons. Maybe she would then come up with the most likely candidate for Larry's last fling. She sensed that the woman lived around here in Whitehorn. Larry had been here about the time the child had been conceived.

If he'd been conceived, she reminded herself as she propped a shoulder against the wall.

Each of her reports, typed neatly, dated, cross-referenced and tucked into manila files, gave a short bio on Garrett's grandsons. She had also included a picture of each of the grown men and kept color copies for herself.

She opened a file. The firstborn, Adam Benson, was thirty-seven years old and an overachiever who had earned an MBA and a reputation for having a chip on his shoulder the size of Montana. There were reasons for his anger—deep-seated and dark. Gina studied the picture she'd culled from his college yearbook. Arrogantly handsome with jet-black hair, steely gray eyes and strong, chiseled features vaguely reminiscent of his grandfather's, Adam was a striking man. He'd worked hard and was determined to leave his mark on this world. Always pushing, never satisfied, he'd become a corporate raider and, even at the age of twenty-three as he stared into the camera, he looked the part.

Gina set his page aside and picked up the next, that of thirty-five-year-old Cade Redstone. Gina smiled. Cade was about as opposite from his older brother as he could be, a real, doggie-chasing, bronc-riding, spur-jangling cowboy whose mother, Mariah Raintree, was a Native American who had once worked as a maid for the Kincaids. The snapshot showed Cade at a rodeo in Texas, astride an ornery Brahman bull. His dark eyes gleamed with anticipation. His bronzed skin gleamed with sweat. Gina suspected Cade would feel right at home on the ranch and would probably give his uptight, older half brother a well-deserved ribbing. While Gina expected Adam to turn on a polished leather heel and leave the Whitehorn ranch immediately upon landing, she suspected Cade would dig his cowboy boots into the gravel, grass and dirt of the spread with gusto and fire.

She set his file aside and picked up the third, that of Brandon Harper, the result of Larry's affair with a Las Vegas showgirl. Brandon's stepfather had been a monster and the boy had lashed out, been placed in foster care, adopted, but had been a juvenile delinquent on a path straight to jail. Luckily he'd been athletic and, under the guidance of a coach or two, had avoided jail. He, like Trent, had made his millions on his own.

The photo she'd found of Brandon had been taken just last year at a social event in Lake Tahoe. Dressed in a black tuxedo with a teal vest, he was standing in the foyer of a high-rise hotel, an illuminated fountain spraying upward as a backdrop, a gorgeous model clinging like a piece of expensive jewelry to one arm. Brandon's smile was as cold as his ice-blue eyes. A Rolex watch peeked from beneath his sleeve and his black hair had been perfectly cut. His features were sharp, bold and guarded. While the woman he was with fairly beamed, Brandon looked as if he had ice water running through his veins.

Gina tossed his folder aside and shook her head. This was getting her nowhere in a hurry. The common link between these half brothers was their good looks, very different yet hinting of a Native American ancestry hidden deep in their gene pool. Their mothers were all beautiful, but from different walks of life. Adam's biological mother had been a cheerleader who had died while giving him birth. Cade's, a pretty housekeeper. Brandon's, a flashy dance hall girl. Young and beautiful and obviously not immune to Larry Kincaid's charms, whatever they had been.

The next file was a double. The Remmington twins. Blake and Trent. Gina's foolish, foolish heart twisted a bit. Living this near to Trent was a mistake. Each night she tossed and turned, thinking of him lying next door. She remembered their lovemaking in the DeMarco Hotel in Dallas and the other times he'd kissed her, his lips seeming to brand her own.

"Don't even go there," she warned herself, but her mind was already wandering from the job at hand to the feel of his skin against hers, the warmth of his hands, the magic of his breath against her flesh.

She swallowed hard and opened the file. Two pictures of nearly identical men stared back at her. Blake was dressed in a white lab coat with a stethoscope slung around his neck. A bright-eyed boy of about three was seated on Blake's bent knee. The floppy-haired imp sported a cast that ran down a chubby leg and he grinned widely as he clutched a one-eyed teddy bear to his chest.

Blake obviously enjoyed his career and the children he cared for. She wondered why, during his marriage, he'd never become a father.

Her stomach clenched at the thought. How ironic that she might be carrying Trent's child. She glanced at her watch, checked the date and sighed. This wasn't how she'd planned to become a mother and yet the thought that a baby—Trent's baby—might be growing inside her was exhilarating. She hadn't thought much about settling down but she'd always wanted children.

And yet she was terrified. The fact that she hadn't yet made the time to buy a pregnancy test convinced her that she was in major denial.

She looked down at the file folder to Trent's picture. It was a far cry from his brother's. Oh, their features were nearly identical, but that was where the likeness ended. Everything about them from their personalities to their attitude toward life appeared to be in diametric opposition to each other.

The snapshot said it all. Trent stood in front of a

gusher, a brazen slash of a smile cutting through two days' worth of dark beard. His eyes were blue and triumphant, his hair longer than the current trend and blowing in the breeze. No hard hat for the owner of the company. Pride was etched into the set of his jaw, naked challenge flared in his eyes as he stood, arms folded over his chest, the tails of his denim shirt flapping in the wind. Rugged. Wild. A force to be reckoned with, Trent Remmington was at home in designer suits or faded jeans, a man, she was afraid, she could so easily learn to love.

She gasped. *Love?* She thought she could *love* him? Now where did that ludicrous thought well from? She barely knew the man, for crying out loud, and just because... just because she thought she might be carrying his... Her stomach clenched and she suddenly had trouble breathing. She'd always been a reasonable woman and not one to think that sexual attraction necessarily meant love. But if she was pregnant—

Rap! Rap! Rap!

She glanced up and found Blake leaning against the doorjamb. "Want to take a break?" he asked.

"A break?"

"I've got to drive into town and could use a little company. Besides, you know the town and can point me in the direction of the nearest grocery store. I promised Suzanne I'd pick up some of the supplies she forgot earlier."

"What about Trent?" Gina asked, dumbfounded.

"He's busy." Blake's smile was positively infectious. "Besides, you're prettier."

"I—I don't know," she started, then decided why not? She was getting nowhere fast as it was. "Sure. Just give me a minute."

"I'll meet you in the foyer." He disappeared and she

told herself that any personal involvement with any of the Kincaid sons was a mistake, but then, she'd already made the worst of all. She yanked the rubber band from her hair, swiped at the wavy red locks with a brush, slapped some lipstick over her lips and grabbed her purse. Slinging the strap over her shoulder, she breezed down the stairs, nearly running into Trent in the process.

It was funny, she thought, that no matter how much the twins looked alike, she knew instantly which one she was facing and it wasn't just a matter of clothes— nope, it was attitude.

"Going somewhere?" he asked, stopping on the stairs.

"Into town."

His lips compressed. "With Blake." It wasn't a question.

"He wanted me to point out the some of the sights."

"That should take all of two minutes."

"You could come along," she invited with a lift of her shoulder.

His eyes narrowed a fraction. "I'll take a rain check. Have fun."

Was he being sarcastic? Probably. Trent continued up the stairs and Gina sped down the remainder of the flight.

"That's the Branding Iron, a local nightspot," Gina said as Blake steered his plush car through the streets of downtown Whitehorn. Melodic notes of soft jazz whispered through the speakers and the leather interior smelled new.

Blake hitched his chin toward the bar as they passed. "Ever been inside?"

"Just once, to interview the bartender and waitresses. Your father—"

"If you're talking about Larry, let's call him by his name, okay. 'Father' just doesn't seem to fit."

She snorted. "I heard the same thing from Trent."

"So it really is true—great minds do think alike," he joked as he drove past Whitehorn Memorial Hospital and the statue of Lewis and Clark positioned near the front of the building. Tall cottonwoods surrounded the structure and street lamps illuminated the grounds. "I'd always thought that was a fallacy."

"Take a right here." She pointed to the next corner.

"Voilà," he said as the grocery store appeared. Two pickups, a dented station wagon with duct tape holding a taillight together and a Mercedes convertible were parked in the asphalt lot. As Blake cut the engine, a tall, silver-haired man in a sharply pressed suit strode out of the store. Anger and something else—desperation?—pinched the corners of his mouth and he swept the Acura a dark look. In one arm he toted a single paper bag of groceries, but his shoulders were bent with the load of his bad attitude.

"Jordan Baxter," Gina said as Jordan pressed his keyless lock and the lights of his convertible turned on. Opening the door, he slid behind the wheel.

"Who's he?"

"A man you want to avoid. The bad blood between the Baxters and the Kincaids goes back for generations."

Blake laughed. "A family feud. Like the Montagues and Capulets?"

"Not quite so highbrow," she said, smiling at his Shakespearean reference. "More like the Hatfields and the McCoys, I'm afraid."

"Are you? That surprises me. You look like the kind of woman who's not afraid of anything."

"There is no such animal," she said as Jordan threw his Mercedes into reverse. The convertible's sleek finish appeared nearly liquid in the incandescent glow of the street lamps. With a well-tuned roar, the Mercedes took off.

She reached for the door handle, but Blake didn't move. He was fiddling with his key chain with one hand, the fingers of the other hand still poised on the wheel. "Before we go inside," he said, "I'd like to ask you something."

Her muscles stiffened. His teasing attitude had disappeared along with his boyish smile. "Shoot."

"Okay." Turning his head to stare at her directly, he asked, "Are you in love with my brother?"

Chapter 10

Blake's question followed Gina around like a lost puppy. *Are you in love with my brother?* Who knew? She'd managed to laugh at his suggestion and hurry out of the car into the store, but the thought that she might be in love with Trent kept nipping at her heels, trailing after her, interrupting last night's sleep and waking her in the predawn hours. She'd given up on sleep and decided to face the day. But even now as she stepped out of the shower into the steamy bathroom, her mind spun at the thought that she just might be falling in love.

"Get a grip," she told herself, for today was the day that the sons of Larry Kincaid were due to arrive. All her efforts at locating them would culminate this very morning. She flung a thick peach-colored towel around her body, tucked it over her breasts and used a wash cloth to wipe the steam that had collected on the mirror.

Soon enough she could leave Whitehorn, Montana. And what then?

Click.

The latch on the door sprang and the door itself opened with a loud creak. Holding the towel to her chest, she whirled around. Trent, fully dressed in jeans and a cream-colored shirt with the sleeves rolled up, slipped in. Her towel nearly fell to the cracked linoleum.

"What do you think you're doing?" she demanded in a harsh whisper, her heart hammering wildly.

"I wish I knew."

"What do you mean?"

In answer, he kicked the door shut, latched the lock, then grabbed her. Steam rose in the tiny room lit only by a single bulb in a tulip-shaped fixture over the mirror.

"Are you crazy?" What had gotten into him?

"Probably."

"Now, wait a minute—"

"No." His eyes held hers for half a heartbeat and she was lost. She gulped. His lips crashed down on hers and though she wanted to protest, she couldn't call up a solitary word of refusal. No, damn it, she practically melted. Just like the silly kind of woman she detested. As if of their own accord, her arms slipped around his neck and she willingly opened her mouth to him. She closed her eyes, feeling soft droplets of water drip from the ringlets of her wet hair onto her bare shoulders.

She was crazy. Downright certifiable. And yet she kissed him as eagerly as he did her. She told herself that she was only fanning the fires of a passion that should never have been lit in the first place, but she didn't care. What harm there was had already been done.

Her towel slipped a bit, edging lower, but she was so

caught up in the emotion of the moment, she didn't feel
it surrender to the insistent pull of gravity, nor would
she have cared. Trent was kissing her, devouring her,
and deep inside she heated, her flesh tingling, her breath
shallow and raspy as she pretended they were all alone
in the universe and that loving Trent Remmington was
forever her destiny.

Her eyes fluttered a second then closed in ecstasy
as he lowered his mouth, kissing the crook of her neck
and tugging the towel down until her breasts were exposed. She moaned and leaned against the sink as he
bared one round nipple and a cool current of air from
the open window moved across her skin. Her nipples
puckered in anticipation.

He, running a thumb over one breast, teased and
played with the rosy little bud of the other with his
tongue, teeth and lips until desire pumped liquid fire
through Gina's veins. Hot. Raw. Hungry. She lolled
her head back, her hands at her sides, her fingers gripping the porcelain sink as her knuckles grew white. She
wanted him   more than any reasonable woman would
hunger for a man. The ache deep inside her pulsed in
white-hot beats that pounded through her brain and
evoked a whispered moan from her throat.

Somewhere in the back of her mind she knew that she
should stop him. On this day of days, when the house
would soon be crawling with Kincaids, she needed to
be composed and relaxed, cool and collected. But his
tongue was liquid magic, stroking, touching, caressing.
The serrated edges of his teeth toyed with her skin and
she arched closer to him, wanting more.

"That's it, love," he said, and slowly pulled the towel
away from her to let it pool on the bathroom floor.

Steamy mist hung in the air as he settled onto his knees, his mouth easing lower, his tongue rimming her navel, his hands moving over her abdomen. Calloused fingers smoothed her skin and she thought of the baby that might be growing within her.

His child.

His breath was hot against the damp nest of curls at the apex of her legs. He kissed her there and she moaned again, her skin on fire. With little urging, she opened to him and he kissed her, softly at first, then with more insistence, his lips and tongue sucking and licking, his breath swirling hot within her.

She bit her lip to keep from screaming, felt him lift her legs over his shoulders as she balanced against the sink. His groan reverberated through her, and the entire universe seemed to center deep in the most feminine part of her. As a morning breeze swept through the cracked-open window, chasing away the last remaining wisps of mist, the pressure mounted. Sweat sheened her body. His fingers dug into her skin. Lifted higher and higher, she was climbing, gasping, panting, until she reached the brink and fell over. Her entire body convulsed, the cold porcelain pressed into her hips, the heat of the man she loved breathing fire deep inside.

"Oooohh." Her throat was dry, her skin fevered. She couldn't think, could barely speak. "Trent…oh, Trent."

"Shh, baby, it's okay." His words pulsed through her.

"No… I… Ooooh!" She bucked again and the universe collided. Her hands grabbed his head and held him close. She squeezed her eyes shut and clamped her mouth against the primal scream that threatened to roar from her.

And then it was over. Her body went limp as he slowly

let her legs fall back to the floor. She was dizzy, still spinning.

Straightening, climbing to his feet, Trent dragged her close and wrapped his strong arms around her to cradle her while she drooped against him and pressed her face into his denim-draped shoulder. Spasm after spasm rocketed through her and for a brief second the bathroom seemed to tilt. Standing in bare feet, she clung to him, dripping in sweat, still aching from his lovemaking.

"What— Why…why did you come in here?" she said when some of her equilibrium slowly returned.

"I thought I just showed you."

"Yes, but… I mean…" She rocked away from him and scraped her hair from her eyes with one hand. "Why now?"

"Because you've been avoiding me."

"You noticed."

"Hard not to."

Oh, God, she was stark naked! Reason swept back with a vengeance and she groaned. "I need to get dressed."

"Fine." He flipped down the lid of the toilet and took a seat.

"What? You can't stay here. It's indecent. Someone might see…" He arched an insolent dark eyebrow and she sighed, realizing the point was moot. "Fine. Whatever." She stepped into her panties and hooked her bra behind her back while trying not to notice that he was studying her for all he was worth. "Kind of a reverse strip show, isn't it?"

His Cheshire-cat grin was insufferable. He stacked his hands behind his head insolently. "Maybe later I can rewind the tape and watch it the right way."

"In your dreams."

"Precisely." Her head snapped up to see if he was teasing but his expression was as sober as if he'd been confessing to a priest. His laser-blue gaze burned into hers.

Instantly the heat in her cheeks ignited. She swallowed hard and looked away. What was going on here? Besides acting out some kind of sexual fantasy. Was there more? Or was it her all-too-active imagination? Snatching her shorts and blouse from a hook near the door, she quickly dressed and then, praying that the hallway was empty, unlocked the door and poked her head out.

All clear. She scooped up her nightgown.

"Not so fast." Trent's voice arrested her.

"What?" She glanced over her shoulder.

"What did you and Blake talk about last night?" Now she was imagining just a trace of jealousy in his gaze. Was it possible?

"Everything and nothing. Your name came up."

"I hope in the 'everything' category."

Blake's question ricocheted through her brain again. *Are you in love with my brother?* Her throat was suddenly as dry as the Mojave Desert. She had to get away. "What do you think?" she quipped back at him, her hand on the doorknob again.

"What I think, Gina, is that you're running scared." His words stopped her cold.

"From?"

But she knew the answer before she opened the door and walked briskly along the hallway.

"Me, darlin'. You just don't know what to do with

me," he said loudly enough that the words chased her all the way downstairs.

Amen, she thought. *If I live to be older than Methuselah, I'll never have the first idea of how to handle you.*

Seated around the cold hearth in the living room of the main house, Trent surveyed the newcomer with a jaundiced eye. He was the first of the next batch of Larry's bastards to show up. Dressed in clean, dark jeans, a plaid shirt and a pair of snakeskin cowboy boots, he'd introduced himself as Mitch Fielding. From the small talk that had erupted, Trent learned that Mitch was the youngest of Larry's bastards.

Mitch was a construction worker who lived nearby. A widower with twin six-year-old girls, Mitch was about six feet tall, with sandy hair, tanned skin and intense hazel eyes. He seemed eager to meet Garrett and the rest of the brood and his aw-shucks, rural persona gritted on Trent's nerves. The guy even blushed when he'd met Gina, and Trent had been certain Mitch would wear the toe of his boot out with the shy, country-boy routine. It was enough to make Trent sick, but then, he'd been acting way out of character ever since he'd met Gina.

Any man who looked at her was a potential rival.

Now, as Mitch, seated on the worn couch, gushed on about his daughters and Gina sat with Garrett and Blake listening in rapt interest, Trent wanted to plant himself next to her, throw an arm around her shoulders just to make sure that any and all males who looked in her direction knew she was off the market.

Or was she?

Never in his life had he been confused about a woman, but this one, Gina, made him think twice. He hadn't been this possessive of any woman, not even Beverly when she'd told him she was carrying his child.

His jaw grew hard and he touched the ancient rifle mounted over the mantel, running an experienced finger down the dark barrel of the weapon. For a moment he thought of this morning when he'd heard Gina rise and dash into the bathroom. He hadn't been able to keep himself from following her. He'd planned to just talk to her but she'd been so damned sexy in the steamy room, her wet red hair framing a fresh face devoid of makeup. Her green eyes had rounded, her towel had slipped and suddenly he'd forgotten about saying anything. Even now, remembering her thrown back against the counter, her breasts so white and tipped with perfect peach nipples, he started to grow hard. Closing his mind to the erotic memory, he tried to concentrate on the conversation at hand.

"...so I was glad to get the call," Mitch was saying, his fingers laced, his hands hanging between his knees. "My little girls need to know their roots. Their great-grandpa. Their uncles."

Trent's stomach turned sour.

"I agree," Garrett said, casting a knowing look in Trent's direction. "We're family."

Blake laughed. "Kind of an odd mix, but, yeah, we are a family."

Trent wasn't buying it. Not for a minute.

He suspected Larry's legitimate kids, Collin, the man who was about Mitch Fielding's age, and his daughter, Melanie, might not swallow the "one big happy family" fantasy, either.

He hazarded a glance at Gina, caught her gaze for just a second and realized that the reason he was sticking around the ranch wasn't because of Garrett and his half brothers. Other than idle curiosity about them, Trent really didn't give a damn. No, his attraction to the ranch was solely Gina Henderson.

"…and so once I found out that you all existed, I knew I had to do something," Garrett was saying, standing at the head of the huge dining room table where the newfound illegitimate sons of Larry Kincaid and a few other Kincaid relatives had gathered. All the men had shown up earlier this morning and the tension in the ranch house had been nearly palpable. Strangers who were half brothers, men who had grown up not knowing about their biological father, this ranch, or each other, were understandably wary. Uncomfortable.

Trent was by far the worst.

Half-drunk cups of coffee were scattered over the oak top and a few of the brothers had brought notepads. Trent hadn't. Sitting low in his chair, his arms folded across his chest, he watched the proceedings silently, appearing as if he'd rather be anywhere else on the planet.

Gina had claimed a chair next to Garrett's. The box of paraphernalia and her notes lying open, some tossed around the table as the men perused her work and the mementoes Larry had kept of his children. Adam's report cards; a citation from the juvenile system on Trent; a rodeo ribbon of Cade's; a yearbook with pictures of Brandon scoring half-a-dozen touchdowns; a copy of Blake's application to medical school; a photograph of Mitch and his daughters and, of course, the date book/journal indicating that there was one son missing from the table, a baby boy as yet unlocated—maybe never to be located.

Each man had fumbled through his file and the small pieces of his life that Larry had squirreled away. A range of emotions was on display from wistful smiles to barely controlled rage. Other stares were bored or vacant, as if a silent agony was being reined in.

Gina's throat was tight when she witnessed the pain of rejection some of these men, who all had once been impressionable boys, experienced.

Larry Kincaid should have been castrated, then drawn and quartered for leaving his sons to grow up on their own. But they were here now. And they had questions.

As Garrett spoke, Gina's stomach was in knots. She felt like the proverbial fish out of water. On top of it, she was the reason all these men had been found and found quickly, though, it seemed, there wasn't a whole lot of animosity directed her way.

Except from Trent. He hadn't quite forgiven her for the lies she'd told him in Dallas. Not that she could really blame him, she supposed, but looking at him now, she felt her heart thump deep in her chest. He sat low on his back, regarding everyone with guarded eyes, as if he trusted no one. Which he probably didn't. For a second she thought of this morning, how intimate they'd been, then she looked quickly away and tried to concentrate.

"...so I got together with Wayne here." Garrett motioned to his cousin, seated to his left. Wayne, a lean, wiry man with tanned, lined skin and the same startling blue eyes as Garrett's, half stood and nodded a full head of silvering blond hair. "And along with a few other people who were involved with this ranch, I decided that I'd buy it back and divide it between all of you. Until now Wayne's managed this place, but he lives in town. Rand Harding's our foreman and he and his wife Suzanne are occupying the foreman's quarters. They'll stay on, along with some of the hands who've been working here for years."

He paused to eye each of his grandsons, then continued. "Now, before you all start talking about not being interested in the spread, or not needing it or not even wanting to be bothered ranching, just hold on. I'm thinking the place will be kind of a touchstone, a place you can all own and where you can all connect. Those who want to run it, well, okay, those who want to be silent partners, that's okay, too." Again he hesitated, tapped his fingers nervously on the ancient oak table. "Well, hell, there's no way to say this other than straight out." He looked at each man in turn. "My son Larry didn't do right by any of you and I want to make it up to you and make you feel wanted—all part of the Kincaid family."

Gina watched the men's faces. They were all serious now, staring at the man they hadn't known was their grandfather. Blake and Trent, seated next to each other, acted as if there was a wall between them.

Adam Benson, the oldest, sat next to Wayne Kincaid. Gina wasn't sure she liked the brooding man who hadn't bothered hiding his arrogance. She could well believe that he was a corporate raider by trade. He was wearing a starched white shirt, power tie and sleek navy-blue business suit. Hawklike, he silently observed the scene around him, and Gina could almost see the wheels turning in his mind.

On the opposite side of the table, Mitch Fielding tapped work-roughened fingers on the arm of his chair. His expression was serene, as if all the melodrama of his biological father didn't bother him a bit. With sandy-brown hair, streaked by hours working under the sun, and hazel eyes that were warm and filled with energy, Mitch seem to accept what Garrett and Wayne proposed without much concern. His plaid shirt was clean but worn, his jeans, too, had seen better days, yet he was as unconcerned about his appearance as he seemed about all the fuss about the land.

"You want us all as equal partners?" Adam asked.

"Yes," Garrett said as Wayne nodded.

Adam leaned forward. "Once you called, I did a little research on the place. It's held in trust, right? For a Jennifer McCallum—"

"She's a Kincaid, as well," Garrett interjected. "A cousin, like Wayne here."

"I'm one of the trustees," Wayne said, "but we all voted and have agreed to sell the ranch to Garrett. It's unanimous."

"And there are no liens?" Adam asked, his face a study in concentration.

"No." Garrett shook his head.

Wayne agreed. "We'd already decided to sell the place when Garrett came up with the idea to buy it and give it all to you."

"And you're doing this with no strings attached." Adam's dubious gaze was centered on his grandfather.

"All I ask is that you stay as long as you want, get to know each other, become a part of the family."

"Sounds good to me," Mitch said.

Adam's mouth became a thin line of distrust. "I don't believe in getting something for nothing."

Trent's jaw twitched a bit, as if he'd had the very same thought. He caught Gina's eye, held it for a minute, then leaned back in his chair even further and glanced away.

"I think it's a hell of an idea." Cade Redstone slapped

his hand on the table. Gina guessed it took a lot to in-
timidate this rough-and-tumble cowboy. Ranch-tough,
Cade was a strong-willed, no-nonsense man who had
traveled all the way from his stepfather's spread in Texas.
Cade met Adam's hard glare and didn't back down for
a second. "A hell of an idea," he repeated.

"I didn't say it was a bad idea, I just had a few questions."

"As well you should," Garrett cut in, spreading his
hands as if he were indeed pouring oil on troubled waters. "As well you should."

"Didn't you sell off twenty acres a while back to
the Laughing Horse reservation?" Adam zeroed in on
Wayne.

"That's right. They needed it for a hotel and spa."

"And a casino."

"Maybe," Wayne agreed.

"But it won't have any bearing on the rest of the
land?" Adam wasn't convinced.

"That's right," Garrett answered. He leaned forward
and impaled his firstborn grandson with his own hard
glare.

"Even if it did, we could work things out through the
county," Brandon Harper, the second of Larry's sons,
thought out loud. He stuck two fingers under his collar and loosened his tie. An investment banker who'd
made his fortune on his own, he was used to dealing
with property disputes and seemed to relish any kind of
battle, be it legal or otherwise. Blue eyes, so much like
his grandfather's, held Adam's. He didn't flinch. "It's
not a problem," he said with authority.

Adam wasn't about to back down. Underlying cur-
rents of tension snapped in the air. Every man in the

room had his own personal ax to grind and grind it he would.

"I think Brandon's right." Garrett took charge again. Though the least volatile of any man at the table, he was a force to be reckoned with. "Besides, I didn't call you together to hassle over the legalities of what I'm doing. I just wanted to start us out together, on the same page. Now, Gina here is convinced that there's another boy out there somewhere, a young one, still a baby."

"A boy Larry fathered?" Brandon asked, tossing back a hank of black hair that fell over his eyes.

"Yes." Garrett sighed and tapped his knuckles on the table. "Unless that notation in his journal's a fake. You all saw it there, in the box." He moved his gaze from one grandson to the next. "Now, I'd suggest we all have lunch and get to know each other. I believe Rand and Suzanne have things ready on the back porch."

He scraped his chair back and the others did the same. A few men tried to make small talk. Mitch and Cade were the most outgoing. Blake tried to draw Brandon into conversation while Adam kept to himself and Trent shot Gina a look that reminded her of their encounter in the bathroom. Her skin flushed, but she ignored it and muttered as she passed him, "I think it would be a good idea if you tried to connect with your brothers."

"Half brothers." Scowling, he fell into step with Gina and sighed. "The old man's a fool, you know. All this idealistic, maudlin crap. He feels guilty because his son was a first-class jerk, but that doesn't mean any of us will ever get along or want to have anything to do with each other."

The caustic sound of his words scraped her raw. "It wouldn't hurt you to try, Trent," she said, coming to

Garrett's defense swiftly. Pivoting to face him, she poked a finger at the middle of his chest. "And while I'm giving advice, why don't you lose the attitude, okay?" Her voice escalated passionately. "You're damned lucky to know your grandfather and no matter what Larry might have been, Garrett Kincaid is one extremely earnest, decent, hardworking and fair man. Things could be worse. A lot worse. Think about it!"

With that, she marched out of the dining room, not giving one damn who had heard her outburst. Trent Remmington was the most irritating, exciting, passionate man she'd ever met in her life, but she wasn't going to listen to anyone second-guess Garrett's intentions. And if Adam Benson or any of the other half brothers opened his mouth against Garrett, he'd get a piece of her mind, as well.

Still steaming, she walked through the French doors to a back porch where the afternoon temperature was already climbing. Country music was playing softly from a radio propped on the windowsill. A long picnic table had been covered with a plaid cloth anchored by platters and serving dishes steaming in the shade of the porch's overhang. Suzanne and Rand were smiling as they met Larry's sons. A pretty woman Gina recognized as Janie, a waitress from the Hip Hop Café helped the half brothers load their plates while a weak breeze turned the leaves of the cottonwoods standing guard near the fence line.

The tangy scent of barbecued chicken vied with the aromas of baked beans and garlic bread. Gina's stomach rumbled softly, yet she didn't think she could swallow a single bite. A barrel of ice held soft drinks and bottles of beer, while a coffee urn stood ready at one end of the picnic table. Yellow jackets had already begun buzzing near the overflowing platters, and the dog, ever vigilant, lay just at the edge of the porch, head in his paws, brown eyes bright and expectant as he hoped for a tidbit tossed his way or a scrap to fall to the floor.

"Danged bees," Garrett rumbled, swatting at a pesky yellow jacket that hovered near his head.

"They won't each much," Wayne said.

"They'd better not, or I'll shoot 'em." Rand winked at his wife who rolled her eyes.

"Behave, Rand Harding," Suzanne teased. She glanced at Gina. "I swear sometimes I'm afraid to take him out in public." She touched her husband's chin. "You'd better mind your manners, or I won't let you go to Leanne's wedding." As if she realized Gina might not understand, she scooped up a spoonful of beans and as she plopped them onto a plate added, "Leanne is Rand's younger sister and she's getting married soon. It wouldn't do to have him show what a true bumpkin he is."

"Careful, woman," Rand growled softly, leaning closer to her. "I might just have to show you who's boss."

Suzanne tossed back her head and laughed. Her auburn hair fell down her back in soft waves and a few of the men glanced at her in open admiration. "Oh, right. That'll be the day, cowboy."

Rand's smile was one of wicked amusement and without so much as opening his mouth, he silently conveyed to his wife what he planned to do to her if she tried to tell him what to do. Again, Suzanne laughed in pure, loving delight.

Gina's heartstrings tugged at the playful banter.

"You're the foreman, right?" Cade Redstone, balancing a full plate, asked Rand as he placed a slab of garlic bread on his plate.

Rand nodded. "Yep. You thinkin' about stayin' on?"

"Not just thinkin' about it. I plan to stick around at least for the summer and I want to work. I've been around horses and cattle all my life."

"Consider yourself signed up," Rand said, and clapped Cade on the shoulder.

Trent had sauntered onto the deck and snagged a bottle of beer. Twisting off the top, he started a conversation with Adam Benson.

Well, it was a beginning, Gina supposed.

Gina accepted a plate from Janie, but realized as she smelled the tangy chicken that she wouldn't be able to eat a bite. Her stomach instantly roiled at the sight of the food. She tried to blame it on the tense conversation in the dining room, on the excitement of meeting the men she'd spent days searching for, on being keyed up whenever she was around Trent, but deep inside she suspected her lack of appetite and nausea were from another source.

Enough of this, she thought, angry with herself when she realized that she'd been afraid to find out the truth. It was time to face the future. As soon as possible, come hell or high water, she was going to go into town and stop by the local pharmacy. Once there she'd buy a pregnancy test kit, bring it back to the ranch, and use it. Then she'd know for sure whether or not she was carrying Trent Remmington's baby.

Chapter 11

"So, you've got it bad for the investigator lady." Blake's comment wasn't a question. He stood, leaning a shoulder on the doorjamb, sipping from a long-necked bottle of beer as the newfound half brothers talked between themselves. They'd eaten, had dessert and were now milling around in smaller groups. Wayne and Garrett were about to take some of the heirs on a tour; Adam Benson had disappeared into the house. Gina had ducked out. Brandon Harper had flung a few questions about family history toward the twins, but was now striking up a conversation with Suzanne Harding, so Blake had cornered Trent.

"What makes you think I've got it bad for anyone?"

"It's written all over your face. You couldn't take your eyes off of her during that meeting and, remember, I know you. We're the only two people here who share the same mother." Blake's eyes, so much like his own, held his. "Come on, no more B.S. What's up?"

There wasn't much reason to lie. "As you know, I met Gina a few weeks ago," Trent admitted.

"Why don't we drive into town and I'll buy you a real beer at the Branding Iron? You can tell me all about it on the way." He shoved his hair out of his eyes. "While you're at it, maybe you can explain what makes this ranch tick."

"I didn't think you were interested in ranching."

"I wasn't, but I've changed." Blake frowned and picked at the label on his bottle. "Divorce does that."

"You and Elaine were never right for each other."

"Amen." They both drained their bottles and left them on a table. As they walked out the front door they spied Garrett pointing out the bunkhouse, stable, machine sheds and various outbuildings to the sons of Larry who were interested in the ranch.

Trent wasn't certain he was in that particular category, but he wasn't alone. Benson seemed to want no part of his Whitehorn legacy.

As he and Blake walked to his twin's car, Trent slapped at a horsefly that hadn't figured out the herd was in the west pasture. The warmth of a bright Montana sun beat against the back of his neck and he couldn't help but smile when he spied a frantic white-faced calf, bawling and running awkwardly toward the herd in search of his mother.

Trent slid into the passenger seat. He'd never been particularly close to Blake, but wondered for the first time in his life if that had been a mistake.

Blake slipped into the driver's seat and shoved a key into the ignition. "Can you believe Larry Kincaid is our father? I mean, we've had some time to think about it, but never really discussed it." The Acura roared to life.

"Nope. But then, I was never close to Harold." Trent focused on a copse of aspens in one of the fields. Horses stood head to rump in the shade, their tails swatting at flies, their ears pricked. Coats from dun to black gleamed in the sunlight and Trent, for the first time in his life, felt a bonding with the land. But that was bull. He'd never felt anything close to roots in his life. Just as he'd never been able to settle down with one woman. But staring out the window to the stubble of freshly mown fields, Gina's image appeared in his mind's eye—her quick smile, wavy red hair and flashing green eyes.

Blake snorted. "Mom ran Harold ragged when she was alive." He threw the car into reverse, backed up, then jammed it into drive. "I just wish she'd told us about Larry before she died."

"Would've been thoughtful," Trent agreed, not wanting to think too long or hard on the fact that Barbara Simms Remmington had given up her fight with cancer—one final battle that she hadn't won. "But then, Mom always did things her way."

Blake slipped a pair of wraparound sunglasses onto the bridge of his nose. "Do you think Larry ever thought about contacting us?"

Trent lifted a shoulder. "Who knows? Garrett told me there was a letter once, one that she wrote sometime after she found out she was going to die." He cleared his throat. "Supposedly she told Larry about us but warned him to keep his distance because we'd grown up to be fine young men or some such trash and didn't want him messing things up."

Blake's hands tightened on the wheel as he attempted

to avoid potholes in the rutted lane. Long, dry grass brushed the undercarriage of the low-slung car. "Guess he took her advice," Trent observed.

"Probably didn't want to be bothered with a couple more kids."

"Fine guy, our father."

"The best." Blake slowed for the highway, saw no traffic and gunned it. The Acura sprang forward, wheeling onto the main road, tires spinning gravel before connecting with asphalt.

"So where is this letter?"

Trent lifted a shoulder. "Who knows? I didn't see it in that Pandora's box that Celia—er, Gina passed around today."

Blake's eyes narrowed as he stared through his dark lenses and punched in the radio. Smooth jazz filtered through the speakers. "You called Gina 'Celia'?"

Trent's jaw hardened. It was just like his brother to pick up on any little error. "Just a mistake."

Raising a dark eyebrow identical to his twin's, Blake said, "Better be careful and keep your women straight. One doesn't like to be called by another's name."

"How would you know?" Trent asked, irritated at his brother all over again. That was the trouble with Blake. Any time Trent had felt the slightest bit of brotherly affection for him, Blake would do something anal and irritating and self-righteous. It was enough to remind Trent that he was better off fending for himself.

"Oh, believe me, I know," Blake said, and Trent had a glimmer that there was more to his brother than met the eye, a darker side filled with his own secrets. Well, well, well. They pulled up behind a tractor chugging down the road while pulling a trailer stacked high with hay bales. Blake eased into the oncoming lane, punched it, and the Acura surged past the farmer to settle back into the right lane and eat up the miles.

"I thought you were always a one-girl guy," Trent said as they neared the town.

"For the most part," Blake hedged, and didn't elaborate as he took a corner a little too fast and the tires whined. "But you weren't." He drove over a final rise and the town of Whitehorn appeared, rising out of the ranch land in a cluster of old and new buildings. "So now we're back to it," Blake said, easing off the accelerator as they passed a Welcome To Whitehorn sign followed closely by a new speed limit. "What's the deal with Gina?"

Gina eyed the home pregnancy tests on a shelf in the town pharmacy, decided they were all about the same and tucked a box under her arm. Though she hardly knew anyone in the store, she stupidly felt self-conscious, as if she were wearing a bright neon sign that said she thought she might be pregnant.

"Get over it," she mumbled to herself. People took the tests every day.

But not you. Until last month, you were a twenty-seven-year-old virgin.

Ignoring the gibe, she grabbed a tube of toothpaste, a roll of film, the latest edition of the *Whitehorn Journal* and a bottle of shampoo, then walked to the register. The cashier, who was barely eighteen from the looks of her, was snapping gum and blinking as if she was just getting used to contacts. She took an eternity ringing up the items.

The pharmacist, standing on a raised platform behind a half wall displaying over-the-counter medications, vitamins and herbs, was busily filling prescriptions. Throughout the store country music was playing softly over the whir of ceiling fans.

Shifting from one foot to the other, Gina had her wallet out of her purse and wondered if anyone in Whitehorn had ever heard of merchandise scanners. A skinny man in rimless glasses and smelling as if he hadn't bathed in this century got in line behind her, and another girl, one Lily Mae had pointed out to her as Christina Montgomery, clutching more hair-care and beauty products than she could hold without a basket, stood a few feet from the smelly man.

Eventually the girl at the register had totaled up her bill and sang out the amount. Gina fished in her wallet and came up with a couple of bills.

"Have a nice day," the girl at the register intoned automatically as she handed Gina her change.

"You, too." Gina scooped up her bag and, hoping the damned pregnancy test wasn't visible through the white paper, spied Winona Cobbs flipping through the magazine rack. That was the trouble with a small town, a person couldn't help but run into someone she knew. With a quick smile and wave in Winona's direction, Gina beelined past the latest in foot balms, bath oil beads and denture cleansers to the front door.

Outside the sun was bright, the afternoon warm. It had been nearly an hour since the gathering of Kincaid brothers had begun to splinter apart.

When she'd spied Trent with Blake, nursing beers and surveying the countryside, Gina had run upstairs, grabbed her purse and hightailed it outside to her Explorer, only pausing long enough to make a quick excuse to Garrett. Then she'd driven like a madwoman into town. Her pulse had been hammering, a headache pounding behind her eyes. She'd almost felt guilty, like a convict on the run, as she'd pushed the speed limit through the hills on her way into town.

How foolish. Now, balancing her bag, Gina reached into the purse slung over her shoulder and slipped a pair of sunglasses onto her nose. Searching for her keys, she looked into a deep pocket, not paying attention as she rounded a corner and slammed into a man walking in the opposite direction.

"Oh!" She nearly stumbled. The newspaper dropped from beneath her arm and the bag from the pharmacy slipped from her fingers. Large male hands grabbed her shoulders, keeping her upright, and with a sinking sensation she realized she'd just run smack-dab into Trent Remmington.

She dropped her keys and they jangled as they hit the cement.

Oh, God. The pregnancy test! "I—I didn't see you," she stammered as she felt her face turn a dozen shades of red.

Pull yourself together, Gina.

"I figured that," he said dryly, and to her mortification she realized he wasn't alone. Blake was just a step behind. Blake reached down, stuffed the toothpaste and film that had spilled onto the sidewalk into the bag and handed the sorry-looking sack with its contents back to her.

Gina scrambled for the keys glinting in the sunlight.

"Fancy running into you," she quipped, managing what she hoped appeared to be a nonchalant smile though her heart was drumming a million beats a second. What if he saw the pregnancy test, guessed that she thought she might be carrying his baby? "I, um, I thought I already told you we have to quit meeting like this."

Trent released her. "My thoughts exactly," he said dryly, but no smile toyed at those razor-thin lips. His eyebrows had slammed together and his nostrils flared slightly.

He knew. Oh, God, he knew! "I, um, have to get going. I'll see you back at the ranch."

"I'll look forward to it," Blake said, but he, too, sober as a judge, didn't so much as crack a smile. A horrible, sinking sensation pounded through Gina's already aching head. She was certain that her secret was out. The irony of it was, she didn't know herself if she was pregnant or not.

Garrett had the feeling that something was going to blow. The tension between Gina and Trent was nearly palpable, like the electricity that charges the air just before a thunderstorm breaks.

It was just a matter of time.

He walked to the stables where the smell of horses and dry hay met him. Rand was in the third stall examining a mare who had been favoring a front leg.

"How is she?"

"Ornery," Rand said as he bent the foreleg back and straddled it while keeping one eye on the palomino's head. Though she was tethered, Mandy had been known to take a nip out of man's hide. "As usual." He was poking the inside of the hoof, watching the mare's reaction. As the mare shifted, he growled, "Don't even think about it," then to Garrett, "What's up?"

"Nothing good," Garrett replied as his thoughts turned back to Trent and Gina. It was obvious those two were falling in love, they just didn't know it yet. "I'm going into town later to interview a couple of gals who are interested in doing the cooking out here. One looks pretty good. She's got a son and would like a live-in arrangement. Thought you might pass that information on to Suzanne. Just in case you see her before I do."

"She'll be relieved," Rand admitted. "She's got her hands full with the books, Mack, and Joe."

"How's that son of yours?"

Rand looked up and grinned. Proud as a peacock, he was. "Couldn't be better." The horse shifted and tossed her head. "Oh, no, you don't," Rand said to the mare.

"I'll see you around." Garrett slapped the rail of the stall, then headed outside where the sun was bright. Rubbing the back of his neck, he eyed the parking lot.

The lot was pretty empty. Trent and Blake had driven into town.

So had Gina. Separately.

Probably just a coincidence, and yet the feeling that there was going to be trouble lingered with Garrett as he made his way to his truck. He opened the door and slid into the sun-warmed interior, then poked his key into the ignition. Trent and Gina weren't like oil and water, he decided, ramming the gearshift into reverse, backing up, then nosing the old truck toward the lane. Nope, those two were more like gasoline and a lit match.

A dangerous and extremely volatile combination.

Someone was bound to get burned.

Chapter 12

The beer didn't settle well in his stomach. Jordan had spent nearly an hour nursing his bottle and his frustration at the bar of the Branding Iron. Besides, he didn't fit in with the blue-collar crowd that was beginning to get off work. Half a dozen mill workers and cowboys had sauntered in, laughing and joking, all wearing dirty jeans and relieved smiles that they'd put in their shifts for the day. Talking to each other and catching the barmaid's attention, they filtered through the front door to take up their usual spots in booths, at the pool table, or here at the bar, already eyeing the television screen mounted high overhead in hopes of viewing the latest sporting event while thirstily tossing back brewskies and nibbling on peanuts before going home to the wife and kids.

Jordan caught a few grim looks cast his way from the men huddled over their drinks. Sour grapes, he thought.

These poor working stiffs would never rise above their small-town roots and they were envious of a poor, sickly kid who had. They'd have manure and sawdust on their boots until the day they died. Jordan Baxter had gone from secondhand sneakers to Italian leather loafers.

The door banged open and Christina Montgomery, the mayor's youngest and wildest daughter, flew into the bar. Several of the locals swiveled on their stools to check her out. Petite, curvy, and an outrageous flirt, Christina beelined for the bar. "I'll… I'll have a…" She looked at the bartender and shoved an errant strand of chestnut hair off her face. "A gin and tonic…no…just a…oh, it doesn't matter, a diet soda, I guess!"

"That all?" the bartender asked, and Christina's pouty lips pursed.

"Yeah, yeah, that's all," she said, lifting herself onto a bar stool and, noticing a few male glances cast her way in the reflection of the mirror, she shook out her mane of hair. Dressed in a blue dress with silver earrings dripping from her ears, she accepted her drink, took a sip and scowled.

Jordan saw her glance his way and offer him a cunning smile. He wasn't interested and looked away, but Christina wasn't rebuffed, just turned her attention to a young cowboy seated in a corner booth. His ears actually turned red as he blushed, but Christina didn't stop there. With a walk that drew a man's attention, she took her drink and sauntered slowly to a table near the back of the room. The girl was pure sex and she knew it, flaunted it.

Her father, Mayor Ellis Montgomery, had a major problem on his hands whether he knew it or not. But it wasn't really any of Jordan's business.

He tossed a few bills onto the bar, slid off his stool and realized that he'd been so caught up in his silent anger at the Kincaids, he'd barely touched his drink. Well, he sure as hell wasn't going to down it now. He made his way to the front door.

It opened in his face and two men he'd never seen before stepped inside. In an instant he recognized them as Kincaids. And twins at that. Tall and broad-shouldered, they both had the piercing blue eyes, dark hair, and arrogance that had always run deep in Kincaid blood. Probably a couple of Larry's bastards.

"Excuse me," the one with the less harsh expression said as they passed. He was dressed as if he planned to spend his afternoon at the golf course. *Get real, buddy,* Jordan laughed to himself, *there ain't no country club here in Whitehorn.* The other one, in faded jeans and a shirt with rolled-up sleeves, didn't say a word, just gave Jordan a cursory glance that made his blood boil.

Jordan couldn't help himself. "Don't tell me," he said, "Kincaids."

Mr. Nice Guy nodded and smiled. "Looks that way. Blake Remmington." He extended his hand and added, "My brother, Trent."

Jordan ignored the fingers stretching in his direction. "Just give the old man a word of advice. He can't sell something that isn't his."

The hand fell. "Pardon me?"

"You heard me."

"Who're you?" The arrogant one was narrowing his eyes suspiciously.

"Garrett Kincaid's worst nightmare."

The twins exchanged glances, then smiled as if in on a private secret.

Jordan's blood boiled.

"Are you the local town thug?" the hard-ass named Trent asked. "If you are, you'd better get some new threats."

"Just give him the message."

Trent looked ready to jump down Jordan's throat. *Good. Take your best shot, bastard, I'll have you up on assault charges so fast your head will spin.*

The cooler one, Blake he'd said his name was, placed his hand over his brother's arm, as if to restrain him. "Look, Mr....Baxter, is it? I don't know what your beef is, but peddle it someplace else, okay? We're not interested."

That did it. Jordan's barely reined-in temper snapped. "You will be," Jordan said, and shouldered open the door.

Yep, they were bastards, both of them. Jordan couldn't make his way out of this joke of a watering hole fast enough.

Outside, he breathed deep of the fresh air, then squinted against the sunlight and tried to shake off the knowledge that he should have held his tongue. Warning the Kincaids was a mistake. It was better to strike first, be a coral snake rather than a rattler. No reason to tip his hand, such as it was, but running into Larry's bastard twins, he'd been blindsided and wanted to lash out. He'd been foolish. Angry with himself, Jordan shoved his hands deep into his pockets.

Jaywalking, he cut through the park and zigzagged down a couple of alleys to his air-conditioned office. He instantly felt better. Here he was king. Lord of his particular castle.

"Hey!" His daughter Hope offered him a wink and a smile that melted the ice around his heart. "You okay?"

"Why shouldn't I be?"

"I don't know, but you look—" she lifted a shoulder "—bugged, I guess would be the best word. Let me guess, you heard more gossip about the Kincaids."

She was teasing him, but he couldn't keep from saying, "I just had the pleasure of literally running into a couple of Larry's bastards."

Her shoulders sagged a bit. "You'd better get used to it, Dad. Whitehorn isn't exactly a metropolis."

"Yeah, yeah, I know." But it griped him just the same. "So, anything happening around here?"

"Not much, but what there was, I managed to handle," she said, needling a bit. "I am capable, you know."

"I know."

Hope paused, squared her shoulders and from her desk chair looked her father steadily in the eye. "I hope you do, Dad. Sometimes I wonder."

"And why's that?" he asked, barely listening as he flipped through the envelopes on her desk.

"Because you don't seem to trust me."

Jordan's head snapped up. "It's not about trust, Hope. It's just that you're young and—"

"And not as tough as you think I should be," she filled in, sighing loudly. "Yeah, I know. The Baxter princess. Or heiress, or whatever it is you call me when you think I can't hear you."

"It just takes time." It was a phrase that rolled easily off his tongue, one he used whenever they had this particular discussion, which they seemed to be having a lot more often lately. Frowning he eyed the return address of one of the legal-size envelopes in his hand. "You know that."

"Yeah, yeah, 'Rome wasn't built in a day.' 'Patience is a virtue.' 'All good things come to those who wait.' 'With age comes reason.' I've heard 'em all before."

"Right," he said, moving toward the door to his office. His interest had been caught by the envelope he'd shuffled to the top of the stack.

He closed the door and ripped open the envelope. As he scanned the letter from a relative of George Sawyer's, the now-deceased lawyer who had drawn up the letter of intent from Jordan's uncle Cameron, Jordan Baxter started to smile. He rested a hip on the edge of his desk and felt a steady flow of elation run through his blood. At last there seemed to be some justice. The letter stated that while finally going through old papers that had sat in the attorney's basement for years, this relative had discovered a box of old legal documents, including the missing letter from Jordan's uncle, Cameron Baxter, willing Jordan the ranch and offering him the right of first refusal to any sale before Cameron's death.

Jordan's heart nearly stopped. He flipped over the page and saw the very document in question. Old and yellowed, smelling faintly of must, it stated all too clearly what Jordan had maintained for years.

His throat suddenly tightened as old emotions tore through him. Vividly he remembered his sixteenth birthday and his uncle Cameron promising him the Baxter place and handing him a copy of this very letter.

"Hot damn," he muttered, his mind spinning out possible legal scenarios as he tried to wrest the old place back from the Kincaids. In the end even his uncle had screwed him over, selling the place to the Kincaids and telling Jordan he'd never even given him the document. Since Jordan's only copy had burned in the fire that had taken his mother's life, he'd had no proof to the contrary.

"Stupid old bastard," he said, knowing that Cameron had somehow bribed George Sawyer to lie about the letter of intent, as well.

When Jordan had confronted his uncle about the sale of the property to the Kincaid family, Cameron had sighed heavily.

"What about the first right of refusal?" Jordan had demanded.

"I'm sorry, son," Cameron had said, placing a fatherly hand on Jordan's eighteen-year-old shoulders, "but I don't remember ever saying I'd give you first option." He'd spit a long stream of tobacco juice at the fence post near the old pump house. "'Sides, what could you do now, you're just a kid. I know how you feel about the place, but the plain fact of the matter is, I'm about broke. Got to sell."

Jordan had been thunderstruck. He'd swallowed hard, all his hopes and dreams sinking as fast as the lowering sun that had gilded the grassland and reflected in the windows of the old ranch house he loved.

"Tell you what I'll do," Cameron had said, "I'll see that some of the money ends up in your hands, to pay for college."

"No way. You promised. You signed a legal document."

For the first time he'd seen the vein throb beneath the brim of Cameron's dirty straw hat. "Then prove it," the other man had said. "Find the damned paper and take it to a judge."

"I will. I'll go to George Sweeney. If he's worth his salt, he's got a copy."

"I wouldn't count on it," Cameron had warned, and the hairs on the back of Jordan's neck had prickled in premonition. Sure as shootin', when he'd called the attorney late that night, George, not only Cameron's lawyer but his poker buddy as well, had claimed no knowledge of any paperwork concerning the ranch.

Jordan had been beaten.

Until now.

A cold smile twisted his lips. Nearly thirty years later, Jordan Baxter studied the yellowed, musty-smelling document with his uncle's signature scrawled across the bottom. His headache disappeared. Everything, it seemed, had changed when he'd ripped open this envelope. Justice and destiny had just met head-on.

He wasn't a scared, poor kid from the wrong side of the tracks any longer. At forty-six he was a millionaire many times over and a man to be reckoned with. The Kincaids were about to learn that lesson.

It was about time.

He reached for the phone and dialed his own attorney. Yep, the Kincaids's ship of fortune was just about to be turned into the wind. And Jordan Baxter was at the helm.

She was pregnant.

No question now, Gina thought as, seated on her bed in her room, she stared at the indicator strip. It was early morning, shafts of sunlight streamed through the open window, the sounds of the ranch filtered inside. Somewhere far off a rooster crowed, answered by a lark's song. Squirrels chattered, a lonely calf bawled and an engine rumbled to life.

A few minutes earlier she'd locked herself in the bathroom, taken the test and waited for the results.

They were most definitely positive.

Now what?

Flopping back onto the bed, she experienced a gamut of emotions. Elation, happiness, fear, joy, worry.

A mother! Gina Henderson, you're going to be a mother! Her heart pounded in anticipation and she couldn't stop a smile from toying with her lips.

The clock in the main hall struck seven, sending reverberating chords through the house. From the kitchen she heard the sound of voices and forced herself to her feet. With an odd mix of elation and dread, she regarded herself in the mirror mounted over her bureau. Twenty-seven and pregnant. That part sounded fine. Wait a minute, twenty-seven, pregnant and *unmarried.* There was the glitch.

Yet women had babies on their own all the time. Single mothers were a very viable part of society. Her hand rubbed the flat area of her abdomen. This wasn't the way she would have chosen to have a child. No, she'd always embraced the fantasy of husband who worked nine-to-five, a Cape Cod–style house surrounded by a white picket fence, a dog and cat... Oh, well. Her apartment in L.A. was large enough for her and the infant and she had some money saved, so she could take time off after the birth. Later she'd move and go back to work with Jack and—

And what about Trent?

She sighed, picked up a brush and absently ran it through her hair until it crackled. Surely he deserved to know about his child. Eventually. Once things had died down here at the ranch and all the Kincaid half brothers had settled. She'd go back to L.A., allow him time to get used to being part of this new piecemeal family and then, once she was through the first trimester of her pregnancy and the danger of miscarriage had diminished significantly, she'd call him with the happy news that he was about to become a father.

He had the right to know about the child; he didn't have the right to tell her what to do about it. She glanced out the open window and saw Mitch Fielding and Rand Harding in one of the paddocks with some of the steers milling in the early morning light. Garrett, with Brandon Harper in tow, joined them and they all four were quickly involved in a discussion. Laughter rippled upward in the clear morning air and somewhere nearby the dog let out a sharp bark.

The lace curtains billowed and she thought fleetingly that this ranch would be a perfect place to raise a child. In her mind's eye she saw a dark-haired boy racing through the fields, fishing in the creek, making forts in the hayloft, riding a spirited mustang on the deer trails that wove through the forested hills in the distance. Or maybe a cherub-faced girl with laughing blue eyes, wading and splashing in a favorite swimming hole, running in a field while trying to catch a butterfly, searching the creek for crayfish, learning to ride bareback with the help of her father...

Oh, God, quit this fantasizing right now! This isn't a scene from Little House on the Prairie, *for pity's sake!*

Her throat closed for a second and she felt the sting of hot tears on the backs of her eyelids. From happiness? Or sorrow that the perfect little family she had envisioned for her child didn't exist? "Get over it," she growled, turning from the window. What she should do is call a local clinic, have another test done to verify, and tell Trent the truth. He had the right to know.

"Don't be a coward," she told herself, not even wanting to guess what Trent's reaction would be. Maybe he'd played this scenario half a dozen times with other women. She didn't think he had any children already as she'd delved pretty deeply into his past, known of half a dozen relationships he'd been involved in, but never thought he'd gone so far as to father a child.

Until now. With you.

Setting her brush on the bureau, she decided it would be best to hold her tongue. At least until she'd visited a doctor.

Tap, tap, tap.

Gina nearly jumped out of her skin. Trent! "Just a minute." She threw the contents of the pregnancy kit into a paper bag and stuffed it into the tiny trash basket in her room. She'd get rid of it later in town, so no one found it and asked embarrassing questions.

Oh, get over it, Gina, you're not fifteen, for crying out loud. No one should be going through your garbage, and even if they did, what you do is your business. Yours!

And Trent's!

Well, fine, that much is true, but this hide-and-seek, guilt-riddled routine is beneath you. Way beneath you!

She threw open the door and found herself staring straight into Blake Remmington's blue eyes. Relief flooded through her. Dressed in a casual sweater and slacks, he said, "Thought you might want an escort down to breakfast."

"Thoughtful of you," she said, surprised and warmed at his concern. "But you didn't have to. I could've found my way downstairs."

"I know. But I needed the company."

"In this houseful of half brothers?" she teased.

"Precisely my point."

Already the sound of rattling pans echoed through the corridors.

"Damn, I told Suzanne I'd help her this morning." She'd completely forgotten. From the minute she'd bought the pregnancy test, her mind had been wandering.

"Tomorrow's another day," he said without the hint of a smile.

"I could do the dishes or take care of lunch," she said as she walked out of her room.

"How long are you staying on?"

"Good question. I don't really know because I don't feel like I've really finished my job here, at least not until I find out if that seventh son really does exist."

"Still not sure?"

"Nope," she admitted with a sigh. "But I'd better figure it out soon and wrap it up. My brother is probably buried to his eyeballs in paperwork." *Jack, oh, God, what was she going to tell Jack?* Not that it was any of his business. As they reached the top of the stairs the scents of sizzling sausage and hot coffee rose to greet them. Gina's stomach quivered a bit and she mentally kicked herself. Just because she knew she was pregnant didn't mean that she had to buy into the morning sickness routine.

As they started down the stairs together, Blake spoke. "Besides, I thought you might want to talk about Trent."

"Why would I want to do that?" she asked as she glanced up at him.

He didn't bother to crack a smile. His jaw was as hard

as granite, but he grabbed her hand. "That's what I was hoping you'd tell me."

It didn't take a brain surgeon to realize that he knew the truth. She'd bet her grandmother's diamond ring that Blake suspected she was pregnant. "I think maybe I'd better talk to Trent first," she said as they reached the bottom of the stairs.

"About what?" Trent's voice boomed from behind her.

Gina's heart nosedived as Trent stepped out of the living room, with Cade behind him. She didn't know how much of the conversation Trent had heard.

"What was it you wanted to talk to me about?" he said as Blake let go of her hand. Trent's gaze flicked to the movement; he hadn't missed it.

"I think I'll let you work this one out alone." Blake sent a silent message to Cade, who quickly picked up on it.

"Me, too." Cade nodded toward Blake. "Let me buy you a cup of coffee." They peeled off, heading in the direction of the kitchen where the sound of laughter floated down the hallways of the old house.

"Okay," Trent said, grabbing her elbow and tugging her into the living room where they were alone. "So, shoot, Gina." He folded his arms over his chest, blue eyes narrowed on her and a lock of dark hair fell over one eyebrow. Every muscle in his body was tense, his neck and shoulders stiff. "What is it you want to say to me?"

In for a penny, in for a pound. She swallowed hard, then forced her eyes to meet his. "I just found out this morning."

"What?"

Taking in a slow breath and silently praying for strength, she said, "The truth is that I'm pregnant, Trent. You're going to be a father."

Chapter 13

"You're pregnant," Trent repeated, stunned.

Gina nodded and felt a deep sadness that he didn't wrap his arms around her, twirl her around and whoop. Clearing her throat, she watched the play of emotions on his face. "I just found out. I was suspicious, of course, but I finally did the test this morning and I thought I'd call a local clinic and double check."

"That…that would be a good idea," he said stiffly, and all at once Gina felt this gap between them, as if they were standing on separate sides of an unbridgeable abyss instead of on the faded rug in the living room of the Kincaid ranch.

"I thought you should know." Oh, God, why was this so difficult?

"After you told Blake." His lips compressed.

"Of course not. Blake just happened to see the pregnancy test in my sack from the pharmacy yesterday when I ran into you and several items dropped out. At least, that's how I think he knew—either that or he's psychic. Anyway, he put two and two together."

Trent didn't comment, just looked hard at her, as if searching for a lie somewhere in her story.

"Look, Trent, don't worry, when I get back to California, I'll—"

"Do what?" he said, and anger turned his face a nasty shade of red. His eyes glittered harshly. "You're going to have this baby, damn it."

"You bet I am," she flung back at him and stepped closer, bridging that gap between them. "I was saying that this is a big shock for me, too, and I'm not sure exactly how I'll handle it, but I'm going home, work until delivery, have the baby and eventually find a bigger apartment so I can raise my child."

"Our child."

"Yes."

"You're not going back to L.A."

"What?" She nearly laughed. "That's where I live, Trent."

"And what do you think you'll do there? Be a single mother?"

"I will be a single mother." Was the man dense?

Determination set his jaw. Blue eyes held hers and wouldn't let go. "If you're really pregnant—"

"I am. There's not much question about it," she said angrily.

"Well, you have been known to lie on more than one occasion. Especially to me."

"This is different."

"I'll say." Fury etched the edges of his mouth. "You should have told me earlier."

"I wasn't certain." She glared up at him. "I wasn't going to tell you and then have it turn out to be a false alarm." She threw one arm up in the air. "I don't know what you want me to do. I'd say I was sorry, but I'm not!"

"Good." He shoved stiff fingers through his hair. "We'll get married," he said out loud, as if she had no say in the matter whatsoever. "And...and you'll stay here."

"What?"

"You won't be going back to L.A."

"Are you out of your mind? Of course I'm going back to Los Angeles. In case you've forgotten, that's where I live!"

"Now, wait a minute—"

"No, you wait a minute. Just because I'm pregnant doesn't mean you can bully me or boss me around." Anger spiked her words but deep inside she was hurt.

What did you expect? her mind taunted. *That he would be thrilled? That he would spin you off your feet, buy you dozens upon dozens of roses, get down on bended knee? Foolish, foolish woman.*

"I assume the baby's mine."

His words stung. Like salt poured into the open wound of her heart. "Of course it's yours!" Oh, Lord, this wasn't going well, not well at all.

"Then it's pretty cut-and-dried, isn't it? We'll get married and the baby will have a name."

"Oh, no, what are you saying?" she whispered, shocked. What kind of marriage proposal was that?

"Admit it, Gina, this is what you've been angling for. I thought you were going to shake me down when I first met you and you lied about who you were, as if you didn't know me, then hopped in the sack with me and—"

She slapped him. Hard. "Don't you ever insinuate anything so vile again! Yes, it's true this baby was an accident, unplanned, but certainly not unwanted. I would think that considering your own personal situation, you might have a little more empathy." Tears burned the backs of her eyes, hot, bitter tears but not of shame. Oh, no, just demoralizing disappointment. "I—I didn't mean to hit you. I mean… I did, but I'm sorry." She lifted a hand, then let it fall. "I just hoped you'd understand."

His teeth ground together and a red welt appeared on his cheek. "That's the reason we're getting married."

"No way, Trent," she said, shaking her head. "I hate to sound cliché, but right now, I wouldn't marry you if you were the—"

"Last man on earth?" he said with a snort.

"The universe…and that includes the black holes, okay?"

"No, it's not okay. None of this is 'okay.'" He walked to the window, stared outside and his rigid shoulders slumped. "So just deep-six the theatrics, Gina, or Celia, or whoever the hell you really are. We have a problem and—"

"Correction." Striding up to him, she poked a finger hard against his chest and swallowed against the tears of frustration lodging in her throat. A breeze slipped through the window, toying with Trent's hair, caressing her hot cheeks. "We have a baby," she said, her voice lower than normal. "It's not a problem. At least, it's not for me."

"The solution is to get married."

"Are you out of your mind? Have you heard a word of

our conversation?" It was her turn to be flabbergasted. She held both of her hands near her head, palms out, as if surrendering. But she wasn't. "I think we should both slow down a minute here, okay? Marriage? You're talking *marriage?* Oh, come on. We don't even know each other well enough…we can't get married, I mean…think about it, Trent, you live in Texas and I'm in L.A. I have a job—no, make that a career to consider."

He winced when she mentioned her work. "I'll take care of you."

"You'll 'take care of me'? Oh, God, don't even suggest anything so remotely archaic, okay?" Her head was spinning, her pride wounded to the core, her pain deepseated. She placed a hand over her abdomen, as if she were protecting her child because Trent's reaction was all wrong. All wrong. "I'm not some frail little insecure woman, you know, no hothouse flower who can't stand on her own two feet, a woman who doesn't feel complete without a man. No way. I'm not going to marry someone out of some sense of duty." Her temper inched skyward. She longed to hear him tell her he loved her, that he wanted to spend the rest of his life with her, that together the three of them would become a close-knit family, the kind neither she nor Trent had ever experienced. But this, this pathetic reasoning, wasn't even a proposal.

Worse, he thought she'd tried to shake him down, to blackmail him into this. What a joke, a horrible, horrible joke.

"The baby needs two parents." He was adamant when he turned his eyes back to look at her, some of his anger appeared to be replaced with concern.

"Two parents who love him and each other," she agreed, glaring at him, her heart aching as she bared her soul. "Two people who want him." Again she pressed on her stomach. "Not a couple of people who throw in together because the innocent child just happens to be coming along. No way."

"Listen to me, Gina. This is my child, too." He grabbed her then, his steely fingers wrapping around her arm. Beneath the anger in his eyes she saw deeper emotions and a pain she didn't begin to understand. "Like it or not, I have a say in it." Grooves deepened at the edges of his mouth and his eyebrows slammed together. "So what're you holding out for? Money? Is that it?"

She gasped. "Is that what you think?" Disappointment burrowed deep in her soul, gnawed at her heart.

"As I said, I felt this was some kind of shakedown from the beginning."

She nearly slapped him again. Instead she yanked her arm away and felt the weight of disappointment heavy on her shoulders. "With you it's always about money, isn't it?" she whispered sadly, then steeled herself, straightening her spine and tossing her hair from her eyes. "Well, it isn't for me. Believe it or not, it never has been. If I'd been interested in 'shaking you down,' I would have found a better way to do it, believe me. Now, listen, I've said all I have to say. I've got a job to do here and I intend to do it, after which I'm going back to California."

"Just like that?"

"You bet. And as for you, don't you have some oil wells that need drilling somewhere? You know, like Texas or Wyoming, or the Yukon? I hear they're finding gushers in Siberia. Maybe you should go and check it out." With that, she turned on a heel and stalked down the hall, anger radiating from her in furious, hot waves.

How could he be so callous? And how could she care

for a man who thought she was capable of such dirty, underhanded, vile— "Stop it," she ordered herself. There was no reason to dwell on any of his motivations. Maybe he was just in shock. But it didn't matter.

She could take care of herself. And a baby.

In fact, she'd make a helluva mother and probably a halfway decent dad. At that thought her heart twisted, but she told herself that her once-idyllic Norman Rockwell envisionment of her life and marriage would have to be adjusted.

She was going to become a mother.

Rubbing his stinging cheek, Trent watched her march off in a tornado of self-righteous ire. His thoughts were going in a thousand directions all at once. A baby? What would he do with a baby? What would he do without one? The kid wasn't even here yet and he felt this swelling sense of propriety and something else, way beyond pride, a newfound fear for the unborn child. Now, Trent was vulnerable.

And he'd made a mess of things with Gina, but she'd blindsided him. He walked out of the living room and upstairs, then paused at the doorway to her bedroom. He looked inside to the mussed bed where she'd slept. The scent of her perfume still hung in the air. Was it his imagination or did that one room seem to have more sunshine than any other part of the house? Why did her off-key singing amuse rather than irritate him? What was it about her that made her sexy without a drop of makeup or a comb through her hair?

Hell, he had it bad. Blake, damn him, was right. Trent couldn't get Gina out of his mind. He walked to his room and picked up his wallet and keys. Stuffing them into his pocket, he started down the stairs.

How could he possibly be a father? What did he know about parenting? Larry Kincaid, his biological sire, had been worse than a cad, a man he'd never known, a gambler, cheat, womanizer who had kids and never bothered to even meet them. No, Trent thought angrily, he wouldn't make the same mistakes—be as distant and uncaring as that bastard had been. Nor would he be a dishrag the likes of Harold Remmington. That guy... well, he'd been little better than Larry.

But Garrett... Trent imagined the older man had been a helluva dad even though his own son, Larry, had ended up a mess. Trent didn't have a clue as to how Garrett's daughter, Alice, had turned out. No matter, it wasn't because Garrett hadn't been in there pitching, doing the best he could, spending his life trying to be the best damned father in the world.

Trent knew it instinctively.

On the landing, he paused as the reality of the situation hit him with the force of a fist to his chest. Gina was pregnant. With his kid. His throat tightened. Memories of another time and place washed over him in painful ripples as he thought about Beverly, haughty and beautiful, telling him he was going to be a father. For such a short time he'd been buoyed with new, exciting feelings of paternity. Elated, he'd imagined his son's or daughter's birth, toddling years and elementary school highs and lows, but his bubble had been burst, pricked by the evil, lying tongue of a woman he'd never loved.

But this time was different.

He'd make sure of it.

Trent took one step toward the kitchen, then stopped

himself. It wasn't just because of the baby that he was feeling this way, he realized. It was because of Gina. Like it or not, he was falling in love with her and he had been since the first time he'd laid eyes on her nearly two months earlier.

He'd just been kidding himself.

The tension in the room was so thick you could cut it with a butter knife, Garrett thought as he finished his stack of waffles and carried his plate to the sink. He, Gina, and Larry's sons had crowded around the kitchen table and discussed the operations of the ranch. Garrett had explained that each of the heirs would own a portion of the spread, but some might want to be silent partners. Others would want to be a part of the day-to-day operations.

Cade had assured Garrett that he would stay on, and Mitch had agreed to work on the spread, as well. Brandon hadn't committed as yet, nor had Adam, who seemed edgy and anxious to leave. Probably had some unsuspecting corporation to gut, Garrett thought unkindly. Adam was the one who could really use this place to get in touch with his heart, but then, it was Adam's decision.

Garrett handed his empty plate to Suzanne, who was loading the dishwasher, then refilled his coffee cup. He took a sip and walked back to the table where his grandsons were beginning to disperse. Blake had been quieter than usual, as if something was bothering him, yet he'd decided to stay on at the ranch, at least for a while.

Trent had been downright silent for most of the meal. If he'd decided how involved he wanted to be here in Whitehorn, he was keeping it to himself. He'd been more intense than usual, brooding in a dark way. He'd cast a few looks in Gina's direction and she'd met his gaze coldly.

Lover's spat, Garrett guessed.

Gina, usually fresh-faced and smiling, hadn't been herself these past few days. This morning was the worst. She'd barely eaten, jumped up and offered to help Suzanne with the dishes, and generally been preoccupied for the past hour.

Probably because of Trent.

The unspoken words hanging between those two had been as cold as the Ice Age.

Garrett had hoped that whatever was between them would have eased off a mite, but it seemed as if just the opposite were true. If anything, they were more bristly with each other than ever.

Something was going on.

And he was damned sure he wouldn't like it. He finished his coffee and set his cup in the sink. Cade and Mitch followed suit; they were two who weren't interested in sitting around the table. Adam had agreed to look over the property, but Garrett was afraid Larry's firstborn was only going to eye it to see how much it was worth.

"Guess I'd better mosey out and check on the stock," Garrett said to Suzanne. "Rand's probably already waiting on me."

"Well, don't keep him. He's supposed to be fitted for a tuxedo today. He's part of Leanne's wedding party, you know."

At the mention of a wedding, Gina's back stiffened. Quickly she untied her apron.

"How's Rand taking it that his baby sister's getting hitched?" Garrett asked Suzanne.

She laughed. "I think he's relieved. And Bill's a great guy. Rand's best friend."

"Then he should be pleased," Garrett said. "I'll see that he makes the fitting." Garrett reached for his hat and noticed that Trent's face muscles had tightened and Gina's skin had blanched a bit at the talk of the upcoming wedding.

What the hell was going on? As far as he could see, they didn't even know the people involved. "Oh, by the way, I've found someone to take on the chores around here," he said to Suzanne. "I'll let you know when she can start. She's a real nice gal with a baby of her own."

"Great," Suzanne said as she turned back to the dishes. "Not that I don't love working here from dawn until dusk," she teased.

Trent downed his coffee, glanced at Gina, then, expression grim as all get-out, said to the room at large, "I'll be in the den. I've got some calls to make." Without another word, he stormed out of the kitchen, his boot heels ringing down the hallway.

"I wonder what's got into him," Suzanne remarked, and Gina bit her lip as she hung her apron on a hook near the back door.

"Bad mood," Blake observed.

"The worst." Gina wiped her hands on a nearby towel. "I think I'll run into town for a while. I'll be back this afternoon." She forced a smile that didn't quite fit her face, then hurried upstairs. A few minutes later, lugging her purse, she raced out the front door. It slammed behind her.

"Talk about bad moods," Suzanne observed. "It seems infectious."

"That it does," Garrett said, watching through the

window as Gina jogged to her Explorer, climbed inside, then roared off down the dirt lane. "Do you know what's going on?" Garrett asked Blake.

"Nope." But the man was a bad liar. He knew something, he just wasn't saying. Avoiding his grandfather's eyes, Blake shoved out his chair and stretched. "I imagine Trent and Gina will figure it out."

"What's 'it'?"

Blake lifted a shoulder.

The phone rang once before Garrett could reach for the kitchen extension; he heard Trent pick up in the den.

"I guess I'd better see about the yearlings in the north pasture," he decided, still bothered about the simmering unspoken battle that he'd just witnessed. "If you're interested, Blake, why don't you come along?"

"I just might."

Garrett stepped onto the porch and started pulling on his boots. He heard a commotion through the screen door and looked up just as Trent shoved it open.

"Jordan Baxter's on the telephone," Trent said, his face muscles stretched tight as tanned leather as his eyes scanned the parking lot. When he saw that Gina's truck was missing, he frowned. He swung his gaze back to Garrett. "Baxter wants to talk to you."

The warning hairs on the back of Garrett's neck raised one by one. He pulled on the second boot and slowly stood, his knees popping a little and the arthritis that sometimes flared in his shoulder beginning to ache. "Somehow I have a feeling this isn't going to be good news."

Fingers tight around the steering wheel, Gina drove on automatic pilot toward town. Images of Trent darted through her mind. She saw him in a business suit, smiling seductively, or in bed, naked, his skin taut, his muscles flexing as he made love to her, or in jeans and a sweatshirt, surveying the Kincaid ranch. Her throat tightened and she battled tears again.

"It's just hormones." She tried to convince herself, dashing the horrid drops from her eyes and sniffing loudly. She had to quit thinking about him. About what could have been.

"Ha!"

He'd proposed, hadn't he?

Done his duty.

Angrily, she took a turn a little too sharply, then eased off on the accelerator. She had a baby to worry about. She couldn't afford to be careless. Never again.

On a whim, she veered east on Highway 17, deciding to visit Winona Cobbs's secondhand store.

The gates were wide open as Gina drove into the dusty lot where junk from the turn of the twentieth century to the millennium had collected around a trailer Winona called home. Ancient, disemboweled cars filled one corner while another was chock-full of used farm equipment. Sheds offered up more personal merchandise, everything from treadle sewing machines to plumbing fixtures to secondhand clothes and shoes.

But Winona wasn't anywhere on the lot. Gina climbed out of her car and walked up the steps of the trailer and knocked on the door. "Ms. Cobbs?" she called loudly, pounding with her fist, hoping to get the woman's attention. "Are you home? Ms. Cobbs?" But no one answered and there wasn't any life in the yard, aside from the honey bees that buzzed around several hives tucked near the fence in one corner of the property.

The psychic apparently didn't believe that anyone would stop by and rip her off.

There was no reason to stay and wait. Winona might be gone for hours, so Gina slid behind the wheel of the Explorer again, tipped a pair of sunglasses onto the bridge of her nose and tried to concentrate on Larry's seventh illegitimate son. She switched on the radio and drove off in a cloud of dust, but her mind kept straying from Larry's baby to the baby she herself had on the way.

Despite a bank of clouds gathering in the western sky, Gina felt her bad mood lighten. She was going to have a baby!

She smiled at the thought of becoming a mother and though Trent's reaction still stung, she hummed along with a Faith Hill song and drove into the town of White-horn, a small speck on the map that was becoming more and more familiar to her.

She spied people she'd met walking along the side-walks or driving by in pickups and cars. She'd learned the back streets and alleys of the town nearly as well as some of the locals. At a stoplight she waited for a couple to cross the street and her heart twisted. A man and woman walked in front of her Explorer, their hands linked. The woman carried her purse and a diaper bag, the man, most likely her husband, was fitted with a front pack wherein a tiny baby, only a few blond curls vis-ible, was resting.

Tears sprang to Gina's eyes and she quickly dashed them away, clearing her throat and reminding herself that she would love her baby enough for two parents. She didn't need a husband. And she didn't need Trent. She still winced when she thought that he'd seen her preg-nancy as a way to squeeze money out of him.

A horn blasted behind her and she realized the crosswalk was clear. Jittery, she pulled up to the Hip Hop and spied not only Lily Mae in her usual booth, but Winona Cobbs seated in a booth near the counter and perusing a paper.

Sniffing back the last hint of any maudlin tears, Gina parked and hurried inside. A bell jingled as the door opened and she was greeted with the smells of coffee, donuts, and frying bacon.

The booths were nearly full, the midmorning crowd hovering over java, pastries and conversation.

Gina didn't waste any time. She walked boldly up to Winona's booth and asked, "Mind if I join you?"

"Not at all." The short, round woman tucked the crossword puzzle she'd been working on into an oversize bag. "Sit," she said, waving to the bench on the other side of the booth. Her bracelets jangled and her bright eyes seemed to pierce straight to Gina's soul. "You're worried about something?"

"A million things," Gina admitted, ordering a glass of iced tea from Emma. "But the reason I wanted to talk to you is because the rumor around town is that you're psychic."

Winona nodded. "I have the gift."

"Then, I was hoping you could help me. I told you before that I think that Larry Kincaid fathered a seventh baby—and I haven't been able to locate him." She reached into her purse and pulled out Larry Kincaid's journal, with the pages open to the notation about the seventh son. She slid it across the table to the older woman. Winona adjusted her shawl and fingered the open page. Closing her eyes, she concentrated, deep grooves etching her forehead. "This is not a fake. You're concerned that it was a notation made after some woman called, a woman with a vendetta intent upon Larry Kincaid, but there is a child, a boy child. The information is correct, but…" Her lips drew hard, her eyebrows pinched together. "But I cannot see how he found out, or who is the mother of the baby."

Winona shook her head, the silvering braid wrapped around her head moving slowly side to side. "The woman who bore Larry's last child prefers to be anonymous."

Gina's heart sank.

"The only sense I get is that the mother is nearby. Somewhere here in Montana. But she is very worried. Not unhappy." Winona opened her eyes and stared at Gina long and hard. "The boy is the light of her life. Just as your child will be yours."

Gina nearly choked on a swallow of coffee. How had Winona Cobbs known that she was pregnant?

The door to the café opened and Christina Montgomery flew into the shop. She took a corner booth and picked up a menu. She looked pale and seemed upset, her blue eyes shadowed.

Winona sighed and her lips folded in upon themselves.

"What's wrong?"

The older woman's expression turned concerned. "I'd have to say that the water here in Whitehorn must be increasing the chances of fertility."

"Now, wait a minute…"

But Winona's eyes were focused on the girl slumped disconsolately at the booth. Christina ordered a soda and stared out the window, her manicured fingers drumming an anxious tattoo on the table.

"She's got the glow, too."

"What glow?" Gina asked. The girl was far from glowing. If anything, her mood was somber and dark.

"A pregnant glow. It's in her aura."

"And you can see it?" Gina asked, unable to hide her skepticism. Though she often ran with her hunches in an investigation, they were usually based on scientific evidence and fact.

Yes, but didn't you, too, come seeking counsel from the psychic? When all else fails...

"Certainly I can see it. Not only in her, but in you, as well."

Gina could barely believe her ears.

"But in Christina's case there's a mist of unhappiness surrounding her."

"'A mist of unhappiness'?" Was this for real?

"Uh-huh." Winona's eyes slitted and for a few seconds Gina had the eerie feeling that the owner of the junkyard was actually reading Christina's mind. But that was crazy. "It has to do with the father, but I can't tell who he is." Winona rubbed the crystal pendant at her neck with calloused fingers. "Oh, there is going to be trouble. Serious trouble. Nothing good is going to come of this."

"How do you know?" Gina asked, and in an instant the older woman turned her eyes away from Christina. Once again they were warm and a smile curved over her uncolored lips.

"I don't know how. As I said, it's a gift."

"Or a curse."

"Depends upon how you look at it. As for Christina, unfortunately I only see pain in her future, but you're a different story."

Gina couldn't help rising to the bait. "I am. How so?"

"It's simple." Winona picked up her cup of coffee and held it to her lips. "In your case you love the man who is the father of your child."

Gina bit her tongue against the argument that leaped to her lips. Because it was true, damn it, she did love Trent. Foolish as it was. "That doesn't mean I don't have my share of problems."

"None that can't be overcome," Winona said sagely as she took a sip of coffee then set down her cup. To Gina's surprise she reached across the table and took Gina's hand in hers. "What you don't understand is that the father of your baby loves you very much."

"No, I don't think—"

"And therein lies the problem. You're not thinking the right way—with faith rather than mistrust. Listen to me, Gina. Whether you believe it or not, the truth is that Trent Remmington, the father of the child you carry, loves you with all his heart and soul."

"You know this?" Gina couldn't believe it. It was too far-fetched.

"And that's not all. You love him, but pride won't allow you to admit it."

Chapter 14

"You goin' somewhere?" Blake asked as he watched Trent stuff all his belongings into his duffel bag.

"I'll be back," Trent said with determination. He glanced around the tiny room he'd called home since landing in Montana, searching for anything he'd need. "You can count on it." He yanked the zipper closed.

"When?"

He met his brother's curious gaze. "As soon as I can."

"Where are you going?"

Trent didn't have time for explanations. He wanted to take care of business, clear his head and return on the first flight he could find. But he had a business to run, and his life to bring into order. "I've got to leave for Houston, A.S.A.P. I just got a call from one of my foremen. There's all sorts of garbage goin' on in the company and it needs my personal attention."

"Such as?"

"Such as talk of a strike, for starters. And that's not the half of it. I've got a couple of wells that'll be shut down in Wyoming and I've got to handle it." His gaze clashed with eyes identical to his own. "I don't know where I'll land or when."

"Sure that's the reason you're takin' off?"

"What're you getting at?" Trent said, bristling.

"Looks to me like you might be running away," Blake accused. "Just like our old man."

Trent hiked the strap of his bag onto his shoulder. Not for the first time would he have loved to knock his smug brother down a peg, but though his fist actually flexed, he slowly uncurled it. This wasn't the time to round on his twin and knock him from here to eternity.

"You don't know what you're talking about."

"I know you're running out on Gina. On the baby."

"Like hell." Trent resisted arguing any further. "I'll call her later."

"Should I give her the message?"

Trent's back teeth ground together. He dropped his bag, turned to face his brother again and said, "Don't say anything, all right? The best thing for you to do is to stay out of this."

"You know, you're taking a chance. She might not wait for you."

"I said, butt out."

"I wish I could. But you're my brother. The only one who's full-blooded. The only one I grew up with. I care what happens to you. To Gina and the baby."

Trent hesitated, felt a damned lump fill his throat. This was not the time to lose focus. "I can take care of myself and I'll deal with Gina on my own terms," Trent said.

"Always the loner."

"Always." But it was a lie. Now there was Gina. And the baby. And the fact was that he had to leave Montana to straighten some things out before he returned. For good. To claim his wife and child, for like it or not, he was going to convince Gina to marry him. But not yet. There were a few ducks that needed to be put in order. He started with Blake. "Look, if you feel the need to bond with a brother or two, I think you can take your pick. Larry left quite an assortment to choose from."

"Right. I choose you."

Trent stopped short. The honesty in his brother's eyes, the pain they'd shared together, was all too visible. His throat caught. He swallowed hard. His voice, when he found it, was raspy. "Find someone else, Blake." With that he grabbed his bag, stopped in the den and snapped his laptop into its case then stormed out of the house. Blake's words echoed in his mind. *You know, you're taking a chance. She might not wait for you...*

He spied Garrett and the old dog near the machine shed. Figuring he'd better take the time to tell the old man that he had to leave for business but that he'd call, he crossed the parking lot and leaned against the fence. As he said his goodbyes, the accusations in Garrett's eyes mirrored those he'd seen in Blake's.

"What about Gina?"

"She was gone when I got the call. I'll phone her later."

"Do that." It was an order. Not a suggestion.

"I will."

"And take my advice," Garrett said, propping up

the brim of his Stetson with his thumb. "Slow down enough to enjoy life. It's over sooner than any of us like to think."

"I'll remember that," Trent said. He was already re-thinking his priorities. He rubbed his cheek where Gina had struck it and knew he'd find a way to make amends.

"Do." Garrett whistled to the dog and strode off.

Trent turned on his heel and strode to his rental car. Ever since Gina had told him he was going to be a fa-ther, he saw the world a little differently. He threw his bag into the back seat of the car. Behind the wheel, he fired the engine and took off, spraying gravel as he fol-lowed the rutted lane toward the main road. Through the passenger window he saw a horse, a lone stallion, head raised, nostrils to the wind, far apart from the rest of the herd. Trent's eyes narrowed on the white stallion for just a second and the animal swung his great head in his direction, ears pricked forward, then reared as the car raced past. The horse was a loner. A rogue. A maverick.

Just like me.

Barely slowing as he entered the main road, Trent shook the image of the stallion from his mind and gripped the wheel with tense fingers. In the past few weeks his entire life had been ripped to shreds, every-thing he'd believed in destroyed. He had a new family, if only he would embrace it; he had a woman he loved, if only he could convince her of that fact; and he had a baby on the way.

This was his chance. If he hadn't blown it already by not waiting for her. But he didn't turn around. He didn't have time because all of a sudden his entire life was looming ahead of him and he was anxious to get on with it. Right now, he had business to attend to, important business. But first on the agenda when the plane touched down in Houston was to visit the jewelry store and pick out a ring with the biggest damned diamond he could find.

When he returned to Whitehorn, he'd find a way to convince Gina that he loved her. If he had to, he'd spend the rest of his life proving it.

Gina tried to shake off the malaise that seemed to cling to her like a shroud. So she was pregnant, so she was alone, so Trent had been gone from the ranch for more than two days without any word from him. So what? She sat on the back porch swing, her laptop beeping that its battery was about to die, and slowly rocked. She looked across the windswept acres and watched the cattle lumber through the dry fields.

She was no closer to finding Larry's last heir than she had been when she'd landed on the ranch over two weeks earlier. Jack was making noise about her returning and though she hated to leave, the truth of the matter was that she was spinning her wheels here. Sooner or later she had to return to Southern California to face the music. Jack deserved to know the truth.

Inside she heard the men collecting. Trent, Adam and Brandon had left, at least temporarily, but Mitch, Cade and Blake had stayed on. Along with Rand and Garrett, they were milling in the living room, waiting for Wayne Kincaid to arrive to discuss legalities concerning the land. From what she could gather, Jordan Baxter was determined to stir up trouble for the Kincaids, making a claim that he had some kind of right to the land. Then there was the press.

For the past few days the phone had been ringing

off the hook, local reporters interested in writing about Larry's sons, all six of them. So far, Gina had avoided being interviewed. If she stayed here much longer, though, she'd have to give some quotes. She'd thought about this and it wasn't necessarily a bad idea. If she admitted she was looking for Larry's seventh son, perhaps someone who knew something about that damned notation in Larry's journal might just come forward.

Her computer beeped again and she snapped it off. She needed to get away from the house, to consider the rest of her life, to find a way to control the ache in her heart whenever she thought about Trent.

She'd returned to the ranch to find him gone—his things packed, his room empty. Blake had tried to reassure her that Trent would return, he'd call, he'd contact her, but she was certain it was a lie.

She walked up the stairs and changed into a pair of jeans and T-shirt. It was true Trent had asked her to marry him, but it had been a reaction, the "right thing" to do. Obviously he'd had a change of heart and taken her rejection at face value. "So what did you expect?" she asked herself as she pulled her hair back into a ponytail and eyed her reflection in the cracked mirror. "Hearts and flowers? Love letters and diamonds? A tortured admission that he couldn't live without you?" She frowned at the woman in the mirror, the woman whose green eyes looked ready to fill with tears. "Get real, Gina. You know better."

But you love him! Face it. You should have accepted his marriage proposal when he offered it. It would have been best for you, best for the baby.

"And it would have been trapping him. No thank you."

She snapped the rubber band in place and took the stairs to the first floor. The men were deep in conversation in the living room and she made her way through the kitchen and out the back door. Needing fresh air and time to herself, she saddled her favorite mare and rode away from the center of the ranch.

"Let's go," she said, clucking to the palomino. With a burst of energy, the horse stretched out, strides lengthening, the wind rushing against Gina's face and cheeks. Tears blurred her eyes and she let them flow, telling herself it was from the fresh mountain air, not because her heart was breaking.

"Run, damn you, run," she said, leaning over the game little mare's shoulders, and feeling the slap of the mane against her chin. Upward, through the trees, along the trail she rode as sunlight and shadows speckled the ground. A jackrabbit hopped across the path, diving into the brambles as they passed.

Gina's heart pounded and she thought of Trent. God, how she loved him, more than was respectable, more than any sane woman should care for a man. Gina, the woman who had vowed to never let a man close to her, to never trust someone who wasn't steadfast, true and dedicated. She'd been looking for the boy next door, a man she could depend on, not a self-serving man like the father who had left her mother with two children to raise. And then she'd foolishly fallen for a maverick oilman, a loner, a rogue who lived his life his own way.

A lump formed in her throat and she steadfastly swallowed it back. Well, it did no good to wallow or cry over a man like Trent Remmington. No, she'd just have to make it on her own. She'd managed to take care of herself up to now; she was certain she could be both mother and father to her child.

The trees gave way to the meadow where she and Trent had nearly made love over a week earlier. Her heart wrenched and again the tears started to flow. Two pheasants flew across the mare's path. Wings whirred, feathers swirled. The horse broke stride and stumbled. Gina pitched forward. Her heart flew to her throat.

She held on to the reins.

Spooked, the mare reared and Gina was thrown back. Then the palomino, as if branded by hot iron, shot forward. "No!" The creek loomed closer. Hoof beats thundered in her eardrums.

Oh, God, no! Gina tried to right herself, but couldn't. She scrabbled for the saddle horn, her head hanging down near the horse's shoulder, her ponytail touching the ground, her right foot caught in the stirrup.

"Whoa!" she cried. "Stop, oh, please—"

She felt the mare's muscles bunch, heard the rush of water.

"Please…no!" The horse sprang, beneath her the creek roared, swift water splashing and tumbling over stones as it cut downhill. The saddle shifted and Gina screamed. Hooves hit the far bank, then scrambled. Dust flew. Her head hit the dirt. Pain ripped up from Gina's hip and exploded in her brain. She screamed and her foot slipped out of her boot.

Thud! She hit the ground hard, every bone rattling in her body. Pain ricocheted up her spine. For a second she was conscious, the darkening sky swirling above her, the ground tilting. She felt something deep within her rend…a warm wetness slide down her jeans.

The baby! Oh, please, God, not the baby! Anything else, but please, please, keep this precious baby alive...

Somewhere she heard the sound of a horse neighing and the barking of a dog, and then as she struggled to find her feet, she felt the warm comfort of darkness seduce her, the blackness at the corners of her vision closing in. Then with a sigh and a profound sadness over her loss, she let out a plaintive moan, wrapped her arms around her body and fell back onto the cushion of grass.

"What do you mean, she's not here?" Trent demanded when Garrett gave him the news that Gina wasn't in the ranch house. Hot, tired, and out of sorts from a whirlwind trip, he'd barely gotten out of the rental car when he'd spied Garrett eyeing the workmen assembling the indoor arena.

"She went off riding earlier this afternoon and hasn't come back yet." Garrett ran a gloved hand along the corner of a two-by-four.

"What time was that?"

"Four, maybe five hours ago." Garrett was chewing on a blade of dry grass. Studying Trent, he shifted the blade from one side of his mouth to the other. "I'm a little worried since she didn't come back for dinner, but I figure she's had a lot on her mind and needs some time alone." His blue eyes were flatly assessing. "I figure she'll be back soon."

Trent wasn't in the mood to wait. He'd done enough of that in the past couple of days. And the times he'd tried to call the ranch all of the lines had been busy with his half brothers either on the phone or the Internet. "I think I'll go looking for her. If I miss her and if she shows up back here, don't let her go anywhere."

"You think I could stop her?"

"You could damn well try." Trent wasn't in the mood for nonsense. He'd spent the better part of the past forty-eight hours kicking himself up one side and down the other for being such a fool. He'd slept maybe three hours in total and was in one bear of a mood, but the ring in his pocket eased his mind. Wherever he found Gina, he was going to tell her how much she meant to him, that pregnant or not, he wanted her for his wife, that he couldn't bear to think of a future without her.

He saddled the roan gelding he'd claimed for his use and took off through the hills. Dusk was lengthening the shadows of the surrounding trees and the sky had taken on a lavender hue.

In his peripheral vision Trent spied the lone white stallion, the solitary horse he'd thought was so like himself. "Not anymore," he vowed as his gelding stretched out, eating up the ground, racing as if against the wind.

"Hey!" He heard Blake's voice and looked over his shoulder. His brother was jogging out of the ranch house and had stopped to talk to Garrett. Another fence he had to mend, Trent thought with a scowl. He saw Blake start for the stables, then turned his attention to the hills. Yep, this place wouldn't be a bad spot to raise a family and it was a middle ground, not Texas and surely not Southern California. Both he and Gina could work from here, take life a little slower and watch their child grow. At the thought of the baby, Trent's chest swelled.

He might not have had exemplary male role models in his life, but there was no reason to think he couldn't be a damned good father. The best. He urged the roan into the woods and up the familiar trail that wound through the pines to the meadow where he and Gina had nearly

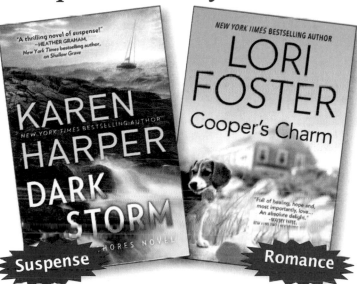

Dear Reader,

Since you are a lover of our books, your opinions are important to us... and so is your time.

That's why we made sure your **"FAST FIVE" READER SURVEY** can be completed in just a few minutes. Your answers to the five questions will help us remain at the forefront of women's fiction.

And, as a thank-you for participating, we'd like to send you up to **4 FREE BOOKS** and **FREE THANK-YOU GIFTS!**

Try **Essential Suspense** featuring spine-tingling suspense and psychological thrillers with many written by today's best-selling authors.

Try **Essential Romance** featuring compelling romance stories with many written by today's best-selling authors.

Or TRY BOTH!

Enjoy your gifts with our appreciation,

Pam Powers

To get up to
4 FREE BOOKS & THANK-YOU GIFTS:

✳ Quickly complete the "Fast Five" Reader Survey
and return the insert.

"FAST FIVE" READER SURVEY

1 Do you sometimes read a book a second or third time? ○ Yes ○ No

2 Do you often choose reading over other forms of entertainment such as television? ○ Yes ○ No

3 When you were a child, did someone regularly read aloud to you? ○ Yes ○ No

4 Do you sometimes take a book with you when you travel outside the home? ○ Yes ○ No

5 In addition to books, do you regularly read newspapers and magazines? ○ Yes ○ No

YES! Please send me my Free Rewards, consisting of **2 Free Books from each series I select** and **Free Mystery Gifts**. I understand that I am under no obligation to buy anything, as explained on the back of this card.

❏ **Essential Suspense** (191/391 MDL GNTC)
❏ **Essential Romance** (194/394 MDL GNTC)
❏ **Try Both** ((191/391 & 191/391) MDL GNTN)

FIRST NAME	LAST NAME

ADDRESS

APT.#	CITY

STATE/PROV.	ZIP/POSTAL CODE

made love. For a reason he couldn't fathom he felt she was there, and the need to see her again, to touch her, to hold her, to promise to love her for all eternity, pounded through his blood.

"Come on, come on," he said urgently, suddenly anxious to find her. The trees gave way and he spied the horse. A smile broke out on his lips and he nearly laughed until he realized the saddle was askew, twisted around the mare's belly.

His gut twisted.

Where was Gina?

He kicked the gelding, spurred him into the field, and his eyes swept the hillside where sunlight was fading fast and the first stars of twilight were beginning to glow.

Then he saw her. Crumpled on the grass, blood at her head, her skin a pasty white. His heart froze, but he kicked the roan and rode like a bat out of hell, jumping down from the saddle before the horse had time to stop.

"Gina! Oh, God, Gina!" Rushing to her side, his blood thundering through his head, he dropped to his knees. "Gina, oh, love…please, please…" His throat tightened and he tried to think. She was breathing, her pulse still strong. The wound on her head was shallow, the blood beginning to crust.

"Gina, can you hear me?" he whispered, his arms surrounding her. "Oh, baby, hang on. I'll take care of you."

"Wh-what?" Her eyelids fluttered open and eyes as green as a spring meadow stared into his. "Trent?"

"Shh." Tears filled his eyes. "You'll be all right. I'll get help."

"Wh-what happened?" she asked, wincing as she moved.

"Stay still. Shh." He pressed his lips to her dirt-smudged and bloody forehead. "You'll be fine."

"But..." She struggled with a memory and then he saw the fear slash through her eyes. "The baby..."

"Will be fine."

"I don't know... I don't think..." And then she was gone again, her eyes closing as he held her to him and noticed the stain on her jeans, the dark red splash that marred the denim.

"It'll be all right," he promised. *And if we can't save this one, we'll have others. A dozen if you want.*

He lifted her into his arms and gently carried her toward his horse. Somehow he'd get her down the hillside and he'd do it quick if he had to carry her every step of the way himself.

"Trent!" Blake's voice rang across the hills and he looked up to find his brother astride the damned white stallion. He was off the horse in an instant. "What happened?"

"I don't know."

"Lay her down so I can examine her and go get help," Blake ordered.

"I can't leave her."

"Like hell, Trent. I'm the doctor, remember. Now go on and get help. She needs to get to a hospital. See if they've got life flight or something."

Trent was astride his horse and racing down the hillside at a dead gallop. His blood ran cold in his veins and his teeth ground together in a jaw tense with determination. He wasn't going to lose Gina now, not when he'd finally found her.

There were voices...so many voices... Gina awoke in the hospital, on a narrow bed covered with soft green sheets. Her head felt as if it had been cracked open and her entire body ached. She winced against the fluorescent light and expected to find a doctor examining her. Instead she found herself staring directly into Trent Remmington's worried eyes.

He blinked against a sheen of tears and managed a smile. "I knew you'd make it," he said, though the crack in his voice belied his words. "You're just too tough to let go that easy."

"Am I?" She felt anything but tough at this moment in time.

"Where am I?"

"The Whitehorn Memorial Hospital."

But there was something wrong, something more, a heaviness and sense of doom she carried in her heart. Then she remembered. "The...the baby?"

"Is fine," Trent assured her. "But I'm not certain about the kid's father. He nearly fell into a million pieces." His throat worked and she felt the sting of tears when she saw the love and raw pain in his eyes. "Everything's going to be fine," he said gruffly. "The doctor said you should make it to term...well, if you follow his instructions."

"I will," she vowed, relieved.

"Good." Trent took her hand in his, frowned at the sight of the IV buried in the back of her wrist. "He also said the best thing for you to do is to marry me."

"What?" she said, then realized it was a joke. "The man must have brutal sense of humor."

Trent winced visibly. "Look, I know what you think about me, and believe me, I understand, but I'd already decided I loved you, needed you and wanted you and... Oh, hell—" he swallowed hard and looked her straight in the eye "—that I couldn't live without you. I went to Houston to straighten things out at the company and—"

"Shh." Blinding pain cut through her heart. "You don't have to do this. Or say anything. Just because I had an accident and nearly lost the baby doesn't mean you're obligated or—oh!" She gasped as his lips crashed down on hers and he kissed the very breath from her lungs.

When he lifted his head, tears sheened his eyes. "I *want* to marry you, damn it. Do you hear me. I *want* to be your husband and the baby's father and even… God, even if you'd lost him, I'd still want you to live with me for the rest of my life."

She wanted to believe him, ached to trust his words, and the raw emotion twisting his features nearly convinced her.

"I'll do whatever it takes," he said, his voice ragged, his soul bare. "You can work. We can live in L.A. Whatever, but I'd like to start out here. Just you and me…and then when the baby comes, the three of us." The fingers over her hand tightened. "I love you, Gina. That's the bottom line. I loved you from the moment I saw you in Dallas."

Her heart felt as if it would burst. Tears drizzled from her eyes.

"Marry me, Gina." His voice cracked with raw, undisguised emotion.

She couldn't say no. Wouldn't have if she could have, because the truth of the matter was that she'd waited for this moment, longed for it, even when her pride had been battered, her bravado masking her pain. "Of course I'll marry you," she whispered, and felt his lips claim hers again. This solitary man loved her and she believed him. His lips molded over hers tenderly, with the promise of tomorrow and when he lifted his head, their future shone in his eyes. "I love you, too."

"I know."

A smile began to stretch from one side of his face to the other.

She actually giggled. This was serious. They were going to get married. She was going to be Mrs. Trent Remmington. She laughed out loud and Trent's deep chuckle echoed around the room. He held her tight and she clung to him. Oh, God, how could she have ever doubted him?

"Glad you're back with us," Garrett Kincaid was suddenly at her bedside, with Blake. "You gave us all quite a scare."

"Especially Trent," Blake added, touching her hand. "Now—" he looked at Garrett "—I think we should let the nurses' station know that the patient has awakened and then these two—" he hitched his chin toward Trent and Gina "—can have a few minutes alone before the real doctor comes along."

"So now you're a fake," Trent said, smiling. "I suspected it all along."

"I'm just not the M.D. in charge."

He and Garrett walked to the door, but Garrett turned and said, "You get better right quick, Gina. You still have another one of my grandsons to find."

"Will do," she promised.

"After you marry me," Trent insisted, and then, next to the hospital bed, he knelt and took her hand in his. "I came back to Whitehorn with this," he said, reaching into his pocket and extracting a ring—a gold band with a single diamond that winked brightly under the harsh hospital lights. "And then I thought that I might not ever be able to give it to you. Maybe I should do this the right way." He lifted her hand and, disregarding the IV drip, slipped the ring onto her finger. "Gina Henderson, will you marry me?"

Tears flooded her eyes. "I don't know what to say. I, um, I think you have me at a disadvantage here." She motioned to the IV stand. "No tellin' what they've slipped into my bloodstream." He lifted that damnably sexy dark eyebrow and waited. "Didn't I already say I would?"

"I'd like to hear it again."

"Okay, Remmington. It's a date. I'd love to marry you," she said saucily.

Again he laughed. "Then we'll make it as soon as possible. Just so you don't change your mind."

"Wouldn't dream of it. As soon as I get out of here."

"You're on, lady." He leaned over and kissed her lips.

Gina's heart melted. God how she loved him.

Footsteps thundered in the hallway. In a second her brother Jack burst through the door. "Gina? My God, I'm sorry I couldn't get here any faster." He strode to her bedside and ignored Trent. "Are you all right?"

"Just fine," she said, seeing the worry in his eyes. "And there's something else you should know—you're going to be an uncle."

"Wait a minute— A *what?*"

"And I want you to give me away."

"Hey, slow down a minute. Are you delirious?"

"Not a chance, big brother. This handsome man here is Trent Remmington. He's about to become your brother-in-law."

Two weeks later Gina stood at the top of the stairs of the Kincaid house. With the help of the local wedding planner, Meg Reilly, she'd managed to put together a quick wedding. All of Trent's half brothers had shown up.

"You look beautiful," her mother said, kissing Gina's cheek as Meg adjusted her veil. All three women's faces were visible in the small cracked mirror over Gina's bureau.

"And you look pretty good for a grandmother."

Her mother pulled a face. "I'm much too young to be a grandmother," she said, then laughed. "But I'm delighted, nonetheless. Now, I think I'd better take a seat downstairs," she said. "I just wish you were going to live in L.A."

"I told you that's impossible. Trent and I agreed to stay here in Whitehorn. And besides, I still have another one of Larry's sons to find, a baby."

"Work, work, work. You'll have a baby of your own to take care of."

"Yes, and he'll probably be born before I find that last one," Gina teased, and thought Meg seemed uncomfortable with the conversation.

"I think it's about time," Meg said with a wistful smile. "Your mother's right. You look fabulous."

"Thanks." Gina glanced out the window to the sprawling acres above which the vast Montana sky stretched. Cattle were grazing and a lone white stallion raced along the fenceline, his head lifted high and proud. She felt as if she belonged here in Montana, on the ranch. With Trent.

The first chords of the piano announced her entrance, so she hurried to the top of the stairs where Jack, as nervous as if he were the bridegroom, waited. "You sure about this?" he asked.

"More sure of it than anything in my life." She descended the stairs, following a trail of rose petals Mitch Fielding's twins had spread.

Jack's arm was steady and as they walked through the French doors to the backyard, Gina smiled brightly. Her family and Trent's family, along with a few of the good citizens of Whitehorn, Montana, had gathered around a hastily built arbor where Trent, dressed in a black tuxedo, was waiting for her. Joy pulsing through her veins, she released Jack's arm and walked forward to join the man who was going to be her husband.

He didn't wait for the reverend's approval, but lifted her veil before the ceremony and placed a kiss upon her lips. "For luck," he whispered, and her heart squeezed.

"Believe it or not, I don't need any," she confided as if no one else could hear. "Today I just happen to be the luckiest woman in the world."

Epilogue

"Well, Laura, that's that. Trent and Gina are married," Garrett said as he stood on the outside of the crowd. Colored lights had been strung on the porch and a band was playing country music. The bride and groom were dancing together, holding each other tight, acting as if no one else in the universe existed, though there were others on the makeshift dance floor with them.

"I didn't expect that, but it's a good thing, and that little great-grandbaby of ours deserves this." He chuckled and refused to think about the fact that Jordan Baxter seemed determined to make trouble for them.

He glanced at the rest of Larry's sons and wondered what would become of them. Cade Redstone had been particularly quiet this evening. He'd joined in the celebration, but hadn't said much, and as Garrett spotted him now, he was seated by himself, his thoughts turned inward.

Garrett sighed. "We can only hope that all of the boys end up as happy as Trent is tonight. I think he might even try to make amends with Blake, you know. Gives his brother the credit for saving the baby's life."

Garrett looked up to the stars. "I sure do miss you, Laura," he admitted, and felt the old familiar tug on his heart, "but then, I know you're watching down on us here." His eyes sparkled. "I wouldn't put it past you to have set this whole scene up yourself. You were always the matchmaker."

Again he looked at the bride and groom. "Well, darlin', this time you couldn't have done better if you'd tried."

* * * * *

Also available from B.J. Daniels

HQN Books

Montana Justice

Restless Hearts

Sterling's Montana

Stroke of Luck
Luck of the Draw
Just His Luck

The Montana Cahills

Renegade's Pride
Outlaw's Honor
Cowboy's Legacy
Cowboy's Reckoning
Hero's Return
Rancher's Dream
Wrangler's Rescue

Harlequin Intrigue

Cardwell Ranch: Montana Legacy

Steel Resolve
Iron Will

The Montana Cahills

Cowboy's Redemption

Visit the Author Profile page
at Harlequin.com for more titles.

INTIMATE SECRETS

B.J. Daniels

This one's for LuAnn Rod, who shared her love of horses with me, and shares my love of snowboarding. See you on the slopes, girlfriend!

Prologue

He looked like the rest of the tourists as he bought a ticket at the small booth on the mountainside. The next tour started in ten minutes. It would be the last tour of the day.

Perfect.

The rays of the sinking sun slanted across the top of the mountain, painting the buildings with bronzed heat. Below, the Jefferson River snaked emerald green through the rocky canyon. On the mountainside, the sagebrush stood dusty gray in a ground already gone dry.

He killed time in the gift shop, passing up a cold beer, ice cream and the usual curios for a schematic of the caverns. With five minutes to spare, he went back to wait by the ticket booth, anxious. Anxious to get deep in the cool darkness of the caves. Anxious to confront an old enemy he knew would be waiting down there for him.

But mostly, anxious to find the one thing he needed, the perfect hiding place.

He'd been bowled over when he'd seen the sign just outside of Three Forks, Montana. Lewis and Clark Caverns 15 Miles. It had been more than fate or good fortune. It had been divine intervention.

A young guide called his tour group, explaining they would have to hike up to the cave entrance. There used to be a small train, but now visitors had to walk. He didn't mind walking the half mile, even uphill along the paved trail, a trail easy enough for his grandmother.

Once inside, there was a two-mile trek and a three-hundred-foot descent, into the bowels of the cave, ending with six hundred rock-carved stairs to the exit.

Perfect.

He quickly got ahead of everyone else, anxious to get inside the mountain. But he also liked the view down the steep mountainside and wondered how many tourists had fallen. Sweat broke out under his arms, ran down his sides.

But it wasn't from exertion. It was pure expectation. He *hated* confined places. Hated anything that reminded him of the root cellar back at his grandmother's farm. The dark, cool, raw earth. The musty, wet-smelling air. The darkness pressing against him, squeezing the life from him. The taste and smell and feel of fear.

Claustrophobia. It was his only failing. But also the only thing that still aroused him to the point of rapture. The ultimate. The little death. It gave him an edge other people didn't have. Would never understand.

He couldn't wait to get inside. He couldn't wait to find exactly what he was looking for. A hole. Something small enough he would have to squeeze through.

A space beyond the hole, far enough off the tour route that no one could find him. A place where he could finish what he'd started.

At the top, he had to wait for the rest of the group. He tried not to be impatient as he stood at the mouth of the entrance and gazed down into the confining darkness. Soon, he thought, soon.

The tour guide led the group through the caverns, pointing out stalactites and stalagmites, flowstone and dripstone. He paid little attention. He knew all about caves. He did listen, though, when the guide spoke about one of the first explorers getting lost, losing his candle and spending three days in the dark, unable to move. The man had been temporarily blind and completely disoriented from the days in total blackness.

More than five hundred feet into the cave, he found what he was looking for. The perfect place to disappear into the blinding darkness.

He hung back in the small room, pretending to admire the iciclelike lime deposits, wondering if the tour guide would miss him. He doubted it, out of a group of more than a dozen. They were all more interested in the rock formations than some nondescript tourist.

The group began to move on. He waited behind a large stalagmite. "Do we have everyone?" the tour guide inquired. No one said anything and the light diminished as the tour moved on, leaving him alone in the dark.

He waited, standing in the dizzying darkness, his face frozen in fear. He loved this part the best. The absolute blackness. The chilling silence. The disorientation that set in within seconds. He thought of the explorer down here without his candle. Trapped. Unable to see anything. Unable to move. And no one to hear his cries for help.

When he couldn't take another second of it, he snapped on the tiny flashlight he'd brought and shone it into the hole he'd found. Small. Just enough room to barely get through. He got down on his hands and knees, then his belly, and taking a ragged breath, wriggled into the narrow tunnel.

He slithered like a snake, deeper and deeper into the confined cavity, squirming around the tight blind corners. Five minutes in, the tunnel ended in a solid rock wall.

He froze. He couldn't go on any farther. Nor could he turn around. This would do just fine. The perfect place to hide a small child.

He started to back out, but his body stuck, now suddenly too large for the cramped rock channel he'd wormed through. Instantly, sweat cloaked his already-clammy body. The constant fifty-degree air raised goose bumps, chilling him. He fought for each breath, but let the panic come, the euphoria of fear.

He tried backing out again. If he'd come through it, he could get out, right? Except he'd come through head-first, and since there wasn't enough room to turn around, he had no choice but to go out feet first. Feet first like a corpse.

Prostrate, he dug in with his toes, inching backward, squeezing through the tight, constricting passage, the claustrophobia taunting him: "You'll never get out. The rocks are compressing, the hole contracting, the mountain closing in on you."

His mouth went dry as dust. He gasped for breath, his heart lunging in his chest. Minutes ticked off like hours.

The tiny flashlight banged against a rock, dimmed, almost went out.

He was breathing hard now, but the air seemed too thin. Maybe he'd made a wrong turn. But he knew better. He struggled for each breath, each inch backward, the hole now endless as eternity. Or hell. His hell.

Then suddenly his toes lost purchase. Nothing but air. Air and space. He shoved himself backward with his hands and slipped through the opening, scrambling out of the hole.

Free.

For a few more desperate moments, he stood in the room where the tour group had left him behind, shining the light across the ghostly rock formations, forcing back the claustrophobia the way he forced back the dark.

He didn't have much time. He gripped the flashlight, suddenly afraid he might drop it. That he might be the one who ended up trapped down here in the deafening darkness.

The irony amused him as much as the bitter taste of his own fear. He stood, just long enough to catch his breath, then hurriedly wound his way through the cold cavity until he was within earshot of the tour group, the worn trail easy to follow. He waited until the guide moved on to the next item of interest before he caught up and fell in with the others.

Then it was over. One last rock-carved wide tunnel and he was back outside again, more than three hundred feet below the entrance, walking down another paved path, smiling smugly, feeling triumphant.

But the euphoria never lasted long.

Fortunately, he'd be back. For the cave's dark, confined allure. For a well-deserved ending to the two years he'd lost. He'd make up for it. In spades. Once he'd snatched the kid, he'd finally get what was rightfully his.

He chuckled to himself as he looked across the mountainside toward Three Forks, Montana. Wouldn't Josie O'Malley be surprised when she saw him. Soon, Josie. Real soon.

Chapter 1

Josie reined in her horse and looked out at the valley that ran spring green to the still-snowcapped mountain peaks.

"Look at that, Ivy," she whispered as she hugged the toddler in front of her, resting her chin on top of her daughter's blond head. "Isn't it pretty?"

The sun slipped behind the mountains, turning the Montana sky a brilliant orange that radiated across the horizon, making the last of the day glow as warm and bright as any Josie had ever seen.

"Pwetty," her fourteen-month-old repeated.

Ivy's hair still had that baby smell, the loose curls a pale blond and down-soft, so much like Josie's own. Ivy looked just as Josie had at that age. Except for her eyes. Instead of being the color of bluebonnets, they were a startling deep, dark brown—just like the baby's father's.

Because of that, Josie never looked at her daughter without being reminded of him—and Texas. Each brought an ache of its own.

As beautiful as Montana was, it wasn't Texas. This time of year, the Texas hill country would be alive with bluebonnets and Indian paintbrush against a backdrop of live oak. The air would be scented with cedar.

So different from Montana. She stared out at the lush landscape and breathed in the sweet scent of pine. The Buffalo Jump Ranch, surrounded by snowy peaks, towering pines and rocky bluffs, was thousands of miles from Texas—and the past.

But more important, she'd found what she wanted to do with her life here in Montana. For the first time, Josie O'Malley felt truly at peace.

The realization startled her. She'd always felt at odds with the diminutive flaxen-haired sprite with the bright blue eyes she saw staring back at her from the mirror. They said she looked like her mother, but her father and brothers assured her she was nothing like sweet-tempered, soft-spoken Katherine Donovan O'Malley had been.

Instead, Josie had a wild spirit, as wild as the Texas land she'd grown up in, with a rebellious temperament her father said came from her namesake, her great-grandmother Josephine O'Malley.

Josie didn't mind the comparison to her great-grandmother, who'd been a Wild West rodeo trick rider. In fact, Josie had clung to her rebellious spirit when her father and older brothers had tried to break it the same way they broke their horses—by trying to break her will. In the end, they'd only succeeded in driving her away.

As she hugged her daughter in the fading light, Josie

realized with more than a little surprise how far she'd come—and not in miles. For the first time, she really *did* feel…ready. Maybe now she could do what she'd sworn on her great-grandmother's memory she would do.

The horse nickered softly beneath them, his ears coming up as he raised his head and sniffed the warm breeze. Suddenly his ears lay back as if he saw something in the trees.

Josie tensed as well, her gaze going past the aspens to the dark edge of pines that bordered the horse ranch to the north. The first shadows of evening had settled in the trees, but she was close enough that she could see him. A man. Standing not fifty feet away. Looking right at her. Watching her and Ivy.

Startled, Josie jerked the reins, making the horse jump to the side, making her lose sight of the man as she held Ivy to her. She steadied the horse, upset with herself for treating the mare with such roughness, and focused again on the pines.

An icy shaft of fear sliced through her, bone-deep, as she stared into the shadows, frantically searching for the man she'd seen. A man she'd recognized.

But no one looked back at her from the shadowed darkness of the trees. Nothing moved. Not the thick, dark branches of the pines. Not the silver-sided, coin-like leaves of the aspens. Certainly not the man she'd thought she'd seen standing there, watching her and Ivy.

The sun slipped behind the mountains, shadows deepening. Suddenly the day no longer felt warm. Or safe.

Josie reined the horse around and, hugging her daughter to her, rode toward the small cabin that had become her home, afraid to look back. At the pines. Or the past.

Afraid to acknowledge who she'd thought she'd glimpsed watching her from the shelter of the trees.

A man who'd been dead for more than two years.

Josie woke with a start, jerking upright, heart pounding, her gaze at once darting to the crib in the bedroom across the hall.

Sun streamed in the window, blinding her. The crib appeared empty. In that instant, the memory of the man she'd seen yesterday in the trees came back, as dark and ominous as an omen.

Then she heard Ivy's sweet laughter. Eyes adjusting to the sunlight, Josie saw her daughter standing in the crib, trying to catch dust motes in her chubby little hands.

Just the sight of Ivy filled her with a wave of relief that threatened to drown her. She got up quickly and took her daughter in her arms, needing to hold her, to assure herself that Ivy was safe.

But the initial fear she'd felt on waking receded slowly, the memory of the man in the pines too fresh. Too real.

Odell Burton was dead. And Josie O'Malley didn't believe in ghosts. But just thinking she'd seen him had shaken her more than she wanted to admit. Especially since at that moment she'd been feeling safe.

As she and Ivy ate oatmeal on the porch in the morning sun, she tried to get back that feeling of peace, however brief, she'd felt the day before. Logically, she knew she'd seen a man—just not Odell.

But the memory of the man watching her and Ivy from the trees still clung to her like the remnants of a bad dream. Something about him had scared her. And Josie prided herself on not scaring easily.

The last time she saw Odell had been on her family's ranch in Texas. She'd turned to find him watching her and realized he'd just come out of the barn. He had an odd expression on his face. He looked almost nervous.

That wasn't like him. She'd known him since they were kids. His father raised rough stock for rodeos down the road from the O'Malley Ranch.

But there had always been something about him— She shivered. His interest in her had always unnerved her. Even when they were kids. Worse, when they were older and he'd realized she wasn't interested in him. Odell had a hard time accepting no. It was probably one of the reasons he'd gotten in trouble with the law at such an early age.

She fed Ivy a few bites of oatmeal, then relinquished the baby spoon, although Ivy was getting more oatmeal on her face than in her mouth.

Josie knew that even thinking she'd seen Odell was some kind of subconscious reminder of everything she still feared from two years ago. She and Ivy were safe. But obviously, her subconscious didn't believe it.

Maybe it was because she'd been thinking about going home to Texas. Just the thought of going home filled her with excitement—and anxiety. It had been two years. She'd broken all ties with her family when she'd taken off the way she had. Not that it could have been helped under the circumstances. Still, she wished things had been different.

Going home meant facing more than Odell's ghost. More than her father and brothers. She couldn't be sure what kind of reception she'd get at the O'Malley Ranch. But at least she knew what to expect from Clay Jackson.

Clay. She closed her eyes for a moment, unconsciously smiling at a distant memory. Clay had grown up on the adjacent ranch, the Valle Verde. He'd been her brother Dustin's age. Six years older, the boys had seen her only as a kid—and a girl at that.

But Clay was always kind to her, and from the time she could remember she'd had a crush on him. When he went away to college, she dreamed of the day he'd return home to the ranch—and her. She knew that once he saw her all grown-up he'd fall for her, just as she'd fallen for him so many years before.

Unfortunately, she thought, her smile fading, he hadn't come back. He'd fallen in love with a woman named Maria and he'd become a deputy sheriff, and he appeared to have no intention of ever returning to ranching.

Then one day he'd just reappeared. She'd looked up and there he was framed against the Texas sky, his broad shoulders blocking out the sun.

Except it wasn't exactly as she'd dreamed. She heard through the ranch rumor mill that the woman he'd fallen in love with after college had run off with someone else, Clay had turned in his badge, and being the youngest, he'd come home to take over the ranch so his father could retire.

He'd just turned thirty. Josie, twenty-four.

Prize-winning horses and Clay, right next door. Unfortunately, she hadn't known then that he'd brought more than just a fine string of horses to the Valle Verde. He'd brought the bitterness of a man who'd lost the woman he'd loved and had sworn never to love again.

She opened her eyes now, all the old regret coming back. She'd naively believed she could heal his broken heart, if Clay would give her the chance. If he'd see her as a woman—and not the tomboy she'd been. He'd once told her she was the wildest thing east of the Pecos, wilder than an "unbroke" stallion.

She hired on in his stables, mucking out the stalls, although she had a degree in ranch management. It wasn't until later that she'd found out Clay had only hired her as a favor to her family. It seemed Clay arrogantly believed he was the man who could handle her. That he would be the one to tame her wild spirit as a favor to her father and brothers.

How wrong he'd been. In the end, he'd only succeeded in spurring her to live up to his expectations—and her foolishness had ultimately cost her dearly.

Clay Jackson had never seen her as anything more than Dustin's wild kid sister. She doubted that would change when they saw each other again.

She looked over at her daughter, who was now banging the high-chair tray with her spoon and dropping globs of oatmeal to the floor with her other hand.

One thing was certain. She was *ready* to go home to Texas. But did she dare?

She turned at the sound of a car coming up the road. "Here comes Millie," she told her daughter.

Ivy stopped banging her tray to look out the porch screen at the approaching car. "Miwillie!" she cried, all smiles.

Josie lifted her daughter from the high chair and wiped her face, kissing the wriggling, giggling toddler's damp, clean cheek when she'd finished.

"Mornin'," Mildred Andrews called as she joined them on the porch. Mildred was short and squat, a small gray-haired woman in her early sixties with a pleasant round face and an ever-present cheerfulness. She made

Ivy laugh. She made Josie smile. There was something so homespun about the grandmotherly woman. And best of all, she loved children—especially Ivy. They'd hit it off immediately, and Josie felt secure knowing Mildred was caring for her daughter. She was the grandmother Ivy would never have.

"I thought I'd take Ivy into the big city," Mildred was saying. The big city Millie referred to was the tiny town of Three Forks, Montana, named for the Jefferson, Madison and Gallatin rivers that joined outside of town to make the Missouri River. "Can I get you anything from the grocery store?"

Josie scribbled down a quick list, the heavy weight of anxiety lightening at just the sight of Mildred. Ivy let out squeals of delight as the older woman took the list and Ivy out to the car. Ivy loved to go "bye-bye."

It wasn't until later, standing on the porch, watching Mildred pull away, Ivy waving and throwing wet kisses from the car seat in the back, that Josie felt a stab of doubt, like a thin blade of ice piercing her heart. She told herself she had nothing to worry about. Ivy was in good hands with Mildred. But she knew that wasn't what worried her. Dead or not, Odell Burton and the past were still haunting her.

She headed for the stables, knowing work would be the only thing that could get her mind off her worries.

By early afternoon, she was feeling better and relieved to see Mildred's car coming up the dirt road in a cloud of dust. Ivy's cherub-cheeked face peered out from the back seat.

Josie walked up the hillside to the cabin where she and Ivy lived, a rustic two-story log structure with a screened-in porch off the front and a deck and stairs off the back of the second story.

From the porch, Josie could see not only the stables and main ranch house, but beyond, across the valley and the Madison River, to the tops of the grain elevators in town.

But the view from the second-story deck off the back was her favorite. She often stood there, looking over the pines to the pale yellow band of sandstone known as the Madison Buffalo Jump. For years, before the Native Americans had horses, the site was used to harvest buffalo on foot.

Josie couldn't imagine a time when buffalo roamed this river valley. She especially couldn't imagine a time before horses. She'd had a horse since birth and had been riding almost as long. She loved horses and understood them in a way she'd never understood men.

Ivy was already out of the car and headed up the steps by the time Josie reached the cabin. She stopped at the car to help Mildred carry in the groceries. A widow, Mildred often stayed over. They'd fallen into the habit of having dinner together, with Mildred surprising them with her favorite dishes.

"Your daughter causes a commotion everywhere she goes," Mildred said, laughing as she lowered a bag of groceries to the table.

"A commotion?" Josie asked, eyeing Ivy as she let the screen door slam behind her.

The cabin was narrow, built tall rather than wide. It ran shotgun style from living room to kitchen with a set of open stairs on the left up to the second-floor bath and two bedrooms.

Josie heard Ivy let out a squeal as she took off across the living room after Millie.

"What did Ivy get into now?" Josie asked with a pretend groan as she set down her armful of groceries, then turned to grab her daughter as she toddled past. She scooped Ivy into her arms and hugged her tightly. She couldn't seem to hug her enough. Everything about the child filled her with awe. Josie never knew she could feel like this. It was the second revelation in her life.

"She was an absolute angel!" Mildred said in Ivy's defense. "It's not her fault that she's so adorable that even good-looking, smooth-talking cowboys can't resist her."

"Good-looking cowboys?" Josie asked, feeling the first prickle of unease as she put the wriggling Ivy back down.

"Even at the store," Mildred continued as she began putting Josie's groceries away. "He just couldn't take his eyes off her. He finally had to come over and say hello."

Josie felt a wave of anxiety flood her.

Mildred looked up and saw her reaction. "Oh, it wasn't like that. He was perfectly adorable. Polite with an accent like yours."

Josie felt the floor buckle under her. Blood drained from her head. Her ears rang. "A Texas accent?"

Mildred looked scared, too, now. She'd paled, her fingers nervously kneading the edges of a box of macaroni and cheese.

Josie could barely form the words. "What did he look like?"

"Oh, Josie, I didn't really pay him much mind," she cried. "He was just a nice-looking cowboy in jeans, boots and a Stetson. I guess he was tall and dark and—" She realized what she was saying. "—and yes, as corny

as it sounds, handsome. But he didn't do or say anything…inappropriate, and with tourists coming through
town all the time—"

"What did he do and say?" Josie asked, trying to keep
the fear out of her voice. Trying not to scare Mildred any
more than she already had.

"He said something like 'Oh, what a beautiful little
girl.' Ivy was giggling. She liked him. Then he said,
'She looks just like someone I used to know. The spitting image. Except for the eyes.' Something like that."

A chill raced up her spine like a Montana blizzard
blowing in. She tried to tell herself it was nothing. Just
like thinking she saw Odell in the pines yesterday.

This had only been a cowboy in a grocery store. Ivy
always attracted attention with that pale blond hair of
hers and her angelic face. And those startling dark eyes.
So why did Josie find herself shaking, fear making her
heart pound and her knees weak with worry?

She saw Mildred frown as if she'd remembered something that disturbed her. "What is it?"

"He *did* ask her name. I didn't think it would hurt
anything."

Josie found breath to ask. "You told him her name
was Ivy O'Malley?"

Mildred quickly shook her head. "I just told him her
name was Ivy."

Josie tried to breathe. She'd kept her name when she'd
left Texas. She'd wanted something of her family to take
with her, something to give her child, and after Odell's
death, she'd believed that no one would ever come looking for her.

But now she realized keeping her name had been a
silly, sentimental and very foolish thing to do. If some-

one from Texas *was* looking for her, she'd made it easy.
So didn't that mean if the man *had* been looking for her,
he'd have already found her? He wouldn't be watching
her from a stand of trees. Or chasing after Ivy in some
grocery store.

"I'm sure it was nothing," she said, trying to reassure
Mildred. Trying even harder to reassure herself.

Mildred looked more worried. "Do you think you
might know him?"

That was the question, wasn't it? Tall, dark and handsome definitely ruled out her brothers. They were tall,
handsome and quite the ladies' men with their Irish
charm, but they were blond like her.

Unfortunately, tall, dark and handsome *did* fit both
Odell Burton and Clay Jackson. But Odell was dead.
And Clay… Well, he didn't know where she was and
didn't have any reason to come looking for her. At least
not one he knew about.

*Don't panic. Mildred's right. It all sounds innocent
enough. So what if he had a Texas accent? Texas is a
big state. So what if he took an interest in Ivy?*

But Josie knew what she really feared. That the man
was somehow connected to Odell Burton and what had
happened in Texas two years ago.

"Did you happen to see what he was driving?" Josie
asked.

Mildred shook her head. "Did I do something
wrong?"

"No," she assured the older woman. "It might be someone I know from Texas. You see, no one back home knows
where I am. I left in a hurry." She smiled at Mildred. "I
found myself pregnant and knew if I stuck around, my
father would either demand a shotgun wedding or shoot

the man. The truth is, he'd have probably shot him." How could she explain the Texas law of the West when it came to daughters? Or for that matter, Texas cowboys and their codes of honor?

"It's none of my business," Mildred said. "I didn't mean to pry—"

"I want to tell you," she said. Mildred needed to know the truth—well at least some of it—to keep Ivy safe. "I didn't want anyone to know about Ivy or who her father was. He was the last thing Ivy and I needed."

"I'm sorry to hear that," Mildred said. "Then you think this man I saw might be looking for you?"

"I don't know," she admitted. But she intended to find out. If the man was still in town. "Would you mind watching Ivy for a little while tonight?"

Mildred readily agreed. "He really did seem like such a nice man."

There weren't many places to stay in a town the size of Three Forks, Montana. As Josie left in one of the old ranch trucks, instead of her own truck with Texas plates, she was thinking about where the cowboy stranger with the Texas accent might be staying.

She figured it wouldn't take much to find him—if he was still around. There was the Sacajawea Inn, a white, wood-framed historic hotel on the north edge of town. Or several motels.

She decided to start with the Broken Spur on the south end of town, but a block before the motel, she spotted a newer black Dodge pickup parked on a side street with the silhouette of a cowboy behind the wheel and Texas plates.

Distracted, she barely missed hitting an older model

Lincoln Continental that sped out of the Broken Spur motel parking lot and pulled in front of her, headed for Main Street.

Her heart was still pounding over her close call when a set of bright headlights filled her cab. She looked in her rearview mirror to see that the Dodge pickup with the Texas plates had pulled out and fallen in behind her.

Flipping up her rearview mirror, she pulled her western hat down and stayed low in her seat, telling herself the truck wasn't following her. Anyone going into town would come this way. It was a coincidence that the truck had pulled out behind her at that moment. Right.

She tried not to look back as she turned left onto Main Street. Downtown Three Forks was only about four blocks long. She went two of those blocks and parked diagonally between two cars in front of the Headwaters Café, the most well-lit part of town and the busiest this time of night.

Immediately she realized that if she got out, she'd be caught in the pickup's headlights like a deer on the highway. She shut off her engine and slid down in the seat, knowing no matter what she did, if the pickup *was* following her, the driver knew where to find her.

Facing the inescapable, she watched the pickup park back up the street a few spaces away. She could see the driver silhouetted behind the wheel, a man wearing a cowboy hat, his face shaded and dark. But she could tell he was looking her way. Her heart lurched, her pulse taking off at a sprint as he opened his pickup door and stepped out.

It had been two years since she'd last seen the tall, broad-shouldered cowboy, but there was no mistaking him or the impact he had on her.

He pushed back his Stetson and glanced in her direction as he walked toward her truck. Her breath caught in her throat. What was Clay Jackson doing in Montana?

Chapter 2

Josie held her breath as Clay started in her direction, her heart pounding. He stepped up onto the sidewalk, the heels of his expensive boots tapping lightly as he walked. He wore a gray Stetson, a western-cut leather coat and jeans. He looked like he belonged here. Or maybe Clay just had a way of looking like he belonged anywhere.

As he neared her truck, she slid farther down in the seat, afraid it would do no good. Of course he'd seen her. He'd been following her! He'd watched her park. He'd know that she hadn't had time to get out of the truck.

She grimaced, realizing she was caught. She waited for him to turn at her front left fender and walk back to her door, maybe tap on the window, or knowing Clay, just stand waiting until she acknowledged his presence.

To her amazement, he didn't slow in front of her truck, didn't come alongside. Instead, he walked to the café entrance, his gaze not on her or the ranch truck at all, but down the street, toward the Town Club bar, where the rusted, dented cream-colored Lincoln Continental that she'd almost hit a few minutes earlier was now parked.

In fact, it was as if he hadn't seen her at all slumped down in the seat, peeking out from under the brim of her hat.

It suddenly hit her. Clay Jackson hadn't been following her! Wasn't looking for her!

She felt a bubble of relieved laughter float up. As far as she could tell he didn't even know she was here in Three Forks.

But if he wasn't looking for her, then what was he doing here?

She watched with interest as he entered the Headwaters Café, took a seat at a front table. He looked out the large picture window in the direction of the Lincoln as a waitress slid a cup of coffee in front of him. The Lincoln hadn't moved, but the driver, Josie noticed, was no longer inside.

She studied Clay, thinking how little he'd changed, as if life had stood still back in Texas, back on his Valle Verde Ranch. While time had flown for her and everything had changed—especially her. And yet just the sight of him still evoked a mix of emotions, regret at the top of the list and an even stronger emotion that she'd spent two years trying to forget.

She rolled down her window and let the cool air rush in, feeling the flush of memory play in her mind like a country-western song, making her ache with a longing of something unfulfilled. An odd feeling, considering the way things had ended.

She forced another memory to the surface, one that firmly put her feet back on the ground and cleared her head of all romantic notions about him. The day Clay Jackson had forbidden her to go near his prized horses other than to clean out their stalls.

But as she watched him now, she knew her problems with Clay ran a lot deeper than his horses. Or her unresolved feelings for him.

She studied him, wondering what he could be doing here. She doubted horses had brought him all the way to Montana.

As she watched him idly sip his coffee, she realized she wasn't going to find out. He wasn't looking for her. Wasn't that enough? She started the truck and backed out, hoping he wouldn't notice her. It hadn't been that long ago she'd wanted more than anything for Clay to notice her. To see her not as Shawn O'Malley's wild daughter but as the woman she'd become.

Funny how times had changed.

Keeping her face turned away, she drove away from the café—and Clay—down to the end of the street and doubled back, taking side streets until she was clear of town.

She told herself that the man Mildred had seen at the grocery store had to have been Clay. But he wouldn't have recognized Ivy as being Josie's. Or guessed who the father was. He had more pressing concerns than a fourteen-month-old toddler with pale blond hair and dark eyes. Or that baby's mother. But just in case, Josie would stay close to the ranch and keep Ivy close as well.

She peeked in on Ivy when she reached the cabin, only to find her sleeping, looking like an angel. She bent down and kissed her warm, plump cheek and breathed in her smell, smiling at the sight of her precious daughter. She felt blessed.

For a few moments, Josie let herself think about Ivy's father, then quickly banished the thought. Some things were best left buried, she thought as she closed the door softly and asked Mildred if she would like to stay over.

Mildred looked tired and worried, but she didn't ask what Josie had found out in town. She readily accepted the invitation to spend the night on the couch. Josie wondered if Mildred stayed because she was concerned about her and Ivy. That would be like Mildred, Josie thought as she went to get the older woman a pillow and some bedding from the closet.

Too restless and wide awake to sleep, Josie went out on the porch and sat down on the step to stare up at the stars.

A pine-scented breeze skittered coolly across her bare arms, making goose bumps rise on her skin. She hugged herself. She'd done the right thing two years ago. The only thing she could do. No reason to start doubting herself now.

But she felt uneasy and knew it was more than just knowing Clay Jackson was in town or seeing some man in the trees the night before. It was the unshakable feeling that her past had come looking for her before she'd finished what she had to do. Before she could go home to Texas and face it as she'd planned.

She leaned back against the step and began counting the stars overhead, anything to distract her from thinking about Clay. Or worse, worrying about why he was in town.

Just an unhappy coincidence.

Right.

She caught the flicker of a light below her on the hillside not far from the stables and the creek.

Must be the owner of the ranch, Ruth Slocum, since she was the only other person here besides Mildred, and Mildred was snoring on the couch.

Josie sat up straighter. The faint light moved like a firefly through the dark. She watched it quickly disappear into the stables. Something must be wrong for Ruth to be in the stables this late at night. Odder yet, why had she come from the creek instead of her ranch house, which was in the opposite direction? Had one of the horses gotten out?

Worried, Josie got a flashlight from her truck and started down the hill.

The moon crested the mountains in a sky shot with stars. The breeze whispered through the tall, dew-damp grass, sending up the sweet scent of spring. Grass pulled at her boots, the night sky at her soul, making her feel small and insignificant.

She pushed open the stable door, surprised to find darkness. Reaching for the light switch, she stopped herself.

Through a crack in the tack room door at the end of the stables, she saw the flicker again of a flashlight, followed by a rustling sound.

She frowned and clicked on her own flashlight, keeping it aimed low at her feet as she moved slowly forward. Ruth wouldn't be rummaging around in the tack room at this time of the night. Not with a flashlight. Ruth had recently broken her ankle; even with her cane and walking cast, she had trouble getting around.

Just as those thoughts took hold—and their possible significance—Josie reached the tack room door. It hung open only a few inches, just enough that she could see a shadow moving around behind it and hear the thump of saddles being dropped to the floor.

But it was another sound that made her freeze. This one behind her. The stable door she'd just come through opened with a rush of cool night air.

Startled, she swung around, banging the flashlight into a post with a resounding thud. The flashlight went out.

From inside the tack room, something fell or was dropped. The narrow beam of light blinked off, pitching the stables into a dense, silent dark.

She could feel the presence of the person who'd just entered the stables but couldn't see him. And she knew someone was still in the dark tack room, closer by. She held her breath, afraid to move.

Suddenly the tack room door flew open and a large, solid body hit her, sending her sprawling to the floor, knocking the air from her lungs. Whoever it was bolted for the nearby back door. A little of the yard light spilled in as a man-sized figure ran out, the door banging behind him.

Before she could get to her feet, someone tripped over her. She heard a loud male curse, then the sound of his body hitting the dirt. He quickly scrambled to his feet and ran toward the back door of the stables. The back door banged open again.

Before it could bang closed, the sound of a car engine roared to life, followed by another male curse. Then the sound of boot heels, slowly working their way back to her as the door banged shut again.

She was on all fours when the stable lights flashed on.

She looked up to see a large cowboy silhouetted against the bright light, his Stetson shadowing his face.

"What the hell?" the cowboy cursed.

She didn't need to see his face. She knew that body and that voice. Had heard that tone used in connection with her on numerous occasions.

Inwardly groaning, she hoisted herself to her feet, and dusting her backside, blinked as her eyes adjusted to the bright light. If anything, this close, he looked more handsome. Dark from his thick black hair to his eyes. His Spanish blood, although two generations removed, still fired passionately in his eyes. Unfortunately, that passion was almost always anger. "Hello, Jackson."

Clay stared in stunned disbelief. He couldn't have been more shocked to see anyone. Hadn't he thought he'd seen her a couple hundred times over the past two years? Each time gave him a start. A jolt of pure electric shock that jump-started his heart and made it take off like an escaped con at the sound of a bloodhound.

"Josie." Even to his ears it sounded like a curse. He stared at her, assaulted with too many thoughts, too many memories and feelings.

Josie O'Malley. After all this time—and looking just as she had the last time he'd seen her. No, he realized as he studied her. She'd changed, although he couldn't put his finger on exactly how.

Her pale blond hair was still short and unruly, as if she'd just run her fingers through it. Her eyes were still that unbelievable blue. Clear as a Texas summer sky but unreadable as if the cool veneer masked a well of secrets. No doubt they did.

And she still had that defiant look, of course. She'd

always been a spitfire. Rebellious, headstrong and willful as a wild mustang. Her father had actually thought Clay could do something with her. It had proved an impossible task. One he'd failed at miserably.

She was still slim and small, about five six in boots, but rounded. Actually more rounded than he remembered.

"What the hell are you doing here, Josie?" he demanded.

"What am *I* doing here?" she snapped, crossing her arms over the breasts he'd just been staring at. "What are *you* doing here is more to the point."

He jerked his gaze away, trying to make sense of this. But after one glance at the rear door of the stables, he narrowed his eyes at her again, seeing things a whole lot clearer. "*You* tripped me."

"Excuse me?" She hadn't lost her Texas twang—or her temper. Her blue eyes fired like forged steel. That was definitely something time hadn't changed.

Her first instinct was to tell him it wasn't any of his business. "I happen to work here."

"Work here?" he repeated, and glanced down the line of stalls.

She knew what he was thinking. That she shoveled manure—just as she had in his stables. What did she care what he thought? It made her more angry, though, that she *did* care.

"You work strange hours," he commented. "Or are you going to tell me that you just happened to be down here in the middle of the night, didn't bother to turn on the lights and just happened to be on the floor to trip me?"

She gritted her teeth, reminded of just how irritating

this man could be. She bit off each word. "I saw a light and someone come in here so I walked down to check. I was just about to find out who when *you* came in and scared whoever it was away."

He raised an eyebrow.

"Whoever it was knocked me down and then you tripped over me," she continued, daring him to interrupt. "But that doesn't explain what *you're* doing here." What *was* he doing here? In Montana? But more important, on the ranch where she worked?

"I'm looking for someone."

She stared at him, her heart pounding. "Anyone in particular?"

"A thief," he said grudgingly. "I've been following him for the past four days. Unofficially, of course."

For a moment she'd thought he'd come to see her—even though she knew from watching him in town it wasn't true. When was she going to quit kidding herself when it came to this man?

"He led me from Texas to this stable."

She didn't like the sound of this. "Why would you follow a petty thief all the way from Texas?" She glanced toward the tack room. To this particular stable?

He frowned. "Petty? I don't think several million in jewels is petty, do you?"

Her heart looped in her chest. Hadn't she feared that the past had come looking for her? Worse yet, in the form of Clay Jackson, the one man she had reason to fear the most.

Did he just imagine the surprise that flashed in her eyes? The worry? God knows, he'd read more in her expression than he should have in the past.

She didn't answer. If anything, she seemed to be

doing her best to look innocent. It was a look she'd perfected, but he knew her too well to fall for it.

"Actually, you know him," he said. Maybe had stayed in contact with him. "An old friend of *yours*."

It was hard to tell if she really did pale under the harsh light in the stable. Maybe he just wanted to see guilt in her eyes. Suspected it. Expected it. The same way he suspected she'd purposely tripped him to allow the thief to get away. After growing up next door to her, he'd have said he knew Josie O'Malley better than anyone.

But two years ago, she'd made him realize that he didn't know her as well as he'd thought.

"An old friend of *mine?*" she asked innocently.

Yes, he definitely glimpsed a crack in her composure. He smiled at her, but there was no humor behind it. Something hot tore at his insides. "You remember Raymond Degas," he said, studying her.

No doubt about it. The last of the color drained from her face.

"Raymond?"

"Come on, Josie," he prodded, his guts on fire. "You had to have heard about the jewel heist two years ago. Raymond and Odell were the number-one suspects. Raymond disappeared. Odell got himself killed. The jewels never turned up."

He felt frustration and anger burn in him. He'd held this woman at arm's length for years until two years ago. After Maria, he'd sworn he'd never let himself feel like that for a woman again.

But Josie had changed that. Damn her, she'd made him want her. Made him want *only* her. She'd dared him to love again, and just when he thought he might take the chance, she'd taken off. Without a word.

What made it worse was she'd disappeared right after the jewel heist.

It would have been suspicious enough if she hadn't been thick as thieves with Odell Burton and his buddy Raymond Degas at the time.

But Clay knew his suspicions ran much deeper. Deeper than he wanted to admit.

He watched her swallow, her gaze sliding away from his.

"I'm afraid I had other things on my mind two years ago," she said. She looked at him again, nothing showing in her face or her eyes now, as if she'd dropped a curtain over her emotions. He recalled the last time he'd seen her do that. Had she been trying to hide something then, too? The thought unnerved him.

But he had her now and he wasn't going to let go until he got the truth out of her. About everything.

Josie watched him glance toward the tack room.

"What do you suppose Raymond was doing in your tack?" he asked.

She didn't answer. She figured Clay had his own theories about that. She was shocked that Raymond had been here at all, let alone Clay.

"Suppose we take a look?" he said, indicating she could go first.

She thought about putting up an argument. Clay had no authority here. Nor did she take orders from him anymore—not that she ever had, without an argument. But she didn't want him forcing the issue by insisting they call the cops or wake up the ranch owner. The fewer people who knew about Clay Jackson and her past, the better. And she had a feeling that the thief hadn't found what he was looking for, anyway.

The tack room had been ransacked, all the tack and saddles pulled down in a heap in the middle of the floor.

"What would Raymond have wanted in here?" Clay said. "Have any ideas?"

Oh, she had lots of ideas, but none she wanted to share with him. She remembered the Lincoln Continental he'd been watching from the café in town. Was it Raymond's? But what would have brought Raymond to Three Forks? "Maybe he was looking for something to steal. You did say he was an alleged thief."

Clay smiled at her attempt at alleged humor. "Kind of a long drive to steal tack."

Had Clay really followed Raymond Degas all the way from Texas? All the way to the stables where she just happened to work? Quite a coincidence, if you believed in them. She had a feeling Clay didn't.

"Anything seem to be missing?" His tone made it clear he doubted it.

"We must have scared him away before he had a chance to steal something," she said, torn between despair and anger as he tried to provoke her.

"Convenient." He was eyeing her as if waiting for her to give him some answer.

Damn you, Jackson, she thought. *I don't owe you any explanations.* Well, at least not any she was willing to make. Including why she'd left Texas the way she had two years ago.

"Convenient that *you* just happened to scare him away when I reached the stables," he said, not willing to let it go. "And what a coincidence that Raymond Degas broke into the stable where you work."

She'd known that was coming.

"On top of that, you just happen to trip me and keep

me from catching him," Clay finished, and crossed his arms, waiting, challenging her.

How much did this really have to do with the robbery? Clay hadn't wanted her, but he hadn't wanted anyone else to have her, either. She felt all that old resentment rising like steam off a geyser.

She thought of Ivy and blew out a long, heated breath. "You believe what you want. You always have."

She turned away and started out of the tack room. She'd clean up the mess tomorrow. "If it was even Raymond," she added.

He moved in front of her, reminding her how fast he was on his feet as he blocked the door, blocked her exit. "It *was* Raymond." His voice was deep and soft and sent a chill through her as she was reminded of another time and place that Clay Jackson had been this close.

"Raymond led me all the way from Texas straight as a shot to you," Clay said, leaning closer, trapping her. "Come on, Josie. We both know what Raymond's looking for."

He was so close she could feel his breath against her cheek, smell his too-familiar male scent. Everything about him seemed to radiate a low-frequency electricity. She felt a buzz when she was around him and always had. But it seemed stronger somehow. More so than she remembered it.

"He's looking for the jewels."

She swallowed but said nothing, her nerves raw with the nearness of him. His body seemed to fill the tack room, making it as hot and sultry as a Texas summer night.

"That's right, you don't know anything about the robbery," he said, his tone clearly calling her a liar. "A rare

collection of rubies, diamonds and emeralds, all irre-
placeable. Intact, the jewelry would be impossible to
fence. Too distinctive. Too easy to track. So what would
the thieves do?"

How would she know? Why would she care? She
knew nothing about getting rid of stolen property. And
why did Clay Jackson *think* she did?

She shook her head, slowly, infinitesimally, afraid
to move too much for fear of touching him. Or worse,
him touching her.

He smiled. A halogen smile against the dark stubble of a day's growth of beard. He leaned so close it reminded her of the last time she'd seen him two years
ago. He'd kissed her beside her barn in Texas. She didn't
need the reminder. Not now. Not anymore.

She held her breath. But he didn't kiss her, although
she did wonder if he, too, had been reminded of that
kiss. Had purposely made her remember.

"It's hard to believe a petty small-time criminal like
Raymond could pull off such a score, isn't it?" he said.
"Even with the help of someone like Odell Burton."

She'd known Clay would get to Odell eventually. "I
heard he was dead."

"Yeah, but he'd have needed an accomplice."

"Raymond."

He shook his head slowly, his smile gone. "I'm talking about someone smart. Someone who knew about
the security plans and knew how to get them. Talk to
me, Josie," he whispered. "Tell me what really happened
that night."

Something in his voice, a slight break that could have
been born of passion or pain, made her wonder which
night he was referring to. She looked into his eyes and

felt that old familiar rush. Like standing on the edge of a cliff. A combination of danger and exhilaration. Fear and longing. Her pulse pounded in her ears. Her heart drummed, the beat accelerating.

"Josie? Are you all right?"

They both turned at the sound of the voice behind them past the open tack room doorway. Mildred stood in the light, her expression worried. In her arms, she held a sleepy-eyed Ivy.

"Ivy woke and was frightened," Mildred said. "We came down to look for you—"

Clay stepped from the doorway and Josie rushed past him to take Ivy in her arms.

"Ma-ma," Ivy said, and snuggled against her.

Josie heard Clay's quick intake of breath as he came out of the tack room. She cradled her daughter to her, bracing herself as she turned and let her gaze rise to his.

He stared at her, then Ivy, his dark eyes wide with shock for the second time tonight. "I knew it," he whispered. "I damn well knew it."

"I understand you've already met my daughter Ivy," Josie said, bracing herself for the inevitable.

He dragged his gaze from Ivy's face to her own. His expression darkened, like a storm rolling in.

"I always wondered why you left Texas in such a hurry," he said, his words striking her like stones. "I guess I know now. At least one of the reasons. Did Odell know he had a daughter? Or is that just another of your well-kept secrets?"

Chapter 3

Josie with a baby! The same little girl he'd seen in town with the elderly baby-sitter he'd mistaken for a grandmother. Hadn't the toddler reminded him so much of Josie that he hadn't been able to resist taking a closer look?

But the little girl hadn't had Josie's incredible blue eyes. Now he realized that was because the baby had taken after her father, Odell.

He should have known. This at least explained part of Josie's hurried departure from Texas. No wonder she hadn't told her family.

He stared at Ivy for a long moment, surprised by the emotions that rushed him. She looked so much like her mother. In fact, she was the spitting image of Josie—except for the eyes.

This could have been my child.

The thought came out of left field, blindsiding him.

Josie hugged Ivy protectively to her, telling herself she shouldn't have been surprised. She should have known he'd see Odell in her daughter. Should have known he'd question if Odell had known she was pregnant. Still, she felt sick inside. What would he do now?

Or was that the least of her worries?

She looked into his angry face, trying hard to understand what it was about her that made him so angry with her. "Odell knew I was pregnant."

That seemed to surprise him. "You told him?"

"He guessed," she admitted.

Clay frowned. "That must have been what the two of you were arguing about that day by your barn. I'm sure Odell wanted nothing to do with a baby."

She looked down at her daughter. Ivy had fallen asleep again, her tiny cherub cheek warm and pink against Josie's shoulder, the dimpled arms locked around her neck. Odell had been furious about her pregnancy. She shivered at the memory of his threat.

When she looked up again, Clay's gaze seemed to soften. "So you struck out on your own. Just the two of you."

Was that grudging admiration she heard in his voice?

"What did you use for money, Josie? I know you didn't take much with you when you left."

So much for admiration. She knew what he was implying. "I *worked*."

"Pregnant?"

"I did what I had to do," she said stubbornly, unwilling to admit how she'd really managed alone, broke and pregnant. Unwilling because she was ashamed of what she'd done. And it really wasn't any of his business.

"You know I'm going to find out the truth."

"My life doesn't have anything to do with you." Even as she said it, she knew that wasn't true. Clay was definitely one of the reasons she'd left Texas.

"We should get the baby to bed," Mildred interrupted.

They both looked over at her. Clay seemed to have forgotten she was standing there, she'd been so quiet. And Josie had been distracted. Clay did that to her.

"Yes, you should get your baby to bed," Clay said. "But you and I aren't finished, Josie. Not by a long shot."

She feared that was true as she slipped past him and headed back up the hill to her cabin with Mildred beside her.

"Who is that man?" Mildred asked when they were out of earshot.

"A neighbor of my family's in Texas. I used to work for him."

Mildred said nothing, but Josie knew the older woman realized there was a lot more to it.

"He's the man I saw at the grocery store," Mildred said. "What does he want?" She sounded worried.

"He's here investigating a robbery."

"He's a policeman?" Mildred asked, sounding surprised but also relieved.

"No, he's a former deputy sheriff, but he's here unofficially." She could tell Mildred feared that he meant her or Ivy harm. "Don't worry. He'll catch his crook and be gone soon."

They walked in silence to the cabin, each lost in her own thoughts.

"You know, I might go on home, if you think you'll be all right tonight," Mildred said when they'd reached the cabin. "With all the excitement, I'm wide awake."

Josie understood perfectly. Mildred said she cleaned when she was upset. Something told Josie that Mildred's house was in for a scrubbin'. "We'll be fine."

Mildred bid her good-night after making certain that Josie had her pepper spray handy.

Josie watched her leave, worrying that Clay's departure wouldn't be that simple. Nothing with Clay had ever been simple. And she now had Raymond Degas to worry about as well.

As Clay left the stables, he heard the high-pitched whinny of a horse. He looked toward the pasture and spotted a stallion standing in the moonlight watching him. The image gave him a start, the horse reminded him so much of Diablo. But while Diablo had been black as midnight, this horse was a blood bay. Like Diablo, though, it stood at least seventeen hands high and had that spirited, wild look in its eyes.

The stallion watched him warily, then took off as if touched with an electric prod, disappearing into the darkness, leaving Clay with one lasting impression. That horse was dangerous. Just like Diablo had been.

But he knew that wasn't why he'd gotten rid of Diablo. Even after the horse had almost killed him, he'd sold him because Diablo reminded him too much of Josie and an unforgettable dream he'd had about both of them.

Once at his truck, he drove up the road, parking out of sight of Josie's cabin. Then, taking his bedroll, he cut through the pines until he could see the cabin without being seen. He tossed down the bag and plopped down on it.

Raymond Degas would be back. Not tonight, probably. But sometime. Clay was betting that Raymond hadn't found what he'd been looking for. And when he returned, Clay intended to be here.

When the lights blinked out in Josie's cabin, he tried to get some sleep, but he couldn't quit thinking about her.

Seeing her again had shaken him, much more than he wanted to admit. She was more beautiful than even he remembered. And the baby—

Odell's child, he reminded himself.

He tried to think about the jewels and his quest for them, rather than Josie. But it was impossible.

He'd often wondered if Josie had somehow been involved in the robbery. Raymond leading him right to her left little doubt that his suspicions about her had been warranted. It gave him no satisfaction, though.

But if she'd been in on the jewel heist, then why was Raymond rummaging around in the stables in the dark instead of just asking Josie for what he wanted?

Clay swore. Unless Josie had double-crossed Odell and Raymond and taken the jewels.

That seemed pretty far-fetched, considering the woman was pregnant at the time. But with Josie O'Malley he wouldn't rule out anything.

He even blamed her for the dream that had plagued him for the past two years. A dream he now thought of as That Damned Dream.

He'd started having the dream after being bucked off Diablo not once—but twice in twenty-four hours. The dream was always the same: Josie O'Malley riding through a creek toward him on the large black horse, the Texas hill country behind her, the horse's hooves throwing up water droplets that hung in the moonlight. Josie coming out of the darkness of the live oaks and into the moonlight, wearing a yellow dress, her shoulders bare, the wet cotton clinging to her skin. She was buck-naked beneath the dress! Her nipples dark and hard, pressing against the soaked fabric as she dismounted and came to him where he'd fallen from the horse, her blue eyes filled with a longing that matched his own.

Definitely a fantasy dream. It disturbed him that he'd had it at all. He'd never thought of Josie like…that. Nor did he want to.

On top of that, the dream mocked him with the incredible impossibility of it. Josie had been riding the horse that had thrown him and then run off—Diablo, his wild green-broke stallion, and she was way too inexperienced to ride a horse like that, let alone one as unpredictable as Diablo.

He'd awoken the next morning, horseless, with a knot the size of Texas on his head, a terrible headache and no memory of what had happened. But with the ground under him instead of a horse, he had a pretty good idea what had taken place.

It had been a fool thing, trying to ride Diablo. Especially in the mood he'd been in. He'd caught Odell Burton in his barn with Josie, gotten into a fight with him and made Josie mad. Although he'd won the fight, he still had the scar where Odell's ring had cut him.

In a foul mood by that time, he'd gotten half drunk and decided to ride Diablo. Not his best decision.

The next morning when he limped back to the ranch, he'd seen Josie—again with Odell, but he'd had the good sense to stay clear of them both.

That's when he started having That Damned Dream. The last thing he'd needed was Josie O'Malley in his dreams. Having her around his ranch was trouble enough without conjuring up the feel, smell and taste of her the moment he closed his eyes.

On top of that, she didn't get over being mad at him from what he could tell. He and Josie had argued enough over how to break horses.

Six weeks later, the jewels were stolen from the Williams Gallery in town where the collection was to go on display. He'd acted as a consultant on the security plans. In fact, he had a copy of the plans in his locked desk drawer at the ranch.

That's when the first inkling of suspicion about Josie started. When Brandon Williams, the jewel collector, called to ask if Clay still had his copy. Williams felt the only way the thieves could have pulled off the heist was with the plans.

When Clay had gone to his desk, he'd found the plans—but someone had been in the locked drawer. They'd used a key, because the lock hadn't been tampered with—and he had the only key.

He'd assured Brandon Williams that his plans were there, keeping his suspicions to himself. Temporarily.

With Odell Burton and Raymond Degas wanted for questioning in the heist, Clay wondered if one of them could have somehow gotten his keys. That seemed impossible. But Odell was always hanging around Josie.

He'd saddled up and ridden over to the O'Malley ranch. Josie was by the barn. Clay wasn't surprised when Odell came out of the barn, looking angry.

He rode toward them, unable to hear their words, but he could see that they were obviously arguing. Odell had grabbed Josie's arm, and she seemed to be trying to fight him off.

Odell spotted him as he rode up and took off before Clay's boot soles hit the dust beside Josie.

"Don't" was all Josie said when she saw him. She was crying and upset.

Without thinking, he'd pulled her into his arms and kissed her. A crazy impulse. He hadn't known it at the time, but it would be the last time he'd see her until today. It had been one amazing goodbye kiss.

After it was over, she'd pulled back, confusion in her gaze. Her eyes had filled with tears. "What do you want from me, Jackson?"

When he didn't answer, she spun on her heel and left him standing with his reins in his hand.

He'd watched her go, fighting the urge to go after her. What *did* he want from her? He'd told himself he didn't know. Getting involved with Josie O'Malley was definitely out of the question. So he'd swung up into the saddle and ridden off, kicking himself for kissing her.

The next day he'd discovered that she'd packed up and left Texas, lock, stock and barrel. At the time, he'd blamed himself. For kissing her. For being jealous and possessive when he had no right. For being angry with her for making him want her. Because by then, he'd realized that he did want her. Like he'd never wanted any woman before. He just wasn't fool enough to confuse that with love and all that went with it.

A week later Odell was killed in a fiery car crash. Raymond Degas had already disappeared, just like Josie. And the jewels had never been found.

He'd been suspicious of Josie's timing when she'd left. But now as he stared down at the cabin below him on the hillside, he didn't kid himself that she wasn't somehow involved, and damned if he'd let any feelings for her or her baby keep him from proving it.

In the wee hours of the morning, he finally dropped off into a bottomless sleep. In the dream, Josie rode to him on a dark stallion, coming out of the creek, her dress wet and clinging to her naked body. A body he knew as well as his own.

Clay woke, heart pounding, drenched with sweat. The bright sun told him it was morning. His aching head and the lingering memory of the dream assured him it wasn't going to be a good day.

Chapter 4

He bathed in the icy creek, hoping the cold would rid him of the images of Josie, her body flushed with desire. But while the freezing-cold water curbed his desire temporarily, it did nothing for his mood.

He called Texas, dialing Brandon Williams's number. Four days ago when he'd called Williams to tell him that he'd gotten a lead on the stolen jewels, the man hadn't been exactly appreciative.

"I'd put that unfortunate incident behind me," he snapped. "Nice of you to call and remind me of my loss."

Williams, a physically fit man in his late forties with a small fortune and an appetite for expensive things, was a pain in the neck. Clay couldn't wait until he could return the jewels to the obnoxious man and hopefully prove to himself that the thieves hadn't gotten the security plans from his desk.

"I got a lead on Raymond Degas."

That had definitely surprised Williams. "Really? Where is he?"

"On the move. I intend to stay with him and see where he takes me."

Williams believed he'd never see his precious jewels again. That was enough of a challenge for Clay, even if he hadn't felt he might be responsible.

"Have you found my jewels?" Williams asked now without preamble.

He gritted his teeth, his already-bad mood darkening. He wished now he hadn't promised to call Williams daily. He wanted to say, "Get the money ready to return to the insurance company," but instead he said, "Not yet." With Raymond out of hiding, Clay had the feeling that it was just a matter of time before he found the jewels, and he couldn't wait to see Williams's face when he handed them to him.

"I'm making progress," he told Williams. "He broke into a local ranch here last night."

"Really?" Williams actually sounded interested.

Clay told him about the tack room break-in, but left out anything about Josie. He didn't want Williams to know that he suspected Josie, let alone that Raymond led him right to her.

"Keep me informed," Williams ordered, and hung up.

Clay turned off his cell phone and cursed. He wanted this over with as quickly as possible. Also, the less time he spent around Josie, the better. He knew Josie felt the same way about him.

He finished dressing and rubbed his jaw. He needed a shave and a decent night's sleep. As he headed toward her cabin, his stomach growled and he added food to his list of needs. He could smell coffee and cinnamon toast. He stopped at the sight of Josie on the porch, having breakfast with Ivy. A shave, food and sleep weren't all he needed.

His conviction to nail her for the robbery faltered as he watched her with her daughter, watched how loving, tender, patient and sweet she was with Ivy.

He smiled at one distinct memory of her as a kid trying to ride some rough stock her father and older brothers had forbidden her to go near. He'd watched her from the fence rail, knowing the minute her father and brothers turned their backs, she'd try to ride that blamed green horse.

She hated anyone to tell her she couldn't do something and she resented her bossy brothers. Unfortunately, that day she'd gotten bucked off and broken her arm. But Clay had always admired her grit.

He frowned and pushed the memory away, reminding himself that she was now in a different trouble league. Jewel theft. And this time, he wasn't silently cheering her on from the sidelines. He was the one who'd have to take her down, and he feared she was up to her pretty little neck in this mess. He just hadn't figured how yet.

When the blue Honda drove up and the woman he'd seen last night in the stables went up to the cabin to stay with Ivy, he followed Josie down to the stables, keeping himself hidden. He figured she knew he'd be around and fairly close, but he didn't want her to see him. Not yet, anyway.

He'd expected her to disappear into the stables for several hours of horse feeding and stable cleaning. Instead she reappeared moments later, leading the wild stallion he'd seen last night toward a round, enclosed pen. The horse jerked at the halter she had on him and snorted and kicked.

His chest constricted. Anyone could see that the stallion was dangerous. Especially in the wrong hands. What did Josie think she was going to do with the beast?

He followed her until she disappeared into the door of the pen, the stallion obviously upset and anxious. On the far side of the building, he found another door. Inside, a small viewing area had been cut out of the side of the enclosure. He opened the door and slipped in. The area was small with a single bench. It ran in front of a long, narrow window that looked down into the pen. He didn't sit but stayed back in the shadows to watch.

Josie stopped in the center of the circular pen to rub the flat of her hand over the horse's forehead, her movements slow, graceful, gentle. The stallion snorted and jerked his head, ears up and back as Josie slid off the halter.

Sensing its freedom, the stallion took off, running around in a circle, obviously nervous and tense.

Josie pulled a coil of light rope from beneath her jeans jacket and let the bulk of it drop to the dirt floor. The horse eyed her, looking as wary as Clay felt. Josie held the stallion's gaze as, from the center of the pen, she began to pitch the line at the horse's flank, sending him cantering around her.

What the hell did she think she was doing? A horse like that could be unpredictable. Dangerous. At any moment, the stallion could turn on her and kill her before she could get out.

"Fool woman," he cursed.

He spun around at the sound of a soft chuckle behind him to find an elderly woman with a cane standing in the doorway. She didn't seem surprised to see him as she let the door close behind her.

"Are you familiar with this type of horse training?" she asked, her voice stronger than he'd expected. She was tall, rawboned and weathered, with sharp eyes and a determined air about her. A horsewoman. She used the cane to maneuver herself over to the window and the bench in front of it. She wore a walking cast on her left ankle and seemed to belong here. He took her for the ranch owner.

"I've heard about it," he said.

She chuckled again as she took a seat on the bench. "Please join me."

He wondered if she had any idea who he was. Or what he was doing here. She didn't seem to care as he sat next to her. Her attention was on what was happening in the ring below them.

Anxiously, he watched Josie pitch the line at the stallion as he cantered around the fifty-foot circle. The horse watched Josie as closely as she appeared to be watching him.

Suddenly she flicked the line in front of him. The stallion swung around and ran in the opposite direction, keeping close to the wall, his eye still on her.

"Watch his inside ear," the elderly woman said as she leaned forward on her cane.

To his surprise, while the stallion's outside ear continued to monitor his surroundings, the inside ear locked on Josie.

"Watch his head," the woman ordered.

The stallion dipped his head, turning it slightly toward Josie, and settled into a steady trot.

"He'll start licking and chewing and running his tongue outside his mouth," the older woman predicted.

Sure enough.

"It's a show of respect," the woman said, looking over at him. "And a willingness to cooperate."

Clay sat up, leaning toward the window as Josie dropped the line, then angled both her body and her gaze away from the horse. The stallion slowed, then stopped to look at her.

Clay held his breath. Josie seemed so small inside the pen with the powerful horse. Too small.

Then she did something Clay couldn't believe. She turned her back on the stallion.

"Fool woman," he breathed, his heart pounding as he feared what the horse would do. "She's going to get herself killed."

"Then you don't know Josie O'Malley," the woman said as she put a hand on his arm to keep him from rising.

The stallion approached Josie from behind, but she didn't turn. Just inches away, the horse reached out with his large head. Clay held his breath, his heart pounding.

The stallion touched his nose to Josie's shoulder. She turned slowly, and he watched as the horse let her rub the spot between his eyes.

Amazing. Josie had this high-strung, unbroken horse eating out of her hand. He stared in disbelief as she turned and walked away and the stallion followed her like a pet dog.

He wouldn't have believed it, especially after seeing the stallion in the corral last night. The horse had had that wild look—the same look Clay had glimpsed in Josie's eyes a time or two.

But now as he watched her, a thought hit him right between the eyes like a brick. The way she handled that stallion... If Josie had been able to tame that wild stallion, then maybe she'd somehow been able to smooth-talk Diablo into letting her ride him.

"Well?" the elderly woman asked, jerking him back from the thought.

"She must have worked with the horse before," Clay said, unwilling to accept what he'd just seen.

"Are you always so skeptical and suspicious?" the woman beside him asked, those keen eyes on him.

"I just know that horses are like women. Unpredictable. Often dangerous. And it's usually a mistake to turn your back on them."

She laughed and held out her hand. "Ruth Slocum. Owner of the Buffalo Jump Ranch. And you are..."

"Clay Jackson," he said, not at all surprised by the strength he found in her handshake.

She slanted her head, still openly studying him. "I understand you're here investigating a crime?"

"Unofficially. I followed a suspected jewel thief to your stables last night." He didn't mention his suspicions about Josie. Not yet.

"I heard someone got into the tack room, but a jewel thief? What would a jewel thief want in my stables?"

"That's the question, isn't it?" he said, glancing down into the pen at Josie.

Ruth Slocum followed his gaze but said nothing.

Chapter 5

"He's certainly a handsome devil," Ruth said as she sat down to the table on Josie's porch.

"Don't say that too loudly," Josie warned as she slid Ivy into her high chair. "It's a bad idea to feed *that* man's ego, and knowing him, he isn't far away."

Her boss smiled. "What about feeding his stomach? I heard it growling while we were watching you gentle that new stallion this morning."

Josie looked up in surprise, almost dropping the bowl of macaroni salad she'd whipped up for their lunch. "Jackson watched?"

"You seem surprised," Ruth said.

She'd known he'd hang around, but she never dreamed he'd have any interest in her work. "He and I never agreed on horse training. Or much of anything else, for that matter." She handed the bowl to Mildred, who was already seated but hadn't said much.

"I think he's here to make trouble for Josie and Ivy," Mildred blurted.

Ruth raised a brow at her friend. "Oh, you do, do you?" She chuckled. "What do you think, Josie?"

She felt the woman's sharp eyes on her as she sat down. "I think he's on a wild-goose chase. But I hope he finds what he's looking for soon and leaves."

Ruth nodded and glanced toward the pines behind the cabin. "Don't you think you should invite him to lunch?"

"With us?" Mildred asked, apparently shocked that her old friend would want to share the table with him.

"Better to have him where we can see him, don't you think?" Ruth said.

Josie hesitated. She could tell that Ruth was taken with Clay, although other than his looks, she couldn't imagine why. But not asking him to lunch would look as if she had reason to avoid the man. Which was true. Or that she had something to hide. Ditto.

She pushed back her chair and went to the edge of the porch. "Jackson!" she hollered. "You might as well come join us for lunch."

Silence.

"Try, please," Ruth whispered.

She mugged a face at her boss but obliged. "Please?"

He came down out of the pines and at least had the good grace to look sheepish.

She couldn't help laughing as she shook her head at him and went to get another place setting.

"Thank you for the kind invitation," he said, tipping his hat to the ladies at the table and giving Josie his best smile when she returned with a plate and silverware.

Ivy giggled and turned shy as he pulled up an extra chair and sat down next to her high chair on the opposite side of Josie.

They talked about the weather, horses and kids during the meal. Mostly Clay charmed Ruth, even softened up Mildred, and did his best to put Josie at ease.

But unlike the other women, Josie knew the threat he posed. She secretly hoped that Clay was wrong. That the man in the stables last night hadn't been Raymond Degas. And that no matter who it had been, it had nothing to do with the stolen jewels. Or Texas.

But, like him, she couldn't pretend it wasn't an amazing coincidence that Raymond—or at least the man Clay believed was Raymond Degas—had led Clay to her.

The one woman at the table whom Clay charmed without any effort was Ivy. She definitely had taken to him, just as Mildred had said after their encounter in the grocery store.

And Clay, to her amazement, seemed to have a real way with the toddler. Who would have known? Josie had never seen him show any interest in children before. Or was it just Ivy?

The thought worried her. She told herself that her daughter just had that kind of effect on people. She was as much a charmer as Clay. It surprised her, though, that Clay Jackson would be susceptible to that charm. Maybe he did have a heart after all. Scary thought.

After they'd finished, Ruth offered to clear the table with Mildred's help. When they'd both disappeared inside the cabin, he asked, "Where'd you learn to break horses like that?"

She looked up from removing Ivy's bib and felt the heat of his gaze. "I don't actually *break* them. I try to gentle them, to gain their trust and confidence so they let me train them."

He smiled. "I'm familiar with the approach. I suppose it works sometimes, if you get lucky."

She felt a surge of anger. "You just can't admit that I might know what I'm doing when it comes to horses, can you?"

He met her gaze and held it, his smile fading, his eyes growing dark and serious. "You were great with that horse this morning," he said, as if the words came hard. "Where did you learn that?"

She busied herself with Ivy again. "I've always loved horses, you know that. I used to watch my father and brothers."

She knew he wasn't buying it. "The O'Malley men don't *gentle* horses."

How true. "I also learned a lot watching your trainers, and I've read about the different techniques. The rest Ruth taught me."

"Really," he said, surprise in his voice. "So you learned some of it in Texas?"

She nodded, wanting to change the subject. "I really need to get back to work."

He got up from the table, studying her openly.

She knew he was wondering if she'd ever worked with his horses. He no doubt couldn't stand the thought that she'd ridden one of them.

She carried Ivy into the cabin. Clay jumped up to open the door and followed her inside, obviously not done with his interrogation.

"Ruth said you'd never worked with that horse before today," he said.

"You don't think *Ruth* would lie to you, do you?"

"It's not that I doubted you—"

Right. She played patty-cake with Ivy, changed her and got her ready for her nap, although Mildred insisted she'd be happy to do it. Josie wanted the time with Ivy. She kissed her daughter and laid her down in the crib.

"Singa," Ivy cried.

Josie glanced at Clay, who had followed her into Ivy's room. She felt self-conscious, but she wasn't going to let him disrupt the life she'd made for them any more than she could help.

She sang Ivy's favorite song, one Josie's father used to sing to her when she was a child. Suddenly she felt close to tears, her homesickness for Texas, the ranch, but especially her father and brothers, acute.

"You have a beautiful voice," Clay said as she turned away to hide her tears and tuck her daughter in.

When she turned back, he was gone, the screen door downstairs banging behind him. Ruth came in to give Ivy a kiss and took Josie's arm as they walked out of the room.

Ruth Slocum had given her more than a job. She'd recognized her love of horses and her desperate need to do something with her life for her unborn baby.

Ruth had advertised for a stable hand, and Josie had driven out to the ranch with little hope that anyone was going to hire her in her obviously pregnant state.

While Ruth showed her around the stables, Josie hadn't been able to keep her hands off of the horses. It had been weeks by then since she'd been around horses. She'd missed the smell, the sound, the sight, but especially the feel of them. Under her palms. Under her saddle.

Later Ruth would tell her that it was her love for

horses that made her offer Josie the job, which included a place to live on the ranch. Within days, Ruth pulled her out of the stables and into the training pen.

In the pen, Ruth had taught Josie more about horses than she dreamed possible and made her realize how much more she needed to learn. Horse training took a lifetime, Ruth had told her, but Josie knew now that it was what she wanted to do with her life, along with raising Ivy. Horses and her daughter *were* her life. She had no regrets about that. Only a deep sense of gratitude to Ruth.

She'd met Mildred through Ruth. The two older women had been friends since grade school. Both had been godsends to Josie. Along with giving her a job and a place to live, Ruth had dug out her son's crib from the attic, and Mildred had collected clothing from her many nieces' and nephews' children for Ivy.

Josie often wondered how she'd have ever made it without both women. She just hoped that one day she'd be able to repay their kindnesses.

"Mind if I offer a little advice?" Ruth asked now.

Josie shook her head.

"Men are like horses," she said. "What works with horses, also works with men."

Josie blinked at her. "You aren't suggesting that I try to…gentle Clay Jackson to a saddle?"

The older woman laughed. "Hell, yes. If you can communicate with a horse by reading his body language and sending similar signals back, why not do the same with a man?"

"I don't have to read Clay's body language, I can read his lips loud and clear," she said, feeling tears close to the surface. "He always thinks the worst of me."

Ruth tilted her head to study her. "What kind of signals are you sending *him?*"

"You don't understand. There was a man in my past—"

Ruth laughed, her weathered face crinkling with humor. "Honey, it's pretty obvious there was at least one man in your past."

Josie had to smile in spite of herself. "There's a lot you don't know about Clay and me."

"And there's a lot I do," Ruth said, squeezing her hand. "Would you give up on a horse after a few failed attempts? You have to school a horse, slowly and gently. Men are no different, honey."

Josie smiled at the idea of schooling Clay Jackson.

"You have a gift when it comes to horses, Josie."

"Yeah, well, believe me, I don't have the same gift when it comes to men."

Ruth laughed and released her hand. "Give it a chance. I think you'll be surprised."

As Ruth left, Mildred settled into the couch with her knitting. She made afghans for her church as part of a blankets-for-the-homeless project and swore that knitting kept her out of trouble. Josie thought she might take it up.

As she pushed open the screen door, she wasn't surprised to find Clay leaning against one of the posts, looking toward the stables. In the distance, Ruth drove off in the golf cart she used to get around the ranch.

"Thanks for lunch. It was delicious," Clay said, never forgetting his breeding or his southern manners. Old-school Texans and cowboys prided themselves on their manners.

"It was Ruth's idea."

"I'll have to thank Ruth the next time I see her."

She groaned, hoping he wouldn't be around long enough. "Don't you have something better to do than follow me around, Jackson?" she snapped irritably as he fell in beside her for the walk down to the stables.

"Nope. You *are* my work, Josie. And believe me, it isn't easy. As a matter of fact, I've been thinking—"

"I'll just bet you have," she said, giving him a sweet-as-penuche smile.

"You really should smile more often," he said. "You're really quite attractive when you're not frowning."

She glared over at him.

"Sorry, just trying to help," he said with a shrug.

"I'll have you know that I've been doing fine on my own. I don't need your help. Or your advice." She started to walk away from him.

He grabbed her arm and pulled her around to face him. "What makes you so damned ornery?"

"I've been bossed around my whole life," she snapped, jerking her arm free. "By my father. By my three older brothers." Her gaze narrowed. "And by you. Everyone knows what's best for me. Even you treated me like I was one of your horses that needed to be corralled."

"I treat my horses very well."

"Oh!" she said, stomping away from him.

He shook his head as he stared at her rigid spine, the proud incline of her head. A woman with a lot of grit. Then he laughed softly and went after her. "A man can't act protective around you."

"It's more than that, Jackson, and you know it."

Damn her. She knew him too well. Although there was a lot she didn't understand about him.

But she was right about one thing. He wasn't here to

protect her. Nor did he have any business trying to tame her in Texas. "I was out of line."

That took some of the wind out of her sails. She'd obviously expected him to make excuses. She slowed, studying him as if she suspected he wasn't being entirely honest.

He couldn't remember a time he'd been more honest.

"I didn't want to see you hurt. Odell Burton was nothing but trouble and you were—"

"Wild as an unbroke stallion? Isn't that what you once told me?"

He wished he could take back some of the things he'd said to her. "Wilder," he admitted. "But I was going to say young, just a kid."

She stopped abruptly and turned, hands on her hips. "Well, I'm not a kid anymore."

"You can say that again!" He let out a low whistle.

She narrowed her gaze at him. "What is it about me that scares you so much?"

He laughed. "Everything about you scares me, Josie."

She shook her head at him, thinking he was joking, and turned and headed on down the hill to the stables.

He caught up with her in two easy strides. "You have to understand, Josie. I care about you. But I'm going to find those jewels and who helped Odell and Raymond steal them. I have the feeling that I'm getting close. I think I'm making some people nervous."

She wagged her head at him, not looking the least bit nervous. "You're so sure of yourself, aren't you, Jackson. But if Odell and Raymond *did* pull off the robbery, why couldn't they have gotten rid of the jewels a long time ago? What would be the purpose in waiting so long? They don't strike me as men with a lot of patience. And if they are the fools you think they are, why didn't they try to fence the jewels?"

He'd already wondered the same thing. "You make a very good argument." And she'd known both men better than he had. All he had was his gut instinct. His gut instinct and Raymond Degas had gotten him this far. Straight to Josie O'Malley. "I *will* find the jewels."

"That's all that matters, isn't it?"

He met her gaze. "Yes. I need to know who stole them and how they did it. I have a theory that the thieves got to the security plans in my office at the ranch."

Nothing showed in her expression, but her eyes seemed a shade darker blue.

"I'm not going back to Texas until I get both. And you're going to help me."

She shot him a disbelieving look. "Why would I do *that?*"

He arched a brow at her. "To prove that you had nothing to do with the robbery. If you have nothing to hide—"

Her gaze narrowed, hotter than a summer afternoon. "I forgot, I'm always guilty until proven innocent with you."

"Raymond didn't get what he came here for," Clay said, angry with her for trying to make *him* feel guilty. "He'll be back. I intend to be here. One way or the other."

"I see," she said, biting off each word. "What is it you want from me?"

What he'd dreamed he'd had one night on a creek bank in Texas. But that was pure fantasy, and most of the time, he knew it. "Just the truth, Josie."

Anger flashed in her gaze. "You sure you can handle the truth, Jackson?"

She had him there. "I also thought you might want me to stay in the cabin so I'd be close by if you needed me."

She laughed. "Well, then you thought wrong," she said, turning her back on him as she stalked away, her hips swaying in her tight-fitting jeans.

Could he handle the truth? He damn sure hoped so.

The afternoon passed slowly, with Clay watching her every move. She finally quit early and went up to the cabin to prepare supper. Clay didn't make any effort to pretend he wasn't watching her like a hawk or that he wasn't still hoping to be invited inside.

Fat chance.

She walked away from him a few yards from the cabin, and when she looked back, he was gone. But not far, she knew.

She made his favorite meal, opening the kitchen window to let the smell waft out to him. Let him eat his heart out. Let him go hungry. Let him suffer.

She'd planned to spend the evening with Ivy, but Mildred reminded her that the two of them were expected over at the neighbor's for a birthday party.

Ivy and the little neighbor girl, Rachel, were the same age, and Mildred often got them together to play. "She gets sick of all us adults around," Mildred would say of Ivy.

Josie didn't want Ivy to go, and Mildred must have noticed.

"We won't be late. It's good for Ivy to be around other kids," Mildred said.

She couldn't argue that. She just felt uneasy. As if a storm were blowing in. But the sky was clear. Not a cloud in the dwindling blue. The only storm that had blown in was Clay Jackson.

After Mildred and Ivy left, the cabin seemed too quiet, especially knowing that Clay was out there. She tried to read, but was too restless to concentrate.

She knew there was only one thing that would relax her. Even though it was getting dark, she headed for the stables.

He liked the dark. The vast emptiness of night. It had a familiar universal appeal. It defied reality. He could pretend he was in Texas. He could pretend he was deep underground.

He felt a small thrill at the thought. But as much as he liked the dark, it didn't do for him what the caves did. He couldn't wait to get back into the caverns. Except next time, he wasn't going alone. Next time he'd have Ivy O'Malley with him.

He smiled at the thought, because it wasn't the toddler he was thinking about but her mother. Ivy was only a means to an end. He'd known for a long time what he wanted. What he deserved. Now he knew how to get it.

He waited until the last of the sun died away before he moved. He preferred moving under the cloak of darkness. Like a vampire coming out of his casket, he felt ready to roam with the disappearing light. He felt an infinity with the night as if it brought him to life and made him invisible. Maybe even invincible.

He definitely felt stronger, more powerful. Ready. Ready to give Josie O'Malley just what she had coming to her. The thought made him salivate. He felt the familiar tightening in his loins, the hammering in his chest. Expectation. He couldn't wait to see her face. She'd taken so much from him.

Eventually he'd take what she cherished most. Take Ivy to a place of endless darkness. And Josie would follow. Josie.

And Clay Jackson.

He swore softly under his breath. Hadn't he always known he'd have to do something about Jackson?

He breathed in the night, shifting his thoughts to something more pleasant. It was hard not to rush his plans. Not to make mistakes.

But part of the fun was the anticipation, the planning. Unfortunately, he had a couple of flies in the ointment he'd have to deal with first. He wouldn't let anyone mess this up. Not again. He was too close.

As he moved through the darkness, the moon shimmered off the rock bluffs behind the ranch. He considered how he would kill Clay Jackson. He just wished he'd done it a long time ago.

Chapter 6

Josie felt a prickling along her neck as she neared the stables. A feeling that she wasn't alone and that someone other than Clay was out there.

She glanced around the ranch yard. Horses shifted restlessly in the corral. A cloud moved across the moon, extinguishing any light. Closer, a breeze ruffled her short hair and sent a chill down her back.

Cautiously she pushed open the door, gripping the flashlight she carried, realizing it made a lousy weapon. Raymond must have come back, just as Clay had predicted.

A sound came from out of the darkness.

"Who's there?" she called out.

Silence. Then she heard the scrape of boots as someone approached, but in the opposite direction from where she'd thought she'd heard something.

A cowboy rounded the corner, his western hat slanted

low over his face. As he shoved the hat back, she half expected to see Raymond Degas's face.

"I figured you'd want to go for a ride," Clay drawled. "I was hoping for an invitation."

Her first instinct was to be rude. But she was too relieved it'd only been Clay. Also, as jumpy as she was, she didn't really mind if he rode with her tonight.

She just needed to get out, to feel the freedom of being on a horse. And she figured she couldn't get rid of him no matter what she did. She might as well have him where she could see him, as Ruth had suggested.

"I guess you might as well," she said, heading for the tack room. "You're determined to hang around, anyway."

He laughed as he joined her in the tack room, filling up the small space with his presence. "With an invitation like that, how can I refuse?"

She shoved a saddle at him, feeling his gaze on her. She didn't dare lift her eyes to his. "You can ride Lady. She's about your speed."

He backed out of the tack room. "You're too kind."

"I'd hate to see you on your backside." Again. She remembered the last time she'd watched him try to ride Diablo at his ranch in Texas.

"I'd think you'd have had your fill of horses for the day," he said as they saddled up.

"I could never get my fill of horses. They're intelligent, graceful and loyal, with a willing nature." Everything that men weren't.

And she'd always loved to ride at night. Now she usually rode in the afternoons, taking Ivy with her. But she missed riding hard and fast under a vast night sky. She used to believe she could outrun her troubles. She didn't anymore.

* * *

The night was dark, only the faint hint of the moon hidden behind a thick bank of clouds as they rode out. No stars. Just shades of darkness splattered across the tall grass.

Clay rode out ahead of her. She'd always loved seeing him in the saddle. He rode tall, assured, as at home on a horse as he was anywhere. Sometimes he seemed to love horses as much as she did. Those times she felt herself soften toward him. A pull stronger than gravity.

She'd felt the same way earlier, watching him with Ivy. Who knew the man could possess such tenderness?

She let the wind blow back her hair as she loped across the field to catch him. The breeze caressed her face, the horse beneath her soothed her, and the night seemed filled with an electric excitement.

He seemed as lost as she was in the ride, his face turned to the black rough line of the mountain peaks and the clouds that hung like a shroud over them, hiding more than the moon from the night, making the vast landscape seem smaller, almost intimate.

They didn't speak as they rode toward the light-colored bluffs of the old buffalo jump. The darkness felt thick with an eager silence as if holding its breath.

Josie brought her horse to a halt at the bottom of the cliffs and climbed down to stare up at the rough rock face. She often rode up here, thinking sometimes she could feel the history that lingered like the dying sun on the rocks. Tonight, though, she felt nothing but the man beside her as Clay dismounted and joined her.

She sensed his body heat as if it were drawing toward her. The masculine scent of him mixed with the smell of leather and horses. Intoxicating. Her body felt alive, everything magnified as if this were her first night here, as if she were experiencing it all for the first time. Seeing it, feeling it, sensing it not only through her own eyes but through his as well.

He was close. Too close. To her. To the truth.

"Thank you for bringing me here," he said, his voice sounding hoarse with unexpected emotion. He knew that this place was special to her, the same way he'd known she'd want to ride tonight. He knew her, better than any man ever had. And yet, he didn't know her at all.

She looked over at him, surprised that he understood what this place meant to her.

He smiled, acknowledging that surprise. But it was a sad smile full of regret.

She wanted to say something, but the moment seemed lost. Was Ruth right? Had she misjudged him? Just as he had her? Was that why it surprised her when he knew anything halfway good about her?

"We'd better get back," she said, mounting up. She hated to cut her ride short, but she realized this had been a bad idea. Being alone with Clay only reminded her of Texas and the past.

She rode toward the Madison River and the ranch, letting the horse run, thankful Clay didn't try to catch up to her or, worse yet, try to talk to her. She didn't like the feeling that she might be wrong about him. Wrong about herself.

She reminded herself why Clay was here. To find the jewels. And the thieves. If she was smart, she'd be very careful. Thinking of Clay as anything other than the enemy would be a huge mistake. One she'd made once before. And look how that had turned out.

She raced through the tall grass, letting the horse go,

the wind roaring past along with the darkness. In the distance she could see the ranch, the yard light glowing.

She headed for it, knowing Clay wasn't far behind, and slowed to let her horse cool down.

But Clay didn't catch her until she reached the ranch yard. She pulled up short when she saw the expression on his face.

"What is it?" she asked in a whisper, his gaze scaring her.

He stared at her as if seeing a stranger. Did he really know this woman? It appeared not. But at the same time, he wondered if he knew her even better than he thought he did. Much better.

"Nothing's wrong," he said, unable to take his eyes off her. "Why?"

She eyed him for a moment, then shook her head and dismounted to lead her horse toward the stables.

"You ride very well," he commented, trying to hide the true extent of his surprise as he dismounted and followed her toward the stables.

He'd never known she could ride like that. He'd watched her gallop across the pasture, the dim moonlight illuminating only her pale blond hair and the light-colored flanks of the horse beneath her. She looked like a spirit, some night sprite. Just the reflection of a woman on a horse riding through the night.

Stunned, he realized he'd seen her ride like this once before. His heart quickened, his pulse pounding at his temple as he remembered Josie in the dream. And then in the pen earlier with the unbroken stallion.

It *was* possible that Josie had ridden Diablo.

The realization hit him hard, filling his head with all the implications. *If* she could gentle a stallion like she had today, *if* she could ride like she had tonight, *if* she *had* ridden Diablo that night in Texas—

"Are you all right?"

Her voice dragged him from his thoughts. He looked down at her. She stood next to him, looking at him with concern in her gaze.

"I'm fine," he lied as he reminded himself of all the reasons that night had been nothing more than a dream. There weren't as many reasons anymore, though. But one good one still remained. When he'd made love to the Josie in his dreams, she'd been a virgin.

The wildest thing east of the Pecos, a virgin? Still, he couldn't shake the image of her on that horse tonight. One with the horse. As confident on a horse as she was with Ivy.

He realized her gaze was still on him, questioning. "I feel as if you cut your ride short because of me. I'm sorry."

She shook her head and looked away. "I was ready to get back."

At least *that* sounded like the truth. He unsaddled the horse and took the saddle into the tack room, which someone had put back in order. He couldn't help wondering what Raymond Degas had been looking for in here.

When he came back out, Josie had put the horses in the corral and stood looking toward the barn on the far side of the stables.

He felt his heart rate jump at the expression on her face. "What?"

"I heard something over by the barn," she whispered, sounding as if she hated to be the one to tell him. Hated that it was happening again. Was it possible she was as confused as he was about all this? "It sounded like it was coming from one of the horse trailers."

"Stay here," he ordered, and took off at a run toward the barn. He was only mildly surprised to hear Josie hot on his heels.

It had to be Raymond, he thought as he slowed beside the barn, wishing he had a weapon. He'd left his pistol locked in his truck, not wanting it around the baby.

He chastised himself for going on the ride. He should have stayed here and watched for Raymond. Except he didn't like letting Josie out of his sight. Because he couldn't trust her. A lie. Because he was worried about her.

That little bit of honesty concerned him. He was letting a woman, who was more than likely a jewel thief— at the least, an accomplice—distract him from what he had to do.

At the horse trailers, he turned to look back at Josie. She had an anxious, worried look on her face that made him wonder if she wanted to talk to Raymond as badly as he did. Maybe more. With Odell dead, Raymond might be the only one who knew where the jewels were. Or he might be the only one alive who could implicate her in the jewel robbery. Blackness bathed this side of the barn, making the horse trailers barely distinguishable. Clay followed the faint rustling sound. Was someone searching one of the horse trailers? It wasn't until he was so close he could touch it, that he saw which trailer it was. Josie's. The one she'd taken when she left Texas.

He'd known she was gone for good when he'd heard she'd taken not only her clothes but her truck, horse, horse trailer and tack.

The consequences of Raymond banging around in

her horse trailer only further fueled his suspicions. He glanced back at her, telling himself he'd be a fool to turn his back on this woman for long.

He had that "I told you so" look on his face, the one that infuriated her so. Was it now her fault that someone was in her horse trailer? She felt sick inside. First the man in the pines. Then someone in the tack room. Now her horse trailer. Why? And who was it? Raymond Degas?

But what worried her most was the look in Clay's eyes when he'd come riding in a few minutes ago. He'd looked as if he'd seen a ghost. As if she'd done something to make him more suspicious of her.

She followed him now, keeping close, hoping against all hope that he was wrong. That whoever was rummaging around in the trailer wasn't Raymond. Wasn't anyone she knew. Didn't have anything to do with the jewel robbery or Texas or Odell or the past. And especially had nothing to do with her.

But she knew it was too much to hope for.

Clay motioned for her to keep back, his expression threatening. She nodded grudgingly and moved back some as he approached the trailer's side door. Her boot toe stubbed something solid and metallic in the tall grass. She bent down to pick up a foot-long piece of galvanized pipe. A weapon.

This time, no matter who came out of that trailer, she planned to be ready. She wasn't going to have Clay say she'd helped the culprit get away. Not again.

He'd reached the side door to the trailer. She watched him grasp the door handle. So sure of himself, so confident that this time he'd catch Raymond. And catch her as well.

She edged back when he wasn't looking, slinking into the darkness behind the trailer, then working her way around to the other side.

Her horse trailer was old with a stall in the back and an antiquated camper of sorts in the front. It had been her father's when he used to show horses. He'd replaced it with newer, fancier ones as his sons took to the road to show the O'Malley Ranch horses. He'd given his old one to her.

It was supposed to be some sort of punishment because she was often at odds with him over any number of things including his methods of horse training. But she loved the old trailer. To her it was a status symbol. She hadn't sold out. She'd held fast, and if an old horse trailer was the price, then it was well worth it.

The only exit other than the locked horse stall door at the back was the door Clay was guarding, but she knew that a person could get out one of the side windows. She also knew she'd left it open to air out the old camper.

From the other side of the trailer came the sound of the door creaking open, followed instantly by hurried movement. Then a cry of surprise, trailed by a loud oath.

She had the pipe raised and ready when the intruder came flying through the torn window screen. She swung on pure instinct, but fortunately missed as a large raccoon took off across the pasture.

A laugh escaped as she dropped the pipe, relieved tension rushing out of her like air from a busted balloon. But as Clay came around the side of the trailer and she caught the embarrassed expression on his face in the yard light, she burst out laughing.

"Raymond got away again," she said between hiccups of laughter. "Only this time I think he was wearing a mask."

"Very funny," he said, dusting at cobwebs on his jeans. "You're in trouble and you and I know it. Sooner or later it's going to come home to roost. Maybe it already has." He turned and started up the hillside without looking back.

She took a deep breath, the truth of his words stilling the laughter. But she couldn't help smiling at the memory of the raccoon flying out the window—and the look on Clay's face.

Her smile faded at the sudden memory of another face. This one staring out of a stand of pines. Watching her and Ivy.

Clay was right. Except her troubles had *already* come home to roost. When he'd blown into town, bringing with him her past mistakes.

The problem was, she didn't know yet what to do about it.

Chapter 7

The breeze made the tall grass ripple like water in the moonlight. She could see Clay's broad back ahead of her. His strides long. Angry. His head down, thoughtful.

Thoughtful worried her.

She felt a pang of guilt when she remembered him today with Ivy. When she thought about him watching her work with the horses. Surprise went without saying. But almost admiration. As if he were finally seeing her. Why now of all times?

She shook off the memories. Her days of mooning over Clay Jackson were long behind her. No more daydreaming about what could have been. She knew where she stood with him. And things between them could only get worse.

She quickened her step, anxious to get back to the

cabin. She never thought of it as home, even after this long. Home was Texas.

As she neared the cabin, she saw that Mildred and Ivy hadn't returned from the neighbor's yet. The realization gave her a start until she noticed that it was still early.

But a nugget of fear lodged itself in her stomach. Who else had blown into town along with Raymond and Clay on this ill wind?

Clay had stopped and now stood by the porch, waiting.

"Thanks for walking me home," she said, breezing past him to mount the steps to the porch. She hoped that was subtle enough. She wanted to be alone. She needed desperately to think, and with Clay so near, he made it impossible.

He said nothing. Nor did he move as she crossed the porch and opened the front door.

As she stepped into the cabin, she started to reach for the light switch and stopped, sensing something different, something wrong.

Clay must have seen her hesitation. He was up on the porch in two strides and at her side, gently drawing her hand away from the light switch.

In a shaft of moonlight that sliced in through the window, she could see that the room had been ransacked. Her only thought was: Thank God Mildred has taken Ivy to the neighbor's.

"Stay here," he whispered next to her ear.

He brushed past her, stepping through that wedge of moonlight to disappear into the shadowed darkness of the cabin. Behind her, she could feel the cooler night air coming in through the still-open door.

She saw Clay move, a dark shadow, large and ominous, toward the back of the cabin. But the noise she heard came from upstairs. A rustling sound. Like the one she'd heard the night before in the stables. Her heart leapt into her throat. Raymond?

Clay must have heard it, too. She saw him start up the open stairs at the left of the living room. He moved quietly, cautiously. Although unarmed, he could be as powerful and deadly as a large mountain cat, she recalled, remembering his fight with Odell that day in his stables.

Unable to stand by idly, no matter what he'd said, she slipped across the living room to where she kept a can of pepper spray. Perfect for the stray grizzly she might meet on horseback. Perfect for the stray thief ransacking her cabin.

Quietly, she retraced her steps, going back out the front door into the night, across the porch and down the steps. There were two ways out of the cabin. Through the front door. Or off the second-floor deck. She didn't think whoever was in the cabin would get past Clay this time to go out the front door. That meant the intruder would go for the deck and the stairs that dropped down into the pines below.

She couldn't keep hoping it wasn't Raymond. This wasn't some random thief here to steal a little horse tack or a few dollars off her bureau.

A cloud cloaked the moon, leaving the sky black as she made her way around the outside of the cabin. The pines stood at the back, the needles even darker than the night. The shadows under them, black as holes and colder.

Josie thought of the face she'd seen looking out of the pine branches across the pasture two evenings ago. Could it have been Raymond? He and Odell *did* look a little alike. Both dark, both tall, but Raymond was definitely not handsome. Maybe the waning light in the pines had played a trick on her. Or just seeing Raymond reminded her of Odell, since they'd been inseparable—except in death, she thought.

The rich smell of pine permeated the late-spring night behind the cabin. She moved to the bottom of the steep stairs that came straight down from the deck.

Carefully, she positioned herself in the trees opposite the last step, suddenly afraid. From this spot, she would see anyone who came down the stairs.

The thought of seeing Raymond Degas again chilled her more than the cool Montana night air. She clutched the pepper spray and waited.

A thud resonated on the second story. Suddenly, the back door slammed open and footfalls hammered across the weathered deck above her, then thudded loudly as they descended the plank steps. Right toward her.

Finally, she'd know the truth. If this man was Raymond. If what she'd feared most was actually coming true.

Another set of boots hit the deck overhead. Clay? He'd never be able to catch whoever was now almost to the bottom.

She held her breath, the pepper spray clutched in her hands, aimed man-high. The moon broke free of the clouds, dappling the deck stairs with silver, distorting the dark shape coming toward her.

He dropped down the last stairs in a flurry of movement. Half running, half falling, hitting the bottom step and stumbling forward—right to her.

It happened so fast. As he fought to get his feet under him, he looked up as if sensing her there. The moonlight fell over his features. Or what would have been his features. A black ski mask flattened his face, making it unrecognizable, monsterlike. Especially the slice of red pressed against the thin slit for his mouth and two marble-size holes for his eyes.

Her finger twitched on the pepper spray trigger.

In that microsecond, their eyes met. His dark and cold and familiar behind the mask. Her heart leapt to her throat, choking back the cry on her lips. He reached out to catch himself. Reached out toward her.

Something glittered in the moonlight. The ring on his right hand. He grabbed the limb right in front of her, the ring just inches from her face.

She fell back against the tree trunk, banging her head. He caught himself on the branch over her head.

Then he was gone, enveloped by the blackness in the pines. Disappearing as if he'd never been there at all.

Before she could take a breath, Clay clambered down the steps, sliding to a surprised stop at the sight of her.

She said nothing, just stared at him, the pepper spray still in her hands. In the distance, an engine turned over. A vehicle sped off into the night.

He swore as he took the pepper spray from her hands, sniffed the nozzle, then tossed it aside. Grabbing her upper arms, he jerked her from the tree branches.

"You saw him?" He sounded angry and frustrated, his tone accusing. "He must have come right past you, so close you couldn't have missed. Why didn't you spray him?"

She looked up at Clay. The moonlight played across his face but couldn't soften the hard lines of his jaw. Nor lighten two-days' growth of stubble. He'd lost his hat.

His black hair shone, a raven's wing tumbling over his forehead. She'd never known a more handsome man.

She had the strangest urge to push herself up on tiptoes and kiss him. To lose herself in his kiss. She yearned to be wrapped in his strong arms. To be safe. To be reassured. To be protected.

But the urge lasted only an instant. There'd be no safety in Clay's arms. No reassurance in his kiss. He hadn't come to Montana to protect her. He'd come to catch a thief. Or two. There was no doubt he thought she'd been one of them.

She looked into his eyes and shivered at the cold, searching darkness she found there. Why did he mistrust her so? And how much would he hate her when he finally learned the truth?

"You could have stopped him," Clay said, his words pelting her like hailstones. "You let Raymond get away. Why?"

She looked away, toward the darkness behind the cabin. Toward the darkness of her past. Her mind felt as numb as her body. Every fear she'd ever had—and some she hadn't even dreamed of—seemed to be coming true.

Clay shook her gently as if to bring her back.

She turned her head to look at him again in the silver web of moonlight that sifted down through the tree limbs.

"It wasn't Raymond," she said, her voice hoarse from the tears that now threatened to close her throat.

He let go of her, stepping back, his gaze hard, unforgiving, unbelieving, reminding her of the last time he'd looked at her like that in Texas. "What do you mean it wasn't Raymond?"

What *did* she mean? Who had she seen? Her mind

refused to let her voice her fear. To say it might make it true.

"He wore a mask," she whispered. And a ring—one she'd seen before.

He pulled her closer, his fingers still locked around her slim upper arms. "A mask? What kind of mask?"

"A black ski mask." The moonlight shone on her face, making her appear even paler, her eyes the light-glazed silvery blue of a sleepwalker.

He wanted to shake the truth out of her, but the tremor he felt in her limbs and the lost look in her eyes stopped him. What had she seen tonight that had terrified her so?

More than a masked man coming out of her cabin. He'd stake money on that.

Was it possible that she really didn't know what was going on? Was that why she was so frightened?

He knew that's what he wanted to believe. That Josie had nothing to hide.

Unfortunately, not even his weakening resolve to nail her to the wall for the jewel theft could make him believe that.

"If there's some reason you're protecting Raymond—"

She seemed to snap out of her trance. Her gaze flew up to his. "The only person I'm protecting is my daughter. Ivy is my *only* concern."

He felt a shock run through him as he looked into her face and saw something that chilled him. The incredible intensity of a mother's love for her child and a desperate need to protect her daughter. Josie would do anything to protect Ivy. *Anything.* Maybe she already had.

"Look, I didn't mean—"

"You have no idea what we've been through," she snapped angrily. "What we still have to get through."

Her eyes glistened shiny with anger and tears. "Don't you think I know my daughter's in danger? What you don't seem to realize is that Ivy's been in danger from the moment she was conceived."

He stared at her. "What do you mean?"

"Odell." She looked away. "He threatened to...hurt her if I went through with the pregnancy."

Clay felt fury burn through him like flames. He wanted to kill Odell and wished he wasn't dead so he could. He looked over the top of her head to the dark pines, feeling like he might explode. It was a good thing Odell was dead. But his best friend Raymond was still alive.

He barely heard the sound of a vehicle coming up the road to the cabin. Mildred bringing Ivy home?

His gaze dropped to Josie's face. It shone in the moonlight, raw with fear. He felt his heart break at the thought of her alone and afraid and pregnant.

"You're right." He hesitated to let her go, as if he might break his only connection to her, a tenuous connection at best. "I don't know what you and Ivy have been through. I only wish you'd have come to me when Odell threatened you." *Come to me before that. Beside the creek.* "I'm sorry."

Her eyes filled with tears as she looked up at him.

He let her go, fighting the conflicting emotions his heart pumped through him. "I have to leave for a while. Can you ask Mildred to stay with you and Ivy until I get back?"

She nodded.

"Are you going to be all right?" he asked.

She squared her shoulders, brushing her knuckles across her cheek at the escaping tears. "Yes."

He picked up the pepper spray from where he'd tossed it and handed it to her. "I have to go," he repeated, as if she gave a damn. Actually, she'd probably love it if he left and never came back. *No such luck, Josie.*

But he had to find Raymond. Had to get to the truth. Now more than ever before. He knew damned well that he'd tailed Raymond from Texas to the Buffalo Jump Ranch—and Josie. Now he just wanted to know why. He wanted to hear Raymond say it.

He'd been wrong about so much. He wanted desperately to be wrong about Josie. But he knew this *had* to be about the jewels. There wasn't any other explanation. Too much money was involved. Too many people. If it really hadn't been Raymond who'd ransacked Josie's cabin, then someone else was also looking for the jewels. He didn't like the feeling that he was the only one who didn't know the score. And Josie O'Malley was right smack in the middle of it all.

"I'll be back," he said as he started across the field to where he'd left his pickup.

She didn't acknowledge that she'd heard him. Not that it mattered. He'd be back, anyway. Hopefully with some answers from Raymond Degas. But he'd be back. One way or the other. Because he wasn't finished with Josie. Only now he wanted to prove her innocence. If he could.

Josie actually did as he'd suggested. She knew she had to do something. She couldn't just keep hoping he was wrong. Not after what had happened the past two nights.

Just the thought of the masked man who'd come flying off her deck chilled her to the bone. Who had he been? She refused to let her mind even speculate—let alone taunt her with the one possibility she couldn't accept. Not yet.

But she also could no longer pretend this would all blow over. She hugged herself, trying to get warm, as she went to meet Mildred.

"How was Ivy?" she asked, smiling at the sight of her daughter's tiny sleeping form in the back of the car as Mildred opened her door and the dome light came on.

"A bit tuckered out," Mildred said. "Me, too. But she has so much fun with Rachel. I didn't let her eat too much cake or ice cream, though."

"I'm sure you didn't." Josie bit back the tears that threatened. What would she have done without Mildred and Ruth?

"What is it, Josie?" Mildred asked now with concern as Josie got her daughter from the car seat.

"The cabin's kind of a mess," she answered as they climbed up to the porch, Josie carrying the sleeping Ivy in her arms. The front door still stood open.

"Oh, my," Mildred exclaimed when she saw the ransacked interior. "Was it the same person who was in the tack room?"

"Probably," Josie fibbed, not wanting to upset Mildred more. "I wish I could tell you what's going on. Clay still thinks someone is looking for missing jewels from a robbery in Texas." She headed up the stairs with Mildred behind her carrying Ivy's things.

"What do you think?" Mildred asked as she helped her slip off Ivy's party clothes and dress the toddler for bed.

"I don't know why anyone would think the jewels were here."

She tucked the blanket around Ivy and leaned down to

kiss her again, loving the warm, baby-soft feel of her. Ivy smiled in her sleep and let out a tiny sigh. Josie smiled down at her through her tears and made a silent prayer.

"Are you afraid this might have something to do with Ivy's father?" Mildred asked.

She looked up in surprise. Mildred had no idea how close she'd come to the truth. "Yes."

"Where is Mr. Jackson?" Mildred asked accusingly.

She checked the baby intercom system Ruth had given her, then the locks on the windows and the back door before she headed down the stairs again. "He had to go into town."

"That's it, I'm calling my friend Charley Brainard," Mildred said, going to the living room phone. "Now, don't you argue."

Josie wasn't about to argue. In fact, she'd just been about to suggest that Mildred call Charley to come stay with them for a while.

Charley Brainard was a huge, likable man, who from what Josie could tell, had quite the crush on Mildred. "I think having Charley come over is a great idea." In more ways than Mildred could imagine. "I need to go into town, and I want to be sure that you and Ivy are safe while I'm gone."

Ten minutes later, Charley drove up the road. By then, she and Mildred had tidied up the cabin, all evidence of the intruder gone but certainly not forgotten.

Mildred went to get Charley a tall lemonade.

"Please don't let anyone in," she said to Charley while Mildred was still in the kitchen. "Anyone at all. You can hear Ivy on the intercom." Or anyone else who might break into the house.

"Don't you worry about that little darling of yours,"

Charley assured her. "Or Mildred, either. I'll take good care of them."

"I know you will. I left the pepper spray on the top shelf, just in case. I won't be long."

"You just take care of yourself," Mildred said, coming in with Charley's lemonade.

Although she knew Ivy would be safer with Charley and Mildred than alone with her, she still had a hard time leaving. But she had to find Raymond. Had to find out what he was doing in Montana. What he'd been doing in her stables. And who had ransacked her cabin tonight.

She had to be wrong. There had to be another explanation. Other than the one that had a death grip on her.

Chapter 8

Josie took the short way to town, hoping to avoid running into Clay. She figured he'd go looking for Raymond with the same intentions she had. Or at least close.

But if Raymond was in Three Forks, she knew she'd be able to find him. Hopefully before Clay.

She took the old road, fighting hard not to panic. There had to be an explanation. For everything that was happening. For what she thought she'd seen tonight. *Who* she thought she'd seen.

At a phone booth just outside of town, she stopped, dug some quarters out of her purse and called what few motels there were, asking for a Texan driving a Lincoln Continental, pretending she'd run into his car and was trying to find the owner. The Lincoln had Texas plates and she'd seen a cowboy in it earlier, but she didn't know the driver's name.

She came up empty in town, where someone like Raymond would have stuck out like a sore thumb. But she wasn't surprised that he'd opted not to stay in Three Forks. He and his Lincoln would be too visible.

And by now he had to know that Clay Jackson was after him. Maybe not just Clay, she thought, remembering the man who'd ransacked her cabin. More people than just Clay might be looking for Raymond.

Because of that, she figured Raymond would hole up. Or take off.

She was betting he'd stuck around, though, and that worried her even more. Raymond wasn't what she'd ever considered a brave man. Nor was he stupid. With this much heat on him, he *should* have run.

If he hadn't, then, Josie wondered why. What was he waiting for? What was he in town looking for? The jewels from the robbery, as Clay suspected? Or something else?

She tried the motels in the surrounding small towns. No luck. Maybe he was camping out somewhere near town. That would make him almost impossible to find, given the number of campgrounds in the area.

Running out of ideas and thinking she'd have to give up, at least for tonight, she remembered the motel up on the interstate. Fort Three Forks. Maybe Raymond would have seen some irony in staying at a fort. Odell would have.

She pocketed the rest of her change and decided to drive out rather than call.

The night had cleared, leaving a full moon and a billion tiny stars to reflect on the water as she crossed the Jefferson River.

As she neared the Fort Three Forks motel, she glanced

across the highway at the Steer Inn, hoping to see the Lincoln. Raymond would have to eat. He'd go for a Montana beef steak, probably chicken-fried, just as Odell would have. Odell. She turned up the heater in the truck, feeling chilled, but not from the night.

No Lincoln at the Steer Inn. Nor parked in front of Fort Three Forks. She pulled around back and looked between the motor homes, hoping she'd get lucky.

Discouraged, she backed up and swung around to leave. Her headlights picked up the shine of a chrome bumper across an expanse of asphalt. She swung the pickup's lights around again, illuminating the white of Texas plates.

The dented, rusted, cream-colored Lincoln she'd seen Clay watching just two nights before sat on the dark side of a large metal building a hundred yards away. In her headlights she could see that the side window on the passenger side was a quarter of the way down, the front left tire looking a little low on air, the windshield cracked. The car appeared empty.

She parked her pickup, raked a hand through her unruly hair and headed for the motel lobby. Raymond wasn't quite as smart as she'd thought. If she'd found him, anyone else looking for him could have, too.

She opened the motel lobby door and stepped in, as the consequences of that thought sunk in. She hoped she wasn't too late.

Laying on her Texas accent a little thick, she tried to get Raymond's room number, knowing he wouldn't have registered in his own name. She came up with a story about being homesick. That much at least was true. And that she'd seen the Texas plates, realized whoever it was was from her neck of the woods and wanted to take them dinner and hear about home.

The girl behind the desk was sympathetic, but she couldn't give out his room number. She offered to ring his room, though, because she remembered him and his southern accent.

Josie watched her. No answer. The girl suggested she leave a message for him.

Josie took the notepad and wrote "Call me" and her number, but she planned to find Raymond before he read it. She'd seen the girl dial room 211.

She thanked her and left, doubling back to take the set of outside stairs up to the open second-floor balcony that ran the length of the rooms. At room 211 she knocked and waited, watching the parking lot behind her over her shoulder.

No answer.

She knocked again. "Maid," she said, hiding the Texan in her accent as much as she could.

Still no answer.

The curtains on the window were closed, but she could see through a crack where the edges didn't quite meet.

She cupped her hands to her face and peered in. The room was dark except for the flicker of the TV screen across the room. It illuminated the only object she could see clearly. The bed. Queen-size. The bright-colored spread hanging off the side, the white sheets crumpled.

She waited, thinking he might have gone into the bathroom. She knew she couldn't wait long. She was too visible up here from both the highway and the parking lot.

But after what seemed like an eternity and Raymond hadn't returned, she looked across the pavement toward the Lincoln, still hunkered away from the lights of the motel in the shadow of the warehouse. Maybe he'd walked across the street to the Steer Inn for dinner.

Her stomach fluttered as she stared at the car, remembering the partially open passenger side window. She would be able to get into the car. See who it was registered to. Or if there was anything inside that would prove Raymond Degas was in Three Forks.

She took the stairs back to the parking lot, trying to convince herself she should wait in her pickup for Raymond to return. But it was getting late and she was anxious to get home to Ivy. She started toward the Lincoln. At least she'd find out if the car was registered to him.

Goose bumps dimpled across her skin as she neared the Lincoln. Just a few days ago she'd been thinking how content she was. She'd actually felt safe, having convinced herself that the past could no longer hurt her. That she could go back to Texas. Soon.

Had she really been that naive?

She reached the dented front fender of the car and looked across the long rusted hood to the windshield. It was too dark to see inside the car even if the windows hadn't been tinted for the Texas heat. She wished she'd brought a flashlight. Even more, a weapon.

Moving down the side of the car toward the partially open side window, she suddenly felt as if she wasn't alone.

No moonlight found this side of the huge warehouse. Nor did starlight. In the distance, cars hummed by on the interstate. Faint laughter rode the breeze over from the motel to echo off the building, leaving a heavy silence. Something moved in the tall grass of the fields off to her left, making her jump. An animal?

Nearer, she thought she heard another sound. Low. Almost a moan. The breeze picked up. She caught a whiff of something. A mixture of mildew, years of road dust and something else, a sharp, coppery smell. Blood.

Her heart drummed, reverberating against her ribs, making her weak and off balance. She stared at the partially open window, but she could see nothing but darkness inside the car.

Run! All her instincts cried for her to turn, run and not look back.

She thought of Ivy and took a step backward, planning to do just that.

But then she heard the moan. A low, pain-filled plea that seemed to hang in the night.

Her pulse thrummed in her ears. The sound *had* come from the car, hadn't it? She glanced off to her left. The lights from the motel and the interstate lit a stretch of open field.

But even before she heard the moan again, she knew it hadn't come from out there.

She stood motionless, her breath caught between her teeth. Only her right arm moved away from her body and toward the car door handle.

It took every ounce of her strength and courage to open the door. The latch clicked, startling her, then the big, heavy door swung out. The dome light flashed on, blinding her for an instant. And the body that had been propped against the door fell out, hitting her legs and sliding to the ground with a heavy thud and a groan.

She let out a startled cry as she recognized the man bleeding at her feet and saw the gun he had pointed at her head.

Three Forks was dead for a Saturday night. Clay had driven past the motel where he'd spotted the Lincoln Continental before, then past the bars and restaurants and gas stations, all without any luck.

The waitress at the Headwaters Café had told him that most tourists wouldn't start rolling in until after Memorial Day. Fly fishermen. Golfers. Families on their way to Yellowstone Park or Lewis and Clark Caverns. A few would want to see where the Missouri began. Most just passing through on their way somewhere else.

That should have made finding Raymond Degas easy. Three Forks wasn't that big. And how many old rusted and dented 1975 cream-colored Lincoln Continentals with Texas plates could there be?

He'd searched the side streets, alleys and driveways of the small town, driving slowly, wondering if he really knew who he was chasing anymore.

Josie had him doubting himself, something he rarely did. Doubts were dangerous for an investigator. When he started questioning his gut feelings, he was in trouble. And as good as dead.

Worse, Josie had him doubting a lot more than his gut instincts. She had him questioning everything. Including whether or not he'd really been on Raymond Degas's trail or someone else's.

Of course the man Clay had been following didn't go by Degas. Or Raymond. He registered under different names and Clay figured the Lincoln was probably borrowed. Or stolen.

But Clay knew a surefire way to prove who the man was. Fingerprints. Degas had had a record since he was a juvie. If Clay could find the Lincoln, he knew he could get a clear print to send to the crime lab in Austin.

He hadn't bothered before because he'd been so sure he had Degas. Now he wasn't sure of anything, especially what had happened two years ago. Concerning the jewel robbery. Concerning Josie.

He kept thinking about her working with the horses in the pen this morning. He'd never seen anyone who was that good with unbroken horses, and he'd seen his share of horse trainers.

Watching her ride tonight like the devil himself was chasing her had left him shaken. Because he'd seen her ride like that before. Only once. On a horse he'd thought no one could ride.

He felt as if he couldn't be sure what was real and what wasn't anymore.

He widened his search to the businesses near the interstate, trying to concentrate on what he *did* know for certain: He'd followed *someone* whom he had reason to believe was Raymond Degas from Texas to Three Forks, Montana. Followed him to the ranch where Josie worked.

Raymond had made it easy, leaving behind a trail any fool could follow.

The thought rattled around in his head like a loose marble. He slowed the pickup, realizing he'd assumed Raymond was a fool. Or that the man no longer thought anyone was looking for him.

But Raymond had disappeared and stayed hidden for almost two years from the cops and Clay, who'd been looking for him. That made Raymond no fool. He had to know that the heat hadn't died on the jewels. So what would make him blow his cover? What would make him leave a clearly marked trail for Clay to follow?

His heart began to pound with a vengeance. He swallowed and slowed the truck to a crawl. For *Clay Jackson* to follow. The anonymous tip about Raymond. The easy-to-follow trail. Had Raymond wanted Clay to follow him to Montana? To Josie?

But why?

He drove down the short road to the Fort Three Forks motel. No Lincoln. He pulled around back to check the parking lot. But instead of finding the one vehicle he'd been looking for, he found the one he'd least expected.

Slowly he rolled down his window and parked alongside Josie's pickup. Empty. What the hell was she doing— He never got to finish the thought.

A gunshot shattered the quiet summer night.

Clay's gaze leapt up at the sound. Through the darkness and his open side window, he saw the Lincoln parked behind the warehouse in the distance. The passenger side door hung open. The glow from the dome light spilled out onto the pavement, onto what looked like a body. No, more than one body. There appeared to be two figures on the ground.

Josie. That's all he could think. Josie and trouble had always gone together. He grabbed his pistol and jumped out, keeping to the darkness as he ran toward the Lincoln.

He slowed, unsure, as he neared the front of the car. The night glittered, a canopy of stars and a large white moon, but none of that light reached the side of the warehouse. Just that small circle of pale gold stealing out of the Lincoln.

As far as he could tell, neither of the figures on the ground had heard him approach. That surprised—and worried—him.

He slowed at the sound. A hoarse, hurried whisper.

Weapon ready, he edged carefully around the front of the car until he could see behind the door hanging open.

He'd been right. Two figures were beside the car on the ground. The smaller one, a woman, knelt over a man sprawled in a pool of blood. He seemed to be trying to tell the woman something.

Clay stepped closer.

Josie lifted her head at the sound of his approach, her face pale and drawn, shock glittering in her eyes. He couldn't tell if it was from seeing him or what had happened before he got here.

He let out a low curse. What the hell was she doing here?

She brushed a wisp of stray blond hair back, her blue eyes too bright in the car's dome light.

He motioned for her to move back from the man on the ground. As she got to her feet, he saw the gun beside the body and hoped to hell it wasn't hers. Or that her fingerprints weren't on it. But with Josie, anything was possible.

Then he stepped close enough he could see the man's face.

Up close, it was clear that Raymond Degas *had* changed during the past two years. He was thinner, his hair long and dirty, his face more pockmarked. But there wasn't any doubt that he was the man Clay had followed from Texas or that he was Raymond Degas.

Raymond stared up, his eyes blank and distant. Blood no longer ran from the bullet hole in his chest.

Although he knew it was useless, Clay leaned over him to check for a pulse. None.

"Is he dead?" Josie whispered.

"Yeah," he said, straightening.

She couldn't seem to take her eyes off of the dead man.

Clay assumed the shot had come from the gun lying beside Raymond, but he didn't like to take chances where murder—and this woman—were concerned.

She stared at Raymond for a few moments longer, then looked up, blinking as if she couldn't bring him into focus. She seemed to notice what he still held in his left hand. A loaded .357 Magnum. Her gaze flicked back up to his. "You don't think *I* killed him?"

Nothing about Josie would surprise him at this point. But cold-blooded murder?

As far as he could tell, she wasn't armed. But what had she been thinking coming here? She should have known that Raymond was dangerous. Obviously his associates were even more dangerous.

"What are you doing here?" he demanded, angry with her for risking her life. But even more angry that she'd even gotten involved with someone like Raymond—and Odell—in the first place. "I thought I told you to stay at the cabin with Mildred and Ivy."

She didn't answer, just looked at him blankly.

"The police aren't going to like that answer," he said, reaching into his coat for his cell phone. He watched her chew at her lower lip as he dialed 911.

"Did you see anyone besides Raymond?" he asked while he waited for a ring.

She shook her head and glanced toward the interstate. A string of lights dotted the highway like tiny gold beads.

The 911 operator answered. He relayed the information to the sheriff's department and hung up.

"You didn't see who shot him?" Clay persisted as he led her away from the murder scene to a bench outside the motel.

She sat down. "I didn't see anyone but Raymond, and I didn't even know it was him until he fell out on the ground when I opened the door. He was bleeding, the front of his shirt was soaked." She looked down at her jeans. They had blood on them. "He fell against me."

"Who fired the shot?" Clay asked.

She shook her head. "I guess *he* did."

"Then he had the pistol in his hand when you opened the door?"

"Yes." She closed her eyes. "It happened so fast."

Didn't she realize the cops would grill her a lot worse than this? "Try to remember exactly what happened."

She opened her eyes and looked over at him. "Can't you just leave me alone for a minute?"

What did he have to do to get this woman to tell him what was going on?

"The cops are going to want to know why you came looking for Raymond," he said, losing his temper. "*Someone* murdered him. It's all going to come out. Everything that you thought you'd left behind in Texas is now coming after you. You can't escape it. Can't you see that?"

More than he knew. She felt herself shiver. She looked away. In the distance she could hear the sirens and see a string of flashing red-and-blue lights headed this way.

Clay was right about one thing. She needed help. She

could no longer pretend that she could handle this alone. Not after finding Raymond the way she had. Not after what he'd whispered to her.

"I want to help you, Josie," Clay said softly, urgently. "I know you're in trouble, and it's getting worse. I heard Raymond tell you something. You have to trust someone. Why not me, Josie?"

Something in his voice tugged at her heartstrings. Tears rushed her eyes, her throat closing over the lump lodged there.

She pushed up off the bench and walked a few feet away, her back to him. She didn't want him to see her tears. Nor could she face him right now.

Why not Clay Jackson? At one time she could have thought of a half-dozen reasons. But right now, she could think of only one. But didn't that make him the last man she should trust with this?

She turned to look back at him, knowing she had little other choice. He wouldn't give up. Eventually he'd find out everything.

She only wished she could have trusted him with the truth in Texas. How different would things have turned out?

"The man who ransacked my cabin, the one I saw coming down the deck stairs—" She could hear the sheriff's department sirens coming nearer. They would be here soon. She dreaded facing the cops, but not more than she did Clay's reaction to what she had to tell him.

She thought of the fear she'd seen in Raymond's eyes. They now shared a common enemy. She had to tell Clay. Warn him.

He seemed to brace himself. She just hoped he could

take the truth, because this was only the beginning and she feared it was going to get a whole lot worse.

"It was Odell Burton."

Chapter 9

Clay stared at her as the sheriff's cars screamed around the turn headed for them, lights flashing, sirens blaring.

"Odell? Odell's dead," he said, as if he had to remind her.

She said nothing.

"You couldn't have seen Odell. It was dark and…" He focused on her. "You said he wore a mask."

"It *was* dark," she admitted. "And he *did* wear a mask, but I saw his eyes and he was wearing his class ring." She looked up, expecting to see the same doubt on his face that she'd heard in his voice. The same doubts she'd had herself. Until she'd found Raymond shot and dying.

Clay was frowning, his brows furrowed, his gaze hard. She *thought* he might remember that ring. It had left a tiny scar at Clay's hairline after Odell had blind-sided him in the stables two years ago.

Few people knew about the scar because it was hidden by Clay's hair. But *she* knew it was there because she'd been the reason Odell had hit him. The tiny scar was a reminder for her of the mistakes she'd made with not one man but two.

Clay said nothing. Couldn't think of anything to say. He remembered that ring, all right. Just as well as he did Odell's lazy, arrogant smile. It had been the smile of a man who had something Clay wanted. Josie.

The assault of memories dug up dark and ugly reminders. Odell was dead. Clay had been at the morgue when Odell's father came in to identify Odell's effects. The ring had been one of them.

"Do you know how many class rings like Odell's there are in the world?" He shook his head and looked away from Josie to the group of uniformed men approaching fast. She was mistaken.

But he couldn't shake the memory of her at the bottom of the deck stairs, her fingers locked on the can of pepper spray, her eyes filled with shock. And terror.

"I know you've never taken my advice in the past," he said under his breath. "But I wouldn't mention this to the cops. At least not yet."

She shot him a look that clearly said "What? The let's-be-honest Clay Jackson suggesting she lie?"

"But of course you'll do as you please. You always have," he added, then stepped forward to introduce himself to the Gallatin County sheriff's deputy.

For the next couple of hours, Clay found himself lost in the surreal activity around the Lincoln. Cop-car lights flashing. Camera bulbs going off. Questions and more questions. The scream of sirens as the coroner arrived. Then the ambulance.

A crowd had gathered and stood barricaded back by the motel. Clay took it all in, never letting Josie out of his sight. Or out of earshot if he could help it.

The instant he'd gotten the chance, he called Judge Branson in San Antonio and, cashing in an old debt, asked the judge to have Odell Burton's body exhumed immediately. Judge Branson wasn't happy about being awakened in the middle of the night, let alone about the urgent request, but he'd grudgingly agreed to do it.

"You'd better be right about this, Clay," he'd said just before he hung up.

Clay would be quite happy to hear that he was wrong. That Odell Burton was six feet under and had been for almost two years. Then maybe both he and Josie could put the man to rest.

"I really need to get back to my daughter," he heard her tell the deputy in charge.

"I understand," the officer said. "Just a couple more questions. Why were you looking for Mr. Degas?"

"I thought I saw him on two occasions at the ranch where I work, the Buffalo Jump Ranch."

"I know Ruth Slocum well," the deputy said, nodding and smiling.

"Both times I didn't get a chance to talk to him," Josie continued. "I thought maybe Raymond had some news from my family."

"You're from Texas, right?"

As if her accent wasn't a dead giveaway.

"The hill country. My family still lives around San Antonio."

The deputy nodded and scribbled in his notebook.

"Neither of you is planning to leave town, right?" he asked, looking up at Clay.

"No," Clay assured him. He wasn't leaving until he got the truth out of Josie, and God only knew how long that would take.

"I'm not going anywhere," she said, but she had that wild look in her eyes again like a horse about to take off over the next hill.

Clay put his arm around her shoulders as he walked her to her pickup.

"You didn't tell him about the break-ins—or about Odell," he said. "I'm not used to you taking my advice. Are you all right?"

They'd reached her pickup, but she didn't want the warmth and weight of his arm and fingers to leave her shoulders. Not yet. It had been too long since she'd felt the weight of a man's arm around her.

She didn't move for a few moments, didn't even look at him for fear he'd see how much she needed him. It didn't matter that she had no right.

"I'm serious," he said quietly. "Are you all right?"

She glanced toward the Lincoln. The ambulance had taken Raymond's body away, but uniformed men still swarmed the area around it. Looking for a murderer.

The night had turned darker, colder. The landscape more lonely. More malevolent. She felt spooked, on edge, nervous. But why wouldn't she? She'd just seen a dead man for the second time today.

She reached into her pocket to dig for her keys. He took his arm back. She could feel his gaze searching her face. She didn't look at him. Couldn't look at him.

Her fingers closed over her keys. She couldn't keep running. Not from the truth. Not from Clay.

"No, I'm not all right," she said, surprising herself. She looked up at him.

A chill seemed to move through her like a restless spirit. Odell. Dead or alive, he and Raymond had brought Clay back into her life. "I know who killed Raymond," she said, her throat hoarse with unshed tears. "He told me."

Clay's jaw dropped. "You aren't going to say—"

"Odell. It was the last thing Raymond said. 'Odell did it.'" Her voice broke. "He's alive, and I'm scared to death that he'll come for me and Ivy next."

He'd been afraid that was what she was going to say.

"Why, Josie? I can understand that Odell didn't want you to have the baby because he didn't want to be responsible for it, but why would he want to hurt the two of you now? Even if he *were* alive, that doesn't make any sense."

He watched her look again at the Lincoln, her eyes filled with terror, but she said nothing.

"I can help you," he pressed. "What is it I did that you think you can't trust me?"

Her gaze jerked back to him.

He looked into the blue depths of her eyes, trying to understand the sadness, the regret. Was it more than getting involved with Odell? More than her fear of the man?

"I have to tell you what happened two years ago," she said, her voice soft as the night breeze.

He felt a jolt. A flash of memory that filled him with fear.

"But I need to be sure Ivy is all right first," she said. She'd already called the cabin. All three times, Mildred had assured her that Ivy was fine. "I need to hold her, Clay."

Clay. Not Jackson. He reached over and took Josie's keys from her hand. "I'll take you home."

He drove toward the ranch, the moon high, the night dark. His head hurt. Too much had happened tonight. Too much remained unresolved. Thoughts flashed in and out like signs caught along the road in the headlights.

Why did Josie have reason to fear Odell? There wasn't any way Odell could have survived the car accident. He'd seen the demolished, burned-out car. He'd also seen Odell's remains at the morgue.

No, Josie was wrong. Odell Burton was dead. But why was she so afraid he wasn't?

They rode in silence, his gaze on the narrow road ahead. Josie's staring out into the darkness.

The sandstone bluffs of the old buffalo jump shone pale tan in the moonlight, making them appear closer as he turned off the paved two-lane highway and onto the gravel road that ran to the ranch. The headlights cut a path through the darkness along the river, making the night seem more empty and the two of them more alone.

Josie looked exhausted, her face ghostly in the jade glow from the dash lights. She let out a long sigh and looked over at him. "I hated Odell."

He raised a brow.

"I've always hated Odell," she said, spitting out the words.

He almost drove in the ditch. "Then why in God's name did you...date him?"

"Date him?" she asked, narrowing her gaze as she glared over at him. "You were the one who thought I was dating him. The truth is, the more I rejected him, the more obsessed he became with having me."

It took him a moment to let that sink in. "But I saw you kissing him—"

"You saw *him* kissing me, and he only did it to get a rise out of you, and it worked," she said, disgusted. "Odell thought you wanted me and he couldn't bear it. Everything with Odell was about winning and losing. He hated to lose. Refused to lose."

He drove in silence the last couple of miles, his hands gripping the wheel, his heart pounding. He didn't dare speak for fear of what he'd say.

He parked between Mildred's car and a pickup he didn't recognize but that he assumed belonged to the Charley Josie had told him about. A single light glowed inside the cabin. Mildred waved from the front window. He saw the relief on Josie's face, heard her breathe a sigh as she got out of the truck and headed for the cabin.

He followed her, feeling shell-shocked. How long had he believed that Josie had feelings for Odell? Or at least that she'd dated Odell because he was wild and dangerous and she was rebelling against her family—and against Clay himself.

But if that hadn't been the case— It made him more than doubt himself. If he'd been this wrong about Josie and Odell, could he be wrong about everything else? But Josie had gotten pregnant with Odell's child. How did she explain that?

He followed Josie into the cabin and thanked Mildred and Charley for watching Ivy while she went up to see her daughter. "I'll take care of them now."

Mildred introduced him to Charley and seemed to hesitate. She studied him, obviously sizing him up.

"I'm worried about Josie," she said.

"Me, too." He walked Mildred and Charley out to

their cars. She opened the door of her Honda but stopped short of getting in.

"Josie told me that the father of her baby wasn't good for her or Ivy and that's why she left Texas, left him." Her gaze locked on him in the light coming from the car. "You seem to care for her and Ivy." She waited as if needing an answer.

"More than you know."

She nodded, her expression stern. "Whatever happened in Texas, it's not too late to make it up to her."

"I hope you're right about that."

Without another word, she got into the car and closed the door. As she pulled out, Charley fell in behind her. The two vehicles disappeared down the road.

Clay turned back to the cabin. He found Josie sitting upstairs next to the crib in an antique oak rocker, her gaze on her sleeping toddler. He couldn't remember Josie ever looking more appealing. Her love for her daughter shone in her eyes and seemed to soften and illuminate her face, making her all the more beautiful.

But he could see the exhaustion in the slope of her shoulders, in the deep blue reaches of her eyes, in the desperation he glimpsed there.

"Come on," he said softly. "Let's get you to bed."

She looked up at him, not appearing surprised to see him. "Clay."

She made it sound like an endearment, her voice soft, breathy. He could get used to her calling him that instead of Jackson.

"I need to tell you the rest."

He nodded. "But not tonight, Josie. In the morning will be soon enough. We can talk then. You need to get some rest."

"You're staying?" she asked, sounding hopeful.

He smiled. "I'll be on the couch if you need me. Don't worry."

"Thank you." Her gaze met his and held it as tenderly as an embrace.

He felt a shock of current run between them. He cupped her cheek in his palm. Her skin felt warm and soft, her gaze almost inviting. He bent closer. She tilted her face up, an open invitation.

His lips grazed hers. Lightly. He wanted to devour her, to taste and probe and take and give back. But he kissed her gently, their breaths mingling.

Her hand suddenly clutched his shoulder. Her fingers dug in as she pulled him down to her. She deepened the kiss, her mouth hot and wet and demanding.

A flash of memory raced through him, teasing his senses. Taunting him. She had kissed him like this before. Not by her barn. But by the creek. In the flickering campfire light. In the dream.

He pulled her into his arms, shoving away the fantasy of Josie for the real thing. Only this moment mattered. Only the feel of her lips. The promise in her eyes. Both so strong he felt empowered, as if this had always been their destiny and nothing on earth could stop it.

Passion, as hot and bright as sunlight, filled him. Heat sizzled over his skin. He lost himself in her eyes, her lips, her taste, her touch, the incredible erotic scent of her. He'd never wanted her more than he did now.

She tugged at his shirt, pulling the tail from his jeans, then ran her hands up under it over his chest. Her cool touch ignited his flesh as her fingertips skimmed over him like a chill.

In the haze of desire, he looked down at her. He saw his own desire reflected in her eyes.

She moaned softly. "Please."

All reason escaped him as she pressed her lips to his, her body, soft and full and ripe, against his.

He swept her up into his arms and headed across the hall to her bedroom. She looped her arms around his neck, her gaze locked on his. He shoved open the door and strode to the bed. As he carefully laid her down, she pulled him on top of her, pulled him into a kiss.

He could think of nothing but her now, his need for her, her need for him as they both struggled to rid themselves of each other's clothing.

Fumbling, he unbuttoned her shirt, drawing it back to reveal the plain white bra against her lightly freckled skin. So prim. So proper. So virginal. The thought shocked him, jarring a memory as he slipped one strap from her shoulder. Then the other. Then peeled away the bra.

Her breasts swelled. Her nipples, hard nubs against his palm.

He bent to suck at her breast. Josie groaned and cradled his face in her hands.

"Clay, oh, Clay."

She pulled away the rest of his clothing and he slowly drew down her panties.

Now, his hardness against her softness, bare skin against bare skin, they locked their arms around each other, bodies melding together with heat and longing.

Josie heard Ivy's cry first. She pulled her lips back from his, her eyes molten steel. "It's Ivy," she whispered. "She's probably wet."

They both listened to see if the toddler would fall back to sleep. The cries grew louder.

"Let me," he said, getting out of bed to pull on his jeans.

"Are you sure?" she asked.

He nodded and grinned. "I'll be right back."

He padded into Ivy's bedroom and turned on the light. "What seems to be the problem, little one?" he asked as he leaned over the crib. She was sitting in the middle of the crib, tears in her big brown eyes.

She smiled when she saw him and babbled something he didn't understand.

He wiped her tears, then checked her diaper. Wet. Just as Josie had suspected.

He laid her down, unfastened the wet diaper, glad to see it was nothing more than that, and applied the moisturized wipe, then slid another diaper under the wriggling toddler.

Ivy giggled and babbled away, kicking her legs and waving her arms and trying to get up, as he tried a half dozen times to figure out how the disposable diapers attached.

Finally, he succeeded and pulled the blanket over Ivy. She had settled back down, her dark eyes flickering closed as he leaned down to plant a kiss on her forehead. What an adorable kid, he thought as he turned out the light and started to leave.

He stopped at the door, glancing back. In the dim light of the night-light he saw Ivy's eyes close. He waited for a few more seconds but she didn't open them again.

He tiptoed back to Josie's bedroom. In the dark, he could see her lying on the bed. But as he neared, he heard the steady, rhythmic breathing.

"Josie?"

She didn't stir.

He stared down at her. As angelic as her daughter. He pulled the blanket up to her chin, covering her delectable naked body and holding his desire at bay. When she still hadn't stirred, he picked up his clothing and headed downstairs to the couch.

Several hours later, shivering and aching for just the nearness of her, he returned upstairs, stripped off his jeans and climbed in beside her. She snuggled against him, sighing softly.

He smiled and closed his eyes, at peace.

Morning broke bright and sunny. Josie stirred and rolled over, seeking the wondrous heat that enveloped her as she'd slept. But the bed was cold and empty. Just as it had always been. She felt an odd desolation, missing something she'd never had. Or had she last night?

She lay on her back, watching the sun play on the ceiling, wishing she could get back the feeling she'd had before opening her eyes. With only a faint memory of the dream to keep her warm, she clung to it, unable to remember anything more than a feeling of being cherished in a cocoon of heat and safety.

Closing her eyes, she tried to remember more, but it was gone. Just like the darkness.

Her eyes flew open at the sound of voices in Ivy's bedroom across the hall. Had Mildred spent the night? Josie tried to remember what had happened last night but couldn't discern reality from dreamland.

Ivy's sweet laugh floated into the bedroom and Josie smiled, some of the warmth coming back. Then she heard another voice. Definitely not Mildred's. She threw back the covers, shocked to find herself naked, her skin flushed.

She stood, the cool morning air raising goose bumps across her flesh as the sound of Clay's voice washed her with heat. She reached for her robe, an uneasy feeling settling in the pit of her stomach.

Last night: Raymond. Murder. Clay. Cops. Cabin. Kiss. Nothing after that but warmth and fuzziness.

She tied her robe around her and moved toward the sound of Ivy's and Clay's laughter. It filled the cabin, as sweet and pure as sunlight, and tugged unmercifully at her heart. The cabin had needed the sound of male laughter. Until that moment, she hadn't realized how much.

Clay's deep, soft voice stopped her at the doorway to Ivy's room. "About this diaper," he was saying as he leaned over her daughter, his large strong hands fumbling with the tabs. His voice as soft and gentle as his movements. "It's a lot easier to put on with a little cooperation from you. You know what I mean?"

Ivy giggled and kicked vigorously, making Clay laugh.

The sight caught Josie completely off guard. Her heart filled like a helium balloon. She loved this man. The thought rattled her. Surely she hadn't admitted it last night to him, had she? She gripped the door frame, remembering the kiss.

What *had* followed it?

Her body suggested something had definitely happened. Was still happening. Just the sight of him seemed to caress her already-sensitive bare skin. Her nipples hardened to points against the fabric of the robe and a heat filled her, making her ache.

"I didn't know you knew how to change a diaper,"

she said, leaning against the doorjamb and trying to act as nonchalant as possible.

Clay looked up in surprise and grinned. "You should have seen me last night. It took a few tries to figure it out, and I still haven't got it down yet."

His gaze lit on hers, sending a shock of desire through her.

She walked over to the dressing table and Ivy. Clay had managed to get one side of the diaper attached. The other flapped in the breeze Ivy was making with her legs and arms. "About last night—"

"No need to apologize," he said, resuming his diaper changing.

Apologize? What did she have to not apologize for?

Ivy kicked and giggled and tried to get up, but he finally got the other half of the diaper ends together. He swooped the toddler up and into Josie's arms, smiling at the two of them as if they made a picture he couldn't resist.

Ivy wrapped her arms around Josie's neck, but her attention was on Clay. She seemed fascinated by him. Ivy hadn't been around many male role models. Not that Josie had ever thought of Clay as a role model for her daughter. Until now. The realization did more than surprise her.

"About last night—" she began again.

"I've been thinking a lot about Odell," Clay said, as if he thought that's what she meant.

Not hardly. Last night's horror had been blurred by waking up this morning, all warm and fuzzy, along with her body's continued reaction to Clay since she'd gotten up.

"I called a judge in Texas to get permission to open

Odell's grave, and I had his dental records picked up."
Clay obviously had pull in high places. "With a little
luck, we'll know by this afternoon—"

"Did we make love last night?" she interrupted.

He looked up in surprise, his eyes widening. A lazy
smile played at his lips. "You don't remember?"

"No, I don't," she admitted.

"I'd like to think that if we'd made love you'd remember," he said, sounding as if he was only half joking.

She met his gaze, her tongue stuck to the roof of her
mouth for a moment. She licked at her lips but had the
good sense not to say anything.

"Ivy interrupted us," he finally said. "I went to check
on her. By the time I got back, you were sound asleep."

She nodded, feeling as if there had to be more. Or
maybe her body had just ached for more. "I thought I remembered you in bed with me," she said as she put Ivy
down, then tugged the robe tighter around her.

His smile broadened; his dark eyes bored into hers as
if her words and her movements amused him. "I couldn't
find a blanket, almost froze to death on the couch. I had
no idea Montana was so cold in May." The heat of his
gaze sent a lightning bolt through her. "I finally crawled
in bed with you and got warm."

At least she wasn't losing her mind. Not entirely.

"But nothing happened." He seemed to wait to see
how she felt about that.

"It's probably for the best," she said as she turned toward the kitchen and away from him, not wanting him
to see the disappointment in her expression. "Hungry?
I think I have some elk sausage Ruth's brother made."

Starved, Clay thought. But not for elk sausage. Or
breakfast. He watched Josie walk down the stairs to

the kitchen, pretty sure she had nothing on under the robe. The memory of her naked body pressed against his filled him with a yearning desire to take her back to bed. But that wasn't going to happen, he realized as Ivy came toddling to him.

"Panquakes," she said, gazing up at him with those big brown eyes and that cherub face. "Panquakes?"

Josie called back, "She wants to know—"

"If I like pancakes," he said, sweeping the baby up into his arms as he trailed her mother down to the kitchen.

"I love pancakes," he said, surprising himself by giving Ivy a kiss on her fat little cheek. His gaze lifted to Josie. She seemed a little surprised as well, as if she wasn't sure she knew him. He hardly recognized himself.

He'd come here to catch a thief and recover the jewels. He'd expected to catch Josie in that same net. What had changed his mind about her?

Or had he changed his mind? He studied her for a moment. Did he really believe she was innocent? He damned sure wanted to. Or maybe he just wanted her so badly that it didn't matter.

Either way, it wasn't like him. Not By-the-Book Jackson. He'd changed. Seeing her with Ivy, seeing her with the horses, seeing a woman he hadn't known in Texas. Maybe he just hadn't let himself get to know her.

He smiled to himself, remembering last night. He wanted to get to know her better. She was definitely some kind of rare woman and he wanted her. More than he could have ever imagined he could want a woman again.

Was it possible she wanted him as much as he did

her? He thought about her reaction last night and again this morning in broad daylight. The image of her hard nipples pressed against the thin robe made him groan inwardly.

"I make a mean pancake," he said, desperately trying to get his mind on something else besides her lush body.

"You cook?" she asked in surprise.

He grinned, his gaze dropping from her eyes to her lips.

She ran her tongue over her lower lip, then caught her lip between her teeth. When he met her eyes again, he saw the warning. Please don't do this. Not now. But soon.

"Pancakes," he said, heading for the fridge. "All I need is flour, eggs, milk and a little baking powder."

"Panquakes!" Ivy shrieked.

"I think Ivy better help me," he said, lifting her up onto the counter beside him.

Josie groaned. "You don't know what you're letting yourself in for."

"Got an apron?" he asked.

She pulled one out and held it up. "Ruth made this one for me." It had embroidered flowers and lots of ruffles on it. She arched one fine brow, daring him to wear it.

He'd never been one to back down from a dare, and this morning he'd have done anything to see Josie smile. He took the apron and put it on, making her laugh. He liked to make her laugh. And Ivy, too.

"Want to learn how to break an egg?" he asked the toddler as Josie set about cooking the sausage.

Thirty minutes later, the kitchen looked as though a northerner had blown through. Flour dusted the counter, floor, him and Ivy. Egg ran down the front of the cabinet and batter ringed the bowl in splattered drying drops.

But he and Ivy had fried up a batch of perfectly browned pancakes to go with the elk sausage Josie had cooked.

"Don't worry," he said at Josie's disapproving look at the mess he and Ivy had made. "I also do my own dishes."

She eyed him askance. "What have you done with the real Clay Jackson?"

"Maybe you just never knew him," he suggested seriously.

"Maybe not," she agreed, her gaze holding his for a long electric-filled moment.

They sat down to breakfast, pulling the high chair up between them. Clay watched Josie take her first bite of his pancakes. Her eyes widened in surprise. She looked over at him.

"These are really good," she exclaimed.

He just grinned, having a hard time keeping his eyes—let alone his hands—off her. He couldn't wait to kiss her again. He couldn't wait to get her back into that bed. It was hard to concentrate on anything with her sitting there, naked under the robe, her blond hair bed-mussed, sleep still lingering in her eyes.

The elk sausage was spicy and a perfect complement to the pancakes, as was Ruth's huckleberry syrup.

They ate in a relaxed, companionable silence. It seemed so right, sitting here with Josie and Ivy, eating breakfast, that he hated it when his cell phone rang just as they'd finished.

Judge Branson? Clay answered the call, his body feeling numb and weak. "Clay Jackson."

"You said to get back to you as quickly as possible," the judge said, all no-nonsense. "Had that body exhumed. Sent off samples for DNA testing with a rush request. But I have to tell you, I think it's a waste of good money to run the DNA. Odell Burton's dental records matched the body's."

"What about the ring?"

"No jewelry was buried with the body. Family says they had a break-in a few months ago. Bunch of stuff was stolen, including Odell's ring. By the way, you remember O.T. Burton, Odell's father? Well O.T. says he doesn't want to hear Odell's name again and that this had better be the end of it. Anything else?"

"No, thanks, Judge."

He hung up and stood for a moment without turning around. He could feel Josie nearby and hear Ivy chattering up a storm as if telling her mother a story. He closed his eyes tightly for a moment, in silent thanks.

"Odell's dead," he said quietly as he turned to face her.

"They're sure?"

He nodded. "No mistake. The dental records matched. The judge sent off DNA samples as well, but it's definite. Odell's dead. As for his ring, O.T. says it was stolen along with some other stuff a couple of months ago."

She sank down onto the couch, her body shaking with relieved sobs as she pulled Ivy into her arms. He watched her hug her daughter, washed with an ocean of emotions.

The sound of a vehicle coming up the hill drew his attention to the window. A sheriff's car pulled up beside his pickup and parked.

"Looks like we have company," he said to Josie as the sheriff climbed out and started toward the cabin.

Chapter 10

It definitely *looked* like a map. But Josie didn't recognize any of the pencil markings on the sheet of the once tightly folded paper. Not that there were many markings. Five *X*'s along a line that wound around in a U-shape, almost a circle.

"Have any idea what it might be?" the sheriff asked. He'd taken a seat at the quickly cleared kitchen table, a file folder in front of him from which he'd pulled out a copy of the map he'd found on Raymond's body. "Or if it might have any relevance to Degas's death?"

She stared at the sheet of paper, fear filling her, but nothing on the map looked in the least bit familiar. It looked as if a child had drawn it. Crude. Simple. Frightening in the way the words had been printed. Something in the slant of the handwriting that sent a shaft of horror through her.

The only words on the map were Start by one open end of the line, followed by Pit as the line continued down and around, then Garden, Waterfall, End, Paradise and Finish.

The word End had been circled in red ink.

She shivered, hugging herself as she looked up at the sheriff, and shook her head.

"How about you?" he asked Clay.

Clay shrugged and shook his head.

The sheriff leaned back in his chair and studied Clay for a long moment. "Raymond was wanted in Texas for questioning in a robbery two years ago."

Clay said nothing.

"I understand that the thieves were never caught and the cache of jewels never recovered," he continued, eyeing Clay. "I also know that you used to be in law enforcement and that you still do some consulting work. But you realize you have no authority to investigate a crime in the state of Montana."

"Like I said, I'm on vacation," Clay said with a shrug. "I didn't even know Josie was in the state." His gaze shifted to her. "It's a smaller world than I ever imagined."

The sheriff glanced over at her. He didn't look convinced but didn't press it. He picked up the copy of the map and slipped it back into a file marked Degas.

"We also found a stolen cell phone in Degas's car." He seemed to hesitate before sliding another piece of paper across the table toward them. "From what we can gather, Raymond Degas made three calls from the phone."

She could feel Clay's gaze on her, hard and questioning. Was he thinking that Raymond might have called her? That her number at the ranch would be on the list? Oh, no, could Raymond *have* called her?

Her chest constricted as she looked down at the three numbers printed on the sheet. Relief swept over her. All three phone numbers had Texas area codes.

Then she recognized one of the numbers on the list and her heart stopped.

Clay studied the list as well, but his relief to see that Josie's number wasn't on the sheet of paper was short-lived. He stared down at the phone numbers. He knew all three.

A wave of confusion hit him as his gaze flicked up to Josie's. She'd paled, her eyes wide with shock.

"You recognize any of the numbers?" the sheriff asked.

Clay could feel the sheriff's intent gaze. Lying wouldn't do any good.

"Yes," he said, looking away from Josie and the fear he saw. "They're to the San Antonio area. The first number is the O'Malley Ranch."

The sheriff looked at Josie. Clay saw that the cop already knew who the calls had been made to. He just wanted to know why. So did Clay.

"Any reason Raymond Degas would call your family?" he asked her.

Josie shook her head.

Clay offered an explanation. "To let them know he'd seen Josie and that she was all right?"

The cop's gaze shifted back to Josie. "Your family didn't know where you were?"

"Look, Sheriff—"

"Let the lady answer," the sheriff interrupted him.

Josie seemed to have regained her composure. "To

put it simply, I found myself pregnant. Where I come from that calls for a shotgun wedding. I didn't want to marry the baby's father. So I left. I haven't kept in touch with my family."

"Well, they know now," he said disapprovingly, then he looked at Clay again, waiting.

"The other numbers are to O.T. Burton and the Williams Gallery," Clay said, having done horse business with O.T. and consulting with Williams. "I have no idea why Raymond would call either of them."

The sheriff's smile never reached his eyes. "Funny, but that's what both parties said when I talked to them. I understand Degas ran with one of the Burton boys—Odell? And that both were suspects in the jewel robbery, but Odell is dead. He was killed in a car crash not long after the robbery."

Clay could feel Josie tense in the chair next to him.

"And Brandon Williams, the owner of the gallery, is a collector. It was his jewels that were stolen." The sheriff's gaze locked onto Clay's. "He seems to think you're up here looking for his jewels and the crooks."

Clay didn't bat an eyelash. Didn't speak. Just waited, knowing the cop knew exactly what was going on here. But there wasn't anything he could do about it without proof.

"Do you have any leads on Raymond's death?" Josie asked into the brittle silence.

The sheriff held Clay's gaze for a few seconds longer, then dropped it to the sheet of phone numbers. He slipped the paper back into the file and stood up to leave. "It's still under investigation," he said without looking up. "I may need to talk to you both again." He gave them both a warning look. "Don't leave town."

* * *

Clay stood at the window and watched the sheriff drive away, wondering about the scared look he'd seen in Josie's eyes when she'd seen the map and the phone numbers.

What was it she was so afraid of? Not Odell Burton. He was dead. Then what? Damn the woman. What was she hiding?

He turned at the sound of her footfalls behind him, his head spinning. Maybe Raymond had called the O'Malleys to tell them he knew where Josie was. Maybe. It just didn't feel right. Why would Raymond do that? Unless money was involved. Clay just couldn't see Shawn O'Malley paying someone like Raymond, even for that kind of information.

But what bothered him most was why Raymond called the other two numbers. Odell's father, O.T. Burton, had never had any use for Raymond. Nor much use for Odell, from the sound of it.

But it was the third number, the call to Williams Gallery, that shook him the most.

He'd dialed Brandon Williams's number the moment the sheriff had left. No answer. He didn't leave a message. This was something he wanted to discuss person to person.

As he watched Josie come into the room with Ivy he noticed her worrying her lower lip with her teeth. Was she upset about the calls Raymond had made or the map?

"So you didn't recognize the map the sheriff found on Raymond?" he asked.

Her gaze jerked up to his and he kicked himself for sounding so suspicious. But damned if he wasn't.

Damned if he wasn't getting more suspicious as the days went on.

"I told the sheriff the truth, Jackson. I have no idea what it was. It just—" She let out a sigh and put Ivy down with her toys before heading for the kitchen.

"It just what?" he asked, following her. "Sit down and talk to me. I'm cleaning this up."

Surprisingly, she didn't argue. She sat, kneading her hands nervously in front of her on the table.

"It just gave me a bad feeling, that's all," she said, and put her hands in her lap. "It scared me, but I don't know why."

She fell silent as he began to wash the dishes. "Let me dry, please. I need something to do."

He nodded, studying her as she pulled a clean dish towel from the drawer. Ivy joined them to play in the toy drawer.

"Why would Raymond call Burton," she asked after a moment.

He shook his head, wondering if Raymond had some reason to think Odell was alive—just as Josie had. Maybe Raymond really believed that Odell had been the one who'd shot him. Hadn't Josie thought she heard him say "Odell did it"? Did someone want them to believe that Odell was alive? But why? And who would do that?

"Who identified Odell's body after the crash?" she asked out of the blue.

"O.T. The identification was based on the watch and ring. The body was too burned for anything else."

"Then dental records weren't checked?" she asked.

He shook his head. "It hadn't seemed necessary at the time. But Judge Branson said the records matched."

She nodded and began to stack the clean plates in the cupboard.

He finished cleaning the kitchen with Josie's help. A dense silence seemed to fall over the cabin as they finished.

"There's something I need to do. Would you watch Ivy for me?"

She called from out on the porch, dialing the familiar number, her fingers trembling.

It rang once, then another two times. No one was home.

Someone picked up. "Hello."

Just the sound of her father's voice choked her up. Tears welled in her eyes and her voice broke. "Dad?"

"Josie." It sounded like a prayer. "Oh, Josie, thank God you called."

She couldn't speak.

"Are you all right?"

It wasn't what she'd expected him to say. She thought he'd be angry and upset about her leaving, about her not calling before, about Ivy.

"Yes," she managed to answer, all her homesickness for Texas and her family flooding her with tears. "I've missed you."

"Me, too, baby."

They talked for a long time. She told him about Ivy and her horse training. He told her about the ranch and Texas and her brothers. Then her father grew quiet.

"Josie," he said after a moment. "When your mother died and left me a little girl to raise, I was scared to death. What did I know about little girls? I thought if I was tough on you like I was with the boys…" His voice trailed off. "I'm sorry I wasn't there for you."

"You did fine, Dad. This was something I had to do on my own."

"It sounds like you've done all right."

She wanted to correct him and tell him she'd messed up. Big time. But she hoped that she could right her mistakes before she saw her father—just as she'd sworn on her great-grandmother's memory she would do.

"You know Raymond Degas called here," her father said. "He had some fool notion that Odell was still alive."

Her heart thudded in her chest. "I know. But he was wrong."

"That's good." He seemed to hesitate. "When the sheriff called, he said someone killed Raymond. They find his killer?"

"Not yet."

Silence.

"Are you considering coming home, Josie?"

She desperately wanted to. Wanted her father and brothers to see Ivy. And Ivy to have her family around her. "I want to."

"Good, I was hoping you'd say that." He sounded relieved.

"I just need to finish what I started up here, Dad."

"I love you, Josie. Be careful."

"I love you, too, Dad."

She hung up and let all the pent-up emotions flow, then she dried her eyes and went inside.

He studied her as she entered the living room. She'd pulled on a sweater, jeans and boots when the sheriff stopped by. Clay missed the robe and the way the thin fabric hugged her curves.

"How did it go?" he asked, suspecting she'd called home.

She nodded and smiled through fresh tears. "Dad wants me to come home."

Even a man as stubborn and hard-nosed as Shawn O'Malley had some sense, it seemed.

He wondered about his own good sense. Or if he had any when it came to Josie. He'd made so many mistakes. Last night she'd been in a confessing mood. She'd wanted to tell him something, had seemed desperate to unburden herself.

But he'd stopped her. He'd been afraid of what she was going to say. He knew he'd have to hear it eventually. One way or the other. But not last night.

"Where's Ivy?" she asked.

He'd played with her until she couldn't keep her eyes open. "I put her down for her nap."

"Thank you."

"No problem. I enjoy her."

He thought he saw pain behind her tears. Why did he fear he'd made more mistakes with her than even he knew about? Or worse, that he was about to make another one?

"We need to talk," he said.

She nodded and brushed at the tears.

He reached out to cup her cheek in the palm of his hand, his thumb brushing across her lips, her soft, smooth cheek. "But first, I want to make love with you."

Her gaze never wavered. What he saw in her eyes almost leveled him. She kissed the pad of his thumb, her eyes filled with a need that mirrored his own.

He swept Josie up into his arms and carried her up the stairs to the bedroom, across from Ivy's, all reason and logic and suspicion discarded as quickly as he planned to discard their clothing. He wanted her. And he planned to have her. Right now. Later he'd deal with whatever she had to tell him, he told himself, as he closed the door.

She opened to his kiss, offering her mouth, encouraging him to explore deeper, as if he would find her every secret in the dark recesses. She clung to him, moaning softly as she kissed him back with a matching intensity that aroused and excited him.

This was nothing like the images that had haunted him. Nothing like the slow, sensual way she'd come to him that night in Texas in the dream. This was wild and hot and hurried. Filled with aching need. A fire that could only be put out with more fire.

She unsnapped his western shirt, jerking it open, flattening her palms to his bare skin as if she needed to feel him as desperately as he did her.

He released her lips only long enough to pull the light cotton-knit sweater over her head. His fingers unhooked the no-nonsense bra she wore, releasing her breasts to his waiting hands. He cupped them, thumbing the already-hard nipples, his desire heightening at just the sight of her.

She groaned and reached for his belt buckle, "Please, Clay."

They joined, coupled in a frantic need for release. He filled her and she fulfilled him in a dance as old as life.

When the release came, he felt as if a dam had broken. Not just for him, but for Josie, too, as if this had been the first time in a long time for her as well. A very long time.

They lay holding on to each other as if in a windstorm. But the real storm had passed, hadn't it?

He pushed himself up just enough to look down into her eyes. The last thing he wanted to do was break the connection between their bodies. He had hoped that having her would finally put an end to the years of yearning. But as he looked down at her, he knew he would never be free of her spell. He would want her again and again. He already did.

Her wide blue eyes stared up at him with a look of surprise and wonder and sated peace. Her blond hair curled wetly around her face. Her arms still locked around him as if she didn't want their bodies to separate any more than he did.

He stared into her eyes. A trickle of sweat rolled down his chest to pool in the hollow of her belly button. The breeze from the open window drifted over him, chilling his exposed flesh.

As he looked down at her, one clear thought lodged itself in his brain like a splinter that refused to come out.

"We've done this before," he said, his voice deadly quiet and just as deadly sure.

Chapter 11

Josie stared into his eyes. "You aren't serious?"

He seemed dumbfounded, stunned. He *was* serious.

"You *really* don't remember," she said, staring up at him, as shocked as he looked.

Josie felt her heart lurch. She searched his gaze, wishing for the need, the desire, the fulfillment, the peace she'd seen just moments before. But all the warmth had gone out of his dark eyes. They stared down at her, hard, cold and accusing.

Her throat closed, her mouth dry as dust. He hadn't moved. Their bodies were still united. Slowly, she unlocked her arms from his back, but still he didn't move to let her up.

"Tell me," he whispered.

"Yes, we did this before."

She felt cold suddenly. From his gaze. From the

breeze. She could feel him pulling away from her, although he still hadn't moved.

"When?"

"The night by the creek."

"Which night?" His gaze locked with hers.

All these months she'd thought he'd regretted their lovemaking—and he hadn't even *remembered* it! How could that be? The fall he'd taken from Diablo? Or the booze he'd consumed? Or had he not wanted to remember it, just as she'd originally thought?

"You got into a fight with Odell," she said, watching his face, "and took off on Diablo. You'd been drinking."

He pulled away, leaving an emptiness inside her, heart-deep. The cool breeze rushed over her bare, sweaty skin, chilling her.

Hurriedly she struggled to get into her clothing, needing something between her and the unbearable look in his eyes. Out of the corner of her eye, she watched him dress, his fingers working methodically while hers fumbled clumsily.

"You really don't remember," she said to his rigid back.

"No."

He sounded as cold as she felt. He didn't remember and now he thought she'd lied to him. Kept it a secret. If their lovemaking had been the only secret she'd kept these past two years, maybe then he could understand why she'd done what she had. Maybe then he could forgive her.

But as she finished dressing, pulling on her boots, she looked over at him. He sat on the end of the bed, his face set in granite. He jerked on his boots, the muscles in his arms bulging with the effort. Then he sat, staring straight ahead, his hands gripping the edge of the bed, his jaw set.

No, she thought, understanding and forgiveness were the last two things she could expect from Clay Jackson.

He fought to rein in the rush of emotions. Betrayal. Shock. Hurt. Anger. All bombarding him at once. Blurring his thoughts. Making him sick.

He stared at the wall, gripping the mattress as if it was all that was holding him together, unable To look at her. Unable to corral his thoughts any more than he could the turmoil of emotions.

Realization came slowly, awkwardly. It hadn't been a dream.

He loosened his grip on the bed as he looked over at her. Memories of the night by the creek flashed as bright as falling stars.

"You rode Diablo."

She nodded. "I'd been working with him, trying some of the techniques I'd seen other trainers use, techniques I'd read about."

And those techniques had worked. He remembered the way she'd ridden. No wonder he hadn't been able to believe it. She'd been able to ride a horse he had fought, a horse that had finally defeated him.

"Why didn't you say something the next day?"

Her brow shot up. "I just assumed you preferred to forget it as if it never happened."

The memory of that night had haunted him for two years. But he *hadn't* believed it had happened for so many reasons. Why was that?

He stared at her. Because he'd refused to believe she could ride Diablo. Refused to believe she could ride that well. His lack of faith in her shocked him.

But he knew it had been more than that. If he'd admitted to himself what had happened between them that night, he'd have had to admit how he felt about her.

He raked a hand through his hair, sick inside. He looked at her, her face still flushed from their lovemaking, it all coming back. Everything.

"Why did you come to me that night?" he asked, his voice sounding as tortured as he felt.

She looked away, but not before he'd seen the pain in her eyes. "Surely you know that I've always wanted it to happen." She shifted her gaze back to him. "When Diablo came back without you, I figured you'd been thrown. Without thinking, I got on the horse and rode out to find you."

"And you found me."

She nodded. "You looked so desolate, so hurt, I—"

"You felt sorry for me," he said in disgust.

Her eyes filled with tears and a mixture of emotions that pulled at his heart as she shook her head. "I wanted you," she whispered.

The honesty in her words stunned him. He wanted desperately to reach for her, to take her in his arms, to make up for all the hurt and pain they'd both suffered.

But a memory tugged at him, a feeling of dread at its heels. "That night by the creek, you were a…"

"A virgin?" Her gaze narrowed; tiny sparks flashed in the blue of her eyes. "That was another reason you didn't believe it happened, wasn't it? You refused to believe you might be wrong about me. That I might not be as wild as you were determined I was."

Her accusation hit its mark. Bull's-eye. He *had* believed the worst of her, but he realized now it had been less from her spirited antics and more to do with his own hurt. He'd *wanted* to believe the worst about her. Because he'd felt vulnerable around her. He'd known instinctively she was the one woman who could get to him.

He stared at her proud profile. "It wasn't you. It was me. I was…" The words didn't come easily. "I was scared. After Maria—I didn't want to get involved."

"I know." She turned slowly to look at him, but instead of anger in her gaze, he saw deep sadness.

His chest constricted, his throat went dry. He swallowed, afraid to ask the one question he now desperately needed answered. "Did you and Odell ever—"

"No," she said, anticipating his question. "I never had sex with Odell. I've never made love with anyone… but you."

The realization slammed him back, knocking the wind from him. He gripped the bed again and held on. It took him a moment to finally form the words. "Ivy is my daughter," he said, hearing the truth as he said them.

"Yes."

Josie wanted to recoil from the horrible pain that twisted his handsome face into a mask of despair. He threw back his head and let out a cry that froze her blood. A cry of pure anguish.

She reached for him, needing to comfort him. But he moved away from her before she could touch him.

He backed up against the bedroom wall, his hands out in front of him as if to shield him from her words. "You let me think she was Odell's."

"You're the one who saw Odell in her."

He nodded, his eyes dark and moist. "What was I to think? I didn't remember that we'd made love."

"Didn't you? Didn't you remember any of it?" She saw the answer in his face.

He slammed a fist against the wall with a curse. "Why, dammit? Why didn't you tell me when you realized you were pregnant?"

She didn't want to get into all the reasons. Not now. "Because I believed it wouldn't have been the best thing for me or my child."

"*Our* child, damn you. Ivy is *our* child! I had a right to know. I had a right to decide what was the best for our child."

Her heart pounded. "What would you have done if I'd told you?"

"I would have—" He looked around as if the answer were in this room. He closed his eyes.

"I knew you wouldn't have believed Ivy was yours." Why did he believe it now?

He lifted his head slowly, sadness softening his handsome face. "But once I knew she was mine, I would have married you."

"You would have forced me to marry you whether it was what I wanted or not," she said angrily. The last thing she'd wanted was a loveless marriage. "I did what I thought was best for Ivy and me."

The phone rang, making her jump. She reached for it before it could ring a second time. "Yes?" She listened for a few moments. "Yes, thank you for calling." She hung up and looked at Clay, tears in her eyes. "That was the sheriff. They have a suspect in custody. A man who was seen drinking with Raymond at the Toston bar. They found the murder weapon in the man's car." Odell didn't kill Raymond. Because he was dead. "It's over."

"If you think that, Josie, you're dead wrong."

* * *

He heard Ivy coming awake in the room across the hall. Ivy. His daughter.

Josie wiped her eyes and looked up at him. Neither spoke for a few moments. Ivy let out another cry.

Josie slid off the bed and headed across the hall.

He stood for a few moments, too shaken to move. He could still smell her on his skin. The same way their lovemaking had been branded in his mind. His anger seemed to overwhelm him.

He trailed after Josie, stopping in the doorway to watch her with Ivy. His daughter. Some of his anger dissipated at the sight of her. He tried to tell himself that Josie had done what she thought was right for her baby. Their baby.

But he couldn't. She should have told him. He had a right to know. Ivy was his, too.

He knew he needed time to think. But for the life of him, he had no idea where they went from here. It scared him. Now that he knew Ivy was his, it changed everything. Surely Josie realized that.

He watched her change the toddler, then put her down on the floor. Ivy scrambled over to him, holding out a worn teddy bear in her hand.

He looked into her large, lash-fringed brown eyes and felt a jolt, heart-deep. "Ivy," he whispered as he reached down to pick her up. He could smell her sweet baby scent as he wrapped his arms around her. Tears burned his eyes.

Over Ivy's small shoulder, he met Josie's gaze. But he refused to let her tears touch the wall of ice he'd built around his heart toward her.

He closed his eyes and hugged his daughter to him, awed and humbled and scared.

"She'll be hungry after her nap," Josie said.

He nodded, realizing how little he knew about his daughter. His gut constricted with regret at all he'd lost. Would he ever be able to forgive Josie? Forgive himself?

He followed her downstairs, carrying his daughter, Ivy's face against his, her arms around his neck.

The pull had always been there. He'd felt something for this child the moment he'd laid eyes on her. Had he known but just refused to admit the truth?

Josie couldn't bear to look at him. She busied herself making a peanut butter and jelly sandwich for Ivy.

When she turned, she saw he still held his daughter, his face filled with anguish. She watched him press a kiss to Ivy's cheek, then put her down. The expression on his face as he looked at his daughter broke her heart.

He didn't look at her as he turned and strode from the room, the screen door slamming behind him.

She closed her eyes, willing back the tears, but her heart filled with images of Clay and Ivy. Their laughter mingling. Their dark eyes accusing her.

What had she done?

Two years ago, she'd believed Clay would make a terrible father and an even worse husband. She'd believed he'd regretted their lovemaking and wanted nothing to do with her. Yes, he'd been wrong about her, had purposely thought the worst of her to protect himself from his feelings.

But what she'd done to him was so much worse. She'd kept him from his daughter. She'd underestimated the man she loved.

"I'm sorry, Clay," she whispered after him.

Ivy chattered up a storm as Josie put her into the high chair and fed her. "Everything's going to be all right now." She repeated the words, praying somehow they would come true.

Someone knocked at the front door. Clay. He'd come back. She pulled a peanut-butter-and-jelly-faced Ivy from her high chair and hurried to the door.

But it was Mildred peering through the screen door.

"Are you all right?" Mildred asked.

Josie smiled, but the tears gave her away.

"What did he do now?" Mildred said, going to the kitchen, straight to the coffeepot.

"It isn't what you think," Josie said, following behind her. Ivy wriggled to be put down, but not before Josie cleaned up her face and hands. Ivy hurried to her cupboard to pull out all of the toys.

"You told him, didn't you?" Mildred said, her hands on her hips as the coffee began to fill the pot. "You told him he is Ivy's father."

Her mouth gaped open.

"Oh, Josie, Ruth and I both knew the moment we laid eyes on him."

She stumbled over to a chair and plunked down. It had been a long day. Too much had happened. She rubbed her temples, wondering what Mildred would say if she knew that she'd just made love with him again this afternoon. "I had to tell him."

"Of course you did," Mildred agreed. "I'm sure you had your reasons for not telling him before. What happens now?"

She shook her head. "Oh, Mildred, it's all so complicated."

"Love usually is."

Her gaze froze on the woman. "Love? What makes you think—"

"Oh, please. I'm not *that* old that I don't know love when I see it."

Josie leaned her elbows on the table and dropped her chin into her hands. "Clay and I have always been like oil and water. He's never understood me any better than I did him. Now too much has happened. We'll never be able to get past it. We're all wrong for each other. We always have been and nothing can change that."

"It already has," Mildred said, smiling. "Ivy. Ivy is the best of the two of you. She's proof that with love even two people like you and Clay can find some common ground."

Common ground. Josie thought of their lovemaking. Oh, they'd already found their common ground, all right. A sexual chemistry. But unfortunately that was shaky ground and nothing to build any sort of relationship on.

"Would you like me to stay?" Mildred asked.

Josie shook her head. "We'll be fine. The sheriff has a suspect in custody for Raymond Degas's murder." And Odell was dead. "We'll be just fine." She actually believed it. She got up to give Mildred a hug. "You go on home. I know you have things to do. But thanks for all your help. I really appreciate it."

"Charley asked me into town for dinner," Mildred said, grinning. "You think I should go?"

"Absolutely," Josie told her.

Mildred got a hug and a kiss from Ivy, then left. Josie watched her drive away, wondering where Clay had gone. He hadn't left for good. That much she knew.

The sun had dropped behind the mountains, leaving

the day cool and a little dark. She made a light dinner for herself and Ivy, but opted to eat inside tonight because of the approaching storm. Thunder rumbled off in the distance.

She played with Ivy until the night turned black and the breeze coming through the window smelled of rain. She sensed static in the air she wasn't sure had anything to do with the storm. She couldn't quit thinking of Clay, the ache for him painful. Was he all right?

She bathed Ivy, dressed her in her favorite teddy bear pajamas and put her to bed just before the storm hit. Lightning lit the night outside her bedroom window. She tried to read, but finally gave up and turned out the light. The storm moved closer. Huge splintered bursts of lightning lit the sky, immediately followed by the cannon boom of thunder.

She pulled the blankets up to her chin, hoping the storm didn't wake Ivy and scare her. She wished Clay was here with them.

Finally, rain began to fall and the lightning and thunder moved on.

It was after three in the morning that Josie woke with a start, sitting upright in bed. At first she thought she'd heard something that had woken her. The rain had stopped. No sound came from inside or outside the cabin.

She turned on the lamp beside the bed, slid into her slippers and hurried to Ivy's room, suddenly afraid.

Ivy lay curled under her blanket sound asleep, her arms wrapped around her teddy bear.

Josie stood for a few minutes watching her, reassuring herself that her baby was fine. It must have just been a bad dream.

That's when she remembered what had dragged her from sleep. Raymond's last words. "Odell did it."

She'd thought he was trying to tell her who'd shot him. But he couldn't have meant that. Odell was dead. Then what had Raymond been trying so hard to tell her? Why would a dying man use his last breath if not to name his killer?

It felt like a light going off inside her head. A burst of knowledge, bright and blinding. *Not* "Odell did it." But "Odell *hid* it." The jewel collection.

That is what Raymond must have been looking for, just as Clay suspected. But if Odell hid it, wouldn't it be in Texas, unless—

She sensed movement from the open doorway. Whirling in that direction, she saw a large man in a western hat silhouetted in the doorway.

"Clay?"

But the moment she said his name, she knew it wasn't Clay.

A scream caught in her throat. No one would hear her but Ivy if she screamed. She spun around, frantically grabbing for a weapon in the dim light in the shadowy room. Her fingers closed over the base of a lamp as she heard him behind her.

He was on her before she could swing the lamp. His strong fingers clamped over her wrist and twisted hard. The lamp thumped to the floor.

Something hard smacked the side of her head. Stars splattered across her vision.

"Ivy!" It was her last thought before the darkness took her.

Chapter 12

Clay drove around for hours. Thinking. Remembering. Hurting. An unmerciful weight had settled on his chest, making merely breathing unbearable.

By the time he got back to Josie's cabin, he felt more excitement about being Ivy's father than anger toward Josie for keeping his daughter from him.

He understood why she'd done what she had. Understood the part he'd played. The confusion. The misunderstanding. And he blamed himself more than Josie.

But it didn't make it any easier.

He parked a little way from the cabin. No lights shone inside, not that he'd expected to see any. It was late. Josie and Ivy would be asleep.

He slid down in the front seat, pulled his Stetson down over his eyes and tried to sleep, craving some release from his thoughts. Worse, his feelings. Feelings of love so strong that he thought his heart would burst.

Ivy was his daughter.

And Josie? He didn't want to think about that right now. Couldn't.

Sleep came in fitful spurts, filled with haunting images, the interludes in between packed with waking panic.

His dreams were always the same. Josie riding up to his campfire on Diablo.

Only this time something was horribly wrong.

Just before daylight, he jerked awake, heart pounding, drenched in sweat, his mind suddenly clear. He *knew* how Josie had done it! He knew how she'd gotten the security plans to steal the jewels.

He flung open the pickup door and raced down the hill to the cabin, not caring about the hour, not caring about anything but confronting Josie. If he thought she'd dropped a bombshell on him yesterday, wait until today. And just when he thought it couldn't get any worse.

He pounded on the front door, waiting in the cool shadow of the porch. The moon sneaked toward the dark western horizon as if hoping to avoid the sun that now rimmed the mountain crest to the east. The early-morning darkness felt damp and cool and quiet.

He pounded again, needing desperately to break that eerie silence, to make sense of what had happened two years ago.

Still no answer. She was probably expecting him and had no intention of answering the door. Or she'd taken off. But her truck was still parked in the yard.

He tried the door, surprised to find it unlocked. He

frowned as he turned the knob and the door fell open and he stepped in.

He felt something under his boot soles. His heart took off at a gallop as he flipped on the living room light. On the floor were wood shavings from where the front door had been jimmied open.

His pulse pounded in his ears at a deafening tempo, his heart a thunder in his chest as he took the stairs two at a time.

A muted night-light gleamed from the empty bathroom. He swung to his left and into Josie's bedroom.

The light was on, the covers thrown back on the bed, the pillow balled near the edge, a hollow space still in the sheets where she'd been. But the bed was empty.

He swung around and raced across the hall into Ivy's room, flinging open the door, his gaze leaping to the crib. The first morning light bled in through the window. Even from the doorway he could see that the crib was empty.

A groan. His gaze swung to the dark corner of the room and the figure crumpled there.

He reached her in two strides, dropping beside her, his fingers going to her throat for a pulse, a prayer echoing in his head. "Please, God, please."

He felt a pulse. Strong. Strong like Josie.

She stirred, her eyelids flickering. Her lips moved but no sound came out.

Tears burned his eyes. He took a ragged breath. "Don't try to talk. I'm here. Everything is going to be all right," he whispered as he brushed the fine blond hair back from her face and felt the lump and the dried blood.

Her eyes jerked open. She blinked up at him, all that

blue filled with confusion and pain. "Ivy." The word was only a whisper.

He felt his heart take off again. "Isn't she with Mildred?"

"No!" Josie tried to get up.

He held her down, a lump the size of Texas lodging in his throat as he looked over at the empty crib. "She was here?"

Josie nodded, tears coursing down her cheeks. "He took her."

"Who, Josie? Who took her?"

She began to cry, huge gut-wrenching sobs. "I didn't get a good look at him."

"It's all right."

"No, Clay," she said, trying to get up again. "I have to find Ivy."

He fought to breathe. "We'll find her, Josie. Just lie still for a moment, please."

The phone rang.

He stared down at her for an instant. "Stay here."

He charged into the bedroom, half-falling, half-sliding, and jerked up the phone. "Yes. Hello."

"It's Charley, Charley Brainard. Sorry to call at this hour, but I can't seem to find Mildred. It's just odd. All the lights are on, her car's here and her knitting is in the middle of the floor. I thought maybe something had happened over there, some reason she might have left in a hurry without her car?"

Clay felt the floor drop from under him. "No, we haven't seen her. But I'll let you know if I do."

He'd barely hung up the phone when it rang again.

A deadly silence filled the line, one he could barely hear over the frantic beat of his heart.

"Jackson." The voice was electronic, unrecognizable. "I have your daughter."

Clay could hear Ivy crying in the background and someone trying to soothe her. "If you hurt a hair on her head—"

"You are in no position to threaten me," the voice snapped. "Listen carefully. I have Ivy and her baby-sitter."

Mildred?

"If you ever want to see Ivy again you will tell no one. No police. Don't underestimate me." Ivy's crying grew louder, and he realized that the voice on the other end of the line had moved closer to the toddler.

"Ivy. Let me talk to her." To his surprise the caller put the phone next to Ivy's mouth and ear. "Ivy?" The crying slowed. "Ivy. Ivy, honey." She stopped crying but still whimpered. He could see her in his mind's eye, her face red and tear-stained, her cupid's bow lips thrust out, eyes wide. His eyes. "Listen, sweetheart." His voice broke. "It's going to be all right. Can you hear me. It's…"

"Clay." He heard a sound behind him and turned to see Josie stumble into the room.

"Your mommy is here."

He handed the phone to Josie but stayed beside her so he could hear.

"Ivy? Ivy, darling."

He closed his eyes at the sound of Ivy's sweet voice. Then the electronic voice came back on.

"Jackson?"

He could hear Mildred in the background. She sounded scared but was trying to comfort Ivy.

"I'm here," he snapped, as angry as he was afraid.

"Who are you? What the hell do you want?" How do you know Ivy is my child?

"I want the jewels," the eerie, unreal voice said. "Josie has them."

Clay looked over at her. She *had* the jewels. Just as he'd suspected. And now someone had kidnapped their daughter for those damned rocks. He gritted his teeth, his gaze boring into her.

She shook her head, her eyes wild as she covered the phone. "I don't have the jewels," she whispered frantically. "You have to believe me, Clay. You of all people."

He stared at her, blinded by his anger, by his need to protect his child. Their child. Josie wouldn't lie about this, not with her daughter's life at stake.

The electronic voice was saying, "I'll call back with instructions for the trade tonight. If you—"

"Just a minute," he interrupted. "What makes you think Josie has the jewels?"

Silence. He feared the caller had hung up.

"The jewels had better still be in her great-grandmother's rodeo saddle where they were. And don't try to tell me that she doesn't have it. She'd never part with that saddle." Static. "Get the jewels and wait for my call. If you tell anyone, especially the police, you will never see your daughter again. Is that understood?"

Clay's gaze was still locked on Josie. His chest tightened. "Yes, I understand perfectly."

"One more thing." The electronically disguised voice set his nerves on edge. "You are to bring Josie O'Malley with you. No argument."

Clay felt a blade of pure ice sink into his heart. "Josie will be there."

"Do I have to remind you what will happen to the kid if you and Josie don't come alone?"

"No."

"Good. And don't forget the jewels or try to pull anything."

Who had taken Ivy? Someone who knew him. Knew Josie. Knew them both well. If he hadn't known better, he would have sworn that Odell Burton had come back from the grave.

"You'll get your jewels," he said through gritted teeth. "Just don't hurt my daughter. Or I'll kill you."

The line went dead.

"Oh God, Clay," she cried as she watched him hang up the phone. Her baby had been kidnapped. By some monster who thought she had the jewels in her great-grandmother's saddle?

She tried to hold back the hysteria, the irrational need to just sit and cry or scream and beat the wall with her fists. She had to keep her head. She had to help her baby.

Clay hadn't moved. He stood, his eyes closed, his hands clenched into fists at his side, his face twisted in pain.

"Clay?" She reached for him, needing him to tell her that it was going to be all right, that they would get Ivy back, that he'd help her.

But when his eyes opened, she saw that it was much more than pain that burned in the darkness. Much more than anger.

"I know how Odell got the security plans," he said, his voice as hollow and strange as the man's on the phone.

Her heart stopped and it took all she could do to will it to keep beating. She'd lost everything. Clay would never believe her now. Not that he would have two years ago.

"It isn't what you're thinking."

He raised a brow. "You have no idea what I'm thinking."

"You think I betrayed you that night by the creek in Texas."

"Didn't you? Didn't you seduce me for my keys so you could get the security plans for Odell? That was the real reason you made love to me, why you came down to the creek, wasn't it? The damned jewels."

She opened her mouth but no words came out. Weakness seeped through her limbs. Not now. Don't let this be happening now. Her head ached. But nothing like her heart. Ivy. Oh, Ivy. They had to find Ivy. They had to get her back.

She needed Clay to help her find their daughter. But he didn't trust her. He thought she'd seduced him for the security plans. That she'd endangered their child for the jewels. Or for Odell. Did he think she'd lied about that, too?

She looked at him, wanting to scream and cry and beat his chest to make him see that they had to trust each other. Now. For Ivy's sake.

Somehow she found the words. "I didn't know anything about Odell's plans to steal the jewels. That night when Diablo came back riderless, I rode Diablo because I was worried about you." She didn't tell him that she'd come to his ranch, looking for him. Dressed in a yellow sundress, feeling foolish and sexy and ready to do anything to get him to notice that she wasn't a kid anymore.

He said nothing. His gaze was unforgiving.

"I didn't just want you that night. I was in love with you. I had been for years."

He flinched, his gaze darker, harder. A muscle jumped in his jaw.

"When I crossed the creek, I saw you, sitting with your back against the trunk of that live oak. I saw something in your eyes. Or at least I believed I did. Heartache. And desire for me. I thought I recognized it because of my own."

She hoped he'd say something. But still he remained motionless, rigid with anger.

"I made love to you because I wanted you and I thought you wanted me, too. It was so incredible. I thought it had changed everything." She looked up and saw impatience in his gaze.

"I had fallen asleep in your arms," she continued, realizing that if he didn't believe this much, he sure as the devil wasn't going to believe the rest. "I woke near daylight to see Odell. He had something in his hand. I started to wake you, but he stopped me by holding up your keys, then slowly putting them back in our pile of clothing and leaving. I didn't know that he'd already taken the keys, made a copy of the security plans and was returning them when I caught him."

"He just happened to know I wouldn't be wearing my jeans that night beside the creek?" Clay said. "You expect me to believe that? How did he know where to find me?"

"He told me after the robbery that he'd followed you," she snapped, her nerves taut. "He'd planned to get the keys from you, one way or the other. My showing up just gave him a less confrontational way. This way he could hurt us both."

Tears welled in her eyes. She willed herself not to cry. She had to think of Ivy. Getting Ivy back. If Clay didn't believe her, then there was nothing she could do about that. There never had been.

He said nothing, but some of the anger seemed to dim in his gaze.

"It wasn't until after the robbery, before you caught Odell and me fighting outside my barn, that he told me what he'd done. How he'd implicated me in the robbery."

"Why would he do that?" Clay asked.

She looked at him and saw that he really didn't seem to understand the relationship the three of them had had.

"He wanted to hurt me, the way he felt I'd hurt him by making love with you," she said. "Unlike you, he knew I was a virgin and he knew why. He knew that you were the only one I wanted. He saw me losing my breakfast by the barn and guessed that I was pregnant with your baby. He knew you'd never believe me about the keys. He was determined that you wouldn't win." She let out a laugh that was so close to a sob her eyes filled with tears. "He thought you *wanted* to win me. He didn't know it had all been for nothing."

Clay looked away, battered by an onslaught of conflicting emotions. "So you ran?"

"I only thought of my baby. Our baby. I was determined to protect her. At all costs. I was afraid of what Odell would do. He swore he'd hurt her."

"But then Odell was killed," Clay pointed out. "You could have returned to Texas. You could have told me the truth."

"I didn't hear about Odell's death until a few months ago. I'd been planning to come back to Texas as soon as I had the money. I'd made a promise on my great-grandmother's memory that I would go back and try to make things right."

Clay didn't know what to think. She'd thought she loved him? His heart desperately wanted to believe she'd seduced him for any other reason than the jewels.

And that she hadn't told him the truth to protect Ivy.

If only he'd known about the baby. About Odell's threat. Maybe this wouldn't be happening now. What would Odell have done if Josie hadn't run? Would he have hurt her or her baby to keep Ivy from being born? Or would he have gotten the jewels out of the saddle, gotten caught, and this would have all been over?

"Let's get your great-grandmother's saddle," he said, not wanting to think let alone talk about that night right now.

But when he looked over at her, he saw her eyes widen. He felt a chill race over him. "Where is the saddle, Josie?"

"Oh, God, Clay. It's not here."

He felt his veins turn to ice. "What do you mean, it's not here? The kidnapper was sure you'd never part with it."

"No, I wouldn't. Under normal circumstances. You asked how I was able to make it, pregnant and alone with no money. I pawned the saddle. It was the only thing I had of any value."

He felt light-headed. The room seemed to spin. He pulled her to him, hanging on for dear life. "You lost it!"

"No," she cried. "I just can't get my hands on it quickly. The pawn shop is in Bozeman and I don't have enough money saved yet."

He let go of her. "Money is the least of our problems. I'll pay to get it back. Let's just hope the jewels are still inside."

"How did they get there?" she cried.

"I thought if anyone would know, it would be you," he said coldly. "Get dressed. We can have a doctor check your head where you were hit. Then we'll be waiting at that pawnshop the moment it opens."

She felt as if she might fly into a million pieces. She hurriedly pulled on her clothes, her head aching, her heart pounding, fear making her weak and sick and crazy.

Clay drove them out of the ranch and headed toward Bozeman, thirty miles to the east. The sun shone blindingly bright in a cloudless blue sky. It should have been raining and dark and cold, the way it was in her heart.

But part of her held on to a small thread of hope. Maybe Clay didn't believe her, but he was helping her. She'd never needed him more than she did now, but she could feel the wall between them. They'd never trusted each other. Nothing seemed to have changed. Except now Clay knew that Ivy was his daughter. And he blamed her because a kidnapper had her. Had taken her for some jewels she hadn't known were hidden in her great-grandmother's saddle.

"Clay, please talk to me. Say something."

"Let's just get the jewels. Then we can talk about what to do."

Dust coated the pawnshop's windows, making it appear dark inside. Clay parked the truck on the side of the building. A bell tinkled over the door as they walked in. The place was a clutter of once-valued things that had been turned into ready cash. He just hoped the saddle was still here.

Josie pulled out her claim stub and handed it over the

dirty counter to a tall, thin man with a bad complexion. He studied it for a moment.

"I want to pick up my saddle," she said nervously.

Clay could almost hear the thumping of her heart over his. Almost.

The man nodded and disappeared through a curtain into the back of the shop. Clay waited anxiously for him to return.

The clock on the wall ticked off the minutes.

The place was hot and smelled of too many people and their things.

When the man finally pushed through the curtain with the saddle under one arm, Clay could have kissed him.

Clay slapped a half-dozen bills down on the glass counter. "Will that cover it?"

The man looked up, studying Clay from under hooded eyes. "Got any identification?" he asked Josie.

She dug in her bag and showed him her Texas driver's license.

Slowly he picked up the money from the counter, counted it and put it into the till. Then he lifted the saddle, bypassing Clay to hand it to Josie.

She hugged it to her, tears welling in her eyes, and Clay followed her out the door.

"I should never have pawned it," she said as they walked to the truck.

He opened the door for her and hurried around to slide behind the wheel.

"You did what you had to do to survive. Your great-grandmother would have understood. She would have been proud of you, Josie."

He heard her crying softly as she held the saddle in her arms as if she held her daughter.

As he drove out of Bozeman, he watched his rear-view mirror. But no one seemed to be following them. He could hear Josie working at the saddle.

"Are they in there?" His voice broke.

A sob burst from her, then the tearful words, "They're here. Oh, thank God, they're here."

He let out a small sigh of relief. They had a long way to go. But at least now they had the damned jewels. And to think at one time, he thought once he found the jewels it would be over for good. How wrong he'd been.

Josie stared at the pile of sparkling jewels, hating them, hating Odell. "I'm scared, Clay."

He didn't say anything for a few moments. Then she looked over at him. His gaze shifted from the road to her. The cold, hard darkness she'd seen in his eyes was suddenly gone. He looked as scared as she did.

He loves Ivy, too.

With tears in his eyes, he pulled her over to him. She snuggled into him, desperately needing his warmth, his strength, desperately needing him. The father of her baby.

She closed her eyes and breathed in the scent of him, surrounded by his strong arms, protected. In his arms, she believed they would get Ivy back safely. In his arms, she believed they could conquer anything.

They reached the cabin with plenty of time to spare but hurried inside to wait for the call.

"The night Raymond died, I thought he'd whispered 'Odell did it.' But with Odell dead—" She looked over at him. "Raymond must have said 'Odell *hid* it.' The bag of jewels. I saw Odell coming out of my barn six weeks after the robbery. He said he'd been looking for me, but at the time, I thought he seemed…odd."

"That's probably when he put the jewels in the saddle."

"He just hadn't expected me to leave Texas like I did. He must have told Raymond where he'd hidden them before his death." She hesitated. "Clay, with both Raymond and Odell dead, then who has Ivy?"

Someone who knew where Odell had hidden the jewels. Someone who knew Clay. Knew her. Someone with a grudge against them.

He shook his head. "Someone Raymond or Odell told."

She nodded, but she could tell he was as scared as she was. The worst part was that they had no idea just who they were dealing with. Or what lengths he would go to. Why didn't the kidnapper call?

When the phone rang, they both jumped.

It took them both a minute of confusion to realize it was Clay's cell phone that was ringing.

"Jackson?" the voice demanded.

Clay shook his head at Josie to let her know it wasn't the kidnapper. "Judge Branson." His chest felt like someone had dropped a piano on it.

"We just got the DNA tests back. I'd put a rush on them for you." The judge let out a sigh. "The lab already had a sample of Odell's DNA from an earlier arrest. Jackson, that body in the grave—"

He knew. He'd known the moment he'd heard Judge Branson's voice on the other end of the line.

"We don't know who the hell it is, but it's not Odell Burton."

Chapter 13

Josie saw it in Clay's body language. In the way he hung up the phone, his head bent, the weight of the conversation heavy on his broad shoulders.

When he looked over at her, she felt the floor drop out from under her. "Odell's alive."

Clay pulled her into his arms. "At least now we know who and what we're up against," he said, sounding almost relieved.

Her worst fears had come true. Odell Burton had her child. A child conceived by a man Odell hated and born to a woman he'd sworn to destroy.

"Oh, Clay, he'll kill her if he hasn't already."

"No, Josie," he said, pulling back to look into her face. He shook her gently, until her gaze locked with his. "He's just using Ivy to get to us. We have the advantage, though. We know Odell. And he doesn't realize that we're on to him."

She struggled to find hope in his words, in the fierce, confident look in his eyes. "But Odell knows us, Clay. He'll anticipate anything we do."

"Josie, do you want to go to the police? It's your decision."

She stared at him in disbelief. "All these years of everyone telling me what to do and you pick *now* to let me make a decision like this?"

"I can make the decision, Josie, but you're Ivy's mother. It should be your decision."

She looked into his dark eyes. Ivy's eyes. "Knowing Odell, I'm afraid to do anything that might jeopardize our daughter's life. He's not bluffing. He'll kill Ivy if we call the police."

Clay let out a sigh. "I agree. Odell's too unstable for us to take any chances."

The phone rang again. This time they both knew who it would be.

Josie felt numb as they drove out of Three Forks under a dark, hopeless night sky. The Jefferson River moved along dull as lead under the black rough edge of the mountains cut against the skyline.

She held the backpack with the bag of jewels in her lap, her fingers kneading the silken material, feeling the cold of the rocks beneath. Her emotions ran from hope to hate, from fear to murderous rage. She wanted to kill Odell. She thought she could have with her bare hands.

"We're going to have to work together," Clay said from beside her.

She nodded. She just wanted her daughter back.

Whatever it took. But numb, frozen fear made her want to curl up in a ball and cry and pretend this wasn't happening.

Clay had repeated the kidnapper's instructions to her when he got off the phone. The words had again been electronically altered but now they knew why. Both she and Clay would have recognized Odell's voice.

They were to bring a backpack. It was to contain only two small flashlights, one votive candle, one pack of paper matches and the jewels. Nothing more.

At some point along the way, the backpack would be checked and they would be searched. If they brought anything else, especially any type of weapon, they would never know what happened to their child.

Clay drove southwest past Three Forks, taking Highway 287 toward Ennis. At the junction, he stopped to look under a large stone next to the stop sign. More instructions. He was to take Highway 2 toward Whitehall.

But as he got back into the truck, he let out a curse. "He's leading us to Lewis and Clark Caverns."

Josie felt herself go weak. "I'd forgotten about his fascination with caves." It explained the odd mixture of items they had been instructed to bring in the backpack. It explained—

"The map!" they both said in unison.

"The map the sheriff found on Raymond," Clay said excitedly. "It's the inside of the caverns."

Josie sat up a little straighter, hope rushing through her.

"Do you think you can draw it?" he asked as she snapped on the cab light to dig in the glove box as he drove. She found a pen and a Burger King napkin. "Wasn't Pit the first name on the map?"

"Yes." She quickly drew what she remembered with Clay's help. "Remember the word End circled in red?"

"Yeah. I would imagine that's where he plans to make the trade," Clay said. "And the word, Paradise just before the word Finish."

"He thinks he'll have the jewels," she said, not wanting to voice her real fear. That for Odell, paradise would only be if he'd gotten the jewels, destroyed her and Clay—and won.

Clay found more instructions just before the turnoff for Lewis and Clark Caverns, not that he hadn't already anticipated what they would say. "Go up the mountain and into the caverns. Keep going. More instructions will be posted once inside."

The narrow paved road curled up the mountain in tight switchbacks. The headlights cut a narrow swatch through the dense trees, the darkness close and low.

The road ended in a small paved parking lot. Several small buildings stood against the night sky. Two vehicles sat in the lot. A rental car and an old pickup truck with local plates.

Clay drove in and parked away from both of them. He killed the engine and the headlights. A faint light glowed near one of the buildings.

"Oh, God, Clay, someone else is here," she whispered.

He took the backpack from her, saying nothing as he opened his door and got out. She followed, hurrying to catch up to him. He had the backpack slung over his shoulder and one of the flashlights in his hand. The golden disk of light bobbed across the pavement in front of him as Clay neared the only other light on the mountain.

Just as she caught up to Clay, he stopped and turned to

try to shield her from something on the ground. At first all she glimpsed was the source of the faint light she'd seen from the truck. A flashlight lay on the ground, the beam dim as if the batteries were running low.

Past it, she caught sight of a pair of boots connected to two jeans-clad legs sticking out from behind the building.

Clay knelt down, then straightened. "The security guard," he whispered. "He's dead."

She glanced at the poor man on the ground. Her heart hammered, her pulse thundering at her temple. Odell had already killed once tonight and he had Ivy.

Her limbs suddenly felt as though they were made of stone. She stared at the mountain ahead, too afraid to move. Tears burned in her eyes. She wanted to howl like the wounded animal she was.

She felt Clay's hand on her face. He cupped her jaw and pulled her into him. She buried her face in his chest, absorbing the warm feel of his jacket, the safe feel of his arms around her.

"We're going to get her back," he whispered. "I promise you, Josie. You just have to trust me."

She could feel the steady beat of his heart against her cheek, his arms around her, strong but gentle. Trust, that was something they'd never had. She looked up into his face beneath the wide brim of his Stetson. Steely determination shone in his eyes. But something more. His love for Ivy.

"Trust me?" he whispered.

She straightened and let out a ragged breath. "I trust you."

"We can do this, Josie," he whispered as he brushed a tear from her cheek.

She nodded, catching his large, warm hand and bringing it to her lips before letting him go.

He handed her the flashlight and motioned for her to lead the way up the path to the cavern entrance. She took a step, then another, each growing a little stronger. Instead of looking ahead, she watched only the few feet of path she could see in front of her. One step at a time. Don't think. Just walk.

She did, trying to hold back the horrible thoughts that bombarded her. Trying to keep from looking off the steep drop to her left as the path climbed the mountain. Or looking too far into the future.

She had to believe in Clay. Believe in herself. She wasn't still that scared young girl that Odell had bullied in Texas. But he didn't know that. He would expect her to cower, to beg, to cry. That's the way he liked her.

She lengthened her strides, breathing in the night air, feeling strength in her legs, in her heart. She could hear Clay behind her and thanked God he was here.

The smell hit her first. Dead, cold air, wrought with an age-old dampness.

She slowed. A gaping hole yawned in the side of the mountain. The once locked, barred door that had sealed it shut now hanging open. Ivy's favorite teddy bear hung from one of the bars.

Clay gently pulled the worn teddy bear down, drawing it to his face. It smelled like her. He breathed in the scent of her, then pulled Josie to him, holding them both for a long moment.

Then he handed the bear to Josie.

She was crying softly, but when he met her gaze, her eyes gleamed with determination. His heart ached as he watched her hug the bear to her as she would have Ivy.

He stared into the dark, ominous opening. Unlike what he'd told Josie, Odell had every advantage. All they had was their love for their daughter.

An owl screeched somewhere nearby, giving him a start. In the distance, a car engine droned on the highway below them. Nothing but silence came from within the cave.

Unlike Odell, he'd never liked caves and didn't like the idea of being trapped underground with a madman. Worse yet, the last thing he wanted to do was take Josie in with him. But he knew neither of them had any choice.

Odell was calling the shots. At least for the moment.

"Stay close," he whispered to Josie as he pulled the second flashlight from the pack. "And remember what I said." His gaze met hers for a moment, then he pointed the flashlight beam into the caverns and stepped through the rock arch, with Josie close behind.

Inside, their footfalls echoed off the walls of carved stone. Their flashlights did little to hold back the darkness. Clay moved slowly at first, feeling his way, expecting Odell to ambush them at any time.

They hadn't gone far when he felt Josie clutch at the back of his jacket, grabbing a handful of cloth. Overhead, the ceiling came alive.

She let out a small choked cry as dozens of bats took flight, a scurry of wings and dark movement just inches above their heads.

"You all right?" he whispered back to her.

The hand on his back released its hold.

The path dropped downward in a series of cramped rock steps. At one point, he thought he heard a baby crying. He stopped to listen but could hear nothing but the drip of water deeper in the caverns, deeper in the endless darkness.

Not far in, they passed a shaft that dropped down to an open room. The Pit on the map Raymond had on him when he was killed?

The narrow path wound down another set of tight, steep steps that opened into a room filled with stalactites and stalagmites, then down along a small tunnel.

This time when it opened up, he saw that they were now at the bottom of the pit. Clay stopped to look up, feeling the hair rise on the back of his neck.

"Clay?"

He looked over at her, then where she pointed. A crudely written note instructed them to put down their flashlights, empty their pockets and the backpack onto the rock floor in the stationary beams of light. They were to open the bag of jewels so they could be seen from above, then put everything back and continue into the cave.

"Do as he says." He laid his flashlight next to Josie's and pulled out his pockets, then dumped the backpack contents to the floor.

He couldn't see Odell. He wasn't even sure Odell was up there, on the trail they'd been on just moments before, now looking down at them from the darkness. It made his skin crawl, though. The man had always been on the edge. From what Clay had seen so far, he'd say Odell had now gone off the deep end. He'd progressed from theft to kidnapping and murder. That was one hell of a leap, even for a man who'd faked his own death.

After a moment, he picked up the items from the floor, put them again into the backpack, including Ivy's teddy bear. As he scooped up his flashlight from the floor, he saw Josie's face. The look in her eyes gave him hope. All her maternal instincts burned in her gaze. She was like a mama lion going after her cub.

Not that he would have blamed her if she fell apart, but he was damned glad she hadn't and he was counting on her to hold it together. For their daughter's sake.

He couldn't let himself think of Ivy as they dropped deeper and deeper into the mountain, the air becoming colder and wetter. Bats scurried in front of them, a restless, frantic sound that set his nerves on end.

Water dripped and ran down the sides of the stone walls. Deeper and deeper. The narrow passages opened into rooms filled with rock formations. Rock sculpted by water and time.

He retraced the map in his head. Pit. Garden. Waterfall. End. Paradise. Points of interest? Except for End.

He shone the flashlight across the rock formations, standing like sentries. If he was right, this was the Garden. He hurried along the rock path worn slick by the feet of thousands of sightseers. If he was right, the waterfall would be in the next room.

But when he reached it, there was no running water. He glanced over at Josie. She pointed with her flashlight at a wall of brown flowstone that rippled and ran downward. "The waterfall," she whispered.

He nodded and gave her what he hoped was a reassuring smile. She reached for his hand, squeezed it, then quickly let go as she pointed her light into the darkness ahead.

They dropped down a tight, steep stairway carved in the rocks and into a huge room filled with boulders. The air seemed denser. Colder. He shone his flashlight beam across the expanse.

Eyes. His hand with the flashlight jerked. Slowly, his hand shaking, he scanned the light back across.

The figure sat against one of the stalagmites. For just that split second, Clay thought it was Odell. Then he heard Josie gasp, "Mildred!"

She was tied to the rock formation, gagged and bound. Blinded by their lights, her eyes widened with fear.

"It's us," Clay whispered as he climbed up to her. He kept his eye out for Odell as Josie removed the gag and untied her hands and feet.

"He's got the baby," Mildred cried. "He's got Ivy."

"Do you know where?" Josie asked.

She shook her head. "He left me here and took the baby."

"It's all right," Clay assured her in a whisper. "Did you see where he went, which way?"

She shook her head, and he realized she'd been sitting here in the dark long enough that she'd become temporarily blind and disoriented.

He knew he couldn't leave her here alone. Nor would it make sense to take her with them. He also knew that Odell had anticipated this.

"Josie, give her your flashlight." Isn't that what Odell had planned for the second flashlight? "Mildred, I want you to follow the trail back the way we just came. It will lead you out of here. You mustn't be afraid."

She nodded, looking scared, but tougher than most women her age. "You're going to get him?"

Clay nodded. Or die trying. "When you get out, go to my truck, lock yourself inside and wait for us. The keys are in the truck."

"You want me to go for help?"

"No, that might jeopardize Ivy's life," he said.

She nodded, tears filling her eyes. She took the flashlight and the keys. "I'll wait for you."

He waited until Mildred disappeared back through the cavern, then he looked over at Josie. Her jaw was set, her eyes dark and narrowed.

"Ready?" he whispered.

She nodded.

"I just want you to know," he whispered, "you did the right thing with Ivy." There was so much more he wanted to say to her, but he told himself there'd be time after they got Ivy back. After Odell really *was* dead and gone. This time for good.

"Thank you," she whispered, and on impulse he leaned down to kiss her lips one last time before they got their daughter.

Josie followed Clay, her gaze on the small puddle of light that shone on the rock floor from his flashlight. The cave narrowed quickly, until she had to sit down and slide down a chute, the rocks overhead close and confining, cold to the touch.

Then the rock opened again. Clay flicked the light over a small room filled with stone statues huddled in thick clusters like lawn ornaments.

She knew they had to be getting close to the *X* on the map, which marked End. If they were right—

Off to her left, a faint light flashed on in one of the rock clusters. She swung around and let out a cry as Odell appeared out of the blackness like a ghost.

She clutched at Clay's jacket, but she knew he'd seen him, too.

Odell stood among the tall, misshapen stone forms. The flashlight he held just under his chin shot eerie, pale

light up over his stark features, making it appear that
he'd just crawled from his grave.

"You bastard," Clay swore.

Odell laughed, the sound echoing through the cavern,
and lowered the flashlight. He'd wanted to scare them
and he'd succeeded.

"Put your flashlight down," he ordered, his flashlight in one hand and a gun in the other. He pointed the
gun at Clay's chest, the flashlight beam at Clay's knees.

He waited until Clay obliged, although Clay left the
light on. The beam cut across the rock floor to shine like
a small spotlight on one of the rough rock walls.

Odell moved toward them, keeping the gun aimed
at Clay's chest.

"Let me see the jewels," he ordered.

Clay shook his head. "Where is Ivy?"

Josie saw that Odell had changed in the past two
years. He'd lost weight. His face was gaunt, his eyes
more deep-set, his body rangier. If anything, he looked
meaner. Crazier.

"Not until I see the jewels," he said.

Clay swung the backpack off one shoulder and pulled
out the bag of jewels. He hefted it in his hands, keeping
it out of Odell's reach.

"I hope you brought the other things I told you to,"
he said, then grinned, his dark eyes flashing with evil.
"Of course you did. You want to see that baby of yours
again, don't you, Josie?"

"How could you involve an innocent child in this?"
she cried. For even Odell, this was despicable. "What
have you done with her? Tell me where she is, Odell."

"Listen to you, woman. I don't think you realize who
you're talking to. I'm not your boy Clay here." His eyes

narrowed, his face twisting into an angry sneer. "You talk nice to me if you want to see that kid again."

"Ivy!" Josie called, the sound deafening in the cave. "Ivy?" The frantic sound echoed, then died into silence. "Ivy!"

"Quit that damn yelling," Odell snapped. "She can't hear you. I gave her a little something to help her sleep. Don't worry, I asked a doctor. No matter what you think, I wouldn't hurt *her*. Unless, of course, you make me."

Odell snatched the bag of jewels from Clay's hand. The bag came open and several jewels clattered to the floor of the cave. Odell's flashlight beam dropped to them. "Wait a minute, these aren't—"

Josie didn't hear the rest. Hate as potent as jet fuel rocketed through her. She launched herself at Odell without words, without thought, without fear.

It happened in an instant.

Odell caught the movement out of the corner of his eye. Shock registered on his face; this wasn't the same easily intimidated woman he'd known in Texas.

He tried to swing the gun, to get it pointed at her before she hit him, but without any luck. She hit him hard, barreling into him, propelling him backward into the stalagmites.

He hit his arm on one. The gun clattered to the floor. She pounded at his chest, his face, his head. He caught hold of her, smacking her with the flashlight just as Clay lunged for him.

The blow from the flashlight sent her flying backward. She tripped over one of the stalagmites growing out of the floor and fell hard, banging her ankle as she went down, the pain piercing through her anger.

When she looked up, she saw Clay and Odell wrestling. The gun lay a few yards away, near Clay's flashlight. Trying to ignore the pain, she slid over to it.

She'd almost reached the gun when she heard a loud crack behind her. She turned in time to see Odell's hand holding the flashlight hit one of the stalactites. The light went out, throwing most of the room into darkness. Odell let out a curse.

In the shaft of light from Clay's flashlight on the floor, she scooped up the gun, then the flashlight.

As she turned with both the gun and the light, she saw Clay slam Odell against the rock wall, his hands on Odell's throat.

"Where is Ivy?" Clay demanded. When Odell didn't answer, he threw him against the wall again, eliciting a groan from Odell.

"Don't kill him," she cried, trying to get to her feet. Her ankle wouldn't take the weight. She slid toward them on her bottom, using her good foot to propel her.

The beam of her flashlight lit on Odell's bulging face. "Clay, don't kill him. He's the only one who knows where Ivy is."

He seemed to loosen his hold.

"Listen to her," Odell gasped. "If you kill me, you'll never find the kid."

Clay instantly tightened his fingers on Odell's throat. "But I'll have the satisfaction of killing you."

Odell's eyes bulged. He tore at Clay's hands around his neck to no avail.

"Where's Ivy?" Clay demanded again.

Odell's face twisted in panic.

"Last chance." Clay tightened his grip on the man's throat again.

Odell's eyes went wild. He tried to move his head, but Clay had him pressed against the wall.

"She's—" It came out a hiss.

Clay gave him a little more air.

Odell's gaze flicked off to his right. "In the hole—"

The gunshot ricocheted through the cave, deafening. Odell slumped against the wall. Another shot filled the room.

Josie swung the beam of the flashlight in the direction she thought the shot had come from, pointing the gun toward an exit on the other side of the room.

Something moved, then disappeared around the corner of the cave wall, but not before she'd seen another light.

"Turn off the flashlight!" Clay cried. "You're making yourself a target."

She snapped off the light, her heart thundering in her chest, as the darkness enveloped them. Who in God's name had shot Odell?

She felt Clay's hand on hers. He took the gun, then the flashlight. She heard him move away from her. He shone the flashlight around the room.

Empty. Except for the rock sculptures. And Odell's body on the floor, blood still pumping out of the wound in his chest.

She crawled over to him and took his face in her hands. A slight gasp escaped his lips.

"Where is my daughter? Don't you dare die without telling me. Do you hear me, you bastard?"

"It's too late, Josie," Clay said from behind her, anguish distorting his voice.

"No," she cried, and shook Odell's head in her hands. His eyes fluttered open. She watched him try to focus.

"Where's Ivy?" she cried, her voice breaking. "Tell me, Odell. Tell me, damn you, or may you burn in hell."

He looked up at her as if he might actually see her. "Crawl." The word barely escaped his lips. "Crawl." His eyes closed, and she felt the weight of his head in her hands and knew he was gone.

"Josie?" Clay asked.

She let Odell's head drop back.

"Josie, we have to get out of here. The killer will be back. For the jewels. For us. Do you hear me?"

"I can't walk, Clay. It's my ankle. I think it's broken, but I'm not leaving without Ivy."

He shone the light on her ankle and let out a low curse. "I'll carry you, but we have to leave, Josie. You have to listen to me—"

She shook her head. "We couldn't move fast enough with you carrying me and you know it. The killer would catch us. You have to go after him." She knew that's what he wanted to do. He was only suggesting they leave because he wanted to protect her.

"He might know where Ivy is," she whispered.

"I don't want to leave you."

She could hear the pain in his voice, see it in his face. "You have to, Clay. Otherwise, he'll come back. Like you said, he isn't going to leave without the jewels." Or without killing her and Clay as well.

She watched him look toward the darkness where the killer had disappeared, trying to make up his mind.

"Go, Clay. I'll be all right."

He looked at her, then got to his feet, the decision made. "I won't let him get past me to you. I'll have to take the flashlight, though, Josie. I'll leave you the candle and matches, but the candle won't last long. Use it only when you have to. Stay here. I'll be back for you."

She looked up at him, tears filling her eyes. "I'll be here, Clay. Just come back. Then we'll find Ivy and get out of here."

He touched her cheek, his gaze locked on hers. "There's so much I should have said to you, Josie."

"There'll be time. When this is all over," she whispered, turning to kiss the palm of his hand.

He scooped up the jewels and put them back in the bag. Then he checked Odell's gun for ammunition, shoved it into the waistband of his jeans and, picking up the backpack, removed the candle and matches. "I'll be back," he said, pressing them into her hands.

She smiled up at him. "I'm counting on it."

Before the last of the light from his flashlight disappeared, she lit the candle with trembling fingers. It flickered, illuminating a small circle around her, reassuring her with its paltry light.

She blew it out and held both the matches and the candle in her hands as she scooted back against the cave wall, away from Odell. She stared into the darkness, seeing nothing, feeling only pain. Ivy. The horrible ache for her daughter suppressed even the pain in her ankle.

Crawl. Josie closed her eyes and tried not to think about the darkness. It had a smell, a feel, a texture that closed in the moment the candle went out. She squeezed her eyes tighter shut. Don't waste the candle.

Crawl. She thought of Odell's words. He'd said Ivy was in a hole somewhere. Crawl. She felt a chill scuttle across her skin.

She opened her eyes. Tiny pinpoints of light danced in the darkness. She closed her eyes again, unable to face such blackness. End. That had been the word on the map. Circled in red. Not long after the waterfall.

Could this be where it was supposed to end? Could the hole where he'd hidden Ivy be in this room? That would be like Odell. In fact, she remembered seeing his gaze flick to a corner of the room when he mentioned Ivy.

Carefully, she cradled the candle in her lap and, holding the matches, struck one. The sudden flare of light blinded her for a moment. She thought she'd dropped the candle, but there it was in her lap.

She lit it. The tiny, insignificant light pooled around her. She pushed the matches into her front pocket, then cautiously got up on all fours again. The candle flickered and she knew it wouldn't take much movement for it to go out.

She tried to get her bearings. They'd entered this room from the right. She hadn't noticed a hole, but she couldn't be sure. What she was sure of, was Odell.

Where had they first seen him? He'd have been near the hole. Guarding his prize, his ransom.

It took everything in her not to cry out Ivy's name. But hadn't Odell said he'd given her something to sleep and that calling for her wouldn't do any good?

She didn't know why, but she actually believed he'd been telling the truth. She moved slowly, carefully, holding the candle as if life depended on it.

Moving to where she'd first seen Odell, she shone the light along the wall, looking for a space deep enough to hide a child in.

The hole, when she finally found it, was small, almost round, and appeared deep. The others she'd found had been too shallow. But this one— Her ankle was killing her. She almost welcomed the pain. It distracted her from her real pain as she lay down on her stomach and slid into the hole and began to crawl.

Was Ivy in here? He'd said she was in a hole. He'd said he'd given her something to sleep. He'd said crawl. But he might have been lying. He might have meant something entirely—

She caught the glint of a tiny odd-shaped object on the narrow tunnel floor. Using her one foot, she pushed herself toward it, holding the candle high.

"Don't go out now," she said to the flame. "Not now."

She stopped and looked down at the small button in the shape of a bear's head. Tears rushed her eyes, blinding her. Ivy had been wearing her favorite bear pajamas with teddy bear buttons.

The candle flickered. She looked down at it through her tears and blew out the flame. It was hard to wait until the wax cooled enough that she could put the candle back into her pocket. But she did, moving methodically, carefully, slowly in a darkness that seemed denser, closer, almost suffocating.

She didn't need light, she told herself. She would find her daughter. Closing her eyes, she felt ahead of her, pulling with her fingers, pushing with her one good foot, dragging the other one, the pain almost unbearable.

She turned a corner and had to stop, the pain in her ankle making her dizzy and sick to her stomach and close to blacking out. She laid her head on her arms and wept, afraid she was going into shock. The sobs finally subsided. She thought of Ivy and slowly lifted her head from her arms.

Just a little farther. She could go just a little farther. She had to.

Then she smelled it. Baby powder. The scent seemed to float to her, beckoning her.

Chapter 14

Clay moved through the cave, keeping his light dim and low. His mind raced ahead of him. Who had shot Odell? And why? To keep him from telling them where Ivy was? Or something else?

He frowned, remembering something Odell had said when he'd seen the spilled jewels. "Wait a minute, these aren't—"

What had he been about to say?

Clay stopped, hidden from view behind a space in the rocks, and pulled out the bag of jewels. He'd never seen them before, only in a photograph that Williams had given him after they were stolen.

Shining his flashlight over the glittering mass, he saw with a start that some of them had broken when they'd dropped to the rock floor.

A sick feeling settled in his stomach as he took one

of the larger diamonds and ran the sharp edge across the glass face of his flashlight.

Just as he'd suspected. Paste. His daughter had been kidnapped for a worthless bag of glass.

It took all his willpower not to throw the jewels against the wall. He stared down at them and sucked in his breath as his anger dimmed and realization dawned, blinding bright.

He let out a curse under his breath. It was finally starting to make sense. Odell faking his death. Raymond turning up after two years. The missing jewels. Raymond's calls to Texas.

He pushed the jewels back into the bag, then looked around for a place to hide them.

Then he moved forward, knowing now what was waiting for him. Who was waiting for him. And just how desperate the killer was.

Ahead he heard a sound. The scrape of a boot heel on rock. He clicked off his flashlight and froze. The air suddenly seemed colder. He almost thought he felt a breeze and sensed that the narrow tunnel he was in opened into a larger space just ahead.

He held his breath. Someone was in the next room. He felt it. Thought he could almost hear him breathing. Sense him waiting in expectation.

The killer had the advantage. He knew the landscape in the cave and he knew where Clay would appear.

The darkness had its own ominous feel to it. Just a cold denseness that made it feel alive. He could see where it wouldn't take long in this kind of total blackness to go crazy, to hear the dark begin to whisper things in your ear that would drive you mad.

He reached blindly into the open pocket of the backpack for Odell's flashlight. It was broken and didn't work, but he'd taken it for the batteries just in case he needed them.

He now carefully and quietly unscrewed the end of the flashlight, took out the batteries and stuffed them into his pocket, working as quickly as he could in the dark. Then he twisted the end back on the flashlight. It was still heavy enough to cause a clatter if he dropped it. Or threw it.

Then, making sure he was ready, he moved forward, knowing the killer was ready for him.

Josie hadn't gone but a few feet more in the narrow confines of the hole when she felt something soft. The edge of a baby blanket.

She held her breath as her hand closed over one small arm. Hurriedly her hand went to her daughter's face. She felt warm breath and heard the wonderful sleeping sounds the toddler made.

Her face streaming with tears, she dug out the candle and struck another match. The flame flared, shocking her to see that Ivy lay curled in a cocoon of blankets against a solid rock wall where the hole ended.

A wave of panic swept over her. She felt as if the walls were closing in on them and there wasn't enough air for them to breathe.

But the look on her baby's face calmed her some. She touched her hand to it again, cupping her precious cheek. Ivy stirred a little, sighing in her sleep.

In the light, Josie could see that Ivy lay on a make-shift thin wooden sled of sorts. That's how Odell had gotten her back in here. That meant it would be easier to drag her out.

She noticed something else. An indentation in the wall. If she were careful, she thought she might be small enough to get turned around so she wouldn't have to try to pull Ivy and herself out backward.

The pain in her ankle had intensified. She wasn't sure she could crawl backward. And she knew Clay would never hear her cries this deep in the rock.

She put the candle down, gauging how much wax was left. She had to hurry. Otherwise she would have to do this in the dark.

The maneuver of getting turned around spent all of her energy but she finally managed it. She lay pressed against the rock wall for a moment, watching her daughter in the flickering candlelight.

Then she gave Ivy a kiss, snugged the blankets around her so nothing could get scraped and blew out the candle. Carefully, she put it back into her pocket along with the matches. The first thing Josie wanted Ivy to see when she woke was her mother's face.

Then she began the arduous job of getting them both out. Fortunately, the sled beneath Ivy slid easily along the rock floor of the hole. And this time, Josie knew where she was going and she had her daughter with her.

She felt as though she could move mountains. Just let Clay come back, she prayed. *Just let him live. His daughter needs him. I need him.*

Clay felt the darkness seem to change around him and knew before his hand lost contact with the rock wall of the cave that he'd reached the next room.

He hung back, afraid the killer would suddenly shine a flashlight on him. He dug the batteries out of his pockets, waited for a long moment, then threw the empty flashlight as far and hard as he could.

The flashlight clattered off rock, echoing through the cavernous room. A light flashed on, just as he'd anticipated it would. Off to the left. Back in the stand of stalagmites.

Clay threw a battery at the light and was rewarded with an "umph" and a curse. The light flashed out.

"I want my daughter, Williams," he yelled into the huge room, then dropped to his hands and knees and moved quickly and quietly across the expanse of stone floor that he'd seen in the glow from the killer's flashlight, Odell's pistol still in his waistband.

He didn't want to kill the collector. Not until he got Brandon Williams to tell him where Ivy was.

A shot exploded in the room, the bullet ricocheting off the rocks, then another shot.

Clay stopped crawling across the floor to pull himself up behind one of the taller stalagmites he'd seen in the flash of light, the second battery in hand, his mind reviewing what he'd seen of the room, anticipating where Williams would go next.

He wasn't surprised when he heard a scuffling sound off to his right. He'd hoped to push the killer in that direction. Away from Josie and that part of the caverns.

He threw the battery in the direction the sound had come from. Another shot rattled through the room, echoing against the rocks and followed by an oath and a loud thud as the collector must have fallen over something, too afraid to turn on his flashlight again.

Then another shot. The bullet pinged far off to the left, a wild shot.

"Tell me where my daughter is and I won't kill you,"

Clay yelled, scrambling quickly away the moment the words were out of his mouth.

Two shots followed, then the loud click that Clay had hoped for. The bastard had a six-shot revolver, the most popular weapon in the West. And he was out of bullets.

Clay snapped on his flashlight, counting on Williams's arrogance. It wouldn't even have crossed his mind that he might need another gun.

But he would have more bullets, only Clay had no intentions of giving him time to reload.

He caught the dark figure in his flashlight beam and charged him, like a linebacker dodging through the stone statues.

He could see the man digging desperately in his pocket, his gaze blinded by the light. At the last moment, Williams heaved the pistol at him and tried to turn and run.

Clay ducked the airborne weapon and tackled the man. They went down hard. He heard the man's head hit the solid rock floor with a crack, then Clay was on him.

It only took a moment to realize that the man wasn't fighting him, wasn't moving at all.

Clay swore as he groped on the floor for the flashlight. It had rolled over against one of the rock formations, the beam shooting across the room to the tip of a stalactite hanging almost to the floor.

He grabbed the flashlight and swung the beam to the soft, frightened features of Williams's face. But the collector stared up at him with a blankness that sent his heart into overdrive. Williams was still alive, but the fall and the knock on the head hadn't done him any good.

"The jewels," Williams whispered.

"I don't give a damn about your jewels. Where is my daughter?"

"I don't know anything about your daughter," he whimpered.

Clay felt panic surge through him. "No, damn you. You have to have some idea."

"Odell. That was his doing. All his doing. I just wanted my jewels."

"And I'd have gotten them for you, just like I said I would. You didn't have to kill Odell. You didn't have to try to kill me. Or—" He almost said "My family."

"Please, you have to get me medical attention," Williams whined. "I'm in terrible pain."

"Aren't we all," Clay snapped. He didn't know why but he believed Williams didn't know where Ivy was. All the man had cared about was his jewels and keeping his secret safe.

"You hired Odell and Raymond to steal them for the insurance money...only, let me guess, they got greedy. You risked my daughter's life for nothing!"

"Nothing?" Williams cried. "What about my reputation?"

"Your reputation is in the toilet and you're on your way to prison," Clay said, pushing to his feet.

He picked up Williams's flashlight. The man wasn't going anywhere. Not hurt and in the dark.

"You aren't going to just leave me here?" the collector cried.

"You're damned lucky I don't kill you."

Clay turned, his only thought to get back to Josie, get help. Medical help for her. Rescuers for Ivy. Then they would comb the caverns. The guides would know all the secret hiding places in the caves. He would search every inch of it. They'd find Ivy. They had to.

He almost ran back through the caverns toward where he'd left Josie, a promise on his lips to make everything up to her. First by finding their daughter.

He hadn't gone far when he thought he heard voices. The sound sent a chill through him. His heart pounded harder. He had to be imagining it.

He slowed, suddenly afraid that he might be losing his mind. As he neared the room where he'd left Josie, he saw the flicker of light. The candle he'd left her. He thought she must have been talking to herself. She sat huddled in a corner, the candlelight flickering on her body. Then he saw that she held Ivy in her lap.

They both looked up, their faces glowing in the light, as he stumbled to them. He could barely breathe around the lump in his throat. Or see, his eyes so blurred with tears. How? Where?

He fell to his knees beside them, his heart bursting.

"You found her." It was all he could say as he wrapped his arms around them both and burrowed his face into them, overcome with emotion.

He felt Josie's hand on his face.

"It's all right," she whispered. "Everything is all right now."

"I have to go get help," he said after a few minutes. He didn't want to let them go. Ever.

"Ivy and I will be fine."

The candle had almost burned out. He handed her the flashlight he'd taken from Williams. "I'll be back as soon as I make the call."

She smiled up at him. "I'm counting on you."

Chapter 15

It had to be the longest night of his life.

From his cell phone in the truck, he called for an ambulance and the sheriff. Mildred stayed to meet the rescue team when they arrived and Clay went back to wait with Josie and Ivy.

When they'd finally gotten out of the caverns, he had ridden in the ambulance with Ivy and Josie, while Mildred drove his truck to the hospital to meet them.

In a separate ambulance, the sheriff had taken Brandon Williams. The coroner would take care of Odell. This time he would stay dead.

By the time they reached the hospital, Josie's ankle was swollen and she was drifting in and out of consciousness with the pain medication the EMTs had given her. Ivy seemed fine after her ordeal, her eyes bright with excitement. Whatever Odell had given her seemed to have worn off.

Clay counted his blessings while he waited for the doctors in the emergency room to set Josie's ankle. Ivy had checked out fine. She'd only been given a mild sedative.

Just as the sun was coming up over the Bridger Mountains, Ruth joined him in the emergency room waiting room.

"How are you holding up?" she asked.

He'd had a lot of time to think. About the past. And the future. It was the future that he'd thought about the most while he'd waited.

"Fine," he said, giving her a smile. "Now that I know Ivy and Josie are all right."

She nodded. "You and Josie did great. Mildred told me all about it."

He didn't want to think about how it could have turned out.

"You have a beautiful daughter."

He glanced over at her in surprise, then realized Mildred must have told her.

She laughed. "Only a fool couldn't see that Ivy is yours."

"Yeah, well you're looking at one."

"You're too hard on yourself. You and Josie have that in common. I was hoping Josie would learn something from the horses. You don't force a horse. Maybe it's a lesson even a man as stubborn and narrow-minded as you can learn."

He laughed. "You don't think it's too late for me?"

"Not if you stop acting like a damned fool."

He heard Ivy's sweet laughter and looked up to see

Mildred coming toward her with his daughter. Mildred had taken her down to the cafeteria for breakfast. Pancakes, Ivy's favorite.

Behind them, Josie limped toward him on crutches, her foot and ankle in a large white cast. She smiled at him, and he thought he'd never seen anything more beautiful.

"Ruth is throwing us a little party at the ranch later," Josie said, and looked at Clay, not sure of his plans.

"I'd love to go," he said. "You and I have to stop by the sheriff's office first. He needs a statement from us both."

"Mildred and I will take Ivy on home," Ruth offered. "The sheriff's office is no place for her, and I'd imagine you two have things to talk about."

"Subtle, isn't she?" Josie said after Clay had helped her into his truck.

"She's right, though. We *do* have to talk." He pulled out of the hospital parking lot and headed downtown toward the Law and Justice Center.

She braced herself, afraid of what he was going to say. Her heart didn't dare hope they could work something out with Ivy. At one time she'd feared Clay, as angry as he'd been, would try to take Ivy from her. After what they'd been through, she knew he wouldn't do that.

"There's something I need to say to you," he began. "I'm sorry. I was wrong about so many things."

"You don't have to apologize—"

"Yes, I do. I was afraid of getting involved with you and I suppose it was my clumsy way of keeping my distance from you. But I still got involved with you, anyway. I'm sorry."

She said nothing. He was sorry he'd gotten involved with her. Isn't that what she'd thought all along?

He must have seen her hurt expression. "Heck, Josie, what I'm trying to say is I'm sorry for the past. If I'd just faced my feelings for you none of this would have happened. But I'm not going to let another day go by without telling you how I feel. Not even another minute." He pulled over to the side of the road. "Josie, I want to marry you. I want us to be a family."

She let the words sink in. How long had she waited for this? So why wasn't she jumping up and down? Why wasn't she throwing herself into his arms? She'd trusted Clay with her life—and Ivy's. Why couldn't she trust this?

"I know you love your daughter," she began, but he cut her off.

"You think I want to marry you because of Ivy, so I don't lose my daughter?" He obviously could see that was what was bothering her.

"Josie, this has nothing to do with Ivy. I've thought of little else but you for the past two years. I looked for you in every face I passed on the street. I—" He stopped and shook his head. "Oh, hell." He slid over and, taking her in his arms, kissed her.

"Oh, Clay," she said when their lips parted. She knew she was holding back, but she couldn't help herself. There was still a lot they hadn't resolved.

It didn't take long to give their statements to the sheriff. Brandon Williams had spilled his guts, hoping for a reduced sentence. Just as Clay had suspected, Williams had sold off all of the real jewels separately and replaced them with glass. The jewelry show at his gallery had just been staged to set up the robbery and collect the insurance money.

But Odell and Raymond, probably more Odell than Raymond, had gotten greedy and decided to keep the jewels for themselves. Odell had hidden them in Josie's great-grandmother's antique rodeo saddle just in case anything went wrong.

Things had definitely gone wrong when Josie took off with the saddle. But Odell had also underestimated Williams, not realizing just how desperate the jewel collector was. Williams had hired an unsavory acquaintance of Odell's to kill both Odell and Raymond.

Raymond had gotten away. Odell had gotten the better of the hitman, someone he'd done business with before in stolen goods. That had made it fairly easy for Odell to steal and switch their dental records and then stage his death, using the thug's body, complete with Odell's class ring.

It would have worked. But Odell couldn't stand the thought that Josie had the jewels in her saddle. Or that she had Clay's baby. The two things ate at him until he found her. But he'd wanted Clay, too, in his revenge scheme, so he'd had Raymond lead Clay to Josie and the jewels with an anonymous tip.

It seemed that Raymond had gotten squeamish, though, when he'd realized Odell planned to kidnap Ivy. Or maybe he'd hoped to get rid of Odell and keep the jewels for himself. Whatever his logic, that seems to be when he'd made the three calls to Texas, to tell them that Odell was alive.

He'd been too afraid of Odell to do more, the sheriff speculated. He'd probably also been worried that Odell would try to cut him out of his share.

Whatever his reasoning, he'd underestimated Odell. Odell didn't even wait until they had the jewels. He got rid of Raymond the minute he didn't need him anymore, following him back from the Toston bar to his motel to kill him.

Williams had trailed Clay and Raymond to Three Forks. He had to get those jewels before Odell tried to sell them. Or before Clay got his hands on them. The last thing Williams wanted was anyone to find out that they weren't real.

"Williams was broke," the sheriff told them. "He'd sold off the real jewels for cash to keep up his life-style. They were his to sell. Too bad he didn't stop right there. But he got greedy. Says he had a reputation to uphold." The sheriff shook his head. "Guess he didn't think he'd get caught. Imagine how a fellow with his demeanor is going to do in prison."

Clay could imagine, but he felt no sympathy for Brandon Williams. Or for Odell.

On the way back to the ranch, Clay put the past behind him and thought only of Josie and Ivy. He wanted them both at the Valle Verde Ranch, under his roof. He wanted Josie in his bed. What did he need to do to convince her?

The party Ruth and Mildred threw was nothing short of amazing, considering how little time they'd had to prepare. Josie sat with her leg propped up on pillows, watching the festivities whirl around her. Many of the neighbors had come along with people whose horses Josie had trained.

Ivy was decked out in her party dress, her eyes bright

and shiny. Josie had to fight the urge to hold on to her, to wrap her in her arms and never let go.

Ivy was safe. Finally. She had to trust in that.

It would be hard to leave here. Hard to leave Ruth and Mildred, but she'd already extended invitations to them to come to Texas and both had accepted. Mildred had asked if she could bring Charley. It seemed that relationship had blossomed. Josie couldn't have been happier for her.

So much had happened. She felt overwhelmed. Clay wanted to marry her. Hadn't that always been her dream?

"You look like me," Ruth said, putting her cast next to Josie's. "Except you got a cooler cast. I can't hardly get any sympathy with this wimpy one." She lowered herself into the chair next to Josie, her laugh as warm and caring as her gaze. "Are you all right? Really?"

Josie nodded. "I have Ivy back."

"What about Clay?" she asked.

"He says he wants to marry me."

Ruth nodded. "Remember what I told you the first time you stepped into the pen? Don't let fear hold you back. Just figure the horses are as frightened as you are. Probably more. But if you show trust—"

Josie nodded, her eyes filling with tears. "You'll get it back."

Ruth smiled as she gave her a hug. "You've always been a quick study, Josie."

As Ruth released her, Josie looked up to see two pairs of dark brown eyes on her. Clay stood with Ivy in front of her.

"I want to be the first to sign your cast, if that's all right," Clay asked.

She nodded, her gaze locked with his. How could she deny this man anything?

"Ivy wants to be next," he said.

"She does?" Josie asked with a laugh, and noticed that they both had felt-tip pens in their hands.

Ruth excused herself to check on the food.

"I told Ivy that I didn't even think she knew how to write," Clay was saying. "She tells me I'm sadly mistaken."

He sat down next to Josie and, taking the cap off the pen, leaned over her cast. Ivy got close to watch him, anxious for her turn. Josie couldn't see what he was writing, her daughter's fair head was in the way.

Just having him this close warmed her, made her feel happy. She loved the smell of him, the feel of him, the nearness of him. And she loved the way he was with Ivy. Her heart cried out for her to give this man a chance.

When he'd finished, he uncapped Ivy's pen and let her sign next to where he'd written. Josie watched her scribbles as Clay pretended to read "I love my mommy bigger than the sky, Ivy." He looked up at Josie with feigned surprise. "Not bad for a fourteen-month-old. I think our daughter is a genius. Must take after her mother."

Josie laughed. "I think she got her writing abilities from her father," she said, trying to see what he'd written. She looked down at the words neatly printed and large enough that she didn't have to bend close to see them.

Tears filled her eyes. Her heart swelled. She swallowed and read the words one more time to assure herself that she hadn't read even one of them wrong.

"I love you, Josie. Will you marry me?"

She raised her gaze to his and saw the expectant,

hopeful look on his face. "Clay—" From the silence in the room, she knew everyone was looking at her, waiting.

"Just a minute," he interrupted. "Before you say anything, there is something else, something I didn't think should be said in felt-tip on a cast. Josie, I've never felt like this before. I don't just love you. I admire you. You're everything I've ever wanted and more. I want to spend the rest of my life with you." He stopped. "I'm crazy about you. I know you and Ivy don't need me, but I need you. I love you, Josie."

Tears filled her eyes. Those were the words she'd needed so desperately to hear. But it was the love she saw in his dark eyes that convinced her, love she knew she could trust.

She cupped his wonderful face in both of her hands. "You're wrong, Clay. We both need you. And love you."

The next thing she knew she was in his arms, his lips on hers. Very persuasive lips.

Clay pulled back to look into her face. "I want the three of us to go back to the Valle Verde and build a family. The sooner the better. You can train all of my horses. Please, Josie, say you'll marry me."

"Oh, yes, Clay," she whispered.

She could hear applause. She looked over Clay's shoulder and saw Ruth. Ruth had tears in her eyes as she gave Josie a thumbs-up.

* * * * *

SPECIAL EXCERPT FROM

HQN

When a plane crashes, ex-military cowboy Thorn Grayson uses his training to find it—and the woman in it. But Geneva Davenport isn't a damsel in distress, and together they'll have to fight their way to safety.

Read on for a sneak preview of
Heartbreaker,
by New York Times *and* USA TODAY
bestselling author B.J. Daniels.

Chapter One

Her eyes flew open, her fight-or-flight response already wide-awake. She jerked up in the bed, blinking wildly, terrified and yet unable to believe what she was seeing. Three hulking dark forms appeared out of the shadows of the huge master bedroom. One of the men tripped over her duffel bag on the floor where she'd dropped it. He swore as he kicked it out of the way.

She tried hopelessly to banish the men back into whatever nightmare they'd climbed out of, realizing the stumble must have been what had awakened her.

All she could think rationally was that this couldn't be happening, because these men being here tonight was so wrong.

But before she could open her mouth to speak—let alone scream—the largest of the three intruders reached her side of the king-size bed. Roughly he pushed her down and clamped a gloved hand over her mouth. This was real.

PHBJDEXP0420

She finally screamed, but the gloved hand over her mouth muffled the sound. Not that it would have done any good if she had hollered to bloody hell. There was no one else in the house to come to her rescue—let alone anyone nearby. The house was high on the mountainside overlooking Flathead Lake, surrounded by acres of forest and as isolated as money could buy.

Frantically she shook her head as she met the man's eyes, the only feature not hidden by his black ski mask, and tried to communicate with him that she wasn't the woman he wanted.

"Don't fight me," the man said in a hoarse whisper as he renewed his efforts to hold her down. "We don't want to hurt you."

But she did fight because they were making a terrible mistake and they didn't know it. That realization sent panic rocketing through her system. Her heart banged against her rib cage, her thundering pulse deafening in her ears. She fought to pull the clamp from her mouth.

If she could only explain the error they were making. Failing in her attempts to pull away his gloved hand, she struck out with her fists as her legs kicked wildly to free themselves from the covers. All she'd managed to do was to make things worse. He leaned over her, pressing his body weight against her chest with his forearm, taking away her breath.

"Did you find it?"

Don't miss
Heartbreaker by B.J. Daniels,
available April 2020 wherever
HQN books and ebooks are sold.

HQNBooks.com

SPECIAL EXCERPT FROM

*As teenagers, they couldn't get enough of each other.
So when Sunny Dalton returns to her hometown of Lone
Star Ridge, Texas, and is reunited with Shaw Jameson,
the sparks they both assumed had long fizzled out are
quickly reignited. But too many old secrets lay hidden
below the surface, threatening the happily-ever-after
they've never given up on...*

Read on for a sneak peek at
Tangled Up in Texas,
the first book in Lone Star Ridge from
USA TODAY *bestselling author Delores Fossen.*

Shaw looked up when he heard the sound of the approaching vehicle. Not coming from behind but rather ahead—from the direction of the ranch. It was a dark blue SUV barreling toward him, and it screeched to a stop on the other side of the intimate apparel he'd found lying on the road.

Because of the angle of the morning sunlight and the SUV's tinted windshield, Shaw couldn't see the driver, but he sure as heck saw the woman who stepped from the passenger's side.

Talk about a gut punch of surprise. The biggest surprise of the morning, and that was saying something considering the weird underwear on the road.

Sunny Dalton.

She was a blast from the past and a tangle of memories. And here she was walking toward him like a siren in her snug jeans and loose gray shirt.

And here he was on the verge of drooling.

Shaw did something about that and made sure he closed his mouth, but he knew it wouldn't stay that way. Even though Sunny and he were no longer teenagers, his body just steamed up whenever he saw her.

Sunny smiled at him. However, he didn't think it was so much from steam but rather a sense of polite frustration.

"Shaw," she said on a rise of breath.

Her voice was smooth and silky. Maybe a little tired, too. Even if Shaw hadn't seen her in a couple of years, he was pretty sure that was fatigue in her steel blue eyes.

She'd changed her hair. It was still a dark chocolate brown, but it no longer hung well past her shoulders. It was shorter in a nonfussy sort of way, which would have maybe looked plain on most women. On Sunny, it just framed that amazing face.

And Shaw knew his life was about to get a whole lot more complicated.

Don't miss
Tangled Up in Texas *by Delores Fossen,*
available March 2020 wherever
HQN Books and ebooks are sold!

HQNBooks.com

PHDFEXP0320

HARLEQUIN

Heartfelt or suspenseful, inspiring or passionate, Harlequin has your happily-ever-after.

With new books published every month, you are sure to find the satisfying escape you know you deserve.

SIGN UP FOR THE HARLEQUIN NEWSLETTER

Be the first to hear about great new reads and exciting offers!

Harlequin.com/newsletters